A BLOODSTAINED LIGHT

WILFRED R. BROOKS

First published in August 2021

Edited by: Rachel Rowlands, www.racheljrowlands.com

Book design by Damonza, www.damonza.com

ISBN 978-1-9169028-0-0 (paperback)

ISBN 978-1-9169028-1-7 (ebook)

www.wilfredrbrooks.com

For my dad, Ray.

I miss you, mate.

CHAPTER ONE

MY WIFE, JOSEE, and I were running across the Bridge of Spirits when the first bolt of blue lightning forked across the night sky and illuminated the gloom above the Coiled Sea. The sapphire flare revealed a fifty-foot breaking wave and a mass of churning clouds, fat with ice water, rolling landward, a malicious spirit determined to inflict ruin on the great city of New Capital.

Josee, lagging behind me, weighed down by her long Al'Mayran robe and her heavy boots clopping on the stone flags of the walkway, whooped at the thunderclap that followed.

'I felt that in my feet, Ani, lass. The bridge actually shook,' she said.

'So let's hurry off it,' I said.

'Don't be so dramatic.'

She weaved a path between the abstract and twisting forms of red, blue and gold spirit sculptures that lined the sides of the bridge. When lightning struck again, she raised her voice and directed a lament at the sea: 'The bridges and towers will crumble, New Capital will be torn from the five cliffs, and we will all be swept into the sea where our souls will plead for Xol's mercy.'

'Laugh if you want to,' I said.

'I thought I already was,' she said, catching up with me.

'But a fisherman friend of my uncle's—'

'Was he a wizened but wise old sailor by any chance?'

I raised my finger to wag it at her, but she picked me up and spun me around, a smile spreading across her face, the freckles around her nose and eyes creasing into lines of laughter.

I scowled until she put me down, then I took a breath and continued: 'My uncle's friend reckoned the storm would hit tomorrow. Clearly, it's picked up speed and will make landfall in less than half an hour.'

The drums of the city's hurricane warning rang out, ordering all residents off the lanes and ways, just as the first pellets of hail struck our faces and the sweet smell of ozone swept inland.

'See?' I said, raising my palms to the brooding sky.

'Okay, okay, I guess it's official now,' Josee said, covering her wavy red hair with her hood until her pale features flickered in the moonlight like those of a transient spirit caught between worlds.

I smiled and kissed her as I buttoned my oilskin coat over my suit. She took my hand, and we watched the cobbled plaza of the Al'Mayran arcade below fill with people, spilling out from the taverns and eateries to hurry home. Shopkeepers rushed to collapse awnings and bring in chairs and tables before they blew away. In their haste, they bumped into the fleeing clientele and dropped glasses and vases onto the silver travertine cobblestones. And all the while, their colourful robes buffeted in the gathering wind and flapped in their pale faces.

'Your people will never learn,' I said.

'Ignorant foreigners, eh?' Josee said.

'Ignorance I can excuse. Wilful disregard, I can't.'

'Yes, yes,' she said, grinning at me, her eyes alive with excitement as another thunderbolt turned their emerald glow an incandescent blue.

'See, I was right to board our windows. Admit it, I was right,' I said.

'And Inspector Anika Sulaqua is always right,' Josee said with a snort.

'Are you trying to provoke me?'

Josee laughed and dragged me away. We picked up speed until we were running again, hand in hand, along the bridge, beyond the Al'Mayran arcade to where giant skytowers, connected by bridges to each other and to the cliffs either side, rose from the exposed bedrock of Magila Bay. Another burst of lightning reflected off their shuttered windows and revealed hundreds of advertising banners thrashing in the wind, making the towers – giant, painted, steel and concrete animal figures – come alive in the morphing shadows.

'Someone is fighting up ahead,' Josee said.

To the west, where the Bridge of Spirits stretched across Magila Bay on segmented stone arches, high enough for ships to pass under, a group of adolescents stood in the shadows of one of the spirit sculptures. They were gathered in a half-circle, throwing the occasional punch towards some unfortunate soul or two they had pinned to the northern wall.

'Wait here,' I said to Josee.

'What are you going to do?' she said.

'My job.'

'You know what I mean.'

'I'm just going to give them a scare,' I said. I shimmered the appearance of a long-dead member of my tribe, a giant man with a fearsome face. In life, he had been a gentle being, and I felt a little guilty using his likeness to frighten children. But my own slight form hardly inspired terror in others, and besides, I had seen the glint of a blade in the last lightning flash and wasn't taking any chances.

'Very imposing,' Josee said, eyeing my illusion.

I drew my sword and one of my percussion pistols and charged, howling in the voice of my deceased kinsman. When the assailants, two boys and two girls, all native Kahokeyans, saw me sprinting towards them, their expressions changed from sneering confidence to wide-eyed fear. Nevertheless, they didn't run. They formed a line from the stone walkway to the middle of the cobbled road, and drew their rusted kitchen knives and old-fashioned stone axes.

They had long dirty hair, gaunt faces, missing teeth, and rotten gums. Judging by the animal-skin rags that hung in pieces from their malnourished bodies, they lived in the Depths, an unmerciful hell where the quick-witted and brutal flourished and the weak died young.

The taller girl strode forward, accompanied by one of the boys, who spun his axe in circles. But the younger pair hesitated, shuffling without enthusiasm to stand behind their mates.

'Don't do this,' I said.

But the knuckles of the tall girl's hand turned white as she gripped her butcher's boning knife, and I knew the attack would follow.

The confident lad lifted his axe to strike. I darted to one side and deflected the girl's lunge with my sword. When our blades met, my true self was revealed.

'She's a shimmerer,' the girl cried.

She dropped her knife, and I flicked it into a puddle with the side of my foot. When she bent to pick it up, Josee ran up and lifted her into a powerful bear hug.

'And she's a fucking copper,' the confident lad said.

He lashed out at me again, missed, slipped on a wet cobblestone, and fell. I took the opportunity to kick him in his groin, and he curled into a ball, letting go of his axe and whimpering, where he lay as the unforgiving hail beat his body.

The tall girl gave up resisting and hung limp in Josee's arms, so I advanced on the remaining pair, the younger boy and girl, making for the boy first. He backed away until his behind hit a spirit sculpture. When a burst of thunder, like cannon fire, shook our guts and split the sky, he spun and drove his poorly made axe into the statue, knocking the axehead away. He froze, dumbfounded, staring at the impotent wooden handle in his hand, then he fled into the hail and rain, his long hair trailing behind him.

I sheathed my sword and holstered my pistol, then showed the youngest girl my empty palms. Unlike her leader, the tall girl, who carried a deadly butcher's knife, this child was armed with only a dull vegetable knife that shook in her grip. When, with little conviction, she attacked, I caught her wrist and squeezed until she dropped the knife.

'Are we done?' I said.

She nodded, and I let her run away. When she had gone, I collected the fallen weapons and helped the older boy to his feet. He staggered over to the sculpture, still doubled over and clutching his stomach.

'What am I going to do with you?' I said to the tall girl.

She looked away, her frail body shaking with sobs, so I placed my hand on her shoulder and asked again, but she just shook her head.

'Okay,' I said, taking a couple of shillings from my purse.

The girl stared at me, bewildered, doubting my intentions, unsure whether to accept the gift.

'I haven't got all night, lass, but if you're quick and run to the arcade, you might find a shopkeeper willing to sell you a fair amount of warm food to fill your bellies.'

The lad snatched the coins from my hand and ran off but the girl surprised me and showed her mettle.

'Our weapons. We won't survive without them,' she said, meeting my eye for the first time.

'Don't try this again,' I said, handing them over. 'My pistols are primed and my charity spent. If I were you, I'd find a different trade. You won't live long plying this one – you're not good enough.'

The girl cradled the weapons in her arms and backed away until she appeared little more than a stray phantom, fading into the dark night, a wisp, unable to sustain even an outline in the falling rain.

Their victims were two boys, aged around nine and ten. Like their assailants, they were also Kahokeyan, with typical high cheekbones and almond-shaped eyes. Their raven hair framed plump cheeks and a pair of cleft chins so alike, they had to be brothers.

I had spent too many years walking a police beat to miss the dangerous feral glare in the eldest lad's eyes; he and his brother appeared well-fed for homeless youngsters normally expected to survive on what little food they could steal or scavenge. Their clothing, too, wasn't the usual rags. They wore trousers that had been recently patched, shirts that were in good condition but too big for their narrow shoulders, and soft-soled deerskin shoes with beads and tassels that still shone. Someone was taking the time to care for them, but who?

The youngest appeared largely unhurt, save for a graze on his chin where he'd fallen. His elder sibling, however, had put up a brave fight and received a split lip, a black eye, and a bloody nose as a reward for his courage.

'We've never met a shimmerer before, have we, Hani?' the younger one said.

'Plenty of coppers, though,' the older boy said.

'So you're Hani, but who's this?' I said to the older lad, gesturing to his little brother.

'Don't tell her, Mani.'

I laughed as I ushered the boys to relative shelter behind the spirit sculpture. I held Hani's face and checked his nose with my thumbs.

'Well, lad, it's not broken,' I said.

He shrugged.

'A warrior, eh?' I said.

'You've got to be where we come from,' Mani said.

'Where's that, the Depths?'

No answer.

I flicked Hani a shilling from my purse and said, 'Do you like Al'Mayran puddings?'

Hani caught the coin and glanced at his brother, who nodded.

'We're not going anywhere with you,' Hani said.

'I'm not asking you to,' I said.

'What do we have to do, then?'

'Nothing, flower,' Josee said.

I held my hand up to shush my wife. 'You could tell me where you got those new shoes from?'

'I'm not telling you anything, copper,' Hani said.

'Oh, come on, what does it hurt?' Mani said.

'It's the principle.'

'Such integrity,' I said, taking a small parcel from my coat pocket and unwrapping the waxed linen cloth.

'A lemon slice! Go on, tell her,' Mani said.

'No,' Hani said, folding his arms.

'Can you at least tell me if your shoes were stolen?' I said.

'So you can arrest us?'

'I'm an inspector of murder, lad, and even if I was a uniformed constable, do you think I'd bother locking you up in the middle of a storm?'

'Yes.'

'Were the shoes a gift?'

Mani nodded behind his brother's back.

'From the same person who gave you those shirts and patched your trousers?' I said.

'Either give us the puds or don't, but let us go,' Hani said.

'Okay, lad. I take it you want the lemon slice?' I said to Mani.

'What else have you got?' he said.

Josee chortled and showed him the wrapped ginger and cherry cake she'd been so looking forward to.

'I'll have the lemon slice,' Mani said.

They took their puddings and, without a single thank you, ran east towards Noon Claw.

'Was it wise to let the older ones go?' Josee said.

'No idea. I can't see through the chaos of the Known World any better than you, my love. Xol will reveal all. Maybe they'll learn to murder. If they're lucky, they'll take their places at the driving wheels of the Great Lifts. Most likely they'll be dead within the year. But there's always a chance one of them might find a better life.'

Josee grabbed the lapels of my coat and kissed me. 'Well, Anika Sulaqua, you grumpy little sod, every now and then, you remind me why I married you.'

I flushed, and looked over the bay as a carmine-red glare coruscated from the cliffs.

'That light was red,' I said.

'So?' Josee said.

'This is a hailstorm. Lightning in a hailstorm is blue. Besides, that flash came from the north.'

'What's the difference?'

'It can't be lightning.'

'Oh, Ani, love, by the spirits, let's get home.'

Another burst of carmine set the night on fire and rendered the sky-towers into silhouetted beasts.

'There,' I said, pointing towards the northern end of Noon Claw, near the mainland. 'Did you see that?'

Froth and spray from the Magila Bay waterfall still hindered my view, but through it, nestled high up in the cleft of Noon Claw, where it met the mainland, I could make out the science academy. The giant glass dome of the Octagon Hall flickered red in the dark night, lighting the bay.

'What is that?' I said.

'It reminds me of home,' Josee said.

'That's it. The lights of the Red Mountains. Lifeblood stones,' I said, slapping the top rail of the balustrade.

'It can't be.'

'What else shines that colour?'

'Only the spirits can say. Come, let's go home. I'm getting cold, and I want to run.'

As Josee took my hand, one side of the Octagon Hall erupted, spewing burning debris down the cliff, like embers tumbling from a coal fire.

'Did you see that?' I said.

'What now?' Josee said.

'There was an explosion. Those are flames.'

'Lightning can cause fires,' Josee said.

'That looked more like a gunpowder blast.'

'You're imagining things, Ani. Come on, I've had enough adventures for one night.'

But I wasn't listening. I just stood and stared at the academy, oblivious to the wind and the rain, until Josee dragged me away.

'Come on, Ani, love,' she said. 'You can't know everything.'

CHAPTER TWO

Tʜᴇ ᴡɪɴᴅ ᴋᴇᴘᴛ Josee and me awake all night, so we spent the dark hours talking and making love. Once the storm passed, I fell asleep, just as the dawn turned the black sky a deep shade of blue, the colour of burning gas.

I dreamt about Kahokey, the great winged titan with the head of a bear, who Xol choked to death with his tentacles. When Kahokey fell, his body formed the Kahokeyan continent, and his paw became the five claws of the sacred cliffs, upon which New Capital was built. Then Xol, his body concealed below the surface of the Coiled Sea, stretched his tentacles through the lanes and ways of the city, but whether he intended to strangle or embrace his children, I couldn't say.

I saw Shona, my love from my adolescence, adrift in the sea with me. I tried to swim to her, but she floated out of reach. Her face was ashen and rotten, although her eyes were open. She lifted a fetid arm and pointed south. I caught a brief glimpse of a terrible armada before I was blinded by a red light that set the sea ablaze and burnt the flesh from my bones.

I jerked up, wide awake, breathing heavily, the bed sheets damp with sweat and clinging to my skin. I disturbed Snuggs, Josee's little magpie cat, who lay on the bed cleaning his paws. He glared at me with indignation.

'Fuck you too, Snuggs,' I said.

He twitched and jumped onto the rug to play with a little toy mouse on a string.

'Sorry, Snuggs,' I said, wiping my eyes.

He rolled onto one of Josee's robes, stretched, and stared at me in expectation. I kicked the bed sheets away and crawled off the mattress to kneel beside him and rub his belly.

'Where's your mam, Snuggs?' I said. 'On the southern balcony, already painting, eh?'

Josee had opened all the shutters and windows, letting in a pale yellow light and a gentle sea breeze that carried the pungent odours of brine, mild sulphur, and fried fish from a thousand hot pans. The roar of the wind had gone with the storm. The voices of fishermen and women rose from the docks below, along with the songs of gulls and sandpipers, announcing they had survived the night, and the vibrations of flowing water, coursing down lanes, drainage pipes and aqueducts, splashing into giant cisterns and dripping from the rooftops of every home, shop and business in the Five Claws.

I left Snuggs wrapping himself in Josee's robe and poked my head out of the window to scold my wife for the disarray in which she kept our home. But I lost heart when I saw her squinting with focus, one brush between her teeth, another at work on her easel. She wore nothing but her undergarments: shorts and a thin tunic, the hem of which rested on her hips. She had piled her hair into a messy bun, revealing her freckled neck and shoulders, and her face was dotted with paint from her fingers, which she often employed on her canvass instead of a brush.

She took a step back to reflect on her efforts, noticed me, and took the brush from her mouth.

'Morning, love,' she said.

I nodded.

'Sleep well?' she said.

I shook my head.

'Bad dream?'

I nodded again.

'You know, it's these sparkling exchanges that keep our marriage alive.'

I laughed and bowed through the window.

'Good morning, my beloved bride,' I said.

'Ah, she eases from silence into sarcasm,' Josee said, that mischievous glint in her eye. 'Go on, try for genuine sentiment, I dare you.'

'That was genuine. You are my bride and my beloved. Satisfied?'

'Maybe. But I'm still not convinced. Demonstrate it.'

'How about I cook you breakfast?'

'That's a start.'

'Anything in particular?'

'Surprise me,' Josee said.

Our flat was the uppermost of thirty in Horizon's Outlook, built around the far western pillar of the Magila Bay bridge. As a result, there was no centre to our home, just four wings with a balcony or terrace along each side that afforded us panoramic views of the Coiled Sea and the city.

I picked up Josee's clothes from the bedroom floor and stowed them away as best I could in her wardrobe until I found the blue-and-golden silk gown I had taken as my own. I slipped it on and made my way out along the eastern wing, stubbing my toe on a painting in the den.

I cursed my wife's name and shouted, 'Can't you tidy up after yourself?'

'What was that?' Josee said from the southern balcony.

'You heard,' I said, limping into my light and airy study with the figures of Xol and his sister Zalema Josee had carved to imitate the expressionist, cube-like style of my tribe.

I turned onto the narrow northern hallway and into the kitchen. Even though the windows were open, the air was thick with the aromas of smoked fish, salted meats, dried herbs, pickled vegetables and sweet preserves, all packed onto shelves and sills and stockpiled in the adjacent pantry.

I threw some wood and wool firelighters and some kindling into the oven stove, struck a match and lit a fire. While it burned, I ground some coffee beans, counting off the turns of the handle until I reached a hundred. I stepped onto the northern balcony to fetch some wood from the pile. I put a couple of pre-chopped logs under my arm and walked to the eastern corner to assess the storm's impact on Noon Claw.

Sodden advertising banners, torn from roofs and poles, were lying twisted like serpents in roads and gardens. Work carts and carriages had shattered against walls and stairwells, and rainwater streams still flowed from some homes. Even a couple of shops had collapsed, making me wonder if the residents were safe or if they'd been lost, maybe carried from their beds or drowned where they slept.

But I couldn't hear the cries of the bereaved nor spot any death waggons or ambulance carts weaving up and down the cliff, and, tellingly, the aroma of petrichor was far more prevalent than the foul stench of death. Most encouraging of all were the ships still afloat in Magila Bay, not a broken mast in sight, and the flotsam already being swept to sea by the outgoing tide.

I crossed the northern balcony to the western terrace to confirm that Pastnoon Claw, on the other side of the bay, had been similarly lucky. One glance told me it had. Better still, on Sundown Claw beyond, my tribe were singing songs of deliverance as they prepared their fishing boats to set sail. So, I hummed along and said a little prayer of thanks to Xol. Then I walked through the dining room, filled with more of Josee's paintings, into the kitchen, where I put the logs in the oven stove fire and made a breakfast of eggs, fried tomatoes and spinach.

Snuggs wandered in and made a nuisance of himself until I fed him some fish in his bowl on the western terrace.

'You're a pain in the arse, Snuggs,' I said as I untied the gateleg table where I had battened it down.

'Don't talk to my baby like that,' Josee said, sauntering onto the terrace to smack my behind.

'You love him more than you do me,' I said, heading to the kitchen via the dining room to fetch our breakfast.

'He isn't as bad-tempered,' Josee shouted after me.

'I'm not bad-tempered,' I said, when I returned to the terrace.

Josee's eyes widened with amusement as I placed the breakfast plates on the gateleg table. She sat down and took her first bite. 'Not bad,' she said, stuffing another forkful of eggs into her mouth.

'Then make it last.'

'What did you dream about?'

'It doesn't matter.'

'Tell me.'

I sighed.

'Shona,' I said.

'Oh, I'm sorry, love,' Josee said, with a gentle smile.

'She was floating dead in the water, as usual. Her eyes were open but this time she was trying to show me something,' I said, sitting down and nursing my coffee.

'Oh, poor love. She was probably on your mind because we crossed the Bridge of Spirits.'

'Maybe.'

'I mean, your hiding place was there and, of course…' Josee faltered, for once unwilling to be blunt.

'It's where he tossed her body into the sea,' I said, finishing her thought.

Josee smiled, but I looked away, her pity stinging my heart.

'What did she want to show you?' Josee said, after a pause and a mouthful of spinach.

'Warships. And red lights like those we saw last night. Only these set the world on fire.'

'Sprits preserve us. What made you dream that, I wonder?'

I took another sip of coffee and stared at my mug as I thought.

'I have no idea. An Al'Mayran legend you may have told me about?' I suggested with a shrug.

'None come to mind,' Josee said, concentrating on clearing her plate.

'What about Ameeleyor?

'I don't remember her sailing the ocean,' Josee said, swallowing.

'But she was the only one in your people's history to use lifeblood stones as a weapon.'

Josee laughed. 'Ameeleyor is a myth, sweetheart, as is her fiery lifeblood stone staff.'

'Myths begin with facts. What if Ameeleyor's story is true?' I said, averting my gaze and slicing a runny egg. 'Maybe she really did burn an entire army to death?'

'And I'm supposed to be the whimsical one,' Josee said, gesticulating with her fork.

'You don't believe she lived at all?'

'There could have been an historical figure called Ameeleyor, but I doubt she accomplished all the deeds attributed to her.'

'But the stone in her staff – the story does say it fires a burning red light?'

'What's all this about, Ani?' Josee asked, grinning, her elbows on the table, her hands clasped in mock formality.

'Forget it.'

'The explosion at the academy?'

'I said forget it.'

'Do you think the scientists in New Capital have found Ameeleyor's staff and were giving it a test fire last night?' Josee said, pretending to hold a staff aloft.

'Maybe they were,' I said, trying to suppress the angry tone rising in my voice.

Josee just shook her head and wiped her eyes.

'Why is that so funny? You're married to someone who can shimmer, for fuck's sake,' I said.

'What would you say to someone who claimed to have seen Xol?'

'That's different.'

'How?'

Perhaps Josee was right: a precious stone destroying an army was about as ridiculous as a giant octopus god living in the sea. But I persisted nonetheless.

'Xol is central to our creation myths. His actions made the Five Claws. He's the sea, the earth, the spirit of the city. He's beyond our world. But Ameeleyor was said to live in historical times. She was a person.'

'Doesn't mean she could harness the power of lifeblood stones,' Josee said, resting her chin on her hand and smiling.

'But you do believe the stones have power?' I said, folding my arms.

'I don't believe much, Ani, you know that.'

'Really? So is your spirit in your heart or not?'

Josee shrugged.

'Okay, be non-committal. What about if you died?'

'Anything to get out of this conversation.'

'You wouldn't care if I didn't bother with a lifeblood stone cremation?' I said.

'Well, that's cultural,' Josee said.

'But it really doesn't matter to you? Is that what you're telling me?
When all is said and done, it makes no difference to you how your
remains are disposed of. Your heart could be allowed to decay, and rot,
and break apart, and the spirit inside escape and be lost for eternity?'

'Okay, okay. Enough. My spirit is in my heart and when I die, I want
to be cremated in a lifeblood stone fire, so my heart is burned whole and
my spirit carried by the smoke to the Red Mountains. Satisfied?'

'Your sarcasm is hollow. You know you've lost.'

'Wait, did you hear something?'

'What?'

Josee leapt to her feet, ran to the southern balcony, and looked down
at the Coiled Sea. 'Ani, come here. It's Xol, he's saying something,' she
said. 'What's that, Xol? Okay, I'll tell her.' Josee turned to face me. 'Xol
wants you to shut the fuck up and go to work.'

When I was picking up our empty plates, the doorbell rang, so I
ran into the kitchen. Through the window I could see Cadet Deewhalee
Huno standing on the cantilevered platform on Pastnoon Claw across
from our flat. Sweat was dripping down his forehead and from his long
ponytail, and he was yanking on the bell pull with the kind of zeal the
young employed to impress their superiors. Unfortunately for Dee, his
enthusiasm had the opposite effect on me.

'For Xol's sake, I hear you,' I said, putting the plates in the sink
before opening the door.

'I'm sorry, Inspector, but there's a body. It was found in Rose Town
by the guards. They say it's the first murder in the brothel area in five
years. Can you believe it?'

'Stop shouting official business from the side of Pastnoon Claw and
come inside.'

I unlocked the hand-crank and turned the handle to lower the
drawbridge to the platform. Dee jumped onto the bridge before it was
fully down and, oblivious to the platform shaking, crossed over, striding

forward and swinging his arms in his loping style. When he reached the northern balcony, I turned my back on him and went inside.

'Would you like a cup of coffee?' I said, once he joined me in the kitchen.

'No, ma'am. Sorry, no thank you, ma'am.'

'Don't you like my coffee?'

'No, ma'am. I mean, yes, ma'am. I do like your coffee, that is. But—'

'Then go and sit on the terrace with Josee and I'll bring you a cup.'

'But Chief Inspector Imala—'

'She sent you running here?'

'She gave me money for a cab,' he said, raising his head, his face earnest and proud.

'I hope the horse is in better condition than you are.'

'Please, Inspector.'

'Go and sit down, Dee. And when we're not at work or around other officers—'

'Call you Ani?'

'My uncle would never speak to me again if he heard you call me inspector or ma'am in my own home or, worse still, on Sundown.'

'Yes, ma'am. I mean, Ani.'

'Oh, and Dee?' I said.

'Yes, Ani?'

'Happy Coming of Age Day.'

Dee had been a skinny lad in a police cadet's uniform several sizes too big for him when he first started working in the inspectors' department. Now he had become a man, and that same uniform was threadbare and in danger of suffocating him. Worse still, he looked foolish with his navy-blue tunic coat, meant to hang below the knee, now barely passing his hips.

Josee still had her arms around the lad, wishing him a happy Coming of Age Day and kissing his cheek when I returned to the terrace with an extra cup. Poor Dee was blushing and trying to avert his gaze from my wife. She hardly helped when she stretched and revealed her midriff.

'Tell me about the body, Dee,' I said. 'The dead one, that is. Not Josee's.'

'Ani,' Josee said, reprimanding me and giving me a clip.

We sat at the gateleg table and Dee filled his cup with coffee, coughing to regain his composure. 'The victim is a pale man.'

'Most dead men are,' I said.

'Well, this one was in life. He's an Al'Mayran, a rich, important-looking one at that,' Dee said.

'An Al'Mayran?' Josee said, suddenly interested.

'Xol help us, that's all I need,' I said, standing.

There was no time to set a fire in the boiler, so I washed with cold water before changing into my dark green suit in the bedroom. I hung my baldric over my shoulder, having ensured my three pistols were primed and loaded with shot, and adjusted my sword and dagger. I slipped on my soft-soled deerskin shoes, put my jacket on and used a black ribbon to tie my hair into a ponytail.

Dee and Josee were waiting for me on the northern balcony, chatting about his Coming of Age festival.

'I want to hear all about this murdered Al'Mayran,' Josee said, planting a kiss on my cheek and waving goodbye to Dee and me.

Much to the cadet's relief, the cab driver was waiting for us in Shadow Rise, the little neighbourhood on Pastnoon Claw beyond the cantilevered platform. She was feeding carrots to her chestnut mare and stroking the white patch on the horse's forehead. She was young for a cabbie, but had already adopted the usual surly manner.

'Where to?' she said to me, determining my seniority.

'Rose Town, southern end,' I said.

'Over Magila Bridge okay with you?'

Shortly after, we were leaving behind Pastnoon Claw, and I was inspecting the steel frame and concrete surfaces of the Magila Bay bridge. The structure was undamaged, having resisted the storm well, and folk were crossing the walkways or driving over in cabs and private carriages without any evident care. Even the Magila tribal pillars that faced the Coiled Sea were undamaged. Their depictions of Xol, his tentacles overflowing with pearls, whale tusks and ambergris, remained defiant.

I gazed north and picked out the science academy; there was the merest hint of pink smoke rising and dissipating into the clear blue sky.

'Look at the Octagon Hall, Dee, and tell me if you think there's an open wound on one corner,' I said.

Dee leaned forward and shaded his eyes from the sun. 'Something doesn't look right,' he said.

'No, it doesn't. I don't suppose you saw the red lights flickering in the dome last night, did you?'

'No, Ani.'

Once over the bay and on the top of Noon Claw, we headed north until the incline was gentle enough to negotiate the wealthy upper levels, whereupon we turned south.

'They have a swimming pool,' Dee said, pointing at a particularly grand dwelling, which had its own lane, straddled three levels and was set in grounds bordered with elm and flowering honey-crisp apple trees.

'I guess the sea's not good enough for them,' I said.

We descended past the grid-like pattern of thoroughfares that made up the Negotiated Burroughs, home to many foreign diplomats and their staff, and turned south along the Lanes of Faith, the gambling quarter. The walls and roofs of the windowless yellow-and-red-painted betting houses appeared undamaged by the storm. They would soon be doing good business again. Nothing short of complete obliteration would prevent the owners and their investors from opening.

The driver turned onto a narrow but gently sloping lane which led to Sumaka Way, the main thoroughfare through Bye-Bye Haven's hundreds of taverns, eateries and cheap hotels. Here the damage was more extensive. The area never looked tidy, and many of its oldest buildings had been in danger of collapsing from neglect alone, without the assistance of gale-force winds. A couple hadn't survived, leaving exposed gaps like missing teeth, through which Pastnoon Claw could be seen across the bay. Beer tables had been blown apart and their pieces carried by the wind through painted windows, wreaking havoc amongst bottles of spirits and ales. Sadly, the guff of leftover food, alcohol, tobacco and vomit hadn't been blown away. Nothing, it seemed, would rid the Haven of that stench.

We continued along Sumaka Way into Rose Town, where the hotels became brothels. At night, dazzling lamps of red and blue, and violet and purple, shone along its walkways, and multi-coloured banners flew from every establishment to entice prospective customers inside with promises of hot food, cool ale, and warm fellowship. As long as your tastes lay within the law and guided you to a human soul of consensual age, you would be accommodated and welcomed with all the love money could fake.

The farther south you went, the grander the establishments became and the higher the class of patrons they could attract. These were not the bawdy houses and knocking shops of the northern end, and the Stars and the Sea in particular, housed in an old palace, outside of which the victim's body had been found, was arguably the most elite brothel in New Capital.

Two uniformed constables were standing with a company of Rose Town guards, dressed in dark brown deerskin uniforms and armed with long-barrelled muskets, outside the guards' brick-built cabin, blocking the way. Our driver pulled up to allow Dee and me to climb out.

'Don't go anywhere,' I said to her.

Other than a few fallen roof slates and advertising banners lying on the cobbles, you wouldn't have thought Rose Town had been in a hurricane's path. There was little in the way of fallen tree branches, and the brightly painted stone facades of the brothels, with their inset tribal pillars and intricately carved, erotic friezes, were still intact. Normally, the aromas of spice and incense wafted along the way, masking the stench of sweat and musk, but this morning, I could smell nothing but the sea. The reason was clear: all the windows and doors were closed. And save for the twitch of a violet lace curtain, there were no signs of life.

I said good morning to the constables and the guards as I passed them to inspect the body. The dead man was an Al'Mayran all right. One I thought I recognised but could not place. He was lying on his back with his arms at his sides. His strawberry-blond hair was still tightly held in a ponytail and he wore a traditional Al'Mayran robe with a red and gold swirling pattern of spirits to protect his sacred heart. The design had worked. Someone had slit his throat.

The edges of the wound were neat and smooth and could only have been made by a sharp blade, ruling out the possibility of a freak accident involving flying debris. There should have been a tremendous amount of blood, but the rain had washed it all away, probably with other valuable forensic evidence. Even the collar and lapels of the dead man's robe had been cleansed, leaving behind nothing more than a pink diffused cloud that showed only as a tint in the gold.

He had a strong jawline with a neatly trimmed beard, and, for an Al'Mayran, high and defined cheekbones. His blue eyes were open and, at least to me, seemed to express sadness and regret. By the right eye, there was a deep cut in the shape of a curve. The mark had not bruised, and so must have occurred shortly before death. Here, too, any blood had been rinsed away.

I would have put him in his mid-forties, and, judging by the shape of his well-defined frame, outlined by his sodden robe, he had been in good health, except for the right leg, which was withered.

'Thoughts, Cadet?' I said.

'His robes are expensive. He appears to be wealthy, therefore a likely target for a mugger,' Dee said.

'One working this far south in Rose Town, a few feet from a cabin of guards?'

'It's possible.'

'Why kill him?'

'It happens all the time.'

'Often when the victim resists, resulting in a shooting, a clubbing, a fractured skull, a stab through the heart...'

'You think this is a professional job?'

'That cut is clinical enough. But was the assassin a native Kahokeyan? That's the question,' I said, as a strange glint caught my eye.

I put on my leather gloves, crouched down, pushing my sword and my dagger aside, and took a closer look at the Al'Mayran's right hand. There was a red substance under the nail of his little finger.

'What do you make of this, Dee?' I said.

'Dried blood? Either his, or, if we're lucky, the murderer's?' Dee said.

'Blood doesn't normally remain this bright.' I took hold of the dead man's sleeve and lifted his hand to the sun. 'Is it me, Cadet, or is his fingernail glowing?'

'Possibly, ma'am, but what is it?' Dee said, bending down next to me and shielding his eyes from the sunlight.

'I don't know. Perhaps forensics will be able to tell us,' I said.

'Look, ma'am. There's a small bump on his chest beneath his clothes.'

I parted the dead man's robe and found a cylindrical golden charm on a chain around his neck. It had raised markings that appeared to be Al'Mayran in style.

'Would a mugger miss this?' I said.

I opened the chain's clasp and pocketed the charm. Beside me, Dee breathed in sharply.

'I want Josee to see it before any of our so-called Al'Mayran experts,' I said, searching through the dead man's pockets.

'But it's evidence and should be indexed, ma'am,' he said.

'It will be.'

'But how will you account for the discrepancy in the index dates?'

'There won't be any.'

'Oh, but ma'am—'

'If you're going to report me, Cadet, get on with it. Otherwise, shut up.'

'Yes, ma'am.'

'This, however, you may index as soon as you can.'

I showed Dee a Great Lift ticket I had found. He put on his gloves to examine it while I stood and adjusted my jacket and baldric.

'It's a South-Western Great Lift ticket, issued at seven minutes to ten last night, shortly before the storm hit, assuming the conductor kept the clock on his or her ticket machine properly wound,' he said.

'What else?'

'It's a return, purchased on the top level of this claw.'

'And?'

He thought for a moment. 'It's not punched,' he said. 'He came straight here and died here.'

'A reasonable conclusion.'

Dee cocked his head. 'What other explanation is there?'

'He's a rich man with a lame leg. I would have taken a cab,' I said, gesturing down Sumaka Way.

'Couldn't he have done both?'

I looked up the cliff. 'Rose Town is just a few levels from the top of Noon Claw and accessible by road.'

'Are you suggesting he went to a lower level first, one that's hard to reach by cab alone?'

'Why not?' I said, walking around the body, looking for blood.

'Then how did he come to be in Rose Town, if he didn't return on the lift?'

'Perhaps someone dumped his body here. Let's talk to the guards, see what they have to say.'

The captain of the Rose Town guards was a short, stocky fellow who, unusually for a Kahokeyan, wore his hair close-cropped, a style which enhanced his pit-bull appearance. He had the kind of eyes that never smiled and always seemed to be searching for a weakness in others. His hard-edged persona, however, seemed forced. After all, murder in Rose Town was rare. Failure for a guard to prevent it, a dismissible offence. He might try to hide his anxiety, but I suspected he was shaken.

'How goes it with you?' I said.

He grunted and said, 'I've had better mornings.'

'Who found him?'

'I did.'

I nodded to Dee, indicating he should take over questioning.

'When did you find him, sir?' Dee said, taking out his notebook.

The captain glared at me and said, 'I won't be questioned by a boy whose bollocks haven't dropped.'

'The inspector meant no slight, sir. We all have to learn, and I value your cooperation,' Dee said with a bow.

I held the captain's eye until he relented.

'Whatever,' he said.

'Thank you, sir,' Dee said. 'When did you find the victim?'

'After the storm passed. I left our cabin to inspect the damage and found him like that outside Madam Nita's.' He gestured sharply with his head towards the Stars and the Sea brothel.

'What time did the victim arrive?' Dee said.

'He didn't,' the captain said.

Dee cocked his head, clearly confused.

'That is to say, we never saw him, and we kept watch all night,' the captain added.

I looked at him hard. 'How can you be certain, hiding in your cabin?' I said.

'Sure, we were inside and boarded up, as we had every right to be. There's no rule or regulation to say we have to stand guard in a hurricane. But we have viewing slots in the shutters, and I made sure someone kept watch all night. That man didn't pass us before the storm came, and no one passed during.'

'And yet, he's here.'

'Do you recognise him?' Dee said.

'He's a regular at Madam Nita's, I can tell you that, but I don't know his name. I don't know any of their names. You understand how it is,' the captain said with a shrug.

'Of course. Who does he normally see?'

'Not my job to mark.'

'That won't suffice,' I said, 'not where the murder of a foreigner is concerned.'

The captain looked towards his men and women gathered by their cabin and lowered his voice. 'He saw this young lad, Nakni. Nitushi Nakni. They were close. More than just business.'

'And Nakni works for Madam Nita at the Stars?' Dee said.

'He does.'

'Have you seen either of them today?'

'Well, er, yes, we have,' the captain whispered, staring at the cobles of Sumaka Way.

'When?'

'They left shortly before you arrived.'

'Did they see the body?' Dee said, stooping to meet the captain's eye.

'Couldn't have missed it,' the captain said, his gaze flicking from the brothels to his fellow guards, to the dead man, but never falling on Dee.

'Did they speak to you?' Dee persisted.

'Not a word.'

'How did they seem?'

The captain rolled his eyes. 'I can never read Nita, but the lad was clearly upset.'

'Were they alone?'

'No, they had two young'uns with them, brothers, who do a little work from time to time at the Stars.'

'Brothers?' I said, giving the captain a light slap on the cheek to get his attention and remind him who he was speaking to.

'I think so.'

'How old?'

'Perhaps the oldest is ten.'

'He didn't have a black eye and a spit lip, did he?'

The captain's mouth fell open. 'How'd you know that?'

I shrugged and waited for Dee to resume questioning.

'When did the deceased last visit?' he said.

'He hasn't been since last week,' the captain said, still looking my way.

'Forgive me, sir, but how can you be so sure?' Dee said.

'Counting everyone on guard tonight, we have the last five days covered.'

'But would all your guards remember him?'

Finally, the captain rounded on Dee. 'Can't miss him,' he said, his tone now angry.

'How so?'

The captain put his hands on his hips. 'Because he's fucking lame and walks with a golden cane.'

'A golden cane?'

'Describe it,' I said.

'Thick shank. Flat crown. Curved nose. You know. A cane.'

'But gold. Anything else unusual about it?'

'It's covered in symbols.'

'Al'Mayran symbols?'

'How would I know, Inspector?' the captain said, now almost pleading with me.

'Were they raised?'

'I reckon so.'

'Where is it?' I said, shrugging and making a show of looking around the crime scene.

'I don't bloody know.'

'Could any of your men or women have found it?'

'What are you saying?'

I stepped in close until I could smell the fish he'd had for breakfast. 'That one of them took it.'

'That cane wasn't here when I found him.'

'So we have a dead man who normally walked with a cane somehow sneaking past you without its aid during a storm,' I said, making a note.

'Now you listen—'

I walked away with Dee, past the dead Al'Mayran, and along the cobbled thoroughfare to the plain utilitarian wall blocking access to Salvation's Climb.

Unlike the southern faces of the other claws, which sloped in uneven and jagged forms of varying steepness towards the sea, Noon Claw was sheer and flat at its ocean-facing head – a single vertical stretch of hard rock from base to peak, as if a long-forgotten god had chopped the end away with a monstrous axe. For a few years, the Climb was the crowning glory of New Capital's architectural achievements. Now the steps were deemed unsafe for public use. There were iron gates in place at certain levels to allow workmen to reach sewage and hydraulic pipes. One such opening lay at the end of Sumaka Way and, in theory, it should have been locked, but today, it was hanging open.

'Do you think the lock was forced last night?' Dee said.

'Possibly. But these gates are always getting broken by children. Youngsters play on the steps. The older ones rob folk and use them to make their getaway,' I said. 'Didn't you and your friends ever come here, Cadet?'

'No, ma'am.'

'A good boy, eh?'

'I suppose. Did you come here, ma'am?'

'All the time,' I said, remembering games of hide-and-seek with Shona. 'Foolish, really.'

We entered the cliff-hewn corridor and, making sure not to stray too near to the stone balustrade, which, like the steps, had seen better days, walked past the ruins of small eateries and shops. Their remains resembled stone and concrete snowdrifts gathered against the inner wall.

Along the way, I tried to pick out footprints in the dust but found none. The blood trail I was hoping to discover was also sadly absent. As we approached the stairwell, I peered over the balustrade to inspect the outer flights. There was no indication of recent damage to the nearest, but on the beach below, there was lighter, sandier rubble, which had not long been exposed to the elements.

The protective walls around the stairwell had collapsed, so Dee and I took care as we walked to the other side of the gap and climbed down to the next landing.

'Careful, Ani. I mean, ma'am,' Dee said.

'It's not the internal flights you need to worry about, Cadet. They're carved out of the cliff face. It's the concrete outer flights that are falling to pieces.'

'Do you believe what our elders say, that Zalema summoned the wind to tear the steps down and punish us?'

'Knowing the New Capital contractors, someone just bought inferior concrete to siphon off money.'

Dee laughed.

'Then again, perhaps the old ones are right,' I said. 'After all, our ancestors used to climb the sheer cliff face, without ropes or hooks, as an act of penance. So cutting a thousand-foot stairwell to aid our climb is a bit of a cheat.'

I stepped out onto the granite landing and tapped the balustrade and supporting animal-shaped columns with the side of my clenched fist.

'What are you thinking, ma'am?'

'If you'd murdered a man that close to the end of Noon Claw, what would you have done with his body?'

'I would have thrown it into the sea.'

'As would every other native of Five Claws.'

'Do you think the murderer escaped this way, ma'am?'

'Probably, but did he also come up this way? And was he carrying our dead man, having killed him elsewhere?' I said.

'Why bother to toil up these steps with a body, especially during a storm? As you say, why not throw it into the sea?'

For a moment, I saw Shona's murderer tossing the bag with her corpse inside from the Bridge of Spirits like she was an empty beer bottle for which he no longer had use. I closed my eyes and shook my head until the memory went away.

'Are you okay, ma'am?' Dee said.

Before I could answer, a lone cloud drifted in front of the sun, dimming the cerulean sea and revealing a faint red beam from horizon to cliff. At first, I thought it was a fire on a distant ship, but I realised the light was radiating from the steps.

'Do you see that?' I said.

'Yes, ma'am, but I can't say what's causing it. Doesn't even look real,' Dee said.

The cloud drifted by, the Coiled Sea turned bright blue again, and the faint tint upon her surface vanished.

I started to descend the next flight, then noticed a widening crack between the landing and the first step, so, to Dee's evident relief, I climbed back up to the aisle and we returned to Rose Town.

I had not expected the Stars and the Sea to be open for business, but it was customary for the previous night's detritus to be cleaned away and the rooms given a well-needed airing. Ordinarily, I would have seen the comings and goings of the staff either enjoying their personal time or taking deliveries of fresh food and alcohol. But the doors of the Stars were locked and all the windows closed and shuttered.

I rang the bell, and when there was no answer, I stepped back, looking for any signs of life. The pale blue facade appeared undamaged, the tribal pilasters, with their heads styled to look like Xol, still held up the roof, and the hard bodies of the painted figures depicted in the frieze were still engaged in carnal acts.

'Police. Open up,' I shouted, banging on the door.

Memi, Nita's deputy, poked her head over the sill of a bedroom window and shouted down, 'Nita's not in.'

'Then I'll talk to you. Open up,' I said.

Memi was a tall and straight-backed woman with Kahokeyan hair as black as obsidian. I had known her for years and she was not normally given to nerves, her demeanour being proud, often defiant. Not today. Once she let me inside, she quickly bolted the door shut and, without addressing me, tightened the belt of her turquoise nightgown, folded her arms, and stared at her bare feet, almost stooping.

I smiled and looked around. The hallway, like the other rooms it led to on the ground floor – the saloon, waiting room, dining room and drawing room – was decorated with flourishes of gold leaf, satin, ivory and marble. Its dark varnished floorboards contrasted with the white-painted walls, upon which hung erotic paintings in ornate golden frames. The staircase had been broadened at its foot, and a thick crimson runner laid down. A new crystal chandelier in the shape of an octopus dangled above.

I remembered the hallway as a hub of activity, irrespective of the time of day or whether the establishment was open or closed, but now it was deserted, and the familiar sounds of laughter and giddy conversation absent, replaced only by the odd creak of a floorboard or muffled cough.

'Do you recognise the dead Al'Mayran in the thoroughfare?' I asked Memi as bluntly as I could.

'I've not had a good look,' she said, unable to meet my gaze.

'Is that a no?' I smiled and waited for her to answer.

'He might be a regular. We have a lot of Al'Mayrans come here,' she said.

'This one walked with a golden cane,' I said.

I saw in her eyes the realisation she could not deny knowing the man.

'Yes, we had a regular like that,' she said.

'Name?' I said.

'We didn't ask.'

I sighed at the obvious lie. 'Did he stay last night?'

'No,' Memi said.

'So I won't find his golden cane in one of your rooms?'

'Of course not.'

'Did he have a favourite?'

She shrugged.

'Come on, Memi. Did he prefer men or women, both, anyone in particular?' I said.

'What difference does it make? Do you think one of us would be stupid enough to kill him and leave his corpse on our doorstep?' she said.

'Yes. Beauty is the only constant for sale here. The intellect is variable.'

'That's ridiculous.'

'No, Memi. It's ridiculous to think you can lie to me and expect to be left alone. A client of yours is dead, a foreigner, and without any other plausible suspect, one will be found here. I already know the dead man saw Nitushi Nakni, as do you, so start cooperating. Where is the lad?'

'He left earlier this morning,' she whispered, her eyes cast down.

'With Nita?'

'Yes.'

'Where did they go?'

'To a meeting with Nita's advocate.'

'Did they step over the corpse as they left?'

'Am I supposed to take that question seriously?' she said, unfolding her arms and finally meeting my gaze, her anger igniting her bravado.

'I'll rephrase it. Did Nita and Nakni see the body before they left?'

'I think the guards discovered… him.'

'For Xol's sake, Memi. Do you see how suspicious this appears?'

'It's not like that, Ani. Please, no one here hurt that man. He was kind and respectful to all of us. I'm sorry he's dead,' she said.

'It doesn't matter. You have to do better, because the next time you see me, I may well be in the company of the CIB. Do you think they'll be as patient?'

'Why would they get involved?'

'Because they're High Chief Naka's dogs, and he doesn't like it when important foreign nationals turn up murdered. It's embarrassing. Make no mistake, he'll set the CIB loose, and Xol help you all then.'

Her eyes were wide and wet, her brow furrowed and her hands clenched at her sides. 'I'll tell you this. You've seen him before,' she said.

'Where?' I said.

'An Al'Mayran celebration. I was there escorting an old client. Your wife donated a painting to some group or other.'

'The Commemoration of Deliverance, a fundraiser for Al'Mayran orphans. Artists like Josee were asked to contribute. I remember the occasion, but not him. Did he speak at the ceremony?'

'No. He was reserved. He sat at his table the whole evening and only stood for the toasts.'

'Who did he sit with?'

'A husband and wife, I think, and another woman – all Al'Mayran.'

'Can you describe them?'

'Both women were blond. But the man had black hair like a Kahokeyan's.'

'A Coor'Seyan. They're Al'Mayran but they have Harn blood.'

'This one had a scar on his face.'

'No one else was at their table?'

Memi shook her head. 'No, but the Al'Mayran ambassador was sat at the next table,' she said, emphasising the word 'ambassador'.

'I'Rasnee?'

She shrugged. 'If that's his name.'

'What's the name of Nita's advocate?'

Memi leant forward. 'Deta Hinatse,' she whispered.

'Where's his office?'

'Red Tern Tower.'

'One more thing, Memi. Why did Nita take Hani and Mani with her?'

Memi's mouth dropped open. She shook her head in disbelief. 'How do you know—'

'The names of those brothers?'

'Damn you, Ani. You leave those boys alone, I mean it. They're just innocent children.'

'Innocent of what?' I snapped at her.

'I just mean they don't know anything about this,' Memi said, her tone defensive.

'Like you?'

'Yes.'

'And Nita and Nakni?'

'Of course.'

'Then why would Nita take them to see her advocate? What's she up to, Memi?'

'Nothing. She was taking them to town. It was convenient, nothing more.' Memi wrapped her gown even tighter around her shoulders.

I sighed and looked her up and down. It was no use, I thought. I'd got as much from her as I was going to, at least for now. 'Have it your way,' I said. 'But I want to speak to those brothers. And you'd better pass my warning about the CIB on to Nita. It's for her own good. Now, I want testimony from everyone here.'

CHAPTER THREE

EE REMAINED IN Rose Town to question the residents while the cabbie drove me from the highest level of Noon Claw, across Chief Pawe Skybridge, far above the waters of Magila Bay, towards the skytowers, where Madam Nita's advocate, Deta Hinatse, kept his office.

Along the way, I looked for Nita and Nakni and the young brothers, Hani and Mani, but I didn't spot them. Over two hours had passed since they had left the Stars, and I imagined their business with Hinatse had long since concluded.

We were soon nearing the rooftop plazas of the skytowers, accessible by the skybridges that connected them hundreds of feet above the bay. In this upside-down world, the main entrances were upon the animal heads of the towers while the ground floors were iron and concrete claws, grasping at the sharp bedrock that cut through the water.

The cab turned into Red Tern Tower's rooftop plaza. Once the driver had found a place to park, I told her to wait for me. Then I checked with reception which floor the advocate's office was located on. Not wanting to negotiate eighty-odd flights of steps to the eighteenth, I took a hydraulic lift down.

Hinatse's secretary of letters was a young Kahokeyan man of slim build with a thin moustache who, according to the modern trend, had slicked his hair back with oil. I introduced myself and held my police emblem out until the neck chain strained.

'He's with a client at the moment,' the secretary said.

'How long will he be?' I said.

'The appointment is scheduled to end in ten minutes but—'

'I'll wait that long, no more, then I'm going in. Please tell him that.'

'I can't interrupt—'

'Either you pass him the message, or I will.'

'Yes, Inspector.'

While the secretary was gone, I waited outside on Hinatse's spacious balcony, part of a deep setback below a recessed section of the tower. I gazed at the giant animal representation above me, admired the way the steel and plaster had been moulded to avoid sharp corners and hard edges and resemble a bird, albeit in a very stylised, cubic design, similar to those found on a tribal pillar.

To the south was the ancient Al'Mayran quarter at the mouth of Magila Bay, with the arcade, the park, and the Bridge of Spirits all clearly visible. I leant over the balustrade to watch the ceaseless flow of ships passing under the high-segmented arches of the bridge. Trade, my uncle said, was a force of nature in New Capital greater than any hurricane.

Hinatse's secretary returned, poked his head around the balcony door and said, 'The meeting is almost concluded. Would you like some salt tea while you wait?'

'Please. By the way, do you have a water closet?' I said with a wink.

Hinatse had the body of a typical middle-aged professional. That is to say, he was soft all over without being too fat, and his limbs were thin and unworked. He had kept enough weight off, despite his advancing years, for his jaw to remain defined, and although the skin around his almond-shaped eyes was wrinkled, it had not leathered. He was pale for a Kahokeyan, having spent most of his life indoors away from the elements, and his hands were smooth except for the thumb and forefinger of his writing hand, which, I noted when he dropped his pen, were calloused.

He smiled as he stood to shake my hand, then gestured to the chair in front of his desk. When he took his jacket off, I noticed it was unlined but had neatly finished seams – a hallmark, I had been told, of an expensive suit. He sat down, stretched his arms and adjusted the band that tied his grey hair into a long and loose ponytail.

'What can I do for you, Inspector Sulaqua?' he said.

'What did you discuss with Madam Nita?'

'I'm afraid that's confidential,' Hinatse said with a polite smile.

'Not if it pertains to a murder enquiry,' I said.

'Why do you assume it does?'

'One of her patrons had his throat cut last night. His body was found outside the Stars.'

'And Nita is a suspect?' he said, with an exaggerated tilt of his head.

I put my elbows on his desk and leant forward.

'Everyone at the Stars must be considered. And Nita coming to see her advocate is suspicious. Which is why I need to know what you discussed.'

He mirrored my position on his side of the desk.

'I'm sorry, Inspector, while I have no wish to obstruct your investigation, my first responsibility is to my client. If you can obtain a warrant, I am more than happy to let the courts decide whether or not to uphold Nita's rights.'

'You're making a mistake, Hinatse.'

'It wouldn't be the first time.'

'And you're not acting in Nita's best interests.'

He leant back and laughed. 'But you are?'

'Does that surprise you?'

'Frankly, yes.'

I sighed. 'Give me something. Talk in generalities.'

Hinatse drummed his fingers on the arms of his leather chair as he thought. 'The meeting related to the brothel, that's all I will say. Ask Nita for the details, or else come back with a warrant.'

I threw my testimony scroll on his desk and said, 'Put all that in writing.'

He unrolled the scroll and began to write.

I kept silent as he worked and said nothing when he handed the scroll back to me, but on my way out, I turned to him and said, 'The dead man is Al'Mayran. He was seen at an official function, so my next stop is the Al'Mayran embassy. If he proves to be a diplomat, the CIB will be brought

in. They'll stuff that warrant down your throat and make you choke on it.
Think about that, Hinatse.'

He flinched, gathered himself and stood to bow.

On the way out of Hinatse's offices, I thanked his secretary for the tea.

'Tell me about the two boys Nita brought,' I said.

'They waited here, on the balcony, same as you did,' the secretary said.

'They didn't meet with Hinatse?'

'No.'

'Did the young man, Nakni, mention anything about a dead
Al'Mayran?'

'No. He took a seat in the waiting area and didn't speak at all. He
looked like he'd been crying, so I left him alone.'

'And the boys?'

'They behaved themselves, more or less, whispering to each other in
code. All I could get from them were nods and head shakes, and giggles
from the youngest. I shouldn't be telling you this,' he said, looking towards
Hinatse's office door.

'Don't worry. You haven't breached any privilege. What's your name?'

'Nequa. Oza Nequa.'

'Are you Lo'tse?'

'My grandfather on my mother's side was.'

'Do you still have family on Sundown Claw?'

'Some cousins. I don't know them well. I'm a child of Pastnoon Claw,
eastern face, I'm afraid to say.'

I collected his testimony and said, 'Stay out of trouble, Oza Nequa. A
man like Hinatse doesn't deserve your loyalty.'

The cabbie drove me across Chief Pawe Skybridge to the top of Noon
Claw, then turned north past the theatres of Player's Realm. Here, much of
the detritus left by the storm had been cleared from the arcades, but there
were gaps in the rows of hanging banners, the odd boarded-up window,
and a few missing branches from the elm trees that ran along Palace Way.
Not all was ugly, though. Brightly coloured petals had been scattered like
tiny streamers across the plazas and surrounding greens, spreading their
sweet scent well beyond the flowerbeds.

As far as I could see, the theatres were opening their doors: the ancient sandstone Five Peaks, the traditional wooden and mud-brick Isulo House, and the recently built New Capital Playhouse, its stained glass and steel having withstood the gales as if they'd never blown.

People from all over the hoop of the Known World were gathering for the daytime shows, dressed in their finery. Kahokeyans, mainly retired elders, in stylised, modern versions of deerskin trousers and shirts, all colourfully decorated with embroidered animals, were looking to fill their empty afternoons with gentle diversion. Sitting and queuing with them were wealthy tourists, rich enough to travel for leisure, and merchants, in the city for business, who either had time to spare or were being indulged by their native hosts. There were Al'Mayrans in intricately patterned robes of swirling spirits mingling peacefully with their historic enemies, Harns, dressed in three-piece suits or traditional gowns, and other folk, like toga-clad Demor and dark-skinned Ziopians in white flowing robes.

The picture was similar farther north. Visitors moved between grand stone, marble, and iron houses of art and history or rested in open squares, scolding their bored offspring for their lack of appreciation, while single folk and childless couples grew merry around them.

The cafes, pastry shops, restaurants and pubs were overflowing, the conversation amongst the clientele sitting outside in the sun was loud and cheerful, and the aromas of spices, baked bread and fried fish mixed in the air. The only austere sight was the private clubs of pure-blood Magila and Yawe tribe members, dark stone and iron buildings whose entrances were locked and whose doormen stood guard with surly and entitled expressions on their humourless faces.

The cab got stuck in traffic in Patron's Sanctum while workmen and women cleared a fallen elm from the thoroughfare. As we waited, I watched New Capital's Kahokeyan elite, young heirs and heiresses, murdering their time and spending their unearned wealth.

Once the cab was moving again, the driver took me around Merchant's Plaza and under the Square, the police headquarters, onto Agale Thoroughfare, and past the purpose-built, often oppressive and character-less homes of state, all full of studious but self-important administrators.

Not all the architecture in the north was drab, though. I leaned forward and pressed my face to the window of the cab to make sure I didn't miss the headquarters of the navy, the army, the secret service, and the fire brigade, buildings constructed in sandstone and marble, decorated with tribal pillars intricately carved and painted to depict the usual cast of sacred animals. Farther ahead were the embassies of all the Known World nations and city-states, designed to demonstrate the glory and wealth of their homelands. When I was a child, my uncle would take my cousins and me to see them, and none was more spectacular than the Al'Mayran embassy.

The sprawling, five-storey structure was the epitome of Al'Mayran design: glass domes, high vaulted ceilings, arched windows and spires. Its exterior was a tornado of full-length, non-geometric, low and high relief sculptures, and swirling spirits, painted in carmine-red and gold against a cerulean background.

The driver pulled up beside the large iron gate.

'I know, wait here,' she said.

I laughed and handed her thruppence to buy some lunch. She tipped her cap and drove to a small eatery advertising fresh crab-paste wraps.

Coor'Seyan soldiers, pale-skinned but black-haired and dark-eyed, a result of their mixed Al'Mayran and Harn heritage, were on guard at the embassy gate. They looked splendid in their flowing black-and-scarlet robes as they raised their polished silver-and-gold spears to catch the sunlight.

I introduced myself to one of the guards, a slender woman with salt and pepper hair braided into a bun. She took me to a small, wooden cabin at one side of the gate, inside of which a young lieutenant was poring over paperwork at his desk, a cup of steaming and fragrant spiced tea poised at his lips.

'What's your business here?' the lieutenant said rather stiffly, while inspecting my police emblem. He had nicked the skin around the apple of his throat while shaving, a humanising touch which offset a square-jawed face designed to brood.

'An Al'Mayran has been murdered. He didn't have identification on him, but I have reason to believe he was a diplomat,' I said.

'I see. Wouldn't a formal approach through proper channels be in order?'

'A waste of time. The quicker I can move, the better. All that fish shit will follow in due course, Lieutenant…?'

He smiled and said, 'I'Seth. I see you believe in being direct.'

'Would Ambassador I'Rasnee prefer I solve the murder or dither, worrying about protocol?'

'Quite. Let me think. Obviously the senior staff will need to be advised, but you should start with security.'

'Fine.'

'I will introduce you to Agent Kohee.'

'A Kahokeyan?'

'Yes, a CIB liaison officer with whom we coordinate on security matters.'

'I see.'

'Is there a problem?'

'With the CIB? Always. In my experience, their brutality is only outweighed by their stupidity. But that's fine for now.'

I'Seth ordered the guardswoman to fetch Kohee. When she'd gone, he smiled again and drummed his fingers on the desk, seeming unsure what to say.

'Lieutenant I'Seth, the dead man had a withered leg and walked with a cane, a golden one. Sound familiar?' I said.

'Er, yes, yes it does,' he said. He grew quiet, his mouth half open, his hesitancy to speak clear.

'The name?' I said.

'Perhaps you should discuss this with Agent Kohee,' he said.

'What difference does it make?'

He thought for a moment. 'None, I suppose. It sounds like a man called Areel I'Advay,' he said.

'When did you last see him?'

'Perhaps a couple of days ago. Not yesterday. It was the ambassador's guards, not the regiment, who were at the gate. We share responsibility.' I'Seth looked over my shoulder and said, 'Agent Kohee is here,' the relief evident in his voice.

Had Kohee been a short man, it would have been a tight fit in I'Seth's cabin, but I doubted the giant Kahokeyan could enter, regardless of how many people were inside. I was not surprised that we met him on the gravel path outside.

He stood over six feet tall, and was almost half as broad, making him one of the most impressive physical specimens I had ever seen. He wore his ink-dark hair long and loose apart from a thin band around the temples to keep his face clear. The skin of his broad forehead was shiny and damp, and the curves of his almond-shaped eyes deep. He had a sharp-edged nose and thick well-defined lips resting in a benevolent smile at odds with the black CIB uniform he wore.

Once we were introduced, Kohee broke into a wide grin and shook my hand.

'Please call me Wes,' he said.

'How goes it with you, Wes?' I said, disarmed by his friendliness and thrown by his size.

'Very well, Ani. May I call you Ani?'

I didn't feel I could refuse. Mostly, I just wanted him to let go of my hand.

'You've brought sad news, I hear,' he said, finally relinquishing his grip.

'Indeed,' I said.

'So your purpose here is the identification of the dead man?'

'Not formally, but yes, I want to know about the victim, as much as you can tell me. I'd like to speak to his colleagues, the ambassador's guards, the ambassador himself, and anyone else who might have seen I'Advay over the last couple of days.'

'One step at a time, Ani, please. Come to my office, and we can talk.'

'I'd rather go to I'Advay's office.'

'What reason do you have to believe the victim is I'Advay?'

'Witnesses in Rose Town, where he was found, said he walked with a golden cane.'

'Rose Town?'

I nodded.

'To search I'Advay's office, I think we need to seek permission from—'

'A murder has been committed, Wes. I'm not interested in permission.'

'Well, I'll let you two agree on the way forward,' I'Seth said, backing away into his cabin. 'Agent Kohee, I will notify my superiors in the regiment. I assume you'll advise Captain I'Dreng?'

'Of course. Please, come, Ani,' Wes said, putting one hand on my back and gesturing towards the embassy with the other.

'Who is I'Dreng?' I said.

'He's the captain of Ambassador I'Rasnee's personal guard, and the head of security at the embassy,' Wes said.

'I need to speak with him, too.'

'All in good time.'

'Now is good for me.'

'Please understand, Ani, this is Al'Mayran land. We must respect that reality and proceed with sensitivity.'

I sighed and looked away.

The Al'Mayran embassy had suffered minimal storm damage, although I did spot a couple of spires with missing slates and the stump of a recently felled tree beside a boarded-up window. There was a garden to the south, overflowing with strong-smelling, cherry-red and blue perennials planted in curved lines. I had seen such a design before, and the resultant waves of colour usually rippled in the breeze, as if animated by the spirits they represented. But the wind had ravaged the flowers and torn most of their petals away, leaving them scattered upon the lawn like blossoms in spring.

Beyond the garden, still inside the embassy grounds but within its own perimeter, was the barracks, a hexagonal structure in the design of a motte-and-bailey castle with a fortified gatehouse and keep. Circular towers were built at every corner of the curtain wall, which was extended by parapets and complete with musket and arrow slits. But while the battlements were imposing, they were mostly for show and would not withstand attack. The Al'Mayrans would not have adorned the building with obsidian and gold if it were meant to resist cannon fire, nor would they have replaced the wall along the eastern cliff edge with living quarters.

'What was I'Advay like?' I said to Wes.

'A decent fellow, but I deal with the ambassador's office, mainly. Areel was with the Al'Mayran High Temple.'

There was an elaborately painted, four-seater, roofed carriage waiting along with a company of mounted guards dressed in cowls of navy blue and gold outside the embassy steps.

'Is Ambassador I'Rasnee leaving now?' I said.

'I assume so,' Wes said.

'Good, I want to talk to him.'

'Wait, Ani. We'll arrange a formal meeting,' Wes said.

I'Rasnee emerged onto the grand, columned portico, a guard flanking him on both sides. He wasn't as tall as many of his countrymen, but still cut an imposing figure in his intricately patterned gown, with folds and tails and full sleeves. He had greying, bright ginger hair, tied into a ponytail, and a neatly trimmed beard. His green eyes glowed, his thin lips looked like a red line had been drawn to approximate a mouth, and his cheeks seemed hollow, the flesh stretched over them like pastry hanging off the edge of a baking tin.

'Ambassador I'Rasnee,' I said, shouting up the steps and ignoring Wes's whispered protest.

'Yes?' I'Rasnee said, looking back and forth between Wes and me.

'My name is Inspector Sulaqua of the murder inspectors' department. I'm afraid I have some bad news.'

'Is this really the way, Ani?' Wes said, taking my arm.

'It's quite all right, Agent Kohee,' I'Rasnee said, descending the steps to shake my hand before folding his arms in his sleeves. 'Please tell me, Inspector.'

'An Al'Mayran man matching the description of Areel I'Advay has been murdered in Rose Town.'

'Oh, by the spirits, no,' I'Rasnee said. He placed his hand over his heart, while beside me, Wes looked away and squeezed the bridge of his nose. 'Rose Town you, say?'

I nodded.

'Well, Areel had needs like any other soul,' I'Rasnee said. 'And Al'Mayrans aren't a puritanical people.'

'You do, however, have a taboo about piercing or tearing the heart of another,' I said.

'It is the only crime punishable by death.'

'And why is that?'

I'Rasnee stared at me with an inquisitive expression. 'Why do I suspect you already know the answer, Inspector?'

I shrugged. 'Indulge me.'

'We believe our spirits live in our hearts, and if the heart is opened, either through violence or as a result of decay following death, the spirit is lost to the ether, doomed never to find a home in the Red Mountains,' I'Rasnee said.

'Is it true that someone who damages the heart of another forfeits his spirit also?'

'Indeed. Why this line of questioning, Inspector?'

'I'Advay had his throat cut.'

'Al'Mayrans are not the only people who slit throats. Forgive me, Inspector, despite this horrible news concerning our friend and colleague, which has shaken me, I really don't have much time today.'

'I won't keep you long. When did you last see him?' I said.

'We had a meeting yesterday morning,' I'Rasnee said.

'What cane was he using?'

'Either a red one or that beautiful golden one.'

'Please try and remember.'

'If I were certain, I would say.'

'Fair enough. What was I'Advay's role?'

'Areel didn't report to me, and he very much wrote his own brief. He represented Al'Mayra, specifically the High Temple, on a committee with members from all over the Known World dedicated to – how can I put it? – auditing the present state of magic. Suffice to say, this was an unusually long-term and nebulous mission for an envoy.'

'Could his duties have endangered him?'

'I wouldn't have thought so.'

'Any enemies?'

'None I'm aware of or that he reported to my guards.'

'Did his work ever involve lifeblood stones?'

I thought I saw I'Rasnee's lips curl into a slight smile and his eyes sparkle. 'Not that he ever discussed with me. His staff may be able to help there.'

'Good. I'll need to speak to them. I'd like to find out more by searching his office and his home.'

'If Areel has been found dead in the brothel area, why would his work be relevant?'

I shrugged. 'Anything could prove pertinent.'

'Regardless, for the time being, I'm afraid I cannot permit you access to his office.'

'Why not?' I snapped.

'Please understand, allowing a foreign authority to examine the papers of one of our envoys could compromise our country's security. It is essential that any sensitive material is removed or redacted before I can permit you access. Now, please excuse me, Inspector, I really must be on my way. I'm running late for a meeting with your High Chief Naka.'

'Come, Ani. Ambassador I'Rasnee has no desire to hinder your investigation. His concerns are legitimate and his position reasonable,' Wes said.

'Is it reasonable to tamper with evidence, Wes? Is that how the CIB operates?' I said with sarcasm.

'We operate within the law.'

I raised an eyebrow and looked at Wes hard, but before I could argue, another Al'Mayran man, one of huge stature, taller even than Wes, appeared at the top of the steps.

He walked on crutches and his right foot, which he kept raised from the ground, was heavily bandaged. His limbs were cannonballs of muscle linked by joints of sharp bone. He had wiry, strawberry-blonde hair, pulled into a ponytail that spread like the segment of a fan down his back. His thick jawline ended in a fat chin with a deep cleft. His lips were full but his mouth small, and his nose was little more than balls of excess cartilage glued onto his face. He wore britches underneath a short robe that did not reach beyond the middle of his thighs, with a pattern of nebulous red spirits fading into a brown background.

'Inspector, this is Liam I'Remo, my personal attendant. He was injured last night in the storm,' I'Rasnee said.

'What happened?' I said to I'Remo.

'He fell trying to fix a shutter at my residence. We came here this morning to see our doctor,' I'Rasnee said, answering for his servant.

'Why not a New Capital hospital?'

'Why drain your city's resources when we have our own?'

'Is it broken, Liam?' I said.

'Liam cannot speak, Inspector,' I'Rasnee said.

'I like him already.'

'Now, if I could ask you to coordinate with Captain I'Dreng and Agent Kohee regarding this tragic matter, I would be most grateful. It was a pleasure to meet you, Inspector Sulaqua. Goodbye.'

One of the guards pushed me aside to allow I'Rasnee by. When I tried to follow, I'Remo blocked my way with a crutch and scowled at me. I met his glare, my face flushed with heat, until I'Rasnee said, 'Come on, Liam,' then the giant hopped down the steps and climbed into the carriage with his master.

'Ambassador I'Rasnee,' I said.

I'Rasnee lowered the window of the carriage. 'Yes, Inspector?'

'I don't suppose you'd know anything about the use of lifeblood stones as a destructive force, would you?'

I'Rasnee laughed. 'Other than the legend of Ameeleyor and her staff, no, my dear Inspector, no.' Amusement still evident in his eyes, he said to the driver, 'When you're ready, my friend,' and wound the window up as the carriage pulled forward.

'You do know this is a home of diplomacy, don't you, Ani?' Wes said.

'What of it?' I said.

'I thought you might try using some. Now, come, let's have some tea. There's something I'd like to discuss with you.'

The embassy's circular entrance hall had a marble floor and sculptures set in recesses at intervals within the curved wall. The painted dome above depicted the lifeblood stones of the Red Mountains, shining their light into the dark sky, warming the air and melting the snow to temper the harsh winter. The spirits of the Al'Mayrans' ancestors, free of their bodies' prisons, were dancing in the starlight and watching over the living, who knelt before them in awe and prayer.

'Beautiful, isn't it?' Wes said as we climbed one of the two curved staircases to the top floor.

'Did you see the red light in the academy's dome last night?'

'I did.'

'Same thing.'

'Oh, that cannot be. The stones are sacred. The Al'Mayrans would never let them be experimented on.'

'Are there any stones at the embassy?'

'The altar in the temple, under the watch of a cleric.'

At the top of the stairs was a framed signpost listing the various departments, amongst them the Office of Spiritual and Magical Matters, which, it stated, was in the eastern annex.

A group of Al'Mayrans, clearly in a hurry, came up behind us. I allowed them to pass and separate me from Wes so I could shimmer the appearance of one of I'Rasnee's guards and escape.

Once my illusion was fixed, I followed the signs towards the far end of the embassy, down several flights of steps and through an arched corridor with stained-glass windows, until I reached the eastern annex where I found I'Advay's office.

I considered maintaining my shimmer – after all, an embassy guard could demand access. But what would I say to whoever was inside, and how irregular might it appear? I changed my mind and shimmered the appearance of I'Advay himself, all but guaranteeing I could trick my way inside. But to what end? I'd come to the embassy to confirm he was the dead man. Now Agent Kohee, the ambassador and others knew. How long would I have before I was caught? Minutes? And what would I do with that time? Search an office without knowing what I was looking for and where? Not worth it, I decided. So I checked to see if anyone was watching before revealing my true image.

An Al'Mayran woman, taller and more powerfully built than Josee, answered my knock. She had curls of light yellow hair and eyes of faint cobalt. She was as pale as any Al'Mayran I had ever met with barely a hint of red in her pink lips. The spirits stitched into her robe were gold and every shade of blue, and they frolicked and coiled together until the roots of their individual strands were indistinguishable and lost in the dance. The breeze from an open window lifted the woman's flowing tresses and caused them to billow gently around her head as if she were an ethereal being amongst mortals.

'May I help you?' she said with a gentle smile.

'Is this Areel I'Advay's office?' I said.

'His office, his department.'

'What's your name?'

'Dabreeyor A'Mendayse. I am Mister I'Advay's secretary of letters. May I ask, who are you?'

'Inspector Sulaqua.'

'Inspector?'

I nodded.

'Why are you here?' she said, concern in her voice. Her demeanour changed, too. She bit her bottom lip, furrowed her brow, and covered her heart with her hand.

'Perhaps I should come in, and you should sit down,' I said.

'Oh, by the spirits. It's Areel, isn't it? What's happened?'

'Nothing has been confirmed, but a man fitting his description has been killed in Rose Town.'

'Oh, no, by the spirits, no.'

She dropped into a crouch and covered her face with her hands, wiping the tears from her eyes before they spilled.

'Let's go inside,' I said.

'I knew it. I knew it. I just bloody knew it,' she said, beating her chest with her fist.

As I tried to lift her up, a lanky, bronze-haired and clean-shaven Al'Mayran man with unsmiling grey eyes, who wore leggings and a long cowl of navy blue and gold, the uniform of the ambassador's personal guard, entered the annex with Wes.

'What is the meaning of this?' the guard said.

'You must be Captain I'Dreng,' I said.

He nodded and accepted my hand almost begrudgingly.

'What are you doing here, Sulaqua?' he said.

'I need to search I'Advay's office,' I said.

'Unacceptable, as I believe Ambassador I'Rasnee has already explained to you. I would ask that you leave.'

'You can't prevent an investigation.'

'I will conduct my own with Agent Kohee and his CIB colleagues. We will coordinate with your department as and when jurisdiction is established. If you remain on the case, you may be permitted limited access to I'Advay's work. Until then, leave. I won't ask again.'

'Is that a threat?'

'An order.'

My throat constricted, and a band of iron tightened around my temples. 'I am a New Capital inspector of murder, I'Dreng, and you don't give me orders,' I said, squaring up to him. 'Furthermore, you will not be permitted to keep this investigation an internal affair.'

I felt Wes's hand on my forearm, and I noticed my hand was resting on the pommel of my sword.

'Come, Ani, there's no profit in debating this further,' Wes said.

'Perhaps you're right,' I said, allowing Wes to lead me away from I'Dreng, who stood with his hands on his hips, eyeing me with a death stare.

Wes and I left the annex at the far eastern side of the embassy and wandered towards a wooden viewing platform that overlooked Yawe Bay. Neither of us spoke as we leant on the oak railings and took in the spectacle of Treasure's Rock, a cluster of gleaming skytowers adorned with banners and flags, built from polished steel and concrete mixed with gold dust and precious jewels. It was the beating heart of banking and commerce, through which much of the Known World's trade passed like currents in the Coiled Sea. For a moment, I thought I could smell the ink and metal of newly minted notes and coins floating across the waters from the Bank of New Capital, but the bank's dark stone walls were obscured by the towers and we were standing far downwind.

'How did you get away from me?' Wes said, without a hint of anger.

'With ease,' I said.

'No, you disappeared.'

'I was right under your nose.'

'You can shimmer, can't you?'

I smiled but said nothing.

'Need I remind you, Ani, that for over a century, it has been illegal for a law officer to use shimmering to aid their investigation.'

'Thank Xol I'm not a shimmerer then.'

'I could have you thrown off the force,' Wes said, his tone lacking conviction, expressing possibility without threat.

'Do what you must,' I said, unable to prevent a smile from spreading across my face.

'It's entrapment.'

'Not intrinsically.'

'Either way, I assume you know any evidence you uncover while shimmering will be inadmissible. So why take the risk?'

I smiled again and said, 'Tell me about A'Mendayse.'

Wes sighed before he answered, but his exasperation seemed affected, and there was amusement in his eyes. 'She's I'Advay's secretary of letters.'

'So she said. But what's she like as a person?'

'Friendly, kind even, and, as far as I can tell, fond of I'Advay,' Wes said.

'She certainly took the news hard,' I said.

'Listen, Ani, it is I who will likely be put in charge of the investigation, from the CIB side, that is.'

'Let's see if you can cooperate more than the Al'Mayrans.'

Wes sighed again. 'You have a low opinion of the CIB, I see?'

'In general, I find your agents brutal and corrupt, more interested in serving High Chief Naka than the city,' I said.

Wes laughed. 'But what do you really think?'

'Prove me wrong,' I said.

'I'll begin by sharing the details of a strange incident that occurred in the barracks last night. One your sad news may – and I emphasise, *may* – cast in a different light. In all likelihood, it's unconnected to I'Advay's murder, but in the spirit of accord, it should be mentioned.'

'Then spit it out, man.'

'The garden window entrance to Brigadier I'Kalmeen's study was broken in the storm and a young soldier killed when he fell into the glass. I had no reason to doubt the validity of this report, until now.'

'Are you suggesting it wasn't an accident?'

'I won't speculate further.'

'Have you been permitted to investigate?'

'I sought guidance from my superiors. They advised it was an internal Al'Mayran matter.'

'Ridiculous. I need to see that body.'

'I fear we're too late,' Wes said, nodding towards the barracks.

Smoke, irradiated by an otherworldly red glow, was rising above the battlements of the barracks' curtain wall. A lifeblood stone cremation was underway. For the briefest of moments, as the smoke was taken east by the breeze, I thought I saw the light separate, like a distributary channel from a river, and form a new stream that veered north-east on a course towards Al'Mayra.

The cab driver smiled when she saw me crossing Agale Thoroughfare, her frosty disposition having melted since I bought her lunch.

'I got you a crab-paste wrap, but you were longer than I expected. I won't vouch for it,' she said.

'I'll take the risk, and I thank you,' I said, catching the wrap she threw me.

I climbed into the cab and was about to shut the door when a hooded Al'Mayran jumped onto the seat beside me. My reflexes kicked in, and I had one of my pistols drawn and aimed at the Al'Mayran before they could close the cab door.

'By the spirits, don't shoot, Inspector Sulaqua. I have something to ask you, and I didn't want to be seen.' Dabreeyor A'Mendayse pulled her hood down and shook her pale yellow hair loose.

'As a rule, try not to alarm police officers. Would you believe some members of the public wish us ill?' I said with a smile.

'Forgive me. I just thought you might want to accompany me to Areel's home?'

I nodded and told the driver to take us to the Negotiated Burroughs.

'What did you want to speak to me about?' I said, when the cab was moving.

'As you've no doubt just witnessed, we cremate our dead as soon as possible to ensure their spirit enters the Red Mountains. But if there's a delay, we perform a lifeblood stone preservation ritual,' Dabreeyor said.

'And you want this carried out for I'Advay?'

'I want to perform it for my dear friend.'

'Ease your mind. The police have accommodated this request before.'

'Oh, thank the spirits. I can't tell you how relieved I am to hear that.'

The driver turned west off Agale Thoroughfare and down a steep winding carriageway by the cliff edge. The sun was passing over Noon Claw and her rays were reflecting off the windows of the skytowers and the waves of Magila Bay.

'I never tire of seeing that sight,' Dabreeyor said.

'It is spectacular. Where would you get the lifeblood stones for the ceremony?' I said.

'The cleric at the embassy.'

'Would the regiment have done the same?'

'Yes.'

I took out my notebook and said, 'I'm going to ask you a few questions now, Dabreeyor. May I call you Dabreeyor?'

'Of course.'

'When did you last see Areel?'

'Yesterday, before he went to his meeting with Major I'Handdru.'

'At the barracks?'

'Yes. That was in the afternoon, at three o'clock. I left the embassy around five, before he returned.'

'What was the meeting about?'

'The suitability of Al'Mayran defences against magical warfare, considering we have no such capabilities ourselves.'

'That's not entirely true, is it? Not if you include the warrior Ameeleyor, her staff, and the lifeblood stone.'

'That's just a religious tale,' Dabreeyor said, laughing.

I shrugged.

'Sorry, Inspector, I don't mean any offence,' she said.

'None taken. Did Areel study the stones or have occasion to handle them?'

'We all touch the stone altar at the temple.'

The driver pulled up at the northern guard post of the Negotiated Burroughs. I waved my police emblem and Dabreeyor showed her diplomatic pass.

'Will you take over Areel's work?' I said.

'Not without access to his office. I'Dreng has locked me out. Oh, the papers Areel had in there. Every unexplainable act of magic from the Known World detailed and illustrated in his own hand. Maybe Ameeleyor will be allowed in?'

'Ameeleyor?'

'Not the warrior,' Dabreeyor said with a smile. 'Ameeleyor A'Jozaf, an attached secretary to Areel's mission. She's best placed to take over.'

'Where does she live?'

'On Dayna's Lane in Jayson's Haven.'

I looked out of the window as we passed through the Harn area of the Burroughs, all full of wooden houses with simple, clean lines, sliding doors and screens.

'Did Areel have enemies?' I said.

'None that I'm aware of,' Dabreeyor said.

'What about Nitushi Nakni? Did you ever meet him?'

'Areel would hold dinner parties, and Nitushi was often there. I even visited him at the Stars on two or three occasions to cancel or rearrange a date Areel made.'

'Who else attended the dinner parties?'

'Usually Ameeleyor and her husband.'

'Name?'

'Mycale I'Krayag. He's a Coor'Seyan soldier.'

'What are your impressions of Nitushi Nakni?'

'Beautiful but masculine. Proud. Surprisingly thoughtful and well-read.'

'Did he and Areel fight?'

'Not that I witnessed. Nitushi strikes me as a gentle soul.'

'Did they socialise outside in the city?'

'Yes. Plays, exhibitions, they shared a love of the arts.'

'What about cafes, eateries, taverns?'

'I wouldn't be surprised to find out Areel ate in every Al'Mayran establishment in New Capital and many others.'

'Tell me about the golden cane?'

'An affectation Areel enjoyed, although he would never admit it.'

'Did he have it on him yesterday?'

'He often used a wooden one carved into a spirit and painted red. It was either that one or the golden cane, I can't remember which.'

Dabreeyor knocked on the roof of the cab and the driver pulled up.

The thoroughfare was wide and lined either side with silver birch trees. The homes were large, stone and brick builds, covered in brightly painted cavorting spirits, and set back from the walkways in private gardens humming with the buzz of honeybees. The sharp aroma of ginger mixed in the air with the bouquet of flowers and sweet-smelling nutmeg and other fragrant spices used by Al'Mayrans.

I didn't have to ask Dabreeyor where I'Advay had lived: two of Ambassador I'Rasnee's guards stood in front of a fenceless garden bordered by green- and purple-leafed beech trees with branches that curved together like the arms of a dancing troupe. Between their trunks, clusters of nettles and thorny shrubs had been planted to keep snoopers away.

'They got here quickly,' I said.

Upon seeing me, one of the guards vanished down a winding path through the wildflower garden beyond.

'May we pass?' Dabreeyor asked the remaining guard.

'Please wait here, kind lady,' he said.

Dabreeyor turned to me and rolled her eyes. 'I'm worried about Areel's housekeeper, Klareesa. She was like a mother to him, and must be grieving terribly. I want to be with her to offer her my support. After all, I've nothing else to do.'

'I doubt I'll be permitted to see her. Can you ask her when she last saw I'Advay and what cane he had with him?'

'Of course. Anything else?'

I wanted to know if I'Advay had been tense or irritable in his last days, and if the housekeeper believed he was in any danger or had any enemies, but they were the sorts of questions you wanted to ask in person, to be present and look into the eyes of whoever was answering, to search for fear and lies.

'That will do for now,' I said.

The other guard returned with a stocky fellow, no doubt her commander. He was freckled and square-faced with plump cheeks and a deeply creased brow above the bridge of a small and round nose. He was short for an Al'Mayran, almost squat and bordering on fat, and wore his red hair close-cropped and parted to one side.

Dabreeyor bent over to whisper in my ear, 'That's Ryeen I'Delboot. I'Dreng's right-hand man.'

'I'm Inspector Sulaqua,' I said, offering him my hand.

I thought he was nervous, scared even, but it seemed his expression might be permanently fixed in a state of surprise.

'Lieutenant I'Delboot,' he said, taking my hand.

'How did you know about I'Advay?' I said.

'I was with Captain I'Dreng when Agent Kohee informed him.'

'I see. You must have raced down here.'

'I follow my orders.'

'Which are?'

'Not to let anyone in.'

'Anyone, or just me?'

'Anyone not with the ambassador's guards, although Ms A'Mendayse may enter if she agrees to remain in the living area.'

'This isn't the embassy, Lieutenant. This is New Capital territory, and I'm one of her commissioned law officers. You don't have the right to keep me out.'

'Be that as it may, those are my orders, and I intend to carry them out. I hope you will respect that.'

I took Dabreeyor to one side and said, 'I'll find you tomorrow.'

'No need, Inspector, I'll come to you. Where do you live?' she said.

I gave Dabreeyor my address, said goodbye to her, and had the cab driver take me to the South-Western Great Lift platform atop Noon Claw. I overpaid the driver and thanked her for her patience, freeing her of any further obligation. She tipped her cap at me and drove off without saying a word.

By the Great Lift ticket booth, there was an overseer's office, accessible via a battered wooden door covered with splintering blue paint. Inside was a small, windowless and musty room packed with accounts and ancient logbooks that smelt of vanilla. There were two bored Kahokeyans inside, sitting with their backs to one another at dark varnished desks. One of them, a young woman, looked up and smiled.

'Is the overseer in?' I said, pointing up a steep staircase.

Her eyes grew bright with mischief when she nodded. Not paying her any mind, I took the stairs two at a time, using the handrail as leverage to propel me up. And when I burst into the overseer's office, I interrupted his advances towards a female colleague.

I flashed my police emblem at them both and glared at the woman, who was busy adjusting the hem of her dress.

'Out,' I said to her.

The woman hopped off the desk where she had been perched and ran by me, a smirk spreading across her face, barely able to stifle her giggles.

I doubted the overseer was yet thirty, but his inactive role was already expanding his waistline. He stood, flattened the collar of his white shirt, which grew bright in contrast to his reddening face, and tried to button his waistcoat. But he forgot the two sides no longer met, and so he straightened his ponytail before sitting down and trying to regain his composure.

'What can I do for you, Officer?' he said, holding his fist over his mouth and coughing.

'Inspector,' I corrected him. 'If I give you a ticket number, can you tell me which conductor issued it?'

'Certainly.'

I took out my notebook and read him the number on I'Advay's ticket. The overseer jotted it down on a piece of scrap paper, and ran out of his office and down the stairs. I followed him out and was about to take the stairs when I noticed a door at the end of the corridor with a sign reading *Keep Out*. I opened it and was hit by the stench of oil and sweat and the din of clanging chains and straining wood, reminiscent of a ship's hull twisting in heavy winds.

The modern lifts within the city's skytowers may have been mechanised with pressurised water, but the ancient Great Lifts, which could carry a hundred people and a score of cabs and carriages on each of their many decks, were older than hydraulic power, and, as yet, they hadn't been converted. Instead, these beasts relied on the muscle of men and women to turn their winches and raise and drag their weight.

I stepped out onto a metal landing and rested my hands on the iron rail. Below, in the gloom of a lamplit shaft dug into the cliff rock, were hundreds of souls, all gathered around the winch wheel, lined up along spokes the length of ships' masts. They worked together, driving perpetually forward, leaning into the leather-padded timber, always in motion, going nowhere except round and round in circles. The heat rose from their glistening bodies, and their muscles and fibres strained to force the teeth of gears to bite together and slot giant sprockets into chain links the size of a buffalo's torso.

If you lived in New Capital long enough, you started to recognise those who turned the wheel. Their skin was paler than a Kahokeyan's should be, their thighs like tribal pillars and their shoulders like the crowns of anchors. At least, that was their youthful appearance. In old age, they became twisted and permanently hunched over. But if you spent the required four decades in the drive station, you earned the right to take a room in one of the pensioners' homes. There, if you were lucky, you might be rewarded with a few more years of physical pain along with your three meals a day, all the ale you could drink, and a simple uniform with the company's logo stitched onto the breast pocket.

'Inspector, I have that name for you,' the overseer said, appearing behind me.

I took the scrap of paper from him and read the name. 'Where is he working today?' I said.

'He isn't. He's taken a couple of days' leave. I've written the address down for you.'

'Fine,' I said, taking one last look at the wheel and the souls who turned it. Shaking my head, I left with a cloud of guilt hanging over me, the same as if I'd been the only survivor of a shipwreck, left alive to wonder why she had been spared when so many had been taken.

I tried to clear my head by strolling north along Magila Bay View, away from the bustle of Player's Realm and Patron's Sanctum. I took a lane down the cliff, by layers of mansions with ivy pouring like waterfalls from their terraces and private decks.

I cut across Riverlyn Park; folk were having picnics and children were paddling in rivers and playing hide-and-seek in the ruins of abandoned stone mills. As I walked, the perfume scent from the flowerbeds drove the stench of the lifts from my clothes and the guilt from my heart.

In the spring, the dawn chorus of mating birds rang out, but as the summer progressed, their song faded. They could still be seen swooping low beneath the trees and shooting through the banks of narrow rivers. And there were plenty of bees and butterflies and colourful leaf-footed bugs to distract a troubled mind. I even saw a red-spotted furry dog moth the size of a sparrow squaring off against a giant rainbow grasshopper before they went their separate ways, perhaps deciding the day was too beautiful for an argument.

At the northern side of the park, I joined the tourists on Pawe's Lament behind the Magila Bay waterfall. The refreshing mist cooled my skin. Beyond the waterfall, there was a little-known path winding steeply up a stretch of undeveloped cliff face. If you followed it for long enough, you emerged outside the Octagon Hall in the science academy.

It took me the best part of an hour to climb two-thirds of the way, and when I reached a natural landing, overgrown with wild grass and flowers, I sat on a wooden form to catch my breath and take in the bay.

The form was ancient and dilapidated, its seat bowed and covered in moss. When I adjusted my position, I trod on a hard object, the sharp edges of which I could feel through the soft sole of my deerskin shoe. I lifted my foot and found a splinter of stone, charred on one side, the colour of a cherry. I rubbed the scorch marks and stained my fingers, the same as if I'd taken a pinch of chilli powder.

'Well, well, well,' I said, putting the stone in my pocket and looking around.

I discovered more small fragments and larger chunks. All were recently broken and scorched with the curious reddish burns. I followed the trail up the steps, finding more pieces of greater size until I came across about a third of a rectangular block that had, unmistakably, been part of the Octagon Hall.

Centuries of wind and rain made it easy to determine the exposed side, which, I noted, had no singe marks except along the cracked edges. The internal side might have been used to contain a fire in a pit. Whatever force destroyed the wall, it came from inside the building.

I raced up the cliff with renewed energy, only slowing as I approached the top. Droplets from the nearby waterfall looped and spun in the breeze, falling upon me and mixing with perspiration, causing my clothes to stick to my skin and my ponytail to become glued to my neck. I wiped my brow and crawled up the last few steps, taking care to raise my head only a little above the edge of the flat break.

The academy sat nestled in the natural cleft where Noon Claw curved into the mainland, below the high chief's residence, the Wooden House. Of all the buildings making up the New Capital Science Academy, the Octagon Hall was the most impressive, with its grand glass dome, ornate curving lines and marble walls that appeared to ripple and bring the depictions of Xol and its friezes dancing to life.

Scientists were lying in the gardens to the west, stretched out on their long, brown leather lab coats, eating fried bread wraps. Not far away at the nearest entrance were two guards, clad in deerskin, who stood chatting, partially obscured from my view by the stone animal columns of the portico. But I was more interested in the workmen and women, busy either boarding up the gaping hole in the wall or constructing the scaffolding ready for the permanent repairs to get underway. I tried to hear what they were saying but the thunder of the waterfall drowned their voices out.

The hole in the wall was an upside-down keyhole, seared red all around the edges. The great dome above was intact and devoid of any burn marks. And if further proof were needed that lightning had not caused the damage, the blast's direction was evident from the rubble, lying spread out like the leaves of an open fan, across the lawn near where I crouched spying from the cliff face.

A bird call, a sharp, high-pitched Magila tribal signal, penetrated the waterfall's din. Startled, I looked for the guards and saw them running in my direction. I considered trying to escape down the path, but I was a police officer and had every right, as I saw it, to enter the grounds of the academy. Apparently, the youngest of the guards, a tall and rangy fellow with a long black Kahokeyan mane, disagreed with me. He dragged me up onto the lawn by the lapels of my suit jacket.

'Who are you?' he said, drawing his axe from the belt of his traditional loincloth.

My throat tightened, and I heard the clang of the Great Lift's chains. I took hold of his shirt, spun, and dropped to my knees, pulling him over my shoulder. I sprang up and flipped him onto his back with his legs dangling over the cliff edge. I drew a pistol and, keeping hold of his collar, rammed the muzzle under his chin.

'My name is Inspector Sulaqua of the New Capital Police Force, and I have a mind to empty your head of what little brains there are rattling around in there.'

'Easy, Sulaqua,' his partner said, slowing to a trot as he approached.

I heard my old fencing instructor's advice: *blow the candle out, Ani, blow the candle out*, or in other words, don't let emotion be your downfall. Remain calm. Remain focused. I took a breath and looked up at the other guard.

He was an older, more well-built man, with a shaved head and an amused glint in his eye. No doubt he was entertained by the sight of his young comrade neutralised so easily by one so tiny.

'What are you doing here?' he said.

He grabbed the police emblem that hung from my neck and pulled the chain taut, almost causing me to topple forward.

'Out for a stroll,' I said.

'Just getting a little exercise, is that it?'

'Sure.'

There was the patter of soft-soled boots upon stone. Twenty or more guards, all dressed in deerskin trousers, sleeveless shirts, and loincloths, were racing down the hill and across the narrow bridge over the waterfall from the Wooden House.

'Shit,' I said, under my breath.

'Shit indeed, Inspector,' the older guard said.

When his comrades arrived, he took his place within the semicircle they formed around me. Once in position, they took out their axes and daggers as their commander, a stout woman with a tattooed face, stepped forward. She eyed me with suspicion and curled her top lip.

'Let him up,' she barked.

With slow, smooth movements, I slid my pistol back into its holster and stood, showing her the palms of my hands. The young guard leapt to his feet and leaned forward to glare into my face, placing his nose inches from mine.

'Have you tried mint tea? It's good for bad breath,' I said.

'Okay, enough of that. You've no business being here,' the commander said, drawing the young guard away.

'She was studying the damage,' the older guard said, nodding in the direction of the Octagon Hall.

'I'll take her to the Wooden House, see what the high chief has to say.'

'And if I refuse?' I said, resting my hand on the grip of my pistol.

The guards let out a battle cry and advanced towards me, adopting positions of attack.

'The high chief it is,' I said.

The Wooden House, located at the end of Agale Thoroughfare east of the academy, where the Kahokey river split into the Yawe and Magila Bay waterfalls, appeared to have been constructed with timber. But it was an ivy- and moss-covered illusion, a spurious natural facade wrapped around concrete and steel, meant to provide the citizens of New Capital with a sense of continuity, like an ancient echo still resonating. It was even kept free of advertising banners.

There were no ramparts or battlements, no curtain wall or fence, just plenty of warriors to defend the tapered northern end of the thoroughfare. Several had formed a line on the moss-covered portico along the threshold of the great doors. The commander with the tattooed face nodded and they made a passageway with their bodies leading into the entrance hall.

Inside, ivy covered the walls, encouraged by the sun shining through the smokehole in the roof. The only decorative features were the carved pillars and tribal banners hanging from the rafters. Seating forms ran along the skirting on all sides, with more benches laid out in a square around an open fireplace that gave of the fresh scent of mint.

Only the commander accompanied me to the inner courtyard beyond, where a giant wooden sculpture of Xol with his tentacles wrapped around the Five Claws was erected. As in my dream, I could not tell whether he was embracing or strangling the residents of his city, and perhaps it did not matter. After all, as any child coming of age will tell you, there is little difference.

Hundreds of warriors stood to attention along the perimeter of the open square, hands behind their backs, staring straight ahead while two men were engaged in a game of handball in one corner. The older player was not in uniform. He wore plain loose-fitting animal-skin trousers and a long-sleeved cotton shirt with a raven's talon embroidered on the chest. He had drawn his greying hair into a ponytail and wrapped a kerchief around his head to soak up the sweat. He was small but agile, and despite the years he had on his opponent, he moved if not quicker then with more assured purpose. When the ball went out of play, he ran, almost like a boy, to collect it. It was only then, as he crouched and looked my way, that I realised it was High Chief Naka.

He came bounding over, tossing the ball in the air, and offered me his hand. I took it without thinking, noting his small features gave his face an unremarkable appearance, no more intimidating than his stature. I had only ever seen him in portraits and sculptures, and I had difficulty accepting that this rather innocuous-looking, middle-aged man was the most powerful soul in the Known World.

'What brings you here, Officer?' he said.

'Inspector,' I corrected, adding 'Sir' as an afterthought.

'Yes, yes.'

The commander whispered in the high chief's ear and left with one final glare in my direction. Although her expression didn't strike fear into my heart, the wide grin spreading across her master's face unnerved me to the point of shame and made my guts turn.

'Interested in lightning damage, are we, Inspector?' Naka said.

'I didn't see any,' I said.

'What a pity, having climbed such a long way up a dangerous path to study the strike on the academy.'

'Is that what happened? Looked like an explosion to me.'

'Your concern touches me, Inspector, but rest assured there were no fireworks in the hall last night, Xol preserve us.'

'How do you account for the blast radius?'

'I'm not a scientist, Inspector. I don't have to, and, thankfully, neither do you. What department are you in, may I ask?'

'I'm investigating the murder of an Al'Mayran, in all likelihood an envoy. Perhaps you know him. Areel I'Advay?'

'I never had the pleasure, but Ambassador I'Rasnee mentioned his probable passing in our meeting today. That makes you Inspector Sulaqua?'

'I'Rasnee mentioned me, too?'

'Sulaqua. That's Lo'tse, isn't it?'

I nodded.

'Do you live on Sundown Claw?' he said.

'No,' I said, acid rising in my throat.

'Still, I wager you have family there. For whom do you work?'

'Chief Inspector Imala.'

'Ah, I know Imala, and I'll be sure to pass my compliments to her.'

'Sir?'

'For training an officer who exhibits such dutiful care. Anyway, good day to you, Sulaqua.'

With a smile and a nod, he spun on his heel and strode away, tossing the ball. My heart was beating fast. I thought its pounding might break my chest, and I told myself not to press him further, and to leave while I could.

'What about the lights?' I called.

Naka leaned his head back and regarded me, a faint smile curling on his lips. 'What lights?' he said.

'The red ones in the dome,' I said.

'Oh, those. They're nothing special, just the consequence of what my scientists call the amber effect. Although the lights always remind me of trying to catch a thunder fish.'

'They remind me of lifeblood stones.'

Naka's eyes widened with amusement, and he could no longer contain his smirk. 'Yes, yes, Sulaqua, very true.'

CHAPTER FOUR

As I walked away from the Wooden House, my thoughts spun like an eddy, valueless and without structure. So I ordered a coffee and a sweet cake from the first cafe I saw and sat under the awning on the walkway of Agale Thoroughfare. My hand was shaking and my saucer was awash with spilled coffee. I closed my eyes and slowed my breathing, trying to relax my neck and shoulders and loosen the knots of tension. *Blow the candle out, Ani, blow the candle out.* But rattled or not, the truth was evident. The high chief, the most powerful person in the Known World, had lied to my face, the same as any common villain.

As I washed the last of the cake down, I heard a horse galloping. A guard from the Wooden House rode south on a grey mount. Beside me, an elderly couple hailed a cab. I barged them aside before they could climb in, flashing my police emblem and letting insufficient apologies fall from my mouth.

The sun was arching west, purpling the sky above Pastnoon Claw, and from the south, a scattering of clouds were advancing, bringing shining silver rain with them. Traffic was growing heavy with folk travelling home from work, but the grey rider weaved his horse between carriages with admirable skill, pulling ahead before disappearing from sight altogether.

We were nearing the Al'Mayran embassy, so on a hunch, I knocked on the roof of the cab and ordered the driver to pull up opposite the gate. I remained in the cab and stared through the side window. The messenger was untying the reins of his horse from a hitching post north of the embassy steps.

'Drop me off outside Merchant's Plaza,' I said to the driver.

We took the western underpass below the Square, a one-way tunnel, wide enough for one carriage. And a passing rider. The messenger from the Wooden House didn't hesitate. He flew past, eliciting much profanity from the cab driver, which echoed off the tunnel roof.

When we emerged, rain was falling, growing heavier by the time we pulled up at the rank in Merchant's Plaza. I turned the collar of my jacket up before paying my fare, and queued at a street vendor to buy a bag of boiled sweets, my belly rumbling, set off by the aroma of freshly cooked seafood infused with gentle herbs.

I hurried across the plaza, dodging umbrellas and diving between awnings for cover before crossing the busy road to the Square's yard. I took the steps to the entrance hall two at a time and almost bumped into the Wooden House messenger striding out.

'How goes it with you?' I said.

He scowled and wiped sweat and raindrops from his brow but neither answered nor stopped.

'I'm well, I thank you,' I said to his back.

The Square's entrance hall was as familiar to me as the flat I shared with Josee or the house I had grown up in on Sundown Claw. Usually, I paid scant attention to the high vaulted marble ceiling with the mural of Xol, or the brightly coloured tribal pillars, carved into sacred animals, or even to the names of fallen officers chiselled into its clean white walls. But today the hall brought to mind the first time I entered the Square, aged thirteen, to report Shona's murder.

On that day, to ensure I wouldn't draw attention to myself, I shimmered the appearance of a police constable I had seen leaving. Despite my disguise, several passing officers and administrators had stared at me as I checked the information board for the location of the murder department. Then, as now, I chose not to take the grand central staircase or the hydraulically powered chains of paternoster lifts, looping constantly between floors. Instead, I slipped through a small service door and down a narrow spiral stairway.

I wasn't sure why I had chosen to tell Imala about Shona. Back then, my chief inspector was young, a junior inspector, and nothing about her particularly exuded kindness or approachability, certainly not her rigid posture or the way her round-rimmed wire spectacles magnified her unblinking and inscrutable eyes. Perhaps I related to her slight build? Either way, it was her desk I stood next to, waiting until she saw me stop shimmering and reveal my true self.

All the other officers jumped to their feet when I changed appearance. Some yelled out and clutched their chests or reached for their pistols. Not Imala. She barely flinched. Maybe her eyes widened a little, and I even think a faint smile may have fluttered across her lips. What I remembered most of all was the way she pointed to the chair across from her and said, 'Please have a seat,' in the same manner she would have addressed a wealthy adult. It did not matter to her that I was a small child in homemade sealskin clothes.

But young Inspector Imala was not waiting for me anymore. Now it was Chief Inspector Imala whose office I headed to, one of a handful along the western wall.

Medele, her elderly secretary of letters, looked up when I entered his dark and cramped ancillary room. As usual, he was surrounded by towers of paperwork, all organised in a system only he understood. He scratched his bald crown and flicked what was left of his hair off his shoulder.

'Oh, do go in, Inspector. I am sure she is expecting you. That is to say, she assumes you will come and go as you please,' he said, with a scowl that caused his lined face to shrivel like a dried apricot.

I said nothing, but placed the bag of boiled sweets on his desk. Medele didn't acknowledge the gift, but the paper rustled as I knocked on Imala's door.

'Come in, Sulaqua,' she said.

'How did you know it was me?' I said, stepping inside Imala's office.

'I saw you from my terrace.'

The terrace she spoke of was little more than a few square feet of railed-off space outside her office, next to a fire exit over the western underpass. I had found her there numerous times, silently sharing a cigarette with one of the Square's caretakers.

Unlike Medele, she kept her office as tidy and well-presented as her appearance. Everything that could be squared away was, in cabinets and drawers and bookcases. Current paperwork was at right angles in neat rows and columns. Even the paperclips in the dish beside her were separated and straight, all pointing in the same direction.

'Busy day?' she said.

'Always,' I said, sitting down without an invitation.

'So I've heard.'

I nodded but didn't speak.

'I'd even go as far as to say you've outdone yourself. It's not every day one of your proteges manages to insult a foreign nation and anger the high chief of the way,' she said.

'Are you proud?'

'Don't joke with me, young lady. What in Xol's name were you doing at the academy?'

'You just receive a message?'

Imala threw a folded piece of paper, spinning, towards me. I opened it and read it out loud:

Dear Chief Inspector Imala,

May I compliment you for training such a sedulous police officer? I am, of course, referring to Inspector Sulaqua, whom I had the great pleasure of meeting today.

Xol only knows what veiled clue she unmasked that led her to the academy and to my humble abode, but I am profoundly glad she discovered it. How else could I have assuaged her concerns regarding the red lights that of late have been seen shining from the Octagon Hall?

I believe I eased her troubled mind, but if any doubt remains, let me assure you we are all safe here in the Wooden House, and both she and your good self should not spend any more of your valuable time worrying about us, nor the nature of this harmless luminescence.

Your most humble servant,

The high chief of the way, Isoqua Naka

'What do you make of it?' Imala said.

'What does sedulous mean?' I said.

'Last warning, Inspector. Explain yourself,' Imala said, pointing her finger.

'Did you know there was an explosion at the Octagon Hall last night?' Imala nodded.

'This is a fragment from the blast,' I said, taking the piece of splintered stone out of my pocket and throwing it across the desk.

Imala took out her kerchief, picked the shard up and examined it. 'Scorch marks. Some kind of residue?' she said.

'Dee and I found a red substance under one of the dead Al'Mayran's fingernails similar to whatever is on that rock; left by lifeblood stones would be my guess, although forensics will confirm that.'

Imala reflected for a moment. 'So our victim handled a lifeblood stone before he died, and the academy is running tests on one. Is there any justifiable reason to make a connection?'

'Why would Naka lie about the cause of the explosion?'

'He's a politician,' Imala said with a shrug.

'Even a politician needs a reason.'

'It doesn't matter. The high chief is under no obligation to explain himself to you,' Imala said, wagging her finger. She sighed and rested her hand on her desk. 'Now tell me why you caused trouble at the embassy.'

'There was no trouble. I had good reason to believe the victim worked there. And I was right, as I usually am.' I paused to reset and keep the rising anger from my voice. 'Now I have a name: Areel I'Advay, an envoy with a mission to study magical and spiritual matters.'

'Did you have to be rude to Ambassador I'Rasnee?'

I looked away before answering. 'I asked him a few questions – all justified.'

'And your confrontation with his head of security?'

'It's that smarmy bastard who was aggressive,' I said, hitting Imala's desk and meeting her eye.

'Without provocation?'

'He refused to give me access to I'Advay's office, then his lieutenant prevented me from searching the dead man's home. What was I supposed to do?'

'You still had the crime scene. What did you find there?'

I told Imala about Nitushi Nakni, the envoy's lover, and about his trip with Nita and the two brothers to see her advocate.

'You need to speak to Nita directly,' Imala said.

'I intend to go to the Stars at first light tomorrow.'

'Good. Forget about lifeblood stones,' Imala said, pushing the shard of stone across her desk. 'The missing cane suggests this is either a mugging or a lover's quarrel made to look like one.'

'Muggers don't like storms any more than we do. Besides, if this was a mugging or a lover's quarrel, we're implying the killer is a local, but what self-respecting Kahokeyan killer leaves a body in the middle of the thoroughfare when the cliff edge is a hundred yards away? Why a cut throat, the clinical, premeditated stroke of a professional? How come the Rose Town guards swear I'Advay didn't pass their cabin? He had a South-Western Great Lift ticket on him. Why not a northern one from nearer the embassy? Where was he going? Or where had he been?'

'You're overcomplicating matters. Given your dislike for the wealthy, the political class in particular, I may have made a mistake assigning this case to you.'

'Oh, fish shit.'

'Watch your manners around me, my girl.'

'Don't take that maternal tone with me.'

'Ani, you're biased. You don't want a poor Kahokeyan or a resident of Rose Town to be responsible because your sympathies always lie with them. And I think we both know why you're haunted by bodies being thrown from cliffs.'

'Twenty years later and you still think I'm obsessed with Shona. Give me some fucking credit.' I stood and headed towards the door.

'Sit down, Inspector. You leave when you're dismissed,' Imala said.

I froze, clutching the doorknob, my ears roaring, my eyes burning. I couldn't look at Imala. Instead, I walked past her and onto the terrace outside. I leant against the steel rail, waiting for the beat of my heart to slow and my breathing to ease.

'Blow the candle out, Ani,' I whispered.

Imala came to stand next to me and rolled a cigarette in silence. She struck a match, lit the tobacco end and took a long and deep draw.

'I've sent for Sudeme and Toko,' she said. 'Before they arrive, tell me your theory.'

'I think I'Advay was killed by an Al'Mayran who didn't want to sacrifice his own spirit by destroying his victim's heart. So he slit I'Advay's throat. It's a quick death and it leaves the heart intact. But I'Advay's spirit was still in danger. If a corpse rots, so does the heart. Eventually the organ will break apart and the spirit within will escape. The heart must be preserved until it can be cremated in a lifeblood stone fire, releasing the spirit to the Red Mountains. Someone wanted to perform the ritual, or at least ensure someone else would. The killer carried his body up Salvation's Climb and dumped it in Rose Town. That's why the guards didn't see anyone pass.'

'Who would walk up those steps at any time, let alone at night, in the middle of a hurricane, with a corpse?' Imala said.

'An Al'Mayran might. Dee and I both saw a red glow on the steps.'

'Why the preoccupation with lifeblood stones?'

I hesitated, then whispered, 'Because of what's happening in the Octagon Hall. I suspect they're being turned into a weapon. That's why I went to investigate the explosion.'

Imala snorted. 'Ridiculous. Pure fantasy. And you do realise you're talking about a possible criminal conspiracy between Al'Mayrans and the high chief.'

'If you don't agree, take me off the case.'

'Would that stop you? Stay away from the embassy tomorrow. I'll smooth things over and see if I can arrange access to I'Advay's office and home.'

'Fine.'

'All eyes will be on us, Ani. The CIB will be brought in, and they would love to profit at our expense. Please don't let me down. That's not an order, it's a request from a friend.'

'Yes, ma'am.'

The Square's chief medical examiner and lead forensic pathologist had already taken their seats at Imala's desk by the time we returned to her office. As there was no free chair, I perched on the windowsill behind her.

The two scientists made an odd but complementary pairing. Toko, the medical examiner, was a small man, full of energy, with a habit of making quick and dynamic gestures. He was always immaculately dressed in elegant suits and kept his hair short, well-groomed and slicked back. Sudeme, the lead forensic pathologist, was no slob, but he was languid in movement, overweight, and while his suits were similarly expensive, he was yet to find a shirt that would stay in his trousers. Nor did his ponytail ever seem to behave like it should, requiring constant fiddling, a task for which his large hands proved entirely unsuitable.

'What do you have, gentlemen?' Imala said.

Toko began: 'The Al'Mayran died from loss of blood caused by the cut to the throat, which severed the jugular vein and, crucially, the carotid arteries – a very deep slice indeed. He would have been unconscious within seconds, dead not long after. I doubt anyone could have saved him. Along with the mark on the eye, there are several other abrasions, all received shortly before death, suggestive of a fight or a struggle. In my opinion, they were inflicted by a powerful man, but I will not be putting that in my official report.'

'Time of death?' Imala said.

'No more than seven hours before discovery, probably less. Despite the storm, it was a warm night and a bright morning. He was lying directly in the sunlight and would have been for some time when I arrived.'

'So no earlier than eleven o'clock yesterday evening,' I said.

'Anything else of note, Toko?' Imala said.

'He'd eaten recently and had what appeared to be Al'Mayran spiced lamb stew in his belly, apricots and all. Several years ago, he received a severe wound to the upper right leg, most likely a musket ball or a piece of shrapnel. It ripped the muscle from the bone, preventing full recovery.'

'Could he have taken a staircase?' I said.

'Even with a cane he would have had difficulty.'

'Sudeme?' Imala said.

'Much evidence was washed away by the rain. There were some very faint grass stains on the victim's robe, on the left side, inside and out, but

I was unable to recover any fingerprints. I did, however, develop a series from the left forearm,' Sudeme said.

'How is Agame coming along with the photographic plates?'

'Both the ones he took at the scene and the ones he took of the Al'Mayran's face in the deadhouse are developed and in the process of being printed.'

'I want the man's likeness sent to the Al'Mayran embassy as soon as possible.'

'What about the red substance under his fingernail?' I said.

'We're still testing it,' Sudeme said.

'Best guess?'

'Its colour and luminescent qualities are consistent with lifeblood stones.'

'Check to see if the substance on that rock is a match,' I said, pointing to the shard from the Octagon Hall.

Sudeme looked to Imala for approval, and when she nodded, he wrapped the charred stone in the handkerchief and put it in his pocket.

After he and Toko left, I turned to Imala and said, 'I want fingerprints taken from the embassy staff.'

'Slow down, Ani,' she said. 'Slow down.'

During the cab ride to Horizon's Outlook, I told Dee about my adventures. As I talked, the sun completed her arc, and by the time we arrived home, she was a red grapefruit dipping below the tip of Sundown Claw. My tribe were gathering around the communal fires, frying fish and mussels for Dee's festival.

Throughout the city, lights were burning bright, the animal towers were coming alive in the changing shadows, and in the east, spirals of cloud floated in a murky green sky.

Josee had left the drawbridge down and was waiting on the northern balcony, sitting on the form with a shawl pulled around her shoulders, reading with the help of an oil lamp.

'Well, come on,' she said, when Dee and I crossed the drawbridge.

'What?' I said.

'You know what.'

I shrugged and raised my hands, palms up. I winked at Dee, making sure Josee saw me.

'Oh, for fuck's sake,' she said. 'Who's the murdered Al'Mayran?'

'It's Dee's Coming of Age festival, we're not talking about that.'

'I don't mind,' Dee said.

'Yes you do.'

'Really, I don't mind,' Dee said.

'See?' Josee said.

'No, no, let's get to Sundown. The tribe will be expecting us.'

I started to leave, but Josee grabbed me. I tried to resist, but she twisted my arm behind my back and spun me around as Dee laughed.

'Something funny, Cadet?' I said.

'No, Ani, ma'am,' he said.

Josee bent my hand back until I yelled out. 'Don't tease the lad,' she said.

'Let go,' I said.

'Tell me who the dead man is.'

'Areel I'Advay,' I said. 'Areel I'Advay, for Xol's sake.'

'I don't know who that is,' Josee said, unable to hide her disappointment.

'Well, he was at the Commemoration of Deliverance.'

'Oh, interesting.'

I put my gloves on and took I'Advay's charm from my pocket. 'Don't touch it,' I said. 'This is evidence. I wanted you to see the markings before I indexed it.'

'It's Al'Mayran, but I've never seen anything like it before.'

Josee fetched her sketchbook and started copying the markings down. I gazed at her face as she studied, the smile she ordinarily wore in repose now replaced with a fierce concentration.

'What are you looking at?' she said, when she was finished and caught me staring.

'You.'

She shook her head, supposedly in irritation, but I could tell she was amused. 'The style of these letters is antiquated. No one writes like this anymore and hasn't done so in a thousand years. The lines are more geometric than modern styles.'

'What do they say?' Dee asked.

'Depends on the context, really. For example, this can mean learning, or awareness, or knowledge, or light – many things really. And this symbol can mean to free, as in to release a slave, or to clear, to tidy, or open, to unlock something.'

'What about the charm's shape?' I said.

'Stylised, but its design is compromised for a functional requirement. And the characters are raised in random places with scant regard to aesthetic consideration.'

'You said one of the symbols could mean to unlock?'

'Yes, why?'

'I was wondering if it could be a key?'

'To what?'

'A golden cane,' Dee said.

'Clever lad,' I said.

'Shall we give him his present now?' Josee said.

'Why not?' I said.

'Oh, no, no, that's fine,' Dee said.

'Rubbish,' Josee said, taking the lad's hand and leading him through the kitchen and the dining room into the drawing room. By the time I caught up, Josee was already crouched down, taking the paper-and-string-wrapped parcel from the sideboard. She jumped up and thrust her hands out in one quick motion towards Dee, smiling at me. I laughed and winked at her.

'Thank you both,' Dee said, squeezing his gift through the wrapping paper, clearly unsure what to say next.

'Well, open it,' Josee said.

He laid the parcel down on the settee and untied the knot. When he peeled the folds of paper back, there was the distinctive navy blue of a new cadet's uniform.

'Oh, no, no. That's not right,' he said.

'Shut up, Dee,' I said.

'But...'

His open face contorted, alternating between overwhelming gratitude

and shame at being the recipient of what he no doubt interpreted as charity. Josee looked at me, worried.

'Your old uniform is a disgrace to the department, Cadet. I'm sick
of seeing you in it. You can pay us back when you become a constable.
Is that clear?' I said.

He stood up straight and saluted me.

'Why don't you go and put it on, look smart for your festival?'

Once Josee and I were alone, she leant in and whispered, 'It's a gift,
Ani, not a loan.'

'Don't worry. I'll talk to his sister. We won't take a penny. Let him
have his pride tonight.'

'I love you,' she said, kissing me.

'Me too,' I said, struggling to release the words from my throat.

'Pardon?'

'I love you, too.'

'Bit louder.'

'Oh, fuck off.'

Josee sat on the settee, which was covered in throws, cushions and
her robes, and dragged me down with her. I rested my head against her
shoulder and fell into silence.

'You're deep in thought, love,' she said.

'I'm thinking about the explosion we saw last night. The blast came
from inside the academy. It wasn't lightning.'

'Dare I ask how you know that?' Josee said, putting her arm around
my neck and giving me a playful squeeze.

'Guess.'

'You went there.'

'And what I saw made me think of the warrior Ameeleyor,' I said.

'Ameeleyor again, eh?'

'Tell me about her. Please,' I said, lifting my head off Josee's shoulder
to meet her amused gaze.

'Well, the first story we're taught is of her birth, during which her
mother bled to death. Ameeleyor was born feet first. The umbilical cord
was crushed, and she came into the world lifeless and blue. A passing
cleric heard of her father's grief. When he saw the dead infant, he took the

chain and pendant he wore, which had a lifeblood stone at its centre, and hung it around Ameeleyor's neck. To her father's amazement, Ameeleyor clutched the rock and began to cry. The cleric told her father that as long as she wore the jewel, she would live.

'In another story, Ameeleyor is a young child, and we learn her father is a shepherd. One harsh winter, when he took ill with fever, she went out into the snow and ice to protect his flock from a pack of wolves. They surrounded her and the sheep, so she used the stone to create a dome of light to protect them. The villagers found her the next day, asleep in the mysterious shelter, with all the snow melted away and spring flowers blooming in the long grass.

'Many years later, when the Harn first invaded, she mounted her lifeblood stone on a warrior's staff and fired a searing red light from it to cut the Harn down. The Al'Mayrans were victorious, but Ameeleyor's lifeblood stone was spent, its energy drained, and she died. But from that point on, the Red Mountains shone and welcomed our spirits when our bodies surrendered them.'

I wanted to press Josee about the warrior's staff, it's power, and if there were other examples of lifeblood stones being used as weapons, but Dee re-entered the drawing room, buttoning up his new jacket.

'Oh, by the spirits, doesn't he look handsome, Ani?' Josee said.

'It's a good fit. And it can be adjusted into a constable's uniform. We checked,' I said.

'Thank you both. I'll make you proud,' Dee said.

'You already have. Now, let's make a move,' I said.

'You're not going like that?' Josee said.

'Like what?'

'Armed to the teeth.'

'Fine,' I said, taking my baldric off.

'Go put on your best animal skins.'

'If I must.'

We were running late, so I changed quickly, putting on a pair of plain cobalt-blue leggings and a long over-the-head grey shirt with a turtle embroidered on the chest. Despite Josee's wishes, I tied my fighting dagger to my calf.

The doorbell rang, and I ran to the kitchen. I found Josee and Dabreeyor A'Mendayse, staring into each other's eyes, their hands on the other's heart in the traditional Al'Mayran greeting.

'I see you've met my wife, Josee,' I said, emphasising the word 'wife' more than I'd intended. 'Josee, Dabreeyor was Areel I'Advay's secretary of letters.'

'May his spirit join with those who came before,' Josee said, pressing Dabreeyor's hand to her chest.

They were tactile people, I told myself.

'I'm sorry if I'm intruding,' Dabreeyor said, taking in my appearance, a gleam in her eye, something close to amusement. 'I just thought I'd come and tell you that Klareesa, Areel's housekeeper, last saw him yesterday morning before he left for work and he had the golden cane with him.'

'I see. I thank you for coming out of your way,' I said.

'Were you very close to Areel?' Josee said, keeping hold of Dabreeyor's hand.

'I'd like to think so. I just feel a bit lost without him. I don't know what to do. I can't even go to work. Areel was my work,' Dabreeyor said.

'Well, we were just heading to Sundown Claw for Dee's Coming of Age festival. If Dee doesn't mind, perhaps you'd like to join us.'

'You're more than welcome,' Dee said with a bow.

'Oh, I'd love to, I've never really been to Sundown,' Dabreeyor said. 'Unless, of course, you don't think it appropriate, Inspector?'

It wasn't. But the short pause I took before I answered was long enough for Josee to fix me with a threatening stare, and I capitulated and said, 'It's Dee's festival. If he's happy, I don't object.'

Night had fallen by the time the boat we had hired arrived at the southern tip of Sundown, where my uncle Ezno and my cousins, Etu and Oura, still lived in our family home. It was a traditional cedar wood and stone cabin near a saltwater pool where Ezno used to grow seaweed and farm snails.

Hundreds of my tribe were already gathered near the jetty to welcome us. Dee stood at the bow of the boat, looking proud in his new uniform as the tribe broke into song.

Dee's sister, already crying, embraced him and made a fuss over how handsome he looked; his little niece and nephew hugged his legs; and his brother-in-law shook his hand and patted the lad's shoulder like he was an equal, not a younger sibling. It was up to Dee to find the waiting elders and kneel before them.

My uncle was by his pool adjusting the ropes of seaweed he had strung between giant Kahokeyan grass stalks. He rose to his feet as Josee, Dabreeyor and I approached, and rubbed his left leg.

Like me, he was short and wiry and hard, even though he had long ago entered his middle years and his contemporaries were growing soft and fat. He only had a few black strands left amongst white hair, and I never saw him without a ponytail, so I often wondered if he was balding. As usual, he wore whale gut trousers and a loose overshirt.

I introduced Dabreeyor, who made the mistake of asking him about his seaweed and listened politely as he provided her with a comprehensive answer. Thankfully, my cousin Oura, a younger clone of his father, emerged from the house and interrupted. He greeted Dabreeyor and saved her from further insights into the reproductive cycle of kelp.

Oura hugged me and kissed my forehead.

'They seem to be getting on,' he whispered, when Josee led Dabreeyor away to find food and drink.

'So it seems,' I said.

'Be calm, little sister, be calm.'

'Where's that trouble-making brother of yours?'

As if he'd been waiting for his appearance to be announced, Etu bounded out from the trail leading down to the shore.

'Always on cue, isn't he?' I said.

Etu was a foot and half taller than the rest of us, broad and heavy-limbed too. He kept his hair short and was rarely seen out of cotton shirts and worn leather trousers. He ran over, grinning, with his fishing rod in one hand and a brace of coalfish in the other. I tried to escape but he was too quick. He dropped his rod, picked me up, spun me around and slapped my face with the fish, shouting, 'It's little Narky!'

I wiped the scales from my nose and lashed out at him. He was too big to wrestle, so I punched and kicked him instead. It was the only way to deal with Etu, and I knew I connected, because he dropped me and put his hands up in surrender.

'You go too far,' I said.

'Me?' he said, opened-mouthed, feigning innocence.

I was about to argue when something, or someone, caught his attention.

'Who's the blond Al'Mayran?' he said, eyeing Dabreeyor.

I rolled my eyes, shook my head, and walked away without answering.

The tribe had supplied dozens of banquet and beer tables for the festival. Gradually, everyone took their seats and waited for Dee to summon his courage. He knocked back a glass of whiskey, took a breath and stood.

'First, I want to thank my sister and her family for raising me, and Ani for showing me my future. I will dedicate my life to the police force but will never ever forget I am Lo'tse. I hope I make you proud to be my kin,' he said.

The festivities began with tributes to elders in the form of gifts and speeches. Once these formalities ended, polite conversation began, which soon developed into half-funny stories about Dee's childhood and some moving ones – he lost his parents and his older brother in a storm. Gradually, folk relaxed. Josee was skilled at easing these transitions, but luckily, tonight, we were blessed with two Al'Mayrans to help the celebrations along.

Their earthy accents grew loud as they drank. And they ate in great amounts with little regard for the custom of allowing the elders to start first. Etu caught me watching and fixed me with a serious expression, but his eyes were ablaze with mischief, and although I tried to stifle my laughter, I let out a snorting guffaw.

'Something funny, love?' Josee said.

I shook my head, unable to stop giggling, and was relieved when Etu finally cracked, soon followed by Oura and Ezno and a few of the other elders.

'Am I missing the joke?' Dabreeyor said, not in the least bit abashed.

'I think we're the joke,' Josee said.

'Don't be offended, Dabreeyor,' Etu said. 'We've had ten years to get used to Josee. We first met her at a festival, too, one for shipbuilding.'

'He means they built a ship,' Josee said.

'You should have seen Ani. She was terrified Josee would make a bad impression.'

'Concerned,' I corrected.

'When it came time to transport the timber to the dry dock, Josee volunteered,' Oura said.

'And shocked us by throwing off her robes to work in her undergarments,' Etu said.

'The robes aren't for modesty,' Dabreeyor said.

'Oh, we know that now.'

'What happened?'

'It's heavy lifting,' Oura said. 'But Josee was more than equal to the task. She helped us carry chine logs for the ship's frame.'

'Something Ani can't do,' Etu said.

'I'm a farmer's daughter, I'm used to hard work outdoors,' Josee said.

'You still blistered in the sun,' I said.

'Oh, yes, Ani went running to fetch some balm,' Ezno said, chuckling, 'only to be told by Josee, in no uncertain terms, not to fuss. Even when Ani was a child, I never dared speak to her like that, unless I wanted a broken nose.'

'Later, when we were taking another log up to the dock, my father and I up front, Etu and Josee behind, Etu lost his footing and slipped,' Oura said.

'Fell drunkenly on his backside,' I said.

'Josee dropped into a squat, and we came running to help, but she twitched her shoulder, adjusted her grip, and rose unaided to her feet, bearing the weight of her end alone.'

'And let out an almighty roar as she did,' Etu said.

'Josee made no fuss at the time, nor did she ever refer to the incident again,' Ezno said, raising his beaker to my wife. 'But we've never forgotten, and she has been welcome ever since.'

Someone began to play a fiddle, prompting Josee to leap up and grab

Ezno's hand. 'Come on, old man, let's dance,' she said, dragging Ezno to his feet and leading him away to dance with Dee and his sister.

'How old is Dee?' Dabreeyor said.

'Fifteen today. He's a man now,' I said.

'Ah, he's just a boy.'

'There are those from richer tribes and more powerful families who are twice Dee's age and half the man he already is. He'll be fine.'

'You're very fond of him, aren't you?'

'We're both orphans.'

'Oh, I'm sorry.'

I shrugged.

'Your uncle raised you?' Dabreeyor said.

'My mother was from the Depths. She gave me to my father when I was a baby and we never saw her again. My father was lost at sea not long after, so I came to live with Ezno. Only, he had his own troubles. My aunt had recently died giving birth to a stillborn baby girl. People assume I was a natural surrogate. But how do you replace a daughter?'

'Had you been his natural-born child, would you think of yourself as his daughter?'

'Of course.'

'And would that make you a replacement for the one he'd lost?'

'No, I suppose not.'

'It doesn't work that way. Death of a loved one inflicts a wound to the heart that can never fully heal. The trick is to keep filling the heart with love. From what I've seen tonight, you are his daughter.'

My eyes began to tear up, so I looked away, out over Lo'tse Bay and towards the lights of Pastnoon.

I cleared my throat. 'Either way, when I look back, his stoicism and warmth are testament to a kind of courage few possess, and which, in my opinion, is rarer and more admirable than any displayed on the battle-field.' The tears fell, so I wiped them from my cheeks as fast as I could. 'Forgive me, Dabreeyor, I don't usually talk this way. It's the drink. The other tribes say it's the only way to loosen the tongue of a Lo'tse.'

'My father was killed by the Harn when I was young. I don't have any likeness of him, no photographic plate or painting, nothing to remind me of what he looked like. My mother and I lost everything. Our entire clan had to flee.'

I nodded and fell silent for a moment, unsure what to say. The inspector took over.

'Do you believe your father's spirit lives in the Red Mountains?'

'I have to. Most of my clan are dead. I need to believe they're united.'

We didn't talk for a while, just sat contemplating the sea and the stars and the lamps and fires burning on Pastnoon and Sundown Claws.

'Why are there no skytowers in Lo'tse Bay?' Dabreeyor asked.

'My tribe holds sway on decisions like that, and we vetoed any plans,' I said.

'You don't like the towers?'

'Me, personally?'

She nodded.

'I don't remember New Capital before they were built,' I said. 'My uncle does, and if you let him, he'll tell you stories about returning home after a long voyage to the vista of four wide open bays like lovers' arms.'

Etu, emboldened more than usual by alcohol, finally worked up the courage to ask Dabreeyor to dance. She bowed, took his hand, and together, they went to join the others.

My uncle sat opposite me to catch his breath.

'Maybe we should always invite a couple of Al'Mayrans to these events. I'll bring it up at the next council meeting,' he said.

I had no idea if he were joking or not, but I smiled anyway.

'You seem deep in thought, Daughter,' he said, lighting his pipe.

'New case. Something about it stinks,' I said.

I pulled Ezno's pipe from his mouth, took a drag, and felt the hum of the narcotic reach my head.

'This is illegal outside of religious ceremonies, Ezno,' I said.

'So arrest me.'

'One day I might,' I said, taking another draw.

I left Ezno alone with his pipe and took a stroll down the rocky trail to the small natural landing where I went fishing with my cousins. I sat, folded my arms around my knees and tried to remember Shona's face as I watched a soft red glow from Salvation's Climb slowly fade away and die.

CHAPTER FIVE

THAT NIGHT, I dreamt of the love of my adolescence again. Only this time, I was thirteen, too, and living in the Depths with her and my mother, and I had never started to shimmer. Like a suppressed memory resurfacing to gut punch me, my power asserted control and I couldn't stop casting images of all I knew. My mother, whose face was always hidden in smoke or mist or blinding light, screamed and dragged me outside. The other families we shared a decrepit old house with jeered and spat at me until I ran away, crying and shimmering uncontrollably. Somehow, I found myself on the Bridge of Spirits, in the clutches of the man who murdered Shona. He strangled me instead of her and tossed me into the sea. I floated next to other dead children, welcome neither on the Claws nor in Xol's caverns below.

I woke with a dry mouth and a sore head. Josee was fast asleep beside me, lying spread out on her side of the bed, snoring. I dressed, kissed her forehead and, after feeding Snuggs and grabbing a slice of bread and a spoonful of anchovies for breakfast, left the flat.

The sun had not yet risen by the time I crossed the Magila Bay bridge, but the western sky had turned a shade of the darkest blue, and to the east, a flare of pale and diffused green light hung above the cliffs. Chains of mackerel-scale clouds were sweeping in from the south, their bellies catching the first light of the coming day, making them appear like stray lanterns drifting north from a distant festival.

Rose Town was dead, and smelt like it, the brothels having only closed an hour or two earlier. Sumaka Way was deserted, except for an old, one-eyed mongrel licking up spilt beer and vomit. Someone had left a half-eaten bowl of pulled pork on a windowsill, so I picked it up and laid it down for him. He cowered and ran away until I crossed the road, then returned, his belly close to the cobbles, to eat the pork, never taking his eye off me for a second.

I hammered on the Stars and the Sea's door until, after several minutes of persistent knocking, a young woman, whom I didn't know but had seen yesterday amongst the Star's staff, opened up and scowled at me.

'What do you want?' she said.

'Your boss,' I said, pushing past her.

Inside, the place smelt musty, the odours of the previous night's revelry still in the air – perfume, incense and spice mixed with stale food, alcohol and tobacco along with the unmistakable stench of sweat, sex and masculine musk. All pretence of order and business had been abandoned. The impression I had was that Nita and her family had danced one last time, spitting in the face of their imminent destruction. It was all so fatalistic and unnecessary.

A select brothel like the Stars and the Sea entertained the higher echelons of New Capital society, including business leaders, politicians and law enforcement chiefs. This gave its workers a false sense of their own security and instilled in them the delusion they belonged to the same class they served. They did not. The police chief or CIB director, who knew their names, paid them compliments, bought them gifts to flatter and delight, and held their sweat-drenched bodies in the warm haze of climax, would not hesitate to undermine their self-respect, degrade their souls and break their bodies if law and order, convenient resolution, or self-preservation required it. Surely, I told myself, someone as intelligent and seasoned as Madam Nita understood that.

In my anger, I ran up three flights of stairs to Nita's room. The young woman followed me, tripping on her nightgown before catching up with me outside the door.

'You need a warrant,' she said, trying to sound authoritative. But her voice shook, and her conviction failed her.

'Get used to it,' I said, and kicked the door open.

Nita was asleep in bed with Memi's head resting on her breast and a young man lying face down beside her, his bare backside exposed. I grabbed a jug of water from the bedside cabinet and threw its contents over their bodies. Nita sat up with a scream, throwing Memi to one side. But the young man barely stirred, so I picked up what I assumed was one of his deerskin shoes and whipped it across his buttocks. He raised his head and stared at me, still lost in the haze of a narcotic stupor.

'Out,' I said, hitting him again.

'Ani, in Xol's name, is this necessary?' Nita said, wiping her face.

'Call me Inspector Sulaqua.'

'This is not you.'

'Memi, get this boy out of here.'

Memi was already on her feet and wrapping a sheet around her body. She did not remonstrate with me but silently dragged the lad off the bed, gathered his clothes and handed them to him over his genitals. She ushered him and the young woman out of the room and closed the door behind her.

Nita threw the bed sheets aside and stood naked before me with her back straight, her hands on her hips, glaring at me with disappointment and condemnation. She was short, the same as I was, but less boyish. She had typical Kahokeyan high cheekbones and almond-shaped eyes, a small straight nose and a top lip with a deep and pointed bow like an arrowhead. Her hair was still the colour of ink, but even in the pre-dawn gloom, I could see the lines of time mutilating her face.

I didn't know how old she was, but the story went that she arrived in Rose Town around thirty years ago in a gold-leaf carriage with a chest full of jewels and precious metals. Within an hour, she had bought the Stars and the Sea from the previous owner, a decrepit and lascivious old man, and invited her first clients inside. She had lived there ever since, a self-made queen, always ready to receive the next flock of subjects into her dream realm. Nita summoned her own reality, forging it from sheer will. But now I feared the illusion would melt away like a night-time's snowfall in the first light of day.

She lit an oil lamp and found her robe, a Harn-style garment patterned with childlike stars against a dark blue sky. She put it on, sat at her dressing table and ran a fine-toothed ivory comb through her long hair.

'Why visit your advocate, Nita?' I said.

'None of your business,' she said, splitting her locks in two.

I held my silver police emblem up to her reflection in the mirror. 'What does that say?' I said.

She ignored me and began to knit an intricate fishtail braid, so I grabbed the half-twisted rope and turned her head until she faced the emblem.

'What does it say?' I said.

'Inspector of murder,' she said, pulling away.

'Correct. I'm not the same girl who once walked a beat along this thoroughfare, trying to keep your people out of trouble while they laughed at my efforts.'

'No one laughed at you, Inspector Sulaqua.'

'Regardless. These are not the old days, and I'm not your friend. Answer my question.'

'When you run a brothel, illegality comes to you,' she said, looking away and resuming her braid.

'Try this routine with the CIB, Nita. See where it gets you.'

'I had a client on the night of the murder who was not himself, medicinally speaking. I took care of it, but in doing so, I wondered if I'd been compromised,' she said, her fingers dancing as they wove.

'The visit had nothing to do with Areel I'Advay?'

She tied her plaited tresses off with a thin ribbon and stared at me. 'Who?'

'Don't do that, Nita,' I said.

'Areel I'Advay? Is that the poor man's name?'

'You know it is.'

'Such a shame. A sweet man of vanilla tastes and a steady appetite.'

'You knew him well?'

'No, I was hardly his type.'

'Nakni was. Did I'Advay visit the lad the night before last?'

'No,' Nita said.

'Did you see him at all that night?'

'Not until the morning when—'

'When you were generous enough to spare his corpse a glance as you stepped over it. Why take Nakni with you to your advocate?'

'These days his main function is to act as my personal guard.'

'Wasn't he too distraught to be on guard? I heard he was in tears.'

'We're professionals, but we aren't cold, and I don't tell my children to stifle their feelings for their patrons. Better to love a little and be injured than to hollow out your heart.'

'Emotional young man, is he?'

'Not particularly. He has a good head on his shoulders.'

'Not the sort to become hysterical and slit throats?'

'Why not leave him alone?' Nita said.

'Would you rather I was the CIB? What do you think they're going to do? You and Nakni will be harassed and beaten down until this matter is drawn to some kind of conclusion.'

'Nothing can stop that now.'

'What have you done, Nita?'

'Me? Nothing,' she said, touching her chest.

'You know who killed I'Advay, don't you?'

'Of course not.'

'How about those two brothers, Hani and Mani, do they know?'

'Feral younglings. They come and go as they please.'

'Why take them to see Hinatse?'

'They didn't see him. We took them into town afterwards.'

'Just a fun outing with a grieving man, eh? Fish shit, Nita. Fish shit.'

She smiled at me and ran the back of a finger down my cheek.

I knocked her hand away and said, 'I need your testimony.'

She sighed. 'Neither I nor anyone else in my establishment is going to scribble anything further in your little scroll. Arrest me if you like.'

'Where's Nakni?' I said.

'Why not leave him be?'

'Don't push me, Nita.'

'Down the hall, two doors on the right.'

I hurried to Nakni's room, leaving Nita to dress, hoping to grab a few minutes with Areel I'Advay's love before Nita could follow.

I knocked on the lad's door, imagining him to be a slim and effeminate young man, highly strung and constantly fluttering close to hysteria. I could not have been more wrong. He opened the door before I finished knocking, leaving my fist swinging in the air near his exposed chest. He was over six feet tall, straight-backed and regal in demeanour, with his thick charcoal hair falling down his back. He wore only a pair of wide pantaloon-style trousers and a white shirt hung from his hand.

'Nitushi Nakni?' I said.

He scowled with disdain, walked away, slipping into the shirt, and sat on a cracked, brown leather reading chair. He leaned back and stretched his legs forward and wide, never once looking up at me.

His small room was decorated with paintings and pencil sketches of rivers and mountains. The furniture was all dark stained wood and animal hide. Above the fireplace hung a lance and shield, synonymous with the northern tribes. The curtains, thrown open along with the window, were embroidered in an unmistakably Al'Mayran design of deep crimson and gold.

'Look at me, Nitushi,' I said.

He raised his eyes. They were bloodshot and sunken in dark circles, the result, no doubt, of a sleepless night, spent self-medicating with soporific opiates. I walked behind him and peered out of the window. Sure enough, on the cobbles below lay several screwed-up pieces of wax paper, their illegal powders and pills imbibed many hours ago.

'Who are your tribe, Nitushi?' I said.

He didn't answer, so I repeated the question as I examined the shield above the fireplace.

'I'm Juhuwa,' he said.

'Why aren't you with them for the summer gathering?' I said.

'That's not for me.'

'I meet a lot of feckless young men who can't handle the traditional ways and drift south looking for comfort.'

'I followed the northern deer for several seasons, long enough to know I wanted a different life.'

'I know what you mean. I love being out on a fishing boat with my uncle and my cousins, but I can't do it day after day, season after season. So now I hunt murderers instead.'

'Then I don't know why you're here.'

'Well, most murders are committed by husbands and wives. And lovers. How long were you Areel I'Advay's lover?'

He didn't answer.

'Did Areel buy you those curtains?' I said.

I opened the top drawer of a chest pressed up against the bed.

'Did he buy you this, too?' I said, holding up an Al'Mayran gown.

Nakni was on his feet and over me in seconds, pulling the garment from my grasp. His chest rose and fell as he stared down at me, his face reddening with anger. I opened my jacket to reveal my pistol baldric.

'I was told you didn't have a temper, Nitushi,' I said. 'Did Areel make you angry like this? Is that why you slit his throat?'

He snorted and turned away.

There was a dust-covered writing desk beside the door, a clean rectangular shape on its top where something had recently been removed.

'Been clearing a few things out, Nitushi?' I said.

I'd caught his attention, but he didn't bite.

'Come on, Nitushi, what was on the desk?'

'A book. I lent it to someone.'

I took a closer look at the paintings on the walls. Some were of Northern Kahokey and others were of Al'Mayra, the Red Mountains and the shining lights of the spirits within.

'I see two different hands. You painted the ones of the north – only an Al'Mayran could depict his homeland like this. But who painted the one that's missing?' I gestured towards a tiny hole in the wall where a nail once held a picture. 'Why take it down, I wonder? What could you not bear to look at? Areel's face, maybe? Did you paint him, or was it a self-portrait?'

Nakni's mouth hung open. He blinked and wiped away tears.

'Leave Nitushi alone, Inspector. He doesn't know anything,' Nita said, standing in the doorway.

She'd put on a long, deep blue, cotton drawstring dress, tied around the waist with ribbons and had sleeves of fine lace. Her lips were stained a velvet pink, and she'd painted a band of metallic grey across her eyes. Her armour was in place.

'Stay out of this, Nita,' I said. 'Come on, Nitushi. Talk to me. I know you and Areel were close – you both loved the arts, he took you to galleries and plays and out dining in fancy restaurants. He even introduced his friends, didn't he? Dabreeyor and Ameeleyor and Mycale? So what happened? Did you fall out? Did he end it? Did that make you angry? Did you slit his throat?'

'I could never…' He adjusted his tone and held his temper. 'Leave me alone,' he said.

'Okay, I'll go now, but I want you to think about something. If your story is reasonable, I might believe it, but the CIB won't, and when they're dragging you away, remember I gave you this chance.'

I pushed past Nita and began searching other rooms, through wardrobes and under beds. If a door was locked, I pounded on it until the occupant answered or Nita ordered them to let me in. Some patrons who had stayed overnight were still asleep, including a city chief. He and I swapped brief nods as the young man beside him giggled. Next, I checked the attic and started moving down the brothel floor by floor. Nothing. When I was about to enter the drawing room, Memi came into the hall via the back door. I shook my head and walked into the flagged yard, full of washing hung out to dry. I tapped on the wooden hatch of the stone-built coal bunker.

'Come on, lads, open up,' I said.

The hatch swung open, and one dirty face emerged followed by another. Hani climbed out first and dropped to my feet in a cloud of coal dust. He offered his hand to his younger sibling, who lay on his stomach, rolled clear of the opening, slipped down the angled surface on his backside, and jumped to the ground. I stared at their new shoes with their colourful beads and tassels now stained black forever.

'I see you two survived the storm. How's the nose, Hani?'

The older boy, eyes circled in black like a raccoon, shrugged and looked away as Memi and Nita entered the yard.

'Did you enjoy the puddings? No? How about that lemon slice?' I said to Mani when his brother didn't answer.

Mani nodded.

'What do you do here?' I said.

The younger brother looked at Memi and Nita before answering. 'I work in the kitchen, and I fetch coal, and I throw out the rubbish and clean the steps. Lots of things,' he said.

'Did you come here two nights ago, after my wife and I saw you on the bridge?'

Mani looked at his dirty shoes.

'Did you see anyone? An Al'Mayran or two maybe?'

'Ani, please,' Memi said.

'In Xol's name, why can't you accept I'm trying to help all of you?' I said, turning on Memi. 'Were they here two nights ago?' I switched my focus back to the boys when Memi didn't answer. 'Were you, lads? You can tell me. It's important.'

Hani folded his arms and looked straight ahead while Mani kept his face lowered.

'If you don't know anything, why were you hiding in the coal bunker?' I said.

'We hate the police. They arrest you for nothing,' Hani said, meeting my eye with a stare too fierce for his tender age.

'Not me. I catch murderers, and I want the one who dumped a dead Al'Mayran here during the storm. Did you see the killer?'

No answer.

'What about the Al'Mayran?'

'Yeah,' Hani said.

'What was he doing?'

'Lying dead in the thoroughfare.'

'What about a golden cane? Did you find it? Did you take it? I won't be angry if you did.'

They shook their heads.

'But you saw something, didn't you, Mani?' I said.

'I saw nothing,' Mani said, his voice breaking as he emphasised the word 'I'.

He gasped and stared at his brother, a look of horror on his dirty face. Hani froze for a second, glanced at me, and bolted. I grabbed his shirt, but he bit my hand, tearing the skin and drawing blood. I let go, and he dived through a broken grate into a drainage pipe running along the back of the brothels. I poked my head in and saw him crawling in the direction of the cliff face.

Mani tried to make his escape too, but I blocked his route, grabbed him by his oversized shirt, and handed him to Memi, kicking and screaming.

'That boy better be here when I return,' I shouted.

I ran through the Stars and out onto Sumaka Way, tying a kerchief around my hand as I made for Salvation's Climb. I swung open the broken gate and looked east, shielding my eyes from the sun's wine-coloured rays, now peeking through the forges and mills atop Dawn Claw. Hani was already out of the pipe and on the Climb. I chased him down the stairwell to the nearest landing, where Dee and I stood the day before, and tested the first concrete step of the external flight. It held, but the boy, more sure-footed than I, was flying, and by the time I returned to the relative safety of the shaft one level below, he was far ahead.

'Stop following me. The concrete is falling to bits. You grown-ups are too heavy,' he shouted up.

I was slightly built and barely over five-foot tall, so I ignored Hani's warning, but as soon as I emerged from the stairwell and put my foot on the next concrete step, I felt it loosen. I grabbed the nearest baluster as the entire section crumbled beneath me. My upper body slammed onto the landing, winding me, and my waist folded over the newly exposed edge, leaving my legs dangling. I caught my breath, swung my feet, and rolled onto my back.

'Are you okay?' Hani shouted from below.

'Which other grown-ups have been using the steps, Hani? Did you watch them climb with the dead Al'Mayran?' I said.

'Stop asking questions. Just leave us alone.'

'I can't. A man is dead, and it's my job to find out who killed him.'

'Then your job is stupid.'

'It has its moments.'

I stood and pressed my back into the column at the south-western corner of the landing, readied myself and, with a prayer to Xol, jumped at an angle into the shaft. Upon landing, I bent my knees and tumbled down the steps. Sharp pains exploded where my bones hit stone and I came to a stop with a loud grunt as all the air was driven out of my lungs.

'Get your arse up, Ani,' I said, gasping for breath and ignoring my aching chest.

I heard Hani running west along the next corridor. The sound was enough to spur me on and put the danger out of my mind enough to continue my descent until I reached the cliff path. I followed the lad into a maintenance area cordoned off by a spiked iron fence. I doubted he could have scaled the barrier, so I entered a nearby storm drainage system, via a narrow cylindrical passage city workers used to access the vertical clay pipes behind the steps.

The passage sloped at a forty-five-degree angle and the ceiling wasn't high enough for me to stand. I crouched and shuffled sideways, crab-like, to the intersection with the central duct. Hani was on the ladder below. I grabbed the nearest rung and swung my body out into the dark and fetid shaft.

We passed several levels without speaking, and the only sounds were our strained breathing, the pats of our soft-soled shoes on the ladder, and the occasional scurry of a rat. I was closing the gap but was unsure what I was going to do when I caught the lad. He was too big for me to carry, and if he struggled, we might both fall.

'Hani, I just want to talk,' I said.

'Then what?' he said.

'Nothing.'

'Fish shit. You'll want me to speak in court. My tribe will never trust me again.'

'What if we could find somewhere else for you and your brother to live?'

'And make us go to school?'

'For a little while. Then you can get a job. Do you like the sea? You could find work with my tribe on the docks or on a fishing boat.'

'If working on a fishing boat is so much fun, why aren't you doing it?'

I was about to argue when I slipped and lost my grip. My heel caught Hani's shoulder as I fell. Somehow, he clung on to the ladder as he twisted away. Out of instinct, I pushed my legs and arms out straight, wedging my body in the pipe and checking my fall, tearing the skin off my hands and the hair from my head. I had to manoeuvre around before I could grab the ladder again, and when I did, I flung my arms around the rails like I was embracing kin, and waited for my shaking to subside and the adrenaline to wane.

'Are you all right?' Hani said.

'Fine,' I said between breaths, my eyes clamped shut, my chin resting on a rung.

'I think you're crazy.'

'Me too, lad, me too.'

The ladder vibrated and I knew Hani was on the move again. He was climbing up towards the first available passage. I sighed and forced my aching bones after him. My hands felt like they were squeezing ground glass and my legs like they were lifting lead weights. But I made it to the opening and, with the greatest of care, stepped off the ladder and crawled up the shaft towards daylight.

I emerged on a cast-iron fire escape by the side of Mowate's Towers, a complex of flats built against a sheer stretch of Noon Claw. They were inaccessible by horse and cab but could be reached on foot either from the north or, as Hani had chosen, by a thin series of staircases carved into their facade.

As I ran, the freedom came back into my body, and I began to close the distance by jumping from one flight to the next, cutting off the turning points. By the time we reached Magila Market at the bottom of the towers, I was less than sixty feet behind the lad. But the change in territory worked in his favour.

The market was busy despite the early hour, and Hani was more nimble than I, able to twist between shoppers and stalls. I thought I had him at one point, only for a woman to step back and trip me onto the cobbled surface.

'Watch where you're running,' she scolded.

I held my police emblem above my head and set off again, this time shouting, 'Police, police!' We passed by the entrance to the Al'Mayran arcade, over the track of the South-Western Great Lift, and continued north. Magila Market became the unofficial border with the Depths, a place no law officer should set foot.

Hani and I cleared the southern end of the market, traditionally occupied by stalls selling fresh fruit and vegetables, and entered a less crowded section where the florists set up. I was soon gaining on him when he scrambled onto the top of the stone wall above the level below.

'Okay, lad, that's enough. I have you now,' I said.

He smiled at me and jumped.

Stunned, I pulled myself up and sat on the wall. Hani rolled off the awning of a stall selling imitations of the latest women's fashions. The stall owner, a fat man with a probable case of gout, clipped Hani around the ear. Far from being scared, the boy took time out of his escape to kick the owner's shin before he resumed his flight. As much trouble as this lad was causing me, I was starting to like him.

'Fuck it,' I said.

I had suffered too much injury to my body and my pride to give up. I got to my feet and leapt onto the awning. The stall didn't give way on the first impact. It had just enough strength in its makeshift frame and enough tension in its canopy to fling me back into the air. But when I came down for the second time, the structure collapsed, covering the owner and several of his patrons in its remains.

'Police,' I said, as I struggled up.

Thinking he had frustrated and beaten me with his daredevil leap, the boy hadn't hurried away fast enough. When he heard the stall crumple, he turned and, to his horror, saw me bearing down on him. He set off at pace, and I wondered if there was any limit to his stamina.

Up ahead, past a rank of underfed, miserable-looking horses and worn cabs, was a side lane that wound down to the dock but could be used to access the Depths. As I had feared, Hani took it.

I should have shimmered before I followed him, but I was exhausted, and the tramps, whores and gang members who worked or patrolled the border stared in disbelief as a police officer, an inspector no less, disregarded all tacit but long-established understanding between our tribes and invaded their realm.

This was not my first venture below, but it had been several years, and even I was surprised by the level of decay. Unchecked weeds, moss and creeping plants were reclaiming the urban sprawl for mother nature. It seemed every window was shattered or boarded up or missing entirely. All signage, if it remained, was dripping with rust or splintering and rotting. Bricks and stones and roof slates were cracked or lying in pieces on the ground, and in many cases, entire buildings were at various stages of complete collapse.

The Depths were never fragrant; the air was usually heavy with pungent odours and noxious fumes. But the hurricane had flooded the already stinking neighbourhoods with waste from unemptied cesspits, and I could only imagine with horror the nature of chemical reactions underway all around me. When I took in the deep breaths my body demanded, foul gasses stung my throat and made my head throb.

It was common to see tins and glass bottles piled up in corners. Unfortunately, the contents of these heaps had been redistributed by the winds, making the cobblestone paths I ran along even more treacherous than usual and tripping me up several times. I fell onto the body of a dead boy with an open chest whose haunted eyes reminded me of Shona's. I could do no more for this poor youngster than I could her, so I put them both out of my mind and hurried by.

Up ahead, Hani was about to corner the ruins of an old butcher's shop. So I summoned the last vestiges of my energy and leapt through the shop's empty window frame in an attempt to cut him off. Inside, I ran through a circle of men and women gathered around a hot pan reeking of stale fish guts. I kicked the back door aside and tackled the boy to the ground, landing in a river of excrement. He struggled for a moment, but he was almost as exhausted as I, and soon gave in.

'Okay, lad, it's over,' I said.

'It is for you, hog,' the raspy voice of a heavy smoker said.

No doubt the voice belonged to one of the group whose breakfast I had disturbed. He grabbed my hair and, with shocking force, pulled my head back to expose my throat.

Years of training and discipline kicked in. Muscle memory. I pushed emotion aside, and, as my fencing instructor taught me to, I blew the candle out.

Never panic. Panic kills you.

Act. Don't react.

Never entertain doubt. Doubt precedes defeat.

Be mindful.

Focus on the task at hand.

I had no idea if my attacker intended to deliver a killing blow or simply drag me to my feet, but I wasn't taking a chance. I drew my fighting dagger and stabbed in the direction of his thigh. The blade slid into muscle, the man screamed, and the grip on my hair relinquished.

By the time I turned around, the man had collapsed, his hands on his upper leg, blood gushing between his fingers. My slash must have caught his femoral sheath.

'I'll fetch help,' a younger gang member said, running off.

'I'm sorry,' I said, quietly, to no one in particular.

A pang of guilt penetrated my calm. The wretched lad was no more than twenty years old. His face was covered with what looked like pockmarks, most likely caused by some childhood disease, which no doubt accounted for his strained voice. By his side lay a wooden club, one without any sharp edges. He may have been about to beat me to death or simply threaten me.

I sheathed my fighting dagger and let go of Hani, who took the opportunity to run away. I didn't chase him. Instead, I fell to my knees to attend to the wounded lad by helping his friends stem the flow of blood. But the cut I had delivered was at an angle, and we couldn't fabricate a tourniquet fast enough, nor tie the makeshift cord tight enough around his thigh to prevent him from haemorrhaging.

'Where in Xol's name is your friend?' I shouted at the lean man, who was trying to apply pressure to his friend's thigh.

'This isn't the Uppers, hog. Folk don't exactly come running to help our kind down here,' the lean man spat.

He was right. If we were in the Uppers, even the Mids, an ambulance waggon from a nearby station would have arrived by now, carrying professionals with the right equipment. We had tied a belt around the lad's leg, and I had found a large splinter from a decayed window frame that I used to twist the belt tight. But the strap broke, the blood flowed over my hands, and all I could do was watch the life ebb from the poor soul's disbelieving eyes.

His death broke the spell that had descended upon us, cast by our joint effort to save him. Now that we had failed, his gang turned on me.

Blow the candle out.

I leapt to my feet, drew my sword, and unholstered a pistol, using its barrel to lift my emblem from my neck.

'You don't want to kill a copper,' I said, my voice cracking. The dead lad with the scarred face was still staring at me.

A young woman with short hair and tribal tattoos on her face rose, stepped forward, and took a dagger from the inside pocket of her long coat.

Blow the candle out.

'I didn't intend to kill your friend, and I don't want to hurt you. Let me go, and no one else has to die,' I said.

'Only you,' she said. Her eyes twitched. She was full of nervous energy and kept looking at her friends, who stood and gathered either side of her.

'Easy,' I said. They circled me and forced me up against an old office block now converted into a communal living area.

'Why are you even here?' a tall and lean man said. His hand gripped the hilt of his sword; his eyes were focused, as if he were weighing his options. Was it worth killing me, or was dispatching a hog going to bring him more trouble than pleasure?

'I just wanted the boy. That's all,' I said.

The lean man relaxed his grip. He adjusted his stance and moved backward, signalling an intention to defuse the situation. But the young woman with the tattooed face had other ideas. She made her move, lunging forward with surprising speed to slash at my pistol hand. I stepped back against the wall, just far enough to cause her to miss, and felt the draught on my knuckles as her blade passed. Before she could reorientate herself, I aimed my pistol at her forehead, blinked, and, for a moment, an image of the scarred boy appeared in my mind. He stared accusingly at me, and my sudden guilt made me fire at the woman's right shoulder instead of her head.

It was a mistake. The time for mercy had passed. It would have been safer to kill her. She dropped the dagger but stayed on her feet and remained a threat.

Forget the lad with the scarred face, Ani. You'll never know his intention, but this young woman's is clear. The time for hesitation is over. Kill or be killed. Blow the candle out.

The lean man drew his sword, and I transferred mine into my right hand, letting my empty pistol swing on its strap. His weapon had a cutting edge for slicing at an opponent, whereas mine was designed purely for thrusting the point forward to inflict damage. But he was overconfident and signalled his swing, which I deflected, leaving me with an open line, and I drove the point of my blade into his heart.

That's it. Good. Kill him. Don't take chances. They dealt this hand.

The lean man went down, but in my zeal to shake off my misguided charity, and this time deliver a killing blow, I lost focus and couldn't recover from my lunge. My stride forward took me inside their circle, and they closed in.

I tried to reach for another pistol, but I had no room to manoeuvre, and they grabbed me and shoved me against the wall. They tore my sword from my hand and forced me to my knees. The young woman picked up her dead friend's club and stood over me. Fear shook my body, but I wanted to die well. I said a prayer to Xol and thought about Josee.

'Kineks, no!' a new voice shouted.

The group made way for a broad-shouldered man with a straight back, high Kahokeyan cheekbones, and a sharp jawline. He was well dressed for the Depths in a modern style of suit trousers, a pale cotton shirt, and a knee-length, dark green raincoat.

'Who are you?' he said, pushing the woman with the tattooed face, Kineks, aside.

'Inspector Anika Sulaqua of the Square,' I said.

'Why are you here?'

'In pursuit of a witness.'

'Who?'

'A boy. I lost him.'

'She killed Patomon and Adoette,' Kineks snarled, trying to push past the newcomer and attack me again.

'In self-defence,' I said.

The newcomer nodded. 'Go to the healer, Kineks,' he said, pushing her away.

The young woman held her bloody shoulder, glared at me, and spat in my face before stalking off. Once she left, the others returned to the butcher's shop and began to eat their foul-smelling fish-gut stew.

The newcomer called after them. 'Once you've had your breakfast, get Patomon and Adoette out of the thoroughfare. This place smells bad enough.' He regarded me as I reclaimed my weapons. 'I'm Kononwa. I work for Yoyu. I'll take you to his manor, you'll be safe there.'

'Great,' I said, under my breath.

Chief Yoyu, to give him his unofficial title, was also known as the chief of the Depths. Although he no longer exercised direct operational control, no criminal gang in New Capital could exist or function without his acquiescence. These days he kept himself insulated from everyday activities and was referred to in newspapers as a community leader. He even attended city council meetings. It was rumoured he helped fix the election for High Chief Naka in return for ruling the underworld.

Yoyu lived in a converted warehouse on Magila Bay that used to belong to a private trading company. It was known as Yoyu's Manor and was located front and centre on the dock, facing directly south. Much to the disgust of the bay's wealthiest inhabitants, it could be seen from their windows, balconies and terraces, serving as an unwanted reminder of their own complicity in New Capital's corrupt financial practices. Perhaps as a further slight to them and their often gaudy tastes, Yoyu had had the wooden exterior of his manor painted white, with printed chains of pale turquoise octopuses running around the windows and door frames, a modest, even quaint style, more in keeping with traditional expressions of piety. I was not surprised to find the interior had also been renovated in the same subtle way, with muted but warm colours, reclaimed wood, and the occasional touch of copper.

The chief of the Depths received me on a second-floor balcony; he was having breakfast under the shelter of a large canopy, drinking salt tea and watching the rain sweep in from the south. He had pulled his ashen hair into a tight braid, woven with beads of tiny fish, and he wore loose deerskin leggings and had a white blanket decorated with a pattern of small red octopi draped over his shoulders.

But clothes, no matter how loose, could not hide Yoyu's dangerous proportions, and the slope of his shoulders was like a boulder smoothed by the wear of the tide. He was resting his bare feet on a stool, with his cup and saucer balanced on his enormous belly. He smiled upon seeing me and offered me a chair next to his.

'Ani Sulaqua, what brings you here?'

'Kononwa,' I said.

'My head of security and a formidable warrior, much like yourself. I hope he did not give you the impression this meeting was obligatory. I'm sure he merely wanted to escort one of our city's finest police inspectors to shelter. You are, of course, free to explore the lower levels as you wish, but I cannot guarantee your safety. There are countless poor and desperate people in the Depths, many of whom have come to blame the city's institutions, such as yours, for their misfortunes and may, however misguidedly, seek to exact retribution on one of its servants.'

'Yes, I met some of them.'

'I can see that. You literally have blood on your hands, Inspector.'

I shifted in my seat and closed my eyes for a moment to push away the unwanted images of the scarred young man. 'Thanks to Kononwa, I survived. Although he did appear to be on familiar terms with them,' I said.

'Better to know your enemy. Besides, it is not his job to scour the lanes and thoroughfares for such miserable wretches. It is yours. Perhaps that is why you are here today? Is this some new initiative from the police to tackle crime and corruption in the Depths? If so, it is most welcome, and I would like to offer you my cooperation. Shall we arrange a meeting with your superiors?'

'That won't be necessary.'

'Are you sure? I could set something up. I believe High Chief Naka would be good enough to hear me if it meant we could, at last, bring peace to this troubled area of our great city.'

'I'll bet he would. Your cousin, isn't he?'

'The high chief? Who told you that? No, no, we have a good working relationship. That is all.'

'Just two old Magila warriors, eh?' I was too tired to go on talking in code and too irritated by Yoyu's veiled threats. 'There's no policy change, Yoyu, official or otherwise.'

'So it was a particular case that brought you down here today?' he said.

I nodded.

'Might I still be of some assistance? For whom were you looking?'

'A young lad,' I said with a shrug.

'Describe him.'

'Kahokeyan, about ten years of age, making a nuisance of himself in the Heights.'

'Sounds like work for a uniformed officer to me, not an inspector of murder. How dedicated you must be, and what a great risk you took pursuing a misbehaving boy down here. Next time, may I suggest you liaise with one of my representatives and have him or her accompany you around these regrettably treacherous lanes? I would hate for you to come to any harm. Now, have some breakfast with me, and I'll have a boat take you over to the Al'Mayran arcade, which I believe you are very familiar with. Your wife is Al'Mayran, isn't she? I hope she is well.'

CHAPTER SIX

I followed Kononwa into the mass of sailors, stevedores, draught horses and mules swarming across the docks of Magila Bay, a spiderweb of rigging, masts, yards and swinging booms. From atop a claw, their distinct tasks were lost in the throng. Up close, their individual labours could be appreciated. Lone souls, pairs, and teams were all engaged pulling waggons, pushing wheelbarrows and hoisting the ropes and chains of winches, see-saws, and yards, as well as huge cranes, some fixed to the dock with concrete, others floating on pontoons larger than the average house. Thousands were employed every day in the business of lifting cargo on and off ships that sailed perpetually between New Capital and all the lands circling the Coiled Sea. From the finest Harn ceramics, packed in solid crates, cushioned with straw and wool, to butchered pig carcasses, dumped into heaps with little care. If it were produced in the Known World, it passed through the Claws and had to be moved using muscle and sinew.

Men and women sang as they worked, or shouted orders above the sound of straining timber, mechanical joints, and the din of heavy footsteps that turned treadwheels or pumped water for hydraulic systems. The air was thick with the scent of sweat and dung, only occasionally penetrated by the sweet scent of spices and perfumes from a broken crate.

Kononwa led me past a drydock, containing a half-assembled ship, to a jetty where several small sailing vessels were lashed. He led me to a handsome little cutter, which I helped him unmoor before taking a seat at the bow. I watched as he rowed us, with great skill and concentration, out of the dock.

'Do you belong to one of the original tribes?' I said to him, once we had set sail and were gliding through the water.

'Couldn't tell you,' he said.

'The Depths?'

'Correct.'

'You sail well.'

'Does that surprise you?'

'Your skills could be valuable to someone other than Yoyu,' I said.

'Yoyu isn't as bad as you coppers say. He takes care of those who are loyal to him.'

'He pretends to.'

'I suppose you have to be clever to know that. I guess if I were a smarter man, I wouldn't have to debase myself by working for him.'

'It wasn't my intention to offend you, Kononwa. I'm sorry.'

He stared at me for a moment to see if I were making fun of him, threat in his gleaming black eyes. But the moment passed, and he giggled like a little boy. 'You're very odd,' he said.

'How so?'

'Most coppers wouldn't apologise to my kind.'

'I am your kind.'

'You're from the Depths?'

'My mother was.' I turned away from him to wash the blood off my hands in the bay's waters. 'When did you learn to sail? Not everyone from the Depths does,' I said, wiping my hands on my trousers.

'I got out when I was a youngster for a few years, saw the Known World.'

'And you came back?'

'So it seems.'

'In Xol's name, why?'

'Beats me. Do you always know why you do things, Sulaqua?'

'No, I reckon not. I just think I do.'

We laughed and shared a few fishing stories until we arrived at the

Al'Mayran arcade not too far away from the steps to the South-Western Great Lift.

'Looks like I owe you my life, Kononwa,' I said as he prepared to row away.

'Don't take it personally,' he said with a wink.

'I'm sorry for the boy. Patomon, was it?'

'You did what you had to.'

I sighed and looked to the sky. 'I'm not so sure. I may have overreacted.'

'What about Adoette, the other man you killed?'

'I'm at peace with that. He tried to kill me.'

'But if you hadn't killed Patomon, would you have had to kill Adoette?'

'Perhaps not. But he still had a choice.'

'Why shoot Kineks in the shoulder, then? Believe me, you should have killed her too, Sulaqua.'

'Tell me about it,' I said under my breath.

It was midday when I returned to the Stars and the Sea. The sky had turned a sombre grey and was marbled with black clouds heavy with water. The temperature had risen, and the air had grown sticky. The sea breeze lost its freshness and brought dry sand and the smell of smoke and rotten flesh into the city. In the distance, the horizon to the south-west disappeared behind a curtain of rain.

The brothel was just opening, and the first customers of the day passed me in the hallway. They hid their faces and quickened their step into the drawing room to choose their companions, or upstairs to their pre-arranged appointments.

'Where's Hani? What have you done with him?' Memi said, marching down the hallway to stand over me.

'Hani is no doubt faring better than I. The lad was almost the death of me. Why did he run? What does he know?' I said.

'He's just a scared child.'

'Why is he scared?'

Memi didn't answer but looked past me and smiled at a middle-aged woman who had arrived with a portly, well-dressed man around her age, who I presumed was her husband.

'Fine, have it your way,' I said. 'But if I can find out about those boys, so can the CIB, and they won't allow tender age nor a frail body to hinder their interrogation. Now, where's Mani?'

'Why? What are you going to do with him?' Memi said.

Exasperated, I began to shout. 'I'm sick of the evasiveness and the questions. Give me the boy. Now.'

'But he doesn't know anything, I swear,' she said, putting her hand on my shoulder and pleading with me.

I tried a sympathetic tone. 'By keeping him here, it's you who is putting him in danger. Give him to me, so I can keep him out of harm's way,' I said, placing my hand on hers.

'Lock him up, you mean?'

'He'll be safer in police custody than in the Depths, or here when the CIB arrives.'

'The police, the CIB, you're all the same,' she said, pulling her hand away. 'You just want to use him.'

'He and his brother have information, and if they don't tell me what it is, the CIB will force it out of them,' I said, my voice rising again.

Tears welled in Memi's eyes and her mouth twitched.

I sighed and said, 'How about I take him home with me? I won't put their names in any official report nor deliver them to my department.'

Nita came down the stairs to greet a client I recognised, a man who ran one of the steel forges in Tsowe Bay. He exhibited no embarrassment nor paid any consideration to public discretion. Instead, he threw his arms around Nita and embraced her.

'I want half a dozen young heifers today, Nita. My appetite has returned with my health, and I wish to exhaust myself at great expense,' he said.

Nita laughed, but as she led him away, she cast a concerned look in my direction, and soon returned once the steel man had been shown into the drawing room.

'For Xol's sake, Ani. I have a business to run,' she said.

'I want the boy, Nita. Give him to me. I'll keep him out of trouble for as long as I can. I guarantee he'll be safer with me than here.'

Nita thought for a long time, looked with sympathy at Memi, and took her arm. 'Do it,' she said.

Memi pleaded with her eyes a moment longer, then seemed to accept Nita's final decision. She nodded and walked away, downcast and defeated.

Memi had given the lad a clean set of clothes, which contrasted with his stained shoes. I kept hold of his hand as we waited in the kitchen for her to wrap up some crab sticks and whelks for his lunch.

'They're his favourite,' Memi said.

The boy remained silent while she fussed over him, and he neither returned nor resisted her affections. But his eyes were wide open and alert, his lips tightly shut and turned inwards like his feelings. In his short life, he had already learnt that the world of grown-ups was not kind to children who belonged to the city's dark and hidden places. No wonder they became feral. It was how they survived.

With tears running down her face, Memi hugged him goodbye.

'He's not like his brother,' she said.

'In what way?' I said.

'Not as tough or as cunning; not yet, at any rate. You better keep him safe.'

'I want to keep you all safe, Memi. Talk to Nita. Whatever she knows, whatever she's planning, it won't work. The safest thing she can do is talk to me before the CIB comes.'

'I know, I know.'

'Then make her see it.'

'I'll try.'

'And failing that, you get out. Take as many of these young men and women with you as you can.'

'Take them where? We have nowhere else to go.'

'Find me.'

Mani did not speak as we strolled along the cobbles of Sumaka Way, but I felt the tension in his hand, which I dared not let go of, even though he was too old to be led. I tried to talk to him. I asked him about his mother and father, where he lived, how he and his brother had come to work at the Stars, but the most I could elicit from him was a sullen shrug and the odd grunt.

He brightened up once onboard a Great Lift. And with nowhere for him to escape, I let him run to the western end and peer over its brass rail at the bay below.

'Is this your first time on a Great Lift?' I said.

He shook his head.

'But I wager it's the first time without hiding beneath its benches, away from the conductor?'

He said nothing but smiled and looked away.

'That's okay. My friend Shona and I used to do the same thing,' I said. 'We once stole into a drive station and saw the giant cogs and wheels before a foreman chased us out. I think we ran all the way down Noon Claw and over the Bridge of Spirits to Lo'tse Bay. Once or twice, we even dared to play on Salvation's Climb. You have to be really brave to do that.'

'Hani does it all the time. He's never afraid,' the lad said.

'So I've seen.'

'You didn't catch him?'

'No. But I'm worried about him. Where would he go?'

Mani shrugged and said, 'He knows lots of places.'

I decided to leave it alone for the day. I was tired and in no mood to suffer such a familiar stone-faced attitude from one so young.

I took him to Horizon's Outlook via Malaye's Heart, a small, ancient and near-deserted neighbourhood – covered in traditional murals – that was awaiting renovation. Few people walked through it anymore, except my wife and I, as it led directly to Shadow Rise and the cliff overhang opposite our home.

'You live here?' Mani said, his mouth falling open, exposing a half-chewed whelk.

'Yes, and you're going to stay for a while. Would you like that?' I said.

He shrugged.

The drawbridge was down, and as we crossed over, I called out to Josee. She came running around the western terrace but stopped dead when she saw Mani. She looked briefly at me, and with barely a pause, smiled at the lad and said, 'Hello, Mani, how goes it with you?'

Another shrug.

'Can I have a crab stick? I'll swap you a plate of sweet biscuits and a glass of sugared lemon juice for one,' she said.

I changed into a clean suit and washed my hands and face while Josee served Mani his biscuits and juice on the western terrace. She joined me in the bedroom with a jar of what she called purifying oil, an ointment Al'Mayrans used on wounds that stung like salt.

'Josee, damn it. We need to keep an eye on the boy. He'll escape.'

'I've wound the bridge up and locked the handle, okay?'

'Sorry.'

'Give me your hands, love,' she said.

I obeyed and grimaced as she applied the ointment.

'I assume young Mani is a witness in your case?' Josee said in a knowing tone, an eyebrow raised.

'His brother is.'

'And where is Hani?'

'I chased him into the Depths, but I lost him.'

'Is that where you picked up all these bruises?' she said, prodding one and making me squeal.

'Mostly. Damn it, Josee, be careful.'

'I don't want to know the details, do I?'

I shook my head. 'I'm not sure what to do with the lad,' I said. 'If he's not already in danger, he will be if the CIB find out about him. I'm sorry to impose this on you but—'

'Forget it.'

'I don't think he'll be here for very long. Just until—'

'Forget it. I like children.'

'You never cease to amaze me.'

'Well, that's odd, because I find you entirely predictable, Anika Sulaqua.'

She planted a kiss on my forehead and, once I was dressed, took my hand. We walked onto the western terrace. Mani sat playing with Snuggs, rolling a little padded toy ball past the swing seat under which the magpie cat hid, waiting to pounce.

'I see you've made a friend,' Josee said.

Mani nodded.

'Do you like cats?' Josee said.

'Yes. But we have to eat them sometimes,' Mani said.

'Please don't eat Snuggs. I don't think he'd like it.'

'Your home is weird.'

'I'm glad you think so.'

'I always wondered who lived here.'

'Artists and weirdos,' I said.

'I'm the artist. She's the weirdo,' Josee said, winking at the lad. 'Want to have a look around?'

Mani nodded and stood up, collecting Snuggs from under the swing seat.

'We eat out here a lot, even when it's cold,' Josee said.

'Not in there?' Mani said, pointing at the dining room.

'Sometimes if it's raining we'll have parties in there. If it's just Ani and me, we stay in the kitchen when the weather's bad.'

'Did you paint all the paintings?'

'If they're piled in heaps, she painted them,' I said. 'If they're hung on a wall, probably not.'

'Ani thinks I'm untidy,' Josee said.

'She also painted the walls with Al'Mayran spirits,' I said. 'And the animals from my tribe's stories – octopuses, fish, sharks. She even carved the tribal pillar near the drawbridge to ward off bad spirits and welcome strangers.'

We showed Mani around the flat, and he marvelled at the wonders Josee had collected – strange and ancient art and artefacts, and well-worn furnishings and rugs from around the Known World. He relaxed and his reserve slipped and the questions bubbled to the surface of his young and imaginative mind: 'Where's that from? But what is it? Is that a demon or a good spirit? Is he like Xol or Zalema? But in what way? Is it hot or cold where that one's from? Have you seen a desert or a mountain or a swamp or a jungle? Do they have monsters or sorcerers there? What about their children? Do they all go to school and do they all have parents and homes?'

When the boy was lying on his stomach in the drawing room, flicking through a book with lots of paintings of Al'Mayra, Josee pulled me aside and said, 'I have to go out in an hour. Shall I take Mani with me?'

'No. Could you take him to Sundown?'

'A lot for the lad to take in.'

'Go to Ezno, it'll be fine.'

The rain had grown heavy whilst Josee and I showed Mani around the flat. I fetched my long oilskin coat and my slouch hat from the bedroom and stood on the northern balcony, buttoning the coat and fixing the hat. The sky was blotched dark grey, blackened with rain below the clouds, like soot half rinsed away. The steady hum of water droplets as they bounced off slate roofs drowned out the voices of the sailors and dock workers below. Even the birds had grown quiet and found a place to hide.

Josee popped her head out of the door to say goodbye as I wound the drawbridge down.

'You sure you want to go out in this?' I said.

'Think it'll last?' she said.

'Maybe not,' I said, turning my collar up. 'Put the bridge back up. And don't let go of the boy's hand when you take him to Ezno. He'll bolt.'

'Can't be having that, can we?'

'What's that supposed to mean?'

'Take care. I'll see you later,' Josee said in a cursory manner before she closed the door.

'Wonderful,' I said under my breath.

At the southern foot of Pastnoon Claw, near the docks opposite the Al'Mayran quarter across the bay, were several blocks of affordable flats called Xol's Fortune. The complex had ten thirty-storey high steel and concrete cuboids linked by narrow skyways. They were utilitarian in design with few ornate touches, carved octopi on the corners and bright painted tribal patterns around the windows, but no reliefs or pillars in the facade, no porticos, nor any balconies for the residents to step out on. Still, they appeared well-made and, judging by the pipes and flutes, were fully plumbed. Ordinary New Capital folk could do a lot worse.

Poqua, the Great Lift conductor whose name and address the lift overseer had given me, lived in a block called Cuttlefish Shell. I knocked

on his door and heard at least two bolts slide before the lock turned and
a young Kahokeyan man with short, balding, dark hair opened up.

'Hello,' he said.

'Poqua?'

'That's me.' He nodded, smiled and revealed a set of crooked teeth
too large for his jaw.

'Inspector Sulaqua,' I said, showing him my police emblem. 'Can I
come in?'

'Of course,' he said, letting me by. 'How can I help?'

'You were working Noon Claw's South-Western Great Lift two
nights ago?'

'That's right.'

'Do you remember seeing an Al'Mayran with a golden cane? He had
red hair, a beard and would have walked with a—'

'I remember him, Inspector.'

His direct and honest answer surprised me. 'What time was this?'

'Oh, I'm not too sure. Before the storm came,' he said, gesturing
towards a pair of wooden chairs with padded seats under the window.

'Where did he get on board?' I said, sitting down in one of the chairs.

'Top of Noon Claw,' he said, pointing through the window towards
the claw in question.

'Did you see where he disembarked?'

He pursed he lips. 'The arcade, I think.'

'You're absolutely sure?'

He shrugged and looked apologetic. 'Well, I've seen him many times,
and I could be confusing memories. That being said, likely the arcade.'

'Did he seem nervous, on edge, constantly looking around, maybe?'

'No, but come to think of it, he was a little flushed. You know how
these Al'Mayrans turn pink, Xol bless their hearts,' Poqua said, shaking
his head and laughing as if to say, *foreigners, eh?*

'Indeed. So you've no idea where he might have gone in the arcade?'

'None at all, Inspector.'

'Did you see him return?'

'Not on my deck, no, and I worked until the storm forced us to close.
He could have come back up on another deck, though.'

'Did you see any other Al'Mayrans you thought looked flushed or out of breath?'

Poqua laughed. 'More than I could count, poor souls – running to get home, weighed down by their wet robes.'

'Okay, thank you. You've been helpful.' I gave him my card and stood up. 'If you remember anything else, come to the Square. Leave a message at reception if I'm not in.'

'Can I ask, is the man okay?' Poqua said, rising from his seat with my card in his hand.

'Dead, I'm afraid.'

'Murdered?'

I nodded.

'How terrible. He was always polite, you know. Always said please and thank you. Small moments, but they stick in the mind, if you appreciate that kind of thing.'

I smiled and said, 'Be well, Poqua.'

After leaving Xol's Fortune behind, I was about to take Runner's Trail up to the Bridge of Spirits to cross the bay when, on a whim, I made my way to the base of one of the bridge's pillars where it rested upon Pastnoon Claw. There was a tiny cave, little more than a hole in the bedrock, by the pillar, where Shona and I had built a den. We used to meet there and build fires in the winter and catch fish in the summertime. Most adults couldn't fit inside the entrance, so it was of little use to other vagrants, but perfect for thin-bodied youngsters to hide in secret and share their first kiss.

The opening of the cave was much as I remembered: low and rectangular like the mouth of a letterbox. I sat down on the wet rock and put my feet inside before sliding in, curving my body like a snake. I dropped into the tunnel section and shuffled forwards into the murkiness of the inner hollow.

A crack in the rocks above, which once acted as a smokehole for the fires Shona and I built, let in a faint light from the grey day outside. Once my eyes adjusted to the gloom, I searched for some remnant of my time with Shona: the blanket we shared while huddled by the fire or the pan I had stolen from home that we used to fry the fish we caught. But in the twenty years since I set foot in the cave, countless other children had discovered it, and it was their belongings I found. Nothing of Shona remained.

I left the cave and hurried up Runner's Trail, across the Bridge of Spirits, keeping my hands in the pockets of my oilskin coat and lowering my head to protect my face from the rain. I tried to push Shona out of my mind and refused to look at the spot on the bridge where I had seen her killer throw her body, tied in a sack, into the Coiled Sea.

I hurried by the skytowers in the middle of Magila Bay, casting my eyes north where Jayson's Haven lay, stretching west from the Al'Mayran quarter on a rocky cape, the oldest Al'Mayran neighbourhood in New Capital, and my next stop.

The Haven's focal point was an ancient temple with crooked, painted spires and a crimson dome, which had resisted the pull of gravity for a thousand years to remain standing. Over time, the temple had been encircled by scores of narrow winding residential ways such as Dayna's Lane, home to I'Advay's colleague, who shared a name with the legendary warrior, Ameeleyor. She lived with her family in a four-storey dwelling at the elevated northern end, shielded by self-closing flood barriers.

Ameeleyor A'Jozaf's home was narrower than most, but its golden dome had been converted into another room for extra space. The exterior was painted in swirls of emerald and black, and every window was a mosaic of stained glass, depicting different scenes from Al'Mayra's mythical past. The one that caught my eye showed the warrior herself vanquishing the Harn with her staff of searing red light.

I ran over, keeping my slouch hat secure to shield me from the rain, and hammered on the door with my fist. A girl, around sixteen years of age, answered. She wore violet robes and was tall and broad with dark hair and eyes but pale skin, the unmistakable colouring of a Coor'Seyan.

'Yes?' she said, wedging her body between the door and its frame to prevent my entry, forcing me to remain in the downpour.

'Police,' I said, holding my emblem up. 'I'm here to see Ameeleyor A'Jozaf.'

'That's my mother.'

'Is she in?'

'No.'

There was a long pause, during which the girl seemed unsure whether she should add anything further.

'Where has she gone?' I said.

'I don't know,' the girl said.

'Work?'

'I'm not sure?'

'When do you expect her back?'

Before she could answer, a man with a deep and resonating voice shouted, 'Caysee, who is it?'

'The police, Pa,' the girl said.

'Wait there.'

While Caysee had her head turned, I pushed the door open using my shoulder for leverage and slid past her.

I stepped onto an Al'Mayran rug of typical design – golden spirits dancing on a blood-red background – running along a narrow hallway and up a wooden staircase. On the walls hung various Coor'Seyan weapons – curved daggers and circular blades – between long, richly coloured and variegated curtains, covered in ancient symbols.

A powerful Al'Mayran man appeared at the top of the staircase, wearing Coor'Seyan military robes of black and scarlet. Unusually, he wore his inky hair loose, and it billowed around his head to the rhythm of his gait as he took the stairs two at a time to stand over me. He was clean-shaven, square-jawed, pale and dark-eyed, and he had a scar on his face running from his forehead over his right eye, dividing his nose and curving away from his mouth. He also had a fresh, yellowing bruise on his right cheek.

'Mycale I'Krayag?' I said, taking off my hat.

'Yes. Who are you?'

'Inspector Sulaqua,' I said, showing him my emblem.

'I don't care for you barging into my home like this. What is this about?' he said.

'Areel I'Advay.'

'I see. Then it's my wife you want.'

'Where is she?'

'In the arcade somewhere.'

A little brown-haired girl, no more than six years of age, dressed in yellow and red robes, stood behind her father, wrapping her arms around his leg. The little one's presence calmed I'Krayag, or at least encouraged him to quell the display of temper simmering behind his fierce eyes.

The young girl began to sing an Al'Mayran nursery rhyme and rock from side to side. I smiled and winked at her.

'Please be quiet, Emellee,' I'Krayag said.

'You know about I'Advay?' I said.

He nodded.

'When did you find out?' I said.

'My wife, she went to the embassy yesterday afternoon, quite late,' he said.

'I see. Well, please accept my condolences for your loss.'

He tried to scowl, but a wave of uncertainty washed across his face, and he said, 'Areel was my wife's friend more than mine.'

'Still, it must have been a shock.'

'I am saddened at his passing, but I'm a soldier. Sudden death is both our companion and our trade.'

'Of course. When did you last see Areel?'

He hesitated before answering. 'Last week. He had dinner with us.'

'Where were you the night before last?'

'Here with my son. He was very ill.'

'How is he now?'

'Improving.'

'Glad to hear it. Were you in all night?'

'My wife and I went to see the apothecary.'

'What time?'

'Between thirty minutes past ten and thirty minutes past eleven. Then we both returned home.'

'Which apothecary?'

'Ronayld I'Kryse in the arcade. My wife knows him a little.'

'And he would verify your visit?'

He nodded. For the first time, I noticed the ring around the little finger of his right hand. It was golden and had a deep black bezel, a relief, which depicted a coiled snake. There were faint bruises on his knuckles too.

'Been in a fight recently, Mycale?' I said.

'I spar as part of my recuperation,' he said, folding his arms into his sleeves and hiding his hands.

'I see. When will Ameeleyor be back?'

'I couldn't say. Will that be all?'

'For now,' I said.

I'Krayag almost tripped me in his haste to shut the door, which he slammed in my face.

'Nice to meet you too,' I said.

I returned to the arcade and headed towards the apothecary shop to verify I'Krayag's alibi. The rain had eased and the sun was breaking through the thinning clouds. Her light reflected off the coloured signs and awnings of the stores and eateries surrounding the silver travertine cobblestones of the inner plaza. I shielded my eyes from the sparkling puddles and the rivulets that filled them, and from the claret spraying fountain, the centrepiece of the arcade.

Al'Mayrans were emerging from where they had taken cover, shaking their robes free of excess water and rolling up their hooded cloaks to carry. Proprietors reopened the doors and windows of their establishments. They came outside to wipe tables and chairs, and to clear the pools gathered in their canopies by running brushes along the undersides of the bowed canvases. They chatted with their patrons, laughing and joking as the fragrant aromas of herbs, spices, fresh bread and sugared pastries returned to the arcade.

Josee emerged from a little coffee shop, one of her favourites, a place specialising in sweet biscuits full of currents, cherries and sultanas. I smiled and started to wave, but she reached her hand back towards the open door for Dabreeyor A'Mendayse to take. Together they ran across the arcade, jumping over puddles, laughing with joy. When they reached the Winter Festival Theatre and stopped outside the box office, Dabreeyor ran into the back of Josee and put her arms around my wife's chest.

My stomach dropped, my throat tightened, and a vice crushed my temples. I tried to control my breathing, grew dizzy, and half sat, half fell onto a nearby form. A blur of Al'Mayran robes flapped before me, a swarm of butterflies in a dream of summer. *It means nothing*, I told myself. *They're tactile people, and Josee makes friends with ease.*

I pushed my hat behind my head until it hung by its strap and looked up to feel the soft rain on my face. I took my handkerchief and wiped my brow and my eyes until my heart stopped racing and I could no longer hear the rush of blood in my ears. Then I said a prayer to Xol, hoping I was just a fool, and went on my way.

Unlike many stores and eateries in the Al'Mayran arcade, the apothecary's shop hadn't been redecorated or remodelled in the Al'Mayran fashion. Other than the red stained-glass windows, there were no ornate flourishes. No brightly painted walls or friezes, no turrets or domes – just a plain four-storey stone facade, with a faded green-and-yellow-painted sign, set in one of the arches supporting the Bridge of Spirits.

In the shop window were glass jars, beakers, bottles and desiccators containing medicinal powders and liquids from all over the Known World. Their labels promised remedies to cure gout or to tame an insatiable appetite – all the latest fads in which wealthy people, too fond of indulging themselves, might place their hopes of turning the tide of their declining health.

I opened the door and heard the ring of the sprung brass bell. I was struck by a wave of contrasting aromas of varying intensity and agreeability – banana and copper, sherbet and sulphur, and vinegar and an odour far too close to the smell of cat piss for comfort. On the shelves were more beakers and bottles containing leaves, twigs, roots and mushrooms, along with animal bones, horns and hoofs. But not everything was dead and dry. One section of the shop was home to tanks of snakes, lizards, caterpillars, and cockroaches, crawling over one another in a desperate attempt to go nowhere.

Footsteps creaked on the floorboards above, and down a staircase. A moment later, a barrel-chested Al'Mayran man with a ginger ponytail emerged through a door behind the counter. His robes were muted, pale blues and sage rather than vivid reds or golds, and the cuffs of his wide sleeves were worn and full of holes. He had a large and heavy-looking head, and his skin was grey and hung from his face. His sunken green eyes peered at me through a sickly yellow film, their light dimmed and discoloured.

'Yes?' was all he said by way of greeting.

I was about to respond when Mycale I'Krayag emerged behind him. The tall Coor'Seyan jumped; his eyes flicked to I'Kryse and back to me.

'More medicine,' he said, patting the folds of his robe.

'How did you beat me here?' I said.

'I passed you whilst you sat on a form.'

'You never mentioned you were heading here.'

He said nothing further as he swung the counter's flap up like he owned the place and stormed out, almost knocking the door from its hinges. I stood in the entrance and watched as he disappeared into the gathering crowd.

I turned, stared at the Al'Mayran and said, 'Ronayld I'Kryse?'

'Yes. Who are you?'

'Inspector Sulaqua,' I said, closing the door before taking out my notebook. 'I have a few questions for you.'

'Is this about Areel I'Advay?'

I paused. 'Oh, did you know him?'

'He was a customer. And while he was at the temple, he attended a lecture or two I gave,' he explained quickly. 'I'm sorry for his passing.'

'How did you know?'

'Mycale just told me,' I'Kryse said, gesturing towards the shop door.

'I'm sure you had a lot to talk about.'

'What does that mean?' he said, sounding offended.

'What did you sell I'Advay?' I said, ignoring I'Kryse's question.

'A herbal remedy for pain relief. That leg gave him trouble – poor man. At least he's free of his body's prison now.'

'That's one way of looking at it. Where were you two nights ago?'

'Here.'

'And A'Jozaf and I'Krayag?'

'They helped me prepare the medicine for their son.'

'Do you allow all your customers to assist?' I said.

'I know Ameeleyor. She's not without skill, and I didn't have any

Fa'lyne mixed, which is what their boy needed. So I asked her to bleed some ceparal twigs and steam some peach urchins. As for Mycale, he's a strong man.' Admiration, even wonder, rose the pitch of his voice. His eyes widened as if in awe at the thought.

'Clearly.'

'And well suited to grinding other ingredients.'

'What time did they arrive?'

His tone flattened. 'Around thirty minutes past ten in the evening. They remained here, working, for around an hour.'

'Was there anyone else?' I said, approaching the counter behind which I'Kryse stood.

'Not that I saw, but the bell rang when we were in the back.' He flicked his head towards the rear of the shop. 'Mycale answered. He said it was no one.'

'And did he and his wife leave together?' I said, placing my hands on the counter and staring hard at I'Kryse.

'Yes,' he said, keeping his answer short and holding my gaze.

'In which direction?'

'I assumed they both returned home,' he said with a shrug, briefly looking away at the lizard and insects trapped in their tanks.

'You say you're friends with Ameeleyor?'

'Old acquaintances, really.' He tried to smile. He failed.

'Since when?'

'I used to advise the Al'Mayran Chamber of Spiritual Matters on ancient cures. I met her and Areel there.'

I changed tack. 'Do you keep lifeblood stones?'

I'Kryse breathed in sharply. 'By the spirits, no. I'm not a cleric. I have no grant, nor would I ever apply. Ask at the New Capital Al'Mayran temple if you wish to see a stone. The altar is made available to all.'

'Have you ever studied them?'

He nodded with vigour, the wonder returned to his eyes, and his tone grew enthusiastic. 'I've had the privilege. Remarkable objects, unlike anything I've ever seen or held. They truly contain the spirits of our ancestors.'

'Powerful, then?'

'Indeed.'

'Dangerous?'

He composed himself. 'Oh, by the spirits, no.'

'They couldn't be weaponised?'

'No, and only sinners would try.'

'Thank you for your time,' I said, completing my notes and handing him my scroll to record his testimony in.

As I left Ronayld I'Kryse's shop, he nodded to me and folded his arms in the sleeves of his robe. From outside, I could still see him through the door window, standing in the same position behind his counter, watching me.

I spent a couple of hours in the arcade, asking the staff and owners of various eateries if they had seen I'Advay on the night of the storm. Although some recognised his description, none had seen him for a week or two.

It was late afternoon when I arrived at the Square. The dark clouds and rain had long since passed, leaving a sweet-smelling scent hanging over the city. But the clear azure skies and warm glowing rays of the sun couldn't dismiss the apprehension in my heart as I approached Imala's office. First, I had to deal with Medele, her secretary of letters and loyal gatekeeper.

'She's been asking about you all day,' Medele said, looking up from his desk in his small room, where he often made visitors wait before they could be permitted to Imala's main office beyond. 'You think you're a law unto yourself. Why she puts up with you, I'll never know.'

'At least she has you in her life to bring her joy, Medele,' I said, quickly passing by to knock on Imala's door.

'Where in Xol's name have you been?' she said, as I entered her domain.

I puffed my cheeks out and blew air to show my displeasure as I shut the door to Medele's room.

'Well?' Imala said.

I shrugged.

'You look like you've been to the underworld and back.'

'That's not far from the truth.'

'Oh?'

'I chased those brothers down into the Depths,' I said, sitting down without an invite in front of her desk.

'In Xol's name, why?'

'Because I believe they're witnesses.'

'We don't go into the Depths – ever,' Imala said, punctuating her words by tapping on her leather writing pad.

'Show me where that policy is written down,' I said, gesturing towards an imaginary document.

'Don't be impudent with me. The residents down there don't trust us, and if we start arresting them on their territory, we'll have a riot on our hands, maybe a revolution. Xol forbid they organise around a cause. Do you know I've spent half my day describing your better qualities to the chief who has eased the Al'Mayrans' worries? But while I was putting out one of your fires, it seems you were lighting another.'

'You're saying if my investigation leads me either too far up or down the social ladder, I mustn't follow. That's brilliant.'

Imala sighed but ignored my remark. 'Have you discovered any-thing useful?'

'I talked with Nita. I think she knows who the murderer is.'

'Bring her in.'

'I don't have any proof.'

'Did you tell her it's either us or the CIB?'

I nodded.

'They'll arrest Nakni,' Imala said.

'I'm sure you're right. And I told Nita and him that. But I don't believe he's guilty,' I said.

'For Xol's sake, Ani, why?' Imala said, rubbing her temple.

I leant forward. 'I think Nita might be greedy enough to try and blackmail the killer. That's why she went to see her advocate. He's rotten. I could smell it.'

'She and Nakni may also just be guilty,' Imala said with a faint smile.

'Possibly,' I said, conceding her point with a nod. 'But I visited an Al'Mayran called Mycale I'Krayag, a Coor'Seyan, and the husband of one of I'Advay's colleagues. He wears a ring matching the wound on I'Advay's eye, and he's been in a fight recently. Unfortunately, the ring is regimental and many others will be wearing one.'

'So you've harassed another Al'Mayran, a soldier this time?' she said, her voice acquiring a tone of reprimand.

'I asked him questions,' I said, holding my hands up.

'And?'

'He has an alibi, an apothecary, who I suspect is lying for him. I'Krayag got to him before I could.'

'So you have nothing and you're still obsessing over an unlikely Al'Mayran killer.'

'I didn't even want to speak to I'Krayag.'

'Stay away from him. Focus on Nakni.'

'If you want someone to arrest that lad without proper evidence, find another inspector,' I said, getting up to leave.

'Sodia from the CIB will be here tomorrow. We're going to the embassy. You can come along and make your apologies in person.'

I said nothing and slammed the door on my way out, giving poor Medele a heart attack. Before I left the Square, I stopped by Dee's desk to see how the lad was doing after the previous night's festivities, and found him yawning and struggling to stay awake.

'Come on, Cadet, let's go home,' I said.

'I arrived late this morning,' he said once he managed to close his mouth.

'It was your Coming of Age festival. People will understand. I'm giving you an order. I'll hail us a cab.'

'Yes, ma'am,' he said, yawning again.

'I have to be at the embassy tomorrow, so I want you to go to the arcade. Ask around, see if any shopkeepers, restaurant managers, waiting staff, anyone, saw I'Advay the night he was killed. Check cab ranks, too. I'm convinced he took a cab from the embassy. Find the driver.'

Dee and I spoke very little as we waited for a free cab in Merchant's Plaza, but once we were travelling across Magila Bay bridge, I told him of my day's adventures, and when we reached Horizon's Outlook, I paid the cabbie to take him to Lo'tse Bay. Josee had left the drawbridge down and the kitchen door half open. I shook my head and called out her name as I entered. She wasn't in the dining room or on the western terrace, but voices raised in laughter were coming from the southern wing, so I quickened my step through the drawing room and the bathroom, flinging the adjoining bedroom door open.

Josee and Dabreeyor were standing in their undergarments, surrounded by robes and gowns, which were strewn on the floor, folded over chairs, and thrown onto the bed, along with torn brown wrapping paper and string.

'For fuck's sake, Josee, are you going to clear all this up?' I said.

'When we're finished, yes,' my wife said, the smile dropping from her face.

'What are you doing?'

'Dabreeyor mentioned she didn't bring all her belongings with her to New Capital. We bought her two new robes, and I wondered if there were any I had that she might like.'

'I'm sorry, Inspector, I didn't mean to intrude,' Dabreeyor said with a faint smile, her eyes flicking towards my wife.

'Josee and I need to leave in a few minutes,' I said.

'I see. I'll be on my way, then,' Dabreeyor said, her eyes dimming and her back stiffening.

I sighed, the regret imminent. 'Come to the Square tomorrow afternoon. You'll be able to perform the preservation ritual for I'Advay,' I said.

'That's very kind of you,' Dabreeyor said with a bow.

I folded my arms and watched as she hurried to find the robe she'd been wearing. She packed the new ones with those Josee was lending her, which, I noticed, included a birthday gift from me.

'Here, I have a bag, flower,' Josee said to her.

Flower? I thought, rolling my eyes.

When Dabreeyor was ready, I followed her and Josee to the northern balcony. The two Al'Mayrans kissed and hugged and waved goodbye.

The kitchen was a mess, the sink full of soaking pots, the oak worktops covered in breadcrumbs and pieces of hard and mouldy cheese. I picked up a cloth and began to wipe some of the detritus away.

'Leave it, I'll do that,' Josee said, pushing me aside and grabbing the cloth.

I returned to the bedroom and began to gather the other robes and hang them up or fold and stow them away. Josee followed me.

'I'm not a child. You don't need to clean up after me,' she said.

'Apparently I do,' I said, refusing to look her way.

'I just didn't expect you home yet.'

'Clearly.'

'What's that supposed to mean?'

'Forget it.'

'No. If you've got something to say, say it.'

'What's the point? Let's just go to Sundown and fetch the boy,' I said, stepping out of the bedroom onto the southern balcony.

I tried to calm down by walking around our home via the western terrace to the northern balcony. I crossed the bridge and waited for Josee on the cantilevered platform opposite Horizon's Outlook.

Once Josee had crossed, I wound the drawbridge up behind us and locked the handle, testing it to ensure it didn't rotate. Josee waited for me, but I marched past her. As we walked, she struggled to keep up, burdened as she was by her robe.

My head was pounding, my throat was dry and my face was flushed with heat. The silence between us was heavy and pointed, and we didn't speak a word until after we boarded the ferry and were sitting outside on the deck together, the sea breeze a welcome and soothing balm.

'I saw you in the arcade with Dabreeyor,' I said, fixing my gaze on a returning fishing boat.

'I wondered why you were so angry about an untidy bedroom and a few crumbs in the kitchen,' Josee said.

'Why didn't you tell me you were seeing her?' I said, meeting Josee's eye.

'I knew how you'd react.'

'You didn't give me a chance,' I said, trying not to look sullen.

'Can you see why?'

I picked at a splinter on the wooden seat of the ferry. 'If you'd told me, it wouldn't have been a surprise.'

'Oh, your attitude is my fault, is it?'

'That's not what I meant,' I said, pulling the splinter away.

Josee put her arm around me. 'I'm going to say this once. You have nothing to worry about. I like Dabreeyor as a friend—'

'You barely know her,' I said, playing with the splinter like it was the most important object in the Known World.

'You get to know people by spending time with them,' Josee said, grinding her chin on my shoulder. 'She's lonely and she's grieving, and I'd like to help.'

'Fine,' I said, flicking the splinter over the ferry's rail into the water.

'Clearly, it's not. And you made that obvious to her.'

'I didn't mean to make her uncomfortable.'

'Yes, you did.'

I sighed and looked to the sky. 'Then I'll apologise. Apparently, that's all I'll be doing tomorrow.'

'How about me?'

I paused, swallowed, and whispered, 'Sorry.'

'You've had a rough life, Ani. I understand, I do. But my patience isn't infinite.'

'What's my life got to do with it?'

'Let's drop the subject. I shouldn't have said that.'

'Tell me what you mean,' I said, my voice rising.

'You'll only get angrier.'

'You're talking about my mother, right?' I said, loud enough for those around us to stare or look away in embarrassment.

'Calm down, love. Yes, I'm talking about your mother and your father and Shona. Happy now?'

'Hardly.'

'That makes two of us.'

On Sundown, we found Ezno kneeling with Mani at the edge of his seaweed and snail pool. When he saw us approach, he rose to his feet and rubbed his left knee while repeatedly bending and straightening his leg.

'How goes it with you, my daughters?' he said, his smile fading when he saw our faces.

'Fine, Ezno,' Josee said.

'And you, Uncle?' I said.

'I'm well for an old man. Mani here is good company.'

The boy peered up at Ezno and gave a passable seaman's salute.

'Good,' I said.

'Oura is frying up last night's leftovers for dinner. Are you stopping?' Ezno said.

'Would you like that, Mani?' Josee said.

The lad nodded.

'Let's help set the table.'

Ezno lit his pipe and stood beside me, drawing smoke as the tide came in. Together, we watched the azure fade from the sky, leaving warm-coloured rays of light that painted the sea pink and the algae-covered rocks yellow like dry summer grass.

'What have you done to your hands?' Ezno said.

'Took the skin off chasing Mani's brother into the Depths,' I said.

'Your job is too dangerous.'

'Fishing killed my father.'

'I wasn't being critical.'

'Uncle?' I whispered.

'Yes, Daughter?'

'Am I hard to love?'

He thought for a long moment. 'No, but you find it hard to accept anyone could love you.'

I heard Etu's footsteps but didn't react in time, and he had me in a bear hug and on the ground before I could resist. Once he pinned my wrists to the warm earth, it was over. He started punching my thighs, poking my ribs, and dropping soil, grass, and weeds onto my face.

Oura, Josee, and Mani stopped setting the table to laugh. It was the most cheerful I'd seen the youngster all day. He doubled up and leant on Josee, who caught my eye, smiled and shook her head.

Dinner went well, and Josee and I managed a degree of civility. Afterwards, I offered to help Oura with washing the pots, but he would have none of it. When he'd gone, I stood to pour Josee, Etu and myself another beaker of ale. Ezno politely refused and I sat down. Only then did I notice Mani staring at me. I winked at him and said, 'What's up, lad?'

'How do you shimmer?' he asked.

I laughed. 'How do you walk?'

'I put one foot in front of the other.'

'But how do you make your leg move?'

'I just do.'

'Well, I just imagine the person I wish to appear as, and the shimmer comes.'

Mani screwed his face up. 'You don't change shape?'

'No. It's an illusion,' I said.

'Do it.'

I shimmered the boy's own appearance and his jaw dropped.

'That's amazing,' he shouted.

'Yeah, but it's wasted on her,' Etu said, nudging Mani, who sat beside him.

But the lad lost his inhibitions and ran around the table to sit beside me. 'But you're still you?' he asked.

'Touch me,' I said.

'Hit her. I know I want to,' Josee said with a wink.

Mani pushed his hand out, where he thought the image of his own face was, then blinked and shook his head like he was fighting off a sneeze.

'It's gone, you're you again. For a moment I saw both you and me.'

'That's the schism. Your eyes are telling your mind one thing but your touch another. Your brain needs harmony, and most of the time, it's the illusion that must lose.'

'Be someone else,' Mani demanded.

I looked at Ezno and shimmered his image first, followed by Oura, Etu and Josee.

'Remarkable,' Ezno said.

'She's just showing off,' Etu said.

Next, I shimmered Yoyu, the chief of the Depths.

'Not him, he's scary,' Mani said. I stopped shimmering altogether. 'Do you do it to catch murderers?'

'I shouldn't. It's against the law.'

'Why?'

'A long time ago, a police officer used it in a bad way.'

'But you don't?'

'I try not to.'

'The law is stupid. At least, that's what Hani says.'

'This time he's right.'

'I think I'd do it anyway,' Mani said, folding his arms.

'Well, lad, between you, me and Xol, I use it if it makes sense to,' I whispered.

'I'd shimmer all the time.'

'Me too,' Josee said.

'You wouldn't be able to,' I said with a shake of my head. 'It takes a lot of focused energy to maintain an illusion. And in police work, it's dangerous. I can look like someone, but can I behave like them? And then there's the schism. All someone has to do is touch me, and if their mind can't reconcile what they're touching with what they're seeing, I'm done for.'

'Do you have to have seen someone to do it?' Mani asked.

'Generally, that's how it works. Shimmerers remember faces and appearances. It makes no sense to try and imagine someone.'

'Does it have to be people? What about animals?'

'Higher life forms, you mean,' Josee said, making Etu and even Ezno laugh.

I ignored my family's teasing. 'Depends. Could I maintain the shimmer of a dog on a city thoroughfare where you would expect to see one? Maybe, if I were lucky to stay out of people's way. But a bear, or an elephant, in the same spot, probably not. The further away from who I am, or the more out of context what I'm shimmering is, the harder it is to maintain control. That's why it's best to shimmer a person you've met, especially if you know them well.'

'It's weird.'

'That's me, son, a freak,' I said, looking at Josee, who smiled back.

After dinner, we sat drinking sugared lemon juice on the rocks south of Ezno's home. Then Josee, Mani and I said our goodbyes and wandered to the nearest dock to find a boat to take us across the bay.

On the way up Pastnoon Claw, the stars began to splinter the twilight as the sky in the west turned from dark blue to black. Neither Josee nor I took Mani's hand as we walked. But he didn't stray too far and even led the way back to Horizon's Outlook. He stood still with his back to us and said, 'The drawbridge is down.'

'Oh, yes,' Josee said. 'You definitely raised it, didn't you?' she asked me.

'And locked it,' I said. I placed my hand on Mani's shoulder as I passed him. 'Both of you, stay here.'

'Be careful,' Josee said, drawing Mani close.

I examined the winch handle and saw two fresh scratches around the keyhole. I drew both of my percussion pistols and crossed the bridge, keeping low, out of line of sight from the kitchen window. When I reached the northern balcony, I turned the kitchen door handle as slowly as I could and tried to push. There was no give. The door was still locked.

Keeping my head down, I crept onto the western terrace, peering around the corner and waiting for my eyes to adjust before standing clear. The dining room door was also locked and the curtains still half closed. As far as I could tell, the room was empty. I passed the drawing room and the bathroom and went onto the southern balcony, my heart quickening, sweat dripping from my forehead, greasing my palms. The bedroom door was open.

I put one pistol down, dried my hand on my jacket and repeated the action with the other hand. My breathing sounded harsh in the silence, and every shuffle of my soft-soled shoes on the granite floor sounded like furniture being dragged. I wiped my brow with my forearm and inched forward.

I slipped inside the bedroom as quickly as I could so my body wouldn't be silhouetted against the night sky, and hid behind the bed. I holstered one of my pistols, took the lamp from Josee's bedside cabinet, removed the glass globe and turned the knob to lower the wick, hoping there was enough oil inside the font. I made sure my head was below the top of the mattress and struck a match, lit the wick, and replaced the globe, turning the knob until the lamp stopped smoking. I waited a moment, listening for movement, and when I heard none, I peered around the corner of the bed. The room was empty. I took the lamp with me, checking the den, my study, and the eastern balcony.

After a cursory glance inside the pantry, I lit lamps throughout the flat until I was confident any intruders had left. I waved Josee and Mani over. The lad ran onto the western terrace, leaving Josee and me on the northern balcony. I raised the bridge and locked the handle, staring across the chasm at Shadow Rise.

'Burglars?' Josee said.

'Nothing seems to be missing,' I said.

Mani returned, scratching his head.

'I can't find Snuggs,' he said.

CHAPTER SEVEN

I WISH I COULD say it was concern over the break-in that kept me up most of the night. Vigilance would have been honourable. Instead, every time I fell asleep, I dreamt of Josee and Dabreeyor, running together hand in hand through the summer rain. Eventually, I gave up on rest and stood on the southern balcony to watch the sun rise over the pointed tip of Dawn Claw.

I had made a bed for Mani on the settee in the drawing room, but when I went in to wake him, I found him pressed against the wall behind it, curled up with a blanket and cushion. He jumped when I woke him, and his eyes grew wide and afraid until he got his bearings. Together, we went to call for Snuggs in Shadow Rise, but we received no comforting cry in response.

'Maybe he'll come back later,' I said.

'Maybe someone ate him,' Mani said.

'Cats aren't on the menu in the Mids, son.'

We walked to the bridge in silence, Mani deep in thought, his lips scrunched together and pulled to one side. Before we could cross to the flat, he stood in front of me with his arms folded.

'Ezno said your father's dead?' he said.

'He was lost at sea many years ago,' I said.

'He wouldn't tell me about your mother. He said I should ask you.'

'That's because she was a whore from the Depths. When I was a baby,

I shimmered and scared her, so she gave me away. I don't know if she's alive or dead.'

Mani nodded as if I'd passed a test and let me by.

After a breakfast of fried mussels and seaweed cakes, I left Josee playing with Mani on the western terrace and walked through Malaye's Heart, down the cliff and across the Bridge of Spirits. On the other side of the bay, I took the Great Lift to the top of Noon Claw.

Throughout New Capital, repairs were well underway, and although normality hadn't returned, the people's collective efforts offered hope in unity. Some even carried out their work with a joyful air, no doubt thankful that the storm hadn't claimed their friends and family. Neighbours and fellow business owners were helping each other sweep lanes and ways, board up windows, and plug holes in roofs. Following a decree from High Chief Naka, schools had closed early for the summer holidays, and the sound of children entertaining themselves or joining in with the clean-up added to the good cheer. The sun was out, and people were embracing their altered routines and relishing still being amongst the living.

But I could not savour our deliverance. The weight of the dead pressed on my conscience. Although, truth be told, the real cause of my low spirits was the prospect of a long day, the first of many, dealing with the CIB, starting with the director of murder investigation, Muno Sodia.

'He's already here,' Medele said when I entered the elderly secretary's ancillary room.

'He's early,' I said.

'And eager.'

I nodded and handed Medele a bag of boiled sweets.

'Very kind of you,' he said.

I knocked on Imala's door.

'Enter,' she said.

Sodia was sitting in front of Imala's desk, but he did not turn to greet me, nor did he speak until Imala introduced him.

'Special Agent Kohee mentioned you, Inspector,' he said, once formally presented.

He had a pudgy and round face which could have been put to good use expressing cheerfulness. But like a machine that had broken down and was no longer fit for purpose, when he smiled at me, it was without joy, almost as if he were masking pain.

He had a shaved head, so it was hard to put an age to him, but I believed him to be in his mid-forties. He was short, not much taller than Imala and me, but he was round and stocky and moved with the conviction of self-importance. His every gesture was meant to indicate how busy he was. He wore a well-tailored version of the black CIB uniform, and the silver epaulettes on his shoulders, depicting a pair of crossed axes over a horizontal line of octopi, had been freshly polished.

'Actually, sir, we've met before,' I said to him.

'It is possible, but I meet so many people these days,' he said.

'I spoke at Superintendent Logaka's symposium last year about the rehabilitation of underage offenders,' I said, sitting down on the spare chair next to his.

'Oh, yes. I remember now,' he said, shuffling his chair away, as if I'd brought a foul odour with me that he was desperate to escape. 'You had some sentimental opinions about the use of outings and boat trips as a reward for behaving like human beings.'

'I intended to emphasise the benefits of cooperation in alien environments,' I said. Glancing over the desk, I caught Imala's eye and added, 'I can't have expressed myself well.'

'Sulaqua is my lead in the field,' Imala said, tilting her head towards me.

'And what have you discovered so far?' Sodia said.

'I'Advay frequented the Stars and the Sea brothel. He regularly saw a young prostitute called Nitushi Nakni,' I said.

'Have you questioned Nakni?'

'I have.'

'And?'

'He's a person of interest.'

Sodia snorted and cast a look at Imala. When she didn't respond he stared out of the window and, in a pompous tone, said, 'Seeing as

I'Advay was found dead outside the Stars, I should hope he is of interest to you, Inspector.'

He drew his attention back to me as he spoke, finishing his statement with a glare.

I bowed.

'I shall request a warrant to search the Stars and the Sea,' Sodia said, tapping his knee.

'We don't have the evidence, sir,' I said, looking to Imala for help.

'I have the high chief's ear in this matter and am reporting to him personally,' Sodia said, pausing for effect. When neither Imala nor I reacted, he went on: 'I will have one of my best men interrogate Nakni at CIB HQ. There have already been too many delays in this case. I respect the police force's need to remain on good terms with the communities they serve, and to tread lightly. But the CIB produces results through its application of robust authority.' He hammered the desk with the side of his fist. 'If the whore is hiding anything, we will find it.'

'I believe Nakni loved I'Advay,' I said, playing with my jacket lapels, trying to remain calm.

'If anything, that strengthens the case against him. It wouldn't be the first time a spurned whore lashed out at a client who lost interest.'

I was about to speak again, but Imala was watching me, her face expressionless and her stare fixed. I thought better of it.

'You met with Ambassador I'Rasnee?' Sodia said to me, a look of disapproval spreading across his face.

I nodded.

'A fine man, I've always found, and an ally to New Capital. We must resolve this case quickly for him,' Sodia said, switching his attention to Imala.

'I entirely agree, as does Sulaqua,' she said, bowing her head.

'A swift outcome would suit all,' I said.

'Excellent. Shall we leave for the embassy now?' Sodia said, standing and pulling his jacket down, trying to take in his faint reflection in the window behind Imala.

'Before we go, I need to check in with Sudeme, ma'am,' I said.

'You have ten minutes, Sulaqua. We'll meet you in the entrance hall,' Imala said, rising.

'Yes, ma'am.'

I took a paternoster lift up to forensics and found Sudeme in one of his laboratory rooms, a small space on the corner of the building with two windows and a pair of free-standing, wooden experimentation tables in the centre. Sudeme used the room for fibre analysis, and he was stood at a microscope with one of his assistants, a young woman in a sky-blue lab coat that fell past her knees.

'May I have a private word with you, Sudeme?' I said.

He looked over his spectacles at me and cocked his giant head to one side. 'Please give us a moment alone,' he said to the young woman.

As she left, she scowled at me, no doubt busy and annoyed at the interruption.

'Have I upset her?' I said.

'You upset everyone, Sulaqua. What do you want?' Sudeme said.

I took Areel I'Advay's charm, still wrapped in my handkerchief, out of my pocket and placed it on Sudeme's desk.

'I found this around I'Advay's neck,' I said.

'Why am I only seeing it now?' Sudeme said, unfolding the handkerchief.

'I wanted Josee to look at it.'

'And what do you want me to do with it?'

'Check it for fingerprints and index it with the same date as the other evidence.'

'You're too much.'

'Will you do it or not?'

'Yes, yes, Sulaqua,' Sudeme sighed.

'Is it pure gold?'

'Unlikely. Gold is usually mixed with copper or zinc to strengthen it. This, however, may be an alloy of titanium and gold.'

'Could such an alloy be used to make a cane?'

'Ah, your golden cane, Sulaqua. An absurd notion.'

'What is?'

'That a crippled man would be wandering around New Capital with such a valuable object in plain sight, inviting a horde of potential muggers to take it from him. That's your motive.'

'Have we swapped roles? Are you the inspector now, and I the scientist? Shall I dust that for prints or can you manage?'

'When I do, will I find your prints, like I did on the burnt stone?'

'No.'

'Anything else, Sulaqua?'

'Have you tested the substance on that stone yet?'

'I have.'

'And is it the same as the one found under I'Advay's fingernail?'

'It is.'

'And?'

'What?'

I sighed and said, 'Have the marks been left by a lifeblood stone?'

'Without a lifeblood stone to compare it to, I can only give you my best guess.'

'For Xol's sake, Sudeme.'

'Let me put it this way: I'm not sure what else either substance could be.'

'I don't know what I'd do without you.'

'Please leave my laboratory now, Sulaqua.'

I took another paternoster lift down to the entrance hall. I found Imala waiting there alone.

'Where's Sodia?' I said.

'Comfort break,' she said.

'Any break from him is a comfort.'

Imala took my arm and pulled me to one side, close to a wall and out of earshot of passers-by. 'That's enough, Ani. Remember you're to apologise to I'Rasnee and I'Dreng.'

'How could I forget?' I said, shaking my arm free.

'That's the spirit, Inspector,' Imala said, putting her hands behind her back and bouncing on the balls of her feet.

I crossed my arms and leant on the wall and watched two uniformed cadets, dripping with sweat, run into the hall.

'Why is Sodia leading this case in person?' I asked.

'He's Naka's man, and the high chief is following this inquiry closely.'

'Did Sodia tell you that?'

'At length.'

'I see. Perhaps I'd be better suited to a less high-profile case?'

Imala let out a little snort and put her mouth close to my ear. 'Don't sulk, Inspector. You're my lead in the field because you're the best inspector I have, and you're accompanying me to the embassy on the off-chance your theory about killer Al'Mayrans proves to be true. In return, try not to be pig-headed and show some respect to Sodia, the CIB, and the Al'Mayrans, whatever you may feel. That way, you stand a chance of staying on the case. And whatever your protests to the contrary, I know you want that.'

'Fine. But if I'm right, about Naka in particular, we can't trust Sodia.'

'We couldn't trust him if the high chief had never heard about this case and Nakni had slain I'Advay before an avid audience,' Imala whispered.

'Is he any good?'

'Sodia?'

I nodded.

'He has a talent for administrative cost-saving, self-preservation, and bullying. But in terms of law enforcement, he hasn't had an original thought in his entire career and doesn't want one. Naka will provide all the insights he needs.'

We took Sodia's four-seater carriage to the embassy. Lieutenant I'Seth and the Coor'Seyans were on guard at the gate. I'Seth ordered his scarlet- and black-clad soldiers to line the drive and stamp the butt of their spears on the ground as we passed. Sodia nodded at I'Seth. His nose was in the air, but I rolled my eyes and winked at the young man, eliciting a faint but noticeable smirk.

Special Agent Wesu Kohee was waiting for us at the top of the embassy steps, his hands behind his back, looking up at the sky, as if he were expecting the sun to pass over. When he saw our carriage, he walked down and opened the door for Sodia.

'How goes it with you, Kohee?' Sodia said.

'Well, sir. And with you?'

'Excellent. Better still when we get this business sorted. Shouldn't take too long.'

Wes bowed.

The greetings complete, we followed Wes through the arched doorway, into the entrance hall and up one of the flights of stairs. I'Rasnee's offices were to the north, at the end of a wide corridor lined with murals of former ambassadors, all connected by painted and abstract forms of twisting and flowing spirits. There was a long, peaked skylight to let the sun in and golden horseshoe oil lamps to light the dark hours.

At the far end of the corridor, standing outside the high doors of Ambassador I'Rasnee's offices, were three of his personal guards, recognisable by their brown leggings and blue-and-golden cowls. As we neared them, I realised one was Captain I'Dreng. He didn't appear to be on watch like his subordinates, judging by his stance: arms folded, back against the wall with one leg bent underneath him. His posture had an embittered air, and he didn't stir and stand upright until we were almost upon him, when a causal nod was all we received by way of greeting.

He was clearly familiar with Sodia, but Imala was a stranger to him, and he gave no indication he was going to introduce himself. I was about to perform the task when the weight of civil convention finally moved Sodia to act.

'Captain, this is Chief Inspector Imala,' he said.

Imala offered her hand and said, 'You must be Captain I'Dreng.'

I had given Imala my unfavourable impression of the captain, and I picked up on a slight edge to her tone when she said *You must be Captain I'Dreng*, as if his poor manners had given him away. To be fair to the captain, I think he spotted it too, because he paused and squinted at Imala before accepting her outstretched hand. *Yes, Normain*, I thought, *you have just been insulted.*

We entered the ambassador's outer office, a circular room painted with layers of red and sky-blue glaze. There were two secretaries of letters at work inside, sitting at desks facing each other: a young, redheaded woman and an older man with a greying blond ponytail.

The older man stood and said to I'Dreng, 'They can wait in the antechamber.' He turned to the young woman, and in a sharp manner asked, 'Is that letter almost ready?'

'Two minutes, sir,' she said.

'Take it to the ambassador for signing when you're finished.'

'Yes, sir.'

The older secretary shook his head, picked up a pile of large document wallets from his desk and left.

'The antechamber is through there,' I'Dreng said, pointing at a single door behind where the young woman sat.

Without another word, I'Dreng disappeared into the main office, leaving Sodia red-faced and clenching his fists. The CIB director tutted and, to express his frustration, flung the door to the antechamber open. Imala gestured with her open hand for me to follow, but I said, 'Excuse me, ma'am,' and addressed the young redhead instead. 'Is there a water closet nearby?'

'Through the door and to your left,' she said with a smile.

'Thank you.'

'You're most welcome.'

'Honestly, Sulaqua,' Imala said.

Outside the ambassador's office, instead of turning left as directed, I followed the older secretary along the mural-painted corridor, past the staircase above the embassy entrance, and through a double door. At the end of a narrow hall, he vanished down a set of steps signposted: *Records*.

I had no idea how far away the records department was, nor if the secretary were merely returning the wallets he had borrowed or fetching other documents. He may even have had business elsewhere in the embassy. For all I knew, he might be away from his desk for the rest of the day or for five minutes.

'Fuck it,' I said, and shimmered his appearance.

I was taking a huge risk shimmering the appearance of a man in his place of work, where the halls and corridors were crowded by his colleagues and associates. While I was projecting his face, would I bump into one of his friends? Would they try to place their hand on his heart by way of greeting, only to find my head? If they did, their vision would disagree with their touch, and the schism would form in their mind, sending them dizzy. They would blink, shake their head, and when they looked again, they would see the real me. It was that easy.

I tried to dispel my fears, blow the candle out, but as I hurried back to the ambassador's offices, nodding at the guards as I re-entered, I was plagued by visions of my capture, of the end of my life as an inspector, and, maybe, the end of my freedom. But once inside, my years of training kicked in and discipline took over. The candle was out, and my focus turned to a single objective: finding out what I'Rasnee and I'Dreng were discussing in their last private moments before we met.

'The letter?' I said to the young secretary, mimicking the lofty tone I'd heard her colleague use. I held my hand out, palm up, fingers beckoning with impatience.

She gave me an unfolded piece of paper written, unfortunately, in code. I quelled my disappointment, knocked on the door to I'Rasnee's main office, and entered. I'Rasnee was sitting behind his desk, reading a leather-bound manuscript, I'Dreng perched beside him. Without saying a word, I marched over and handed I'Rasnee the letter, hoping that when we made physical contact, the schism wouldn't form in his mind and create discord between what he saw and what he touched.

'This is fine, Normain,' he said, closing the manuscript and handing it to I'Dreng.

'Not too light on detail?' I'Dreng asked.

'Possibly, but what else is there to say? As long as the people you've chosen can be relied upon,' I'Rasnee said, his gaze remaining fixed on I'Dreng rather than on me.

'They can, Ambassador. Both are from good families, committed to the cause.'

'And how are they under pressure? After all, Sulaqua is clearly bright and rather dogged. Not to mention unpredictable,' I'Rasnee said, signing the letter, folding it and putting it into an envelope.

'Can't she be removed from the case?' I'Dreng said.

'Not unless she gives me enough justification to request it,' I'Rasnee said, striking a pocket match and lighting a candle. 'Let's see what she does.'

I tried to control my anger, but my throat constricted, and I tasted acid. I let out a slow breath and watched, with growing impatience, as I'Rasnee put three beads of sealing wax onto a spoon, melted them over the candle, poured a blob onto the envelope and sealed it shut with his ring. I put my hand out, but he blew on the wax to cool it and waved the envelope in a fanning motion.

My heart rapped against my chest. Perspiration beaded on my forehead. I thought of the older secretary, whose form I was shimmering, and hoped he wasn't on his way back. Why had I taken such a risk? What did I expect to learn?

I'Rasnee handed me the envelope, his hand higher than I anticipated. For a moment, he blinked, the schism taking effect. He shook his head and rubbed his eyes, and while he wasn't looking, I took the opportunity to grab the letter and step back.

'To the high chief, without delay,' I'Rasnee said, blinking his momentary confusion away, his mind reconciled once again.

I nodded, spun, and was almost out of his office when he shouted, 'Wait.'

I froze.

'Yes, sir?' I said, in as calm a manner as I could muster.

'Arrange for a pot of salted tea to be brought to the antechamber.'

'Right away, Ambassador,' I said, blowing out a sigh of relief.

I returned to the outer office, grateful not to find the older secretary sitting at his desk with his younger colleague staring at him in disbelief. I gave her the letter and relayed both of I'Rasnee's orders.

She practically snatched the letter from my hand and ran out. I stood behind the door, waiting as long as I dared to put distance between her and me. All the while, my heartbeat quickened, blood rushed ever louder in my ears, and my brow poured with sweat. I prayed to Xol neither she nor I would cross paths with her colleague, and opened the doors and hurried past the guards, back down the corridor.

I needed to find a place to stop shimmering as soon as possible. The only immediate option was the hall behind the double doors leading to the records department, where I might encounter the man whose appearance I had stolen. I could try to find somewhere else, but delaying it only increased the risk of discovery. I dived through the doors just as the older secretary's head emerged above the bannister at the end of the hall. He noticed me the moment I stopped shimmering his likeness.

'I think I'm lost,' I said.

'Where were you heading?' he said, shaking his head and blinking.

'The water closet?'

'No, no. You should have turned left outside the ambassador's offices.'

'Oh, yes, your colleague did say. Sorry, a lot on my mind. Police work, you know.'

'Not particularly,' he said.

I smiled and waited for him. The two of us walked together in uncomfortable silence back down the mural-painted corridor, at the end of which I nodded to him and went to find the water closet. There, I bolted the door, took my jacket off, rolled up my sleeves, and washed my face.

'In Xol's name, Ani, what are you doing?' I said, staring in the mirror and pulling on the collar of my shirt to let some air in. 'Was that worth it, lass?'

I couldn't tell. I hadn't heard I'Rasnee and I'Dreng discuss anything categorically incriminating. But Xol knows their conversation sounded conspiratorial.

When I had dried my face and recovered my nerve, I returned to the outer office and entered the antechamber. Wes, Imala and Sodia were sitting at a circular table of carved redwood with I'Rasnee and I'Dreng. The captain of the ambassador's guards was tapping his fingers on the leather-bound manuscript he'd been discussing with his master. The young secretary had just placed a pot of salted tea in the centre of the table and was busy distributing wooden cups. To my surprise, once I had taken my seat, I'Rasnee began to pour.

'You will have to forgive my skills. As Inspector Sulaqua knows, my attendant was injured in the storm,' he said, dismissing the secretary with a nod.

'Do you often drink salt tea, Ambassador?' Imala said.

'I've developed a taste for it, yes, and I don't like to impose our spiced fruit teas on a gathering of Kahokeyans. Seaweed cake?'

Although ornately decorated in marble and gold leaf, the antechamber was small and seemed more suited for internal embassy matters rather than official meetings with foreign nationals. In fact, I'Rasnee seemed determined to keep the proceedings informal. He adopted a polite, even ingratiating attitude in contrast with the cunning I witnessed earlier.

I raised my hand to my mouth and coughed. 'Perhaps I should begin by apologising for my behaviour the other day. While I admit I may have been overzealous, I meant no disrespect to either you, Ambassador I'Rasnee, or to Captain I'Dreng,' I said.

I'Dreng remained impassive and unmoved by my contrition, but I'Rasnee raised his hand and waved my apology away.

'It would be a sad world if caring too much was considered a fault in a law officer,' he said.

'Nevertheless.'

'Your apology, however unnecessary, is entirely accepted, Inspector,' I'Rasnee said with a bow. His pencilled-on lips turned upwards as he sat down. He took a sip of his tea and said, 'I've notified Areel's friends and colleagues of his passing and have sent word home. But I'd dearly like to offer those who grieve for him some news of your progress.'

'We already have a suspect. A young lad, I'Advay's partner, who I intend to take into custody,' Sodia said.

'Excellent. May I ask who?'

'I understand Sulaqua has already mentioned I'Advay's habit of visiting Rose Town?'

'She has. And rest assured, it's not a source of any embarrassment.'

'Well, we believe some altercation occurred between I'Advay and this young whore on the night of the storm, culminating in the envoy's murder.'

'I see. Well, I doubt the discovery Areel was paying for solace when he died will sting his kin any harder than the death of a beloved son and brother. When do you expect to charge this young man?'

'He hasn't been arrested yet,' I said.

'But he is your primary suspect, Inspector?'

'He's the only suspect at present, Ambassador. We're still gathering evidence. Of course, it would help if I were allowed access to I'Advay's office and home.'

'You'll find nothing in I'Advay's office to indicate why a whore would kill him,' I'Dreng said. 'And may I remind you, this is Al'Mayran territory.'

'Ambassador I'Rasnee and Captain I'Dreng have no desire to hinder the investigation, Ani,' Wes said. 'They merely wish to remove or redact sensitive material. We're negotiating regarding access to both locations. Please be patient.'

'I'm sorry, Inspector, but I'm a little confused. Are you saying you don't believe Areel's lover to be responsible for his death?' I'Rasnee said, a polite smile on his face.

'Inspector Sulaqua believes in being thorough,' Imala said. 'She agrees with Director Sodia and me that all circumstances at present point to I'Advay meeting his unfortunate demise in Rose Town, at the hands of one of its residents.'

I bowed my head.

'Perhaps we can help in some small way,' I'Rasnee said. 'As promised, Captain I'Dreng has conducted an internal investigation into Areel's last known movements at the embassy and provided his findings in a report. 'Unfortunately, we only have one copy. It was, after all, put together very quickly.'

I'Dreng slid the bound document across the table to Sodia. He made a show of taking his spectacles out of their case and putting them on with affected precision before opening the document and folding the first page flat.

He took his time reading, oblivious to us. Occasionally, he would mutter 'Very good,' or 'Excellent,' while nodding and turning a page. When he was done, he made a point of passing the document beyond me to Imala, who thanked him and handed it straight to me.

The report was light on detail, as I'Dreng expressed to I'Rasnee, but managed to account for most of I'Advay's whereabouts on the day he died, helped, I noticed, by convenient witnesses from the captain's own guards. Were these the trustworthy souls from good families, who were committed to the cause? I wondered.

'So, I'Advay arrives at the embassy at eight o'clock in the morning, as noted by your people at the gate,' I said to I'Dreng. 'Dabreeyor A'Mendayse confirms he entered his offices fifteen minutes later. He has one meeting in the morning, at eleven o'clock, with you, sir, in your office,' I said to I'Rasnee. 'He returns to his office a little after twelve and takes A'Mendayse to lunch in the embassy dining hall. They return to work at a few minutes past one. He leaves for his meeting with Major I'Handdru in the barracks at a quarter to three in the afternoon. But first he briefly sees his friend, Brigadier I'Kalmeen. According to Major I'Handdru, their meeting overruns and I'Advay doesn't leave until a quarter to six. He is next seen at the entranceway to the annex by one of your guards at six o'clock. But he isn't seen again until he leaves the embassy at a quarter past nine. So where was he for those three hours?'

'As far as we're aware, he was in his office,' I'Dreng said.

'Still, it's a long period of time unaccounted for.'

'So?' I'Dreng said, irritation creeping into his voice.

I shrugged, hoping to either provoke him further or let the silence build until he felt compelled to speak. Imala and Wes kept their tongue. Sodia, however, couldn't contain himself.

'Indeed, Sulaqua, so what?' he said.

'So what was I'Advay doing?'

'He had a habit of working late, Inspector,' I'Rasnee said.

'I'm sure that's correct. Did you hear about the death of the Coor'Seyan soldier that night?' I said, looking first at I'Dreng and then at I'Rasnee.

I'Dreng nodded.

'Tragic accident,' I'Rasnee said.

'If it were an accident,' I said.

'What in the Known World are you implying?' Sodia said.

'It's an odd coincidence, that's all.'

'For Xol's sake, this is New Capital, people get hurt in a storm all the time. The ambassador's attendant, for example.'

'Yes, very good point, sir, thank you for reminding me,' I said. 'How did I'Remo hurt himself again, Ambassador?'

'Liam fell, fixing a shutter at my home,' I'Rasnee said.

'What time was this?'

'Between ten and half past that night, just as the storm was picking up.'

'And before that, did you and I'Remo return home together?'

'I saw Ambassador I'Rasnee and his attendant home around six o'clock, then I went to my quarters next door,' I'Dreng said, answering for his master.

'In the Negotiated Burroughs?'

'Yes.'

'And you were there all evening?'

'All night, until I left with the ambassador the following morning.'

'And you, sir, were you at home all evening?' I said to I'Rasnee.

'Yes, Inspector. I'm not normally in the habit of taking air during a hurricane.'

Sodia snorted.

'Of course,' I said, bowing. 'And I'Remo was with you all night, too?'

'Yes, Inspector. And, as Captain I'Dreng said, we all left for the embassy the following morning. Liam saw the doctor, who strapped his ankle. As we were leaving to see High Chief Naka, we met you and learnt the sad news of Areel's passing.'

'The meeting with Naka was pre-arranged?'

'Yes, although you'll forgive me if I don't share what we discussed with you.'

'You know, I saw one of the high chief's people deliver a message to you later that day, after I'd seen Naka myself and inspected the damage to the Octagon Hall. I'm surprised he had anything more to tell you.'

'It was related to our earlier conversation.'

'I fail to see the point in these questions, Sulaqua,' Sodia said.

'Yes, Inspector, I think we've detained the ambassador enough for one day,' Imala said.

'But my door is always open to you,' I'Rasnee said.

'Thank you, sir. I'll remember that,' I said with a bow. 'But before we leave, can someone please arrange for me to speak to the captain's guards? The ones who saw I'Advay?'

'Of course. That will be done.'

'I'd also like to interview Brigadier I'Kalmeen and Major I'Handdru.'

'I'll do my best. But I can't demand the brigadier and the major meet with you.'

'I'm sure you'll be persuasive, sir.'

I stood with Wes and Imala on the embassy's portico while Sodia arranged for his carriage to be brought around. As we spoke, one of the Coor'Seyan guards hurried past us, through the garden, heading towards the barracks.

'There's some confusion at the gates,' Wes said.

He and I shared a glance and ran along the drive to find an Al'Mayran woman knelt at the entrance, crying with her head in her hands. Lieutenant I'Seth was trying to comfort her while simultaneously attempting to remove her from the gateway and a gathering crowd of onlookers.

'Ms A'Soyne, whatever is the matter?' he said.

'Oh, Lieutenant I'Seth, I've been kidnapped. I was so scared. I was sure they were going to kill me,' A'Soyne said.

She was another pale blond with deep blue eyes. But her hair was straight, and her skin freckled. She was in her early forties and had a round face with a small mouth and a broad nose, ending in a near-flat circle. For an Al'Mayran, she was neither tall nor heavy-limbed, and I could believe a strong man or two capable of dragging her away without too much effort.

'Who was going to kill you?' I said, kneeling down with her and I'Seth.

A'Soyne gawped at me, unsure of whether to speak to a stranger or not.

'It's okay, Ms A'Soyne. This is Inspector Sulaqua. She's with the New Capital police,' I'Seth said.

A'Soyne's hands trembled as she pulled her robe around her neck. She closed her eyes and shook her head. 'I don't know who they were. I just don't know.'

'Did you see anyone?'

She shook her head again. 'I was blindfolded.'

'Okay, did you hear their voices?'

A'Soyne squeezed her eyes shut tighter until deep wrinkles formed like the converging lines of a seashell. 'One voice. A man's voice. By the spirits, Lieutenant I'Seth, he kept me drugged. I was groggy. Nothing made sense.'

'I don't follow,' I'Seth said.

'Time.'

'Time? Ms A'Soyne?' I repeated, trying to prompt her.

'Day or night. I couldn't tell. How many days, I couldn't say. And I felt so…' A'Soyne's voice trailed off.

'How did you feel, kind lady?' I said.

A'Soyne opened her eyes and stared hard at me, almost pleading, begging me for answers I couldn't give. 'My body. My body wasn't my own. I didn't recognise my voice.'

'I see. And how did you get free?' I asked.

'I don't know. I woke up this morning inside Jayson's Mausoleum,' A'Soyne said.

'In the Al'Mayran park?' I said.

'Yes.'

'And you came straight here? You didn't raise the alarm in the park or in the arcade?' I said.

'I just ran to the Great Lift. I wanted to be here. I'm sorry.'

Her voice broke. She covered her face with her hands and sobbed.

I gave her a moment. 'That's okay.'

She recovered enough to face me again.

'Where did they kidnap you, kind lady? Can you remember that?' I asked.

'Outside my home.'

'Where is that?'

'The Negotiated Burroughs.'

'When?'

'I saw the date on the park clocktower this morning.'

'Okay.'

'So it had to be the night before last. Yes, I was taken the night before last,' A'Soyne said, punctuating her statement with two firm nods, as if trying to establish some control.

'Two nights ago, Ms A'Soyne?' I'Seth said, a perplexed expression on his face.

'Yes, Lieutenant,' A'Soyne said. As A'Soyne spoke, Imala and Sodia joined us.

'Can you tell me anything about where you were kept – sounds, smells?' I said.

'I heard a crowd. Seagulls. A fiddle. Maybe I was dreaming,' A'Soyne said.

'Did you recognise the tune?'

'It was Al'Mayran.'

'And smells?'

'Lots. Odd combinations that didn't make sense. Damp wood. Mustiness. Fruits and herbs and flowers.' She stared off mid-thought. 'And lots of metal and chemicals. Oh, even the spirits couldn't say. Maybe it was the drug they used on me. But that was alcohol, I swear it.'

I put my hand on her shoulder. 'That's all really useful, Ms A'Soyne. You're doing well. Now, what about the voice you heard, was it Kahokeyan or Al'Mayran?' I said.

'I… I don't know. He disguised his voice. Al'Mayran, I think.'

'But it was definitely a man's voice?'

'Sorry, Inspector, I think that's enough questions for now,' I'Seth said, helping the shaking woman to her feet.

A'Soyne leant on him, and he put his arms around her, cupping her head in his hand as he led her away towards the barracks. I grabbed Imala by the arm and pulled her to one side.

'We need to talk to that woman. Whether this incident is related to I'Advay's murder or not, we have a responsibility here, and we can't allow the Al'Mayrans to manage this internally,' I said.

'Keep your voice down, Ani,' Imala said.

'Oh, for Xol's—'

'I agree with you, but let me handle it. I want to get a forensics team to that mausoleum first.'

'I'm going down there now.'

'I'll come with you,' Wes said.

'Then go. I'll update Sodia,' Imala said.

Wes and I hastened to Agale Thoroughfare to find a cab. Although there were many, and nearly all travelling south, I couldn't see a single one free, so I started running, with Wes behind me, to find the nearest cab rank.

'Who is she?' I said.

'Je'mymor A'Soyne. Brigadier I'Kalmeen's secretary of letters,' Wes said.

'How well do you know her?'

'Hardly at all, but I can tell you she wasn't taken two nights ago.'

'How do you know that?'

'Because I saw her yesterday.'

CHAPTER EIGHT

THE SUN WAS near the crest of her arc and she was warming the city like an oven. None of the high-floating, flat-bottomed clouds hid her rays, nor did they promise a cooling shower. They just hung, almost still in the gentle breeze, appearing more like holes punched through the azure sky. Not that the heat seemed to bother the crowds in the Al'Mayran park.

There were folk from all around the Known World, all either ambling through the lanes at their ease or chatting in groups, blocking where we were running. To avoid them, we cut across the intricately shaped lawns, the fresh scent of cut grass filling my nostrils, making me sneeze, and weaved between the folks sitting and enjoying their lunch. But even the green was busy. I dodged children who ran through the twisting lines of flowers and took care not to collide with older folk, many of whom were looking for a form to sit on in the shade.

Even around Jayson's Mausoleum there was a crowd. People were sitting on its steps, leaning against its spiralled marble pillars, or were gathered around its circular wall. They were nearly all Al'Mayran, their robes and flowing gowns filling the spaces between them. They laughed and joked, debated and argued, some gesturing wildly while others stood with their arms folded in their sleeves.

Wes and I pushed through their mass, sometimes with force, never eliciting much of a response, except the occasional adjustment of a robe which we dragged off a shoulder as we passed.

'The crime scene will be fucked,' I said.

'Perhaps not inside,' Wes said.

At first glance, the mausoleum appeared locked. The high-standing, golden double doors were shut and the handles level. But on closer inspection, the plate of the right-hand-side handle was creased, having been prised away and forced back down. I put my leather gloves on and lifted the plate to peer underneath.

'The cylinder's broken,' I said.

'That took some strength. You can jimmy the plate with a crowbar, but to force it back down without hammering? That's just brute force,' Wes said.

I pushed the handle down and eased the door open. 'It's stifling in here,' I said, as warm air struck my face.

'It's the glass-domed roof. It acts like a greenhouse,' Wes said.

'What do you think you're doing?' a voice behind us shouted.

I glanced over my shoulder and saw a Kahokeyan groundskeeper: a short, round-faced and barrel-chested fellow with waist-long, ink-dark hair tucked behind his ears.

'I'm Special Agent Kohee. This is Inspector Sulaqua. We have reason to believe there's been a break-in here. Can you help clear these people for us? There's a good fellow,' Wes said, holding up his emblem.

'Oh, I see. Don't you worry. I'll sort it,' the groundskeeper said.

Inside, dust and aerosols spun in a hanging orb of yellow light shining from the dome above, revealing the painted, cotton-textured red swirl that rose up the inner wall in ever fainter circles to become a mere wisp pointing to the sky. Jayson's ashes appeared undisturbed in their urn, held in the hands of his own sculpted and painted likeness, which stood in the centre of the chamber. His spirit had long since departed to the red rocks of his homeland.

I walked around him, inspecting the floor until I found a few strands of long blond hair.

'What is it?' Wes said from the doorway.

'Straight blond hairs like A'Soyne's,' I said.

'You'd best come out until forensics arrive.'

I noticed a black hair lying a few feet away.

'Kahokeyan?' Wes said.

'Or Coor'Seyan,' I said.

By the time forensics arrived, Wes and the groundskeeper had tied a rope around the pillars of the mausoleum to keep folk out. I pointed out the hairs I'd found to the company leader and joined Wes outside the perimeter.

'What are you thinking?' he said.

'Are you sure you saw A'Soyne yesterday?'

'Absolutely.'

'Then how do you account for her belief she was kidnapped two days ago?'

'The effect of the drugs. I believe she has lost time.'

'She wasn't drugged before she was taken, therefore, being kidnapped should be the last coherent memory she has.'

'I disagree. With a concussion, you lose time before your injury as well as after. Couldn't certain narcotics have the same effect?'

'True, but let's say she was taken yesterday, not the day before, so after you say you saw her.'

'I did see her yesterday,' Wes said, a hint of frustration in his voice.

'So why would her kidnapping, which happened later, be the only event she remembers from that day? Why not the entire day, or at least a few more moments? Why doesn't she remember seeing you?'

'I know I saw her, Ani. Are you calling me a liar?' Wes said, with a smile that appeared forced.

'No.'

'It's the drugs. Who knows what they did to her mind? Who knows if she's remembering the kidnapping correctly? Perhaps that event was so traumatic, it entered her dreams, whereas the rest of the day just merges with other days.'

'I think she knows when she was taken.'

'Then how did I come to see her the day after? Explain that to me,' Wes said, folding his arms, his biceps stretching his uniform.

'Magic.'

'Magic?' Wes snorted.

'Yes, something called storming.'

'Storming? Isn't that an Al'Mayran version of shimmering?'

'No. Very different. When I shimmer, it's an illusion. I'm tricking your mind. I'm obscured by the mirage, but I'm still me. To storm someone is to steal their body, to transfer your mind and your spirit into their physical shell.'

Wes relaxed and laughed. 'And you think that's more likely than A'Soyne's drugged and bewildered mind confusing the days? I can't wait to tell Sodia. I like lateral thinking but there are limits. But my, you have quite the imagination, don't you?'

'Be quiet.'

'I was only teasing. I meant no offence.'

'No, you big ape, be quiet. I'm trying to listen.'

'To what?'

'Can you hear a fiddle?'

Wes turned an ear to the arcade; an exuberant Al'Mayran tune called 'Dance for Summer' was being played.

'I think I know where she was kept,' I said.

'In Xol's name, how?'

I ran off without answering, under the high vaulted arcade entrance and into the cobblestone plaza. The music was coming from behind the claret fountain, the player obscured by a crowd of listeners. I continued on to Ronayld I'Kryse's apothecary shop below the Bridge of Spirits.

'Here?' Wes said, catching up with me, panting heavily.

He gazed up at the faded green- and yellow-painted sign and the balustrade of the bridge above. He held his hand over his eyes to peer into the red-tinted shop window at the jars and beakers full of eye-catching but likely useless remedies.

'Before we enter, recall what A'Soyne said about the smell of fruits, herbs and flowers, metals and chemicals,' I said.

I opened the door and triggered the sprung brass bell. This time I'Kryse was behind his counter. I turned to Wes and breathed deeply in. He copied me, inhaled the sulphur, and coughed.

'Inspector?' I'Kryse said, his pale green eyes widening.

'This is my colleague, Special Agent Kohee, from the CIB. We'd be grateful if you could let us take a look through your attic window,' I said.

'Why? Whatever for?'

'We're following up on a witness testimony relating to the I'Advay investigation. We're trying to get a sense of the difference in perspective from the bridge compared to the attic. It shouldn't take too long, okay?'

I lifted the counter flap and walked through the opening before I'Kryse could answer. Behind me, Wes was gawking at a tank of lizards.

'Agent Kohee?' I said.

'Coming,' Wes said.

A narrow flight of wooden stairs divided the shop, north from south. We climbed to a dark hallway on the next floor. To the rear, there was a stockroom containing crates of unopened supplies, and, to the front, overlooking the arcade, a tidy office. I'Kryse's living quarters, which included a water closet and kitchen, were on the floor above. His living room was of typical Al'Mayran tastes: ornate rugs and curtains, painted walls and leather furniture. Pictures of Al'Mayra were hung everywhere, all sacred sites, most of them depicting the Red Mountains and their light. In the hallway ceiling, there was a hatchway to the attic.

I stood on the bannister, opened the hatch, releasing a dank fug, and pulled the ladder down. I climbed up and emerged in a mist of red light, pouring in through the small, stained-glass window. The low, unplastered stone ceiling followed the arch of the bridge above it, compromising the available space, which, outside of the red glow, was blackened with shadow.

On the wooden floor were crates of stock, a closed chest with spirits carved into the lid, various tools left in a box, a workbench, some pallets resting against the back wall, an old free-standing oil lamp, a horse's saddle, and a coil of thick rope next to a bare mattress below the window.

I stepped away from the hatch to allow Wes and I'Kryse to climb the ladder into the attic. I bent down near the mattress and flicked the end of the rope with my thumb. It was clean, freshly cut and, judging by the inch-wide, dust-free circle around the coil, a length of it had been recently used. Wes crouched beside me and ran his hand over the mattress. He picked up a strand of wavy blond hair that couldn't have been A'Soyne's.

We looked out of the window, listening to the chatter of the crowds, accompanied by the music of the fiddle, and the song of seagulls perched on the bridge's balustrade.

'Will that be all, Inspector? Only, I have an appointment,' I'Kryse said.

'Yes, thank you. Very revealing,' I said.

We followed I'Kryse out of the attic and back down to the shopfloor. Once Wes and I returned to the plaza, we watched I'Kryse lock up his shop. I asked the CIB agent what he thought.

'The hair wasn't A'Soyne's,' he said.

'Why would it be? Think about it. If she'd been stormed, her body would have been used to infiltrate the embassy while her consciousness was trapped here, in her assailant's body.'

'I can't keep up with you, Ani,' Wes said, shaking his head, his brow creased and channelling rivulets of sweat.

'You didn't see A'Soyne yesterday. You saw her kidnapper.'

'In A'Soyne's body?'

'Clever boy,' I said.

'That's insane.'

'It fits. It explains A'Soyne's inability to remember being at the embassy and why she felt like her body wasn't her own.'

'Because you're saying it literally wasn't?' Wes said.

'Exactly.'

'Even if I believed storming possible, which I'm not saying I do, we have no proof. That leaves us with a cut rope, a dirty mattress, and a hair that doesn't belong to our victim.'

'I know. But what do you really think?' I said.

'It's suspicious.'

'That's a start. Come on, big man, follow me.'

'Where?'

'Jayson's Haven.'

On our way there, I explained to Wes my theory about Al'Mayran killers, lifeblood stones, and Mycale I'Krayag as a possible suspect. But I didn't tell him about Mani.

A tall Al'Mayran woman in her early forties answered the door to

I'Krayag's house. She had wavy, pale yellow hair, almost white, and ghostly blue eyes.

'Ameeleyor, this is Inspector Sulaqua of the Square,' Wes said. 'Inspector, this is Ameeleyor A'Jozaf.'

She was taller than my wife and Dabreeyor A'Mendayse, although she was slimmer, almost thin by Al'Mayran standards. Her robes were emerald, gold and black, the same colours as the house, and the spirits depicted on them were distinct and elegant. She had a long nose with a sharp bridge, and when she took my hand, she leant her upper body away and peered down at me as the faintest of wan smiles flitted over her lips, then vanished.

'Can we come in, please?' I said.

'Of course,' she said, after a moment's hesitation.

She showed us into the living room. The sun's light shone red through the stained-glass window and fell upon a circular rug, patterned in a vortex of spirits. Ornaments of the mythical Ameeleyor sat upon the fire-place mantel, the bureau and the side cabinets. A series of full bookcases ran the length of one wall, and upon the others there hung Al'Mayran landscapes, depicting either the grey rocks of I'Krayag's home or the Red Mountains, alive and bright, in full luminance. Bundles of aromatic sage and frankincense hung from the oil lamps. A single scented candle had been lit and placed on the coffee table before the worn leather settee, where a young lad, around thirteen, lay wrapped in a blanket of crimson and gold. Unlike his father and his sisters, he had the same pale yellow hair as his mother and the same pastel-blue eyes.

'This your boy?' I said.

'Yes. Payval,' Ameeleyor said.

'I hope you're feeling better?' I said to the lad.

He looked towards his mother for approval before speaking. 'Much, thank you,' he said.

'My husband told me you called the other day. I was out shopping, for the sage and so on,' Ameeleyor said.

'My wife hangs them whenever I'm unwell,' I said.

'She's Al'Mayran?'

I nodded.

'I see. You must be familiar with our customs.'

'I'm sure I've much to learn about Al'Mayrans.'

Ameeleyor tilted her head and stared at me with a quizzical expression on her face. 'Well, I assume you're here to talk about Areel,' she said, after a pause.

'We are,' Wes said.

'Would you come out to the back porch? I want my son to rest.'

'Wherever,' I said.

Ameeleyor led us through the kitchen, a small tiled room with a range and a sink full of lunch pots, to the wooden, ivy-covered porch outside. She offered us a seat around a simple round oak table.

The garden was long and narrow and without borders. Beyond it, there was a steep grassy drop covered in wildflowers, with rows of elm trees at the bottom of the incline near the waters of the bay. Caysee, the eldest daughter, sat at an easel in the middle of the slope, painting the skytowers rising above the trees with the eastern face of Pastnoon Claw in the background. I'Krayag was playing hide-and-seek with his youngest girl in the trees and pretending not to hear the child's near constant giggling. When he noticed Wes and me, he scowled and stood, straight-backed, his hands balled into fists.

Ameeleyor folded her arms into the sleeves of her gown and hunched over slightly, turning her head to listen to me.

'How long had you known I'Advay?' I began.

'About five years. We met at the Senate in the chamber for spiritual matters. He was already with the High Temple. The two institutions liaise, and we met at an assembly. When he learnt my husband's regiment was to be stationed here, he asked if I'd like to join his mission.'

'Doing what?' I said.

'I attended the Known World committees with Areel. My knowledge and education complemented his. We would discuss magical theory and carry out research in the Great Library.'

'When did you last see him?' I said.

'Before the weekend,' Ameeleyor said.

'So you weren't at the embassy the day he died?'

'No.'

'And you wouldn't know what cane he was using?'

'No.'

'Where were you the night he was killed?'

'For most of the evening I was at home caring for my son. His condition worsened so, as my husband told you, we went to see Ronayld I'Kryse at his apothecary's shop.'

'Both you and your husband?'

'Yes.'

'You both left your son?'

Ameeleyor scowled and adopted a defensive tone. 'My eldest was here. We didn't go far.'

'When did you leave?'

'About thirty minutes past ten. We stayed an hour, then returned home.'

'Together?'

'Of course.'

'And you were home the rest of the night?'

Ameeleyor nodded. I picked a wavy blond hair up from the table and asked, 'While you were at the apothecary's shop, did you go up to the attic?'

Ameeleyor squinted. 'What an odd question. No.'

'Ever been up there?'

'No.'

I smiled and said, 'Have you heard what happened to Je'mymor A'Soyne?'

'No,' Ameeleyor said, straightening her back and maintaining eye contact.

'She claims to have been kidnapped.'

'By the spirits, is she hurt?'

'Not physically. But traumatised.'

'I can only imagine.'

'Indeed. She claims to have been taken days ago, only several people saw her at the embassy yesterday.'

'How strange,' Ameeleyor said, her voice losing its natural cadence.

'Isn't it? Can you remember what you and Mycale were doing two evenings ago?'

'Apart from fetching more medicine for my son, or household supplies, we will have been here,' Ameeleyor said, gesturing to her home.
'After all, with Areel gone, there's little point in me going to work.'

I nodded, looked at Wes, and tapped my fingers on the table as I
thought. 'Did you and Areel socialise often?'

Ameeleyor tilted her head. 'Quite often.'

'Did you know he visited Rose Town?'

She sighed. 'Eventually he told us.'

'When?'

'When he introduced us to Nitushi Nakni.'

'And what did you make of that relationship?' I said.

Ameeleyor adjusted her robe and pulled it tight around her shoulders. 'At first, I was unsure.'

'Because Nakni is a whore?'

Wes shifted in his chair. Ameeleyor recoiled and puffed her cheeks
out. 'Blunter than I would have put it,' she said.

'What changed?'

'Areel was happy.' She shrugged. 'And I grew to like Nitushi.'

'What did they do together?'

'They enjoyed concerts and plays and fine dining.'

'Any particular establishments?'

'I don't know.' Ameeleyor looked towards her husband playing with
their youngest. 'When Mycale and I ate with them, it was here or at
Areel's home.'

'Why?'

'Out of consideration for my husband.'

'He's shy?'

'Reserved.'

'Do you know Nakni is our prime suspect?'

Ameeleyor cast her eyes down. 'Yes.'

'Do you think him capable of murder?'

'He was too protective of Areel.'

'Possessive?'

'Not at all,' Ameeleyor said firmly, returning my gaze.

I stared at her until she looked away, towards her husband again.

Wes coughed, stood, and bowed. 'I think I'll go and say hello to Mycale.'

'How did you and your husband meet?' I said.

'What has that got to do with Areel?' Ameeleyor said.

'Just curious.'

'Professional habit, I suppose,' Ameeleyor said, wrinkling her nose. 'He saved my life. I was taking part in an archaeological dig on the outskirts of Harnland. A renegade band captured us and Mycale led the rescue.'

'You know Brigadier I'Kalmeen?'

'He and my husband are friends.'

'Really? A warrant officer and a brigadier?'

'Coor'Seyans care little for status, except the kind earned by deeds.' As she spoke, she gazed at I'Krayag and smiled.

My eyes fell on Caysee and I said, 'Your eldest is talented. May I take a closer look at her painting?'

'If she doesn't mind.'

I stood and walked down the slope with Ameeleyor following. Her eldest had sketched a faint outline, placing the nearest skytower so it loomed in the foreground to force a strong perspective, leading to a single vanishing point atop Pastnoon Claw. She had already painted a light wash of azure for the sky, leaving gaps to represent the flat-bottomed clouds, to which she was now applying touches of yellow to add warmth and body.

'Do you mind if I watch?' I asked her.

'If you like,' Caysee said without breaking concentration.

'My wife is an artist.'

'A professional?'

'She's selling quite a lot of her work at the moment.'

'Does she exhibit?'

'Yes.'

'Do you think she'd take a look at some of my work?'

'I'm sure. Although she works in oils mostly. Did you paint any of the pictures in the living room?'

'Most of them. They're of my parents' homes.'

'You grew up near the Red Mountains?' I said to Ameeleyor.

'Yes,' Ameeleyor said.

'Near the spirits, in theory?'

'Yes,' Ameeleyor said, pulling on her robe again.

'Is Ameeleyor a common name there?'

She nodded.

'And your namesake's myth, do you believe it's true?' I asked.

'I believe there's truth in it.'

'Including the staff of light?'

'Who can say?'

'Have you seen the red lights at the academy?'

She nodded.

'My wife said they reminded her of the stones. I thought they were related to the explosion. I wonder if we're both right. What do you think?' I said.

'I really couldn't say, Inspector. Have you asked all the questions you wanted?'

'Almost.'

'Oh?'

'Do you believe in storming?'

Out of the corner of my eye, I noticed Caysee's hand freeze above her canvas.

'Body swapping?' Ameeleyor said, keeping her eyes trained on mine. 'Why ask that?'

'Just trying to account for A'Soyne's lost time. It's just a theory,' I said with a shrug.

Ameeleyor remained silent. Wes climbed the hill with I'Krayag, the latter carrying his little girl, Emellee, on his shoulders and looking with concern towards his wife.

'Let's go,' I said to Wes.

'One moment,' he said.

He reached behind Emellee's head and pretended to pull a penny from her ear. The little girl laughed, took the coin Wes offered her, and said, 'Look Ma, I'm magical like you.' As soon as she had spoken, she grew quiet and looked afraid, like she'd been caught misbehaving.

It was mid-afternoon when I brought Wes down to the inspector's department in a paternoster lift and introduced him to Dee, who smiled, shook Wes's hand and said, 'I look forward to working with you, Special Agent Kohee.'

'Call me Wes.'

'Agent Kohee will do fine, Cadet,' I said.

When we took seats around my desk, Wes knocked the coffee out of a colleague's hand.

'Oh, I do apologise,' he said.

The injured party spun around, his face angry, ready to berate Wes. But upon seeing the giant CIB agent looming over him, he thought better of it and said, 'It had gone cold anyway.' He set about trying to soak up the coffee with his handkerchief, muttering under his breath about there being plenty of meeting rooms in the Square.

I laughed and winked at Dee, who tried his best to suppress a smile.

'Any luck in the arcade, Cadet?' I said.

'The victim was a familiar presence at many of the eateries, but if he dined at one of them the night of the storm, I haven't found it yet. Nor the supposed cabbie,' Dee said.

'May I?' Wes said, picking up Dee's notebook. 'My, such detail.'

'The cadet is very thorough,' I said.

'Pity you chose the police force instead of the CIB.'

'That's a matter of opinion,' I said.

We updated Dee on the day's events and soon settled into a speculative conversation about the case.

When Wes announced his thirst and went to fetch a drink from the department's water fountain, he surprised Dee and me by offering to bring us each a beaker. Curious, I watched him stroll slowly, almost leisurely, through the aisles between desks and across the office.

He took a sudden detour to help Medele, who was burdened with a tower of files, and opened the door to the secretary of letters' tiny room. Next, a chief inspector knocked a pinned-up wanted poster from a notice board. When the chief inspector didn't fix the poster back in place, Wes did so for him, with a shake of his head. When a young female cadet reached the fountain just before Wes, and took a deferential step back to allow him to go first, he insisted, with a warm smile, that she take her rightful place. As if his gesture alone hadn't put the teenager at ease, he stood chatting with her until she crumbled into giggles.

'What are you looking at, Inspector?' Dee said to me.

'A very rare creature, Cadet. One hardly seen in the Five Claws these days.'

'What?'

'A kind and polite CIB agent.'

'Well, statistically, at least one must exist.'

'Then he's Wes.'

A little while later, a clerk from reception tapped me on the shoulder to tell me Dabreeyor A'Mendayse was here to perform the lifeblood stone preservation ritual on Areel I'Advay's remains.

I met her in the entrance hall, close to the reception desk. She was staring into space and biting her lip. She beamed when she saw me, let out a deep breath and clutched the drawstring sack and dark mahogany case she carried to her chest.

'Oh, thank you, Ani,' she said. 'I can't tell you how relieved I'll be when I've carried out this task for Areel.'

'You seem nervous,' I said.

'I am. I've done this before but not often. I'll just be glad when it's done.'

I took her arm and pulled her to one side, out of earshot of the receptionists. 'Dabreeyor, I owe you an apology,' I said.

'Whatever for, Ani?'

'I was short with you yesterday. It was uncalled for.'

'I never thought anything of it.'

'You're very kind. But I apologise nonetheless. I was… ashamed of my—'

'Forget it, Ani,' she said, taking my hand. 'There are far more important things to worry about.'

'Fair enough,' I said with a bow.

I led Dabreeyor down to the deadhouse in the basement, one level below the inspectors' department. As we walked along the lamplit corridor she ran her hand over the wall, where murals of Xol, accepting the dead into his caverns under the sea, had been painted.

'Do you believe Xol is real?' she said.

'No. I just live like I do,' I said.

'A giant octopus god. It's thrilling to think of.'

'Terrifying when you're a child. But I suppose that's the point.'

'Do you have any rituals for your dead?'

'Depends on the tribe, or even the band within the tribe. Lo'tse mostly bury our loved ones at sea – wrap them in blankets with some of their favourite possessions, and set sail. Hundreds of boats, sometimes thousands, attend. We gather above a deep abyss and release our dead to Xol's mercy, pleading with him in song to accept them.'

'Must be quite a sight,' Dabreeyor said.

'No red smoke though.'

Toko, the medical examiner, had laid I'Advay's body on a slab in one of the examination rooms. I could have left him alone to observe Dabreeyor, but I hadn't seen the preservation ritual before and was curious about the details. So I stood with him at a respectful distance to watch.

Dabreeyor placed the drawstring sack and mahogany case, engraved with a design of floating spirits, onto a wheeled table she had drawn alongside the slab.

'If you tell me this could damage evidence, I'll stop it,' I said to Toko.

'No, I have what I need. I'm happy to accommodate this ritual, nonsense though it is,' Toko said.

'Nonsense?'

'The belief the spirit is locked away in the heart for safe keeping, and if the walls of the heart are broken or crumble with decay, it will escape. I've cut open a lot of hearts, Ani. I've never seen a spirit escape. Not once.'

'It's your open mind I've always admired,' I said, rolling my eyes. 'Would it hurt you to live your life acknowledging that a power greater than we understand could exist?'

'That's how I live my life. It's called scientific exploration.'

'Fair enough, but what if that power turned out to be a giant octopus god living in the waters off our shores? Do you really want to take a chance?' I winked at him.

'If you want to talk about risks,' Toko said, 'consider the Al'Mayrans in battle: they put more faith in the red dust they cover their bodies in than the armour they wear. Furthermore—'

Toko lost his words when Dabreeyor undid the sash around her waist and removed her blue robes to reveal her undergarments: a plain sleeveless tunic and shorts.

Dabreeyor was athletic and robust, and her resemblance to my wife grew stronger when she pinned her hair above her head like Josee did when she was painting. But Dabreeyor was not here to create art.

She opened the drawstring sack and took out a bowl, two glass jars, and a flat wooden blade with a dull edge. She sprinkled a pinch of lifeblood stone dust and mixed it with oil in the bowl, releasing the unnatural gleam of the stones.

From the box, she took several steel instruments, plated with silver and gold, that appeared to be both utilitarian and decorative, equally suitable for a hospital theatre or as ornaments in a home. She picked up a scalpel and sliced I'Advay's chest in one swift stroke.

I gasped, and Toko said, 'A sure hand.'

Next, she strapped a jig fitted with a saw and a rotating handle to I'Advay's torso. She pressed down and turned the handle to cut through the breastbone. Once she removed the jig, she opened the envoy's chest with a spreader, cut through the underlying tissue, and severed the arteries and veins connected to his heart. As she worked, she chanted, and tears streamed down her face.

When she had the heart out of its cage and in her hands, she placed it in the bowl and covered it in the lifeblood stone paste. Now that it was gleaming and protected, she slipped the organ back into its cavity, removed the spreader and sewed I'Advay's chest together. Her task complete, the spirit saved, she sighed and smiled at me, her pale blue eyes wet and alight with relief and happiness.

'Thank you,' she said with a bow of her head.

I hadn't eaten since breakfast, so I took Dabreeyor, Dee and Wes to a small eatery, just south-west of the Square at Merchant's Plaza. We sat outside under an awning and shared a bowl of stewed squid and seaweed while watching New Capital's residents traverse the skybridges from cliff-top to tower.

'How do they not fall into the bay?' Dabreeyor said.

'Al'Mayran steel and Kahokeyan skill. That's what my father said, and he helped build the bridges,' Wes said.

'It's not our steel. You forge that. We just supply the iron ore. No, it's the ingenuity I marvel at.'

'Innovation born of necessity. Overcrowding, you see. First, we learnt how to build homes on stilts, cut steps into the cliffs. Later, we needed stronger arches and vaulted ceilings to build on top of and to span the bays with bridges that could support entire neighbourhoods. When that wasn't enough, the towers came.'

'Yes. Like titans rising from the sea,' Dabreeyor said.

'My uncle calls them monuments to wealth,' I said.

'And some paid a higher price than others. When I was a little boy, my father died building one – along with scores of souls in a single collapse,' Wes said.

'Bless his spirit,' Dabreeyor said.

'Perhaps Xol and Zalema have to humble us.'

'But why punish the poor working men and women? It's not their arrogance that needs to be checked,' I said.

Wes shrugged and smiled. 'I was an angry little boy for a while,' he said. 'I'm reconciled now.'

'You lost your father young, too, didn't you, Inspector?' Dabreeyor said.

I nodded.

'And both died plying their trade,' she reflected.

'No. It's the rich who get to die plying their trade. The poor are killed by theirs,' I said, my tone harsher than I'd intended.

No one spoke for a few minutes – each of us seemed lost in thought – and an air of melancholy hung over the table.

'Dabreeyor, what contact do you have with Je'mymor A'Soyne?' I said after some time.

'She performed the same role for Brigadier I'Kalmeen that I did for Areel, so we had cause to correspond and speak to one another,' Dabreeyor said.

'Is she competent?'

'Entirely.'

'You wouldn't describe her as foolish or given to nerves?'

'No.'

'Do you believe in storming?'

Dabreeyor laughed, and almost choked. 'Body swapping?'

I nodded.

'Oh, Ani, we're taught those myths when we're young to keep us in line, but there's nothing to it, at least that I ever saw,' Dabreeyor said.

Beside me, Wes shook his head and laughed.

By the time I went to see Imala, Medele had left for the day, so I dropped a bag of sweets between the heaps of paperwork on his desk.

'How goes it with you, Ani?' Imala said, when I entered her office. She was nursing a glass of whiskey, which normally signified a better mood.

'You tell me. How was my behaviour today?' I said.

'As usual, it left a lot to be desired. But you're still on the case, which is now a joint investigation with the CIB. You're to partner with Special Agent Kohee.'

I nodded.

'The CIB is looking for a quick conclusion. Nitushi Nakni would give them that,' Imala said, looking away.

'The lad's innocent. I would prefer a different inspector be brought in to arrest him if those are your orders,' I said.

Imala dismissed my suggestion with a wave of her hand and took another sip of her whiskey. 'Do you still believe an Al'Mayran killed I'Advay?'

'More than ever. I'Rasnee and I'Dreng are hiding something,' I said.

Imala let out a deep sigh, took her spectacles off and rubbed her eyes. 'I think you're right. But go slow, Ani.'

'Slow won't do Nita and Nakni any good. I need to cast enough doubt on the case against them that even the CIB can't deny it.'

'How?'

'I want Salvation's Climb searched. I think I'll find more evidence of lifeblood stones there. And I think I'll find the cane.'

'And what of the logistics and dangers involved? Entire sections are inaccessible. Whole concrete flights have fallen away. And those that remain may collapse at any time. No, no, we don't have the expertise.'

'Pay for expertise. Bring in specialists. For Xol's sake, this city was constructed on the sides of cliffs. If we can't find capable men and women, who can?'

'You speak of evidence but give me none to justify signing off such an endeavour,' Imala said.

'What if I said I could do it?'

'Perhaps you could. But are you ready to risk your life to prove your theory?'

I thought about how close I had come to dying on the steps the day before and looked away from Imala's unflinching gaze.

CHAPTER NINE

THE LATE EVENING sunlight entered the bedroom through fine sheer curtains, which infused the glow with a tint of sepia where it fell upon the walls and wardrobes, like a stroke from one of Caysee's watercolour brushes. Beside me on the bed, Josee stretched, and I pressed my body into hers to feel the warmth of her pink and freckled skin. I ran my hand over her midriff and circled her bellybutton with my finger, all the while studying her face for proof of sated desire.

Usually, when I made love to her, I did so free of agenda or want of validation. Today, when I had touched her, I saw Dabreeyor caressing her, and my wife responding and grasping at blond hair instead of black. I had brought an imagined rival into our bed, one with whom I could not possibly compete.

Josee played with my hair, picking up strands and letting them fall. 'This needs washing.'

'It'll do.'

'Don't argue. The boiler's lit. I'll run you a bath. Come on, move your arse.'

Once Josee filled the tub with hot water mixed with sea salt and lavender herbs, I dipped my toe in and yelped, 'It's scalding.'

'Rubbish,' Josee said, taking a bottle of laurel oil from the cabinet above the basin and stepping into the tub.

She poured three drops of oil onto her palm, put the bottle on the windowsill and stared at me, waiting, with her hands raised.

I turned the cold tap on to reduce the heat, wafted some of the steam away and climbed in. We sat down and she began to rub the oil into my scalp, making little circular motions with her fingertips. When she was finished, she wrapped her arms around me and held me close.

'How can you still be this tense?' she said.

I shrugged and said, 'I think I've met a victim of storming.'

Josee laughed. 'Load of rubbish.'

'Why is it? I can fool you into seeing someone else, so who's to say storming isn't as real as shimmering?' I said.

'What you do, magical though it may be, is a mirage. Storming, on the other hand, is no illusion. At least, it wouldn't be if it were real.'

'Both abilities are magical. Science, as yet, can't explain them. Shimmering is real, therefore, storming could be too. End of story.'

'But to be able to take over someone else's body, literally replace their mind and spirit with your own. How can that be possible, love? I mean, are you the same person in your new body? If your victim were ill, would you be ill? If my body were taken over, would the one who stormed me be able to paint?' Josee said.

'All good points. I wish I had answers.'

'What's put this into your head?'

'This woman at the embassy was kidnapped, drugged, and held prisoner. She says she was taken two days ago, only she was seen at work yesterday.'

'And you think it's more likely she was stormed, had her body stolen, than the drugs confusing her?'

'That's what Wes, the CIB agent I'm partnered with, argued. But I think being taken is the last clear memory she has. It's everything that came after that's foggy.'

'Drugs can do weird things to a person's mind.'

'You should know.'

Josee squeezed me. 'Very funny.'

'But this woman says she was kept blindfolded, and she felt like her body and her voice weren't her own,' I said.

'There's absolutely no evidence Al'Mayrans could ever storm, and the only texts on the subject are poems and stories, not works of history.'

'That doesn't mean they didn't exist,' I said, twisting my head to see if Josee were laughing at me. 'Shimmering is dying. In time, if there are none of my kind left, will we pass into myth? Will future historians who have never witnessed magic first-hand come to discount all evidence of our existence? At the heart of every legend, there is truth.'

Josee ran the outside of her forefinger down my face. 'I agree. But what is that truth? The legend says stormers emerged from the remnants of the Ghost Clan. And although the clan has disappeared, you still see people like Dabreeyor, whose hair and eyes are close to white. So perhaps they were real and Dabreeyor is a descendant. That doesn't mean her ancestors, if they were the Ghost Clan, could storm.'

'Tell me their story again,' I said, looking forward, resting my head on Josee's shoulder and stretching out my legs, letting them float.

Josee took a deep breath. I felt my body rise and fall with her chest as she spoke. 'They spent their time communing with their own spirits. They meditated for days, sometimes to the point of starvation, even death, until they were able to leave their bodies and realise a collective mind across the entire clan, irrespective of an individual's body or shell, as they would call it. Storming is supposed to be what's left of the hive mind.'

'Why did they disappear?'

'Most left Al'Mayra to seek out other lifeblood stones. There's no other explanation.'

'And so the collective mind was lost.'

Josee squeezed my shoulders. 'But we say, mainly to scare children, that when one descendant meets another, they may be able to swap minds, or one could steal the other's body. My friends and I would play at being stormers, pretending we were each other. It was part of my childhood. I can't take it seriously.'

I was about to speak again when Josee pushed me under the water to rinse my hair. She held me under until I began to struggle, then released me. I spluttered and coughed and squeezed my nose. She laughed, pulled me towards her and began to wash my back with a bar of vegetable oil soap.

After we bathed, I put on a pair of plain deerskin trousers and a shirt with a design of a wine-dark sea dragon on the chest and sat near the corner of the western terrace. I watched the dying light of the sun, no more than a dissolving strip of orange along the horizon, tainted by coal dust and pressed between the dark inky sea and the blackening sky.

It was high tide, and I could hear the gentle lap of the waves upon the foundations of the pillar below; that is until a late-returning fishing boat disturbed a flock of resting gulls, whose angry cries drowned the ripples out.

The fires were alight on Sundown, and the aroma of frying fish and mussels drifted in the air, as did the tang of the spices Josee was using in the stew simmering on the hob.

I happened to look north towards Shadow Rise and saw Etu and Mani running. They didn't appear to be playing, so I raced to the northern balcony and turned the winch handle to lower the bridge.

'Problem?' I said to Etu, when I saw the unusually serious expression he wore.

'I don't know. We saw an Al'Mayran crouched on the cliff edge beyond the wall of the viewing platform in Shadow Rise. You know, where the children's climbing frame is. We think he was watching your flat,' Etu said.

'Don't point. Come in,' I said.

'What's the matter?' Josee said when we entered the kitchen. She moved the pan of stew away from the hottest spot of the oven top and wiped her hands on a cloth.

'Don't turn around but they think someone is spying on us – an Al'Mayran,' I said.

'It's getting dark. How do you know it's an Al'Mayran?' Josee said.

'They had a robe on, black and gold, or blue and yellow, but I swear in Xol's name, it had swirls of spirits on it,' Etu said.

'Definitely,' Mani said.

I put my soft-soled shoes on, fetched my baldric and sword belt and checked my pistols were primed and loaded with shot.

'I'll come with you,' Etu said.

'Stay here,' I said.

'I don't want either of you going,' Josee said.

'I'll come and show you, I'm not scared,' Mani said.

'Thank you, Mani, but that won't be necessary. Etu, if you follow me, I'll shoot your ear off. Understand, cousin?'

'I'm not helpless,' he said.

I handed him my flintlock pistol and said, 'Wind the bridge up and keep watch in case anyone comes here. It could be a trap.'

Etu took the pistol and nodded. 'Don't do anything foolish,' he said.

'Look who's talking,' I said.

The sun was no longer lighting the horizon, the moon had barely begun to wax crescent in the lunar cycle, and the children of Shadow Rise had abandoned the climbing frame for the day. But as I approached the play area and crouched behind the wall at the cliff edge, I could hear siblings in a small stone house laughing, and their neighbours singing and dancing to the tune of a fiddle. A cool breeze blew, lifting my wet hair and billowing my shirt around my neck. I shivered, pulled my collar tight and peered over the wall.

The slope of the claw was uneven, its contours only discernible as a silhouette against the lights of Sundown. The rocks and trees, which provided many spots to perch, were blanketed in shadow. I studied each empty space, watching for movement, trying to mark the outline of a robe or hood, or catch a glint of gold or yellow in the starlight.

I ran the palm of my hand over the ground, searching for a stone. I found what felt like an old tobacco tin and threw it. It was too dark to see it drop, but it ricocheted half a dozen times. A figure squatting on the pointed end of a rock shaped like a tilted wedge reacted to the sound of the tin falling. My eyes adjusted, and I noted the outline of their robe and caught the merest hint, no more than a flicker, of a golden sheen.

'Don't move,' I said, standing and pointing a pistol in their direction.

The figure bolted into the trees and bushes, their robe trailing after them.

'Shit,' I said.

I hopped over the wall and ran along the rocks, clumps of grass, and the brittle earth of the cliff face, praying I wouldn't leap into an open chasm. Occasionally, I slipped down the incline and wondered if this was to be my end – a native of the Five Claws plummeting to her death from a cliff, the same as if I'd been an outsider raised on the grasslands. But Xol was looking after me, and my foot always found a resistant surface.

I reached the thick end of the rocky wedge and turned into the trees, assuming the figure would be far ahead of me. Instead, they were waiting for me to pass, crouched with their hood covering their face, their form indistinguishable from the rocks around them.

They tripped me, and I went down hard, driving the air from my lungs. I tried to rise, but they kicked me in the stomach. As I lay curled up on the ground, a searing pain spreading over my midriff, they shoved my shoulder with their foot and I rolled. I twisted and dug the fingers of my free hand into the earth, firing my pistol into the void. The flash lit the night, and I saw a blue-and-gold-clad figure: I'Dreng or one of his guards, I thought. The darkness swallowed them.

I holstered my empty pistol and got to my feet, scanning the gloom for my assailant. Nothing. I was exposed, too, with the night sky behind me, so I crouched and clambered up the cliff face on all fours. A pitch-black section ahead turned out to be a small cleft, which I slid into on my backside. I had to lean forward to feel for a route up, and as I lowered my head, a carmine-red flash ignited the grass in front of me.

I rushed to put it out, stamping my foot until I smothered the flames. When the fire was extinguished, I looked for the Al'Mayran, but he was gone. I collapsed, gasping for air, my stomach burning where I'd been kicked, as if I'd been pierced by a hot poker.

That night, I couldn't sleep, so I left the bedroom to gaze at the stars from the southern balcony. I spotted a comet and followed its path east over the city. But my eye was drawn by another light: the flame of an oil lamp, flickering in the breeze blowing through Salvation's Climb.

CHAPTER TEN

BEFORE THE SUN rose, I changed into my suit, taking care not to wake Josee, but a shooting pain where I had been kicked caused me to drop my baldric and startle her. She sat upright in bed and said, 'Who's there?' with a panicked strain in her voice that saddened my heart to hear.

'Sorry,' I said.

'You're up early.'

'I couldn't sleep.'

'Ani, are we in danger? Be honest.'

'Maybe.'

'Because of your case?'

I sat on the edge of the bed, trying to read my wife's expression in the faint light before I spoke. 'I think I'm being warned off. But the Al'Mayrans can't tip their hand, or else they might give me the proof I need.'

'Your proof may be your cut throat,' Josee said, with more than a note of reproof in her tone.

'If you're concerned, you and Mani can move in with Ezno.'

'I won't be chased from my home.'

I sighed. 'I don't know what else there is to say. Did Mani mention his brother yet?'

Josee's voice began to strain with anger. 'Nothing that will interest you.'

'That's harsh.'

'Is it?' She paused and I heard her breathing. When she spoke again, she'd calmed a little. 'I just meant nothing pertinent to your case. The lads belong to a tribeless tribe of youngsters called the Vermin who will one day take over the Depths and make a fortune. At least that's what Mani says.'

'Feral younglings like Mani and his brother start as lookouts for the gangs, progress to burglary and mugging. If they demonstrate the necessary skill and lack of remorse for their victims, they move on to breaking bones for debt collectors and eventually graduate to murder.'

'We can't let that happen to Mani.'

Thinking we'd struck a conciliatory note, I risked Josee's ire, and pushed her. 'I need you to talk to the lad about what happened the night of the murder.'

'Will that bring Areel I'Advay back?' she snapped.

'It's my job.'

'Mani is not your job, he's just a boy. One you're using to find his brother so you can exploit him too. And for what? You just want to be proven right.'

She threw off the sheets and stormed into the bathroom. I tried to follow her but she bolted the door.

Before I left, I filled Snuggs's bowl with some tuna, more out of hope than expectation, then left without reconciling with Josee.

I crossed the Bridge of Spirits and made my way to the fish market below the Al'Mayran arcade and onto the wharf. I took the footpath to the pebble beach at the bottom of Noon Claw. The once grand entrance to Salvation's Climb had been enclosed to protect curious citizens and tourists from falling debris, but the fence was damaged, and it was a simple matter of stepping through a gap to reach the steps.

There was plenty of new rubble lying around with lighter coloured sides that had not been exposed to weather. I sifted through the smaller fragments, and overturned the larger ones, but found nothing. I wasn't sure what I was looking for. Did I expect to see a golden cane gleaming in the ruins? I climbed a few flights but soon found breaks in the steps that were too wide to negotiate and turned back. Imala's words about risking my life to prove my theory haunted my thoughts.

Waiting for me on the path just outside the fence, leaning on a rock under an overhang and smoking a cigarette, was a fisherman I recognised. When I was a child, he used to work out of Lo'tse Bay and would often chat with my uncle on the docks and in the markets. He had lost a leg below the knee when lightning split the mizzen mast of the ship he was working on and sent a foot-long splinter into his calf. I couldn't recall seeing him in several years and did not remember his name. His hair was greying, but his body was still hard and his jaw as square and fixed as it used to be. His fishing rod was resting beside him and, in his left hand, he held a brace of coalfish.

'How goes it with you, young Ani?' he said.

'I'm well, and you?'

'I can't complain.'

'I don't recall seeing you for some time.'

'Been around the Known World, following the trade winds, working fishing and freight ships to pay my way.'

'Ah,' I said with a nod.

'How is your uncle Ezno and his boys?'

'Well, I thank you.'

'Does your uncle still go out?'

I smiled. 'What else would he do?'

'Do you ever go out?' he said, one eyebrow raised.

I felt a little judged, as if by refusing to enter the fishing trade, I had abandoned my people's way of life. 'On occasion.'

'Blow the city out of your mind?'

'Something like that.'

'I see you're still on the force?' he said, nodding to the police emblem hanging from my neck.

'Yes, sir.'

'Working on a case, I expect?'

'Always.'

'Looking for clues in the rubble of the steps, were you?'

I shrugged and smiled without confirmation or denial.

He took a long drag on his cigarette and took his time blowing the smoke out. 'Well, you aren't the only one,' he said, looking at the horizon.

'Oh?'

'Two Kahokeyans, twin brothers I'd say, and an Al'Mayran were doing the same as you when I arrived. I watched them from the jetty.'

'What did they look like?' I said, taking a step forward and putting my hands on my hips.

'The brothers were alike, short and lean, climbers' builds if you ask me. They had long hair, greying a little. I'm sure I've seen them before, a fair few years ago now, though. I want to say they're from Ulawe's Perch; somewhere deep on the west side of Pastnoon at any rate.'

'And the Al'Mayran?'

'Kept his hood up.'

'Are you sure it was a he?'

He thought before answering. 'I reckon so, but I couldn't be certain. It was dark, but his robe wasn't as bright as some I've seen. Blues and greens, I think.'

'A uniform?'

'I wouldn't have thought so.'

'Was he tall, short, thin, fat?'

The man whose name I couldn't remember shrugged. 'Average height for an Al'Mayran, maybe six foot. Bit hefty.'

'Did they find anything?' I said, flicking my head towards the steps and the rubble.

'Not that I saw. Anyway, I thought you'd want to know.'

'I thank you.'

'Tell your uncle Yitaqui will visit him.'

'You'll be welcome, Yitaqui.'

'I know that, Ani. I know.'

My stomach was empty and growling. But the queasiness rising from my gut to the back of my throat couldn't be explained by hunger alone. I shouldn't have left home without speaking to Josee again. I stopped off at the Al'Mayran fish market to buy a jar of her favourite spicy krill paste and fresh seaweed cakes before returning to our flat.

I was surprised to find the drawbridge down and the kitchen door open. Inside, around our kitchen table, sat Memi and six young workers from the Stars and the Sea: four women and two men, none over twenty years of age. Josee was brewing a pot of coffee while Mani showed them his kite.

'How goes it with you, Memi?' I said, placing the bag of krill paste and seaweed cakes on the worktop beside Josee. My wife peeked inside the bag, smiled at me and shook her head.

'The CIB is at the Stars,' Memi said.

'What? Now?' I said.

'One of the guards saw them marching down Sumaka Way with armoured waggons like a bloody army. I was teaching my pupils their spellings and numbers in Nita's office when they broke the doors down. We ran out of the back and into the Heart of Solace next door. We left through there and no one paid us any mind as we passed. Oh, Ani, they're tearing the place apart and arresting everyone. Did you know they were coming today?'

'How many warnings did you need, Memi?'

'I know, I know. I'm sorry.'

'You can't stay here, Memi.'

'What? You said—'

'I know what I said. Josee, I have to get up there. Can you take Memi and her friends to Ezno? Tell him they need to be kept out of sight. He can take them out on a damn boat if he has to.'

'And Mani?' Josee said.

'I want Mani with us.'

She folded her arms and raised herself above me, but I held her gaze and didn't flinch.

'Fine,' she said.

So much for reconciliation.

The doors of the Stars and the Sea were hanging from their top hinges by the time I arrived. CIB agents were emerging with bags of coins and cash, jewels and precious metals, and boxes of account books along with several handcuffed residents who had been either too dim-witted or too hungover to run. Men and women in black uniforms were shouting and prostitutes were screaming. Crying children were being lined up while they watched their mothers and fathers being led away. One woman was lying in the street, semi-conscious, her eye black and her nose broken. A short, barrel-chested agent was standing over her, yelling, as her little boy buried his face in her neck.

Wes was there, hanging back, keeping his distance from the unfolding scene. His head was bowed, and he was staring at his feet. But when he saw the injured woman and her child, he stormed over and pushed his colleague aside.

'Shame on you, Sewati,' he said.

He helped the woman to stand and gave her his handkerchief to press against her nose. He picked up her little boy and comforted him before handing him to a female agent who rolled her eyes in disgust.

'What's the point of this?' she said.

Wes shrugged and shook his head. He spotted me and wandered over, unable to meet my gaze.

'It's for the best,' he said, as he stood beside me.

'Best for who?' I said, looking up at the sky to the south. A covering of grey clouds was approaching.

'These are terrible places, filled with exploited and brutalised men, women and children.'

'The Stars? Exploited maybe, brutalised no. And as for these people's children, they were a damn sight safer an hour ago.'

'This is no environment in which to raise a child. To think they're safe from predators here is just naive.'

'Nita and Memi don't peddle children, that I can guarantee you. And the young ones are better off here than in the Depths, where a child's body is bought and sold the same as any other. For Xol's sake, Wes, I spent years building a relationship with these people.'

'For what good? They denied knowing I'Advay's name.'

As Wes and I argued, two agents dragged Nita out of her home. Her hair was loose, her face free of makeup, and her gown was open from the waist up, exposing her breasts.

'Wait,' I said, stepping in front of the agents before they could bundle her into an armoured waggon.

'Who in Xol's name are you?' one of the agents, a gangly stooped fellow with a pock-marked face, said, pushing me aside.

'She's Inspector Sulaqua, and she's my co-lead in the field on this investigation,' Wes said, putting his arm on the man's shoulder.

'Why is she being arrested?' I said.

'She's an accomplice to murder,' the gangly agent said.

'Do you have a warrant?'

'Of course,' he said, smiling and winking at Wes.

'Any evidence?' I said.

'Don't you worry, we'll get it out of her.'

I closed Nita's robe and knotted the sash tight around her waist. Then I removed the band from my hair and used it to tie her own into a neat ponytail. When our eyes met, I tried to read Nita's thoughts, but saw nothing except a hint of resignation. I didn't speak to her. I couldn't find the words, so I helped her into the waggon instead.

Nakni was wrestled out, struggling and kicking at his captors. His face had been beaten, and the blood from his broken nose was splattered all over his bare chest. His eyes were manic, full of rage as he cursed the CIB. An agent appeared behind him, holding a small wooden box aloft.

'Love letters from I'Advay to the whore,' the agent said. 'We found him trying to burn them.'

I thought of the spot on the writing desk in Nakni's room where the dust hadn't settled and cursed myself for not searching the Stars more thoroughly.

The agent was older than the rest, around fifty, with silver hair. His weathered face was lined with creases that curled around a permanent scowl.

'Who's that?' I said to Wes.

'Special Agent Unaduti. Sodia's man.'

'I thought Sodia made you lead in the field?'

'He did, nominally at least. Some of these agents will answer to me. But many will only follow Unaduti's orders.'

'So you have no power to stop this?'

'Even if I did, I'm not sure I would.'

Nakni broke free from his captors and tried to run with his hands cuffed behind his back. But the barrel-chested Sewati tripped him, and the lad fell, face first, onto the hard cobbled road. Sewati and three other agents surrounded him and pummelled him with their truncheons until he lost consciousness.

Unaduti saw my face and laughed. 'What's wrong, Inspector, no stomach for subduing a criminal?' he said.

'Criminal or not, he's of no use to me dead,' I said.

Unaduti sneered and ordered Sewati to throw Nakni into the waggon.

'Animals!' Nita screamed at the agents.

Unaduti slapped her with the back of his hand.

Upon seeing Nita degraded, I felt the sudden crush of a clamp around my temples and my face burned. I grabbed Unaduti's ponytail and dragged him to the ground, pressing my knee to his throat. I ran my fingers over the grip of my percussion pistol as images of Unaduti, dead at my feet, a hole in his head, his brains running into the grooves between cobblestones, flashed through my mind. He tried to get up, so I pushed down harder and covered his nose and mouth.

I barely heard Wes saying my name above the furnace raging in my ears, but it was enough to pull me out of the red mist. I stood up and walked away.

Blow the candle out, I thought, but I always found my rage harder to control than my fear.

'Where are you going?' Wes said, catching up with me.

'None of your business, Kohee,' I said.

'Come now, Ani, we should be working together.'

'Is this working together?' I said, gesturing to the chaotic and violent scene.

'I give you my word this wasn't my idea.'

I ignored him and strode north, no destination in mind, needing to get away from the CIB before I killed one of them. But Wes stuck by my side, keeping step.

'Has Sodia told you to follow me?' I said.

'Of course he has.'

His honesty caught me off guard, and I examined his open face for artifice. If he were playing me for a fool, he was a skilled performer.

'Come, let me buy you breakfast,' he said with a smile.

Wes and I walked to Merchant's Plaza, and I ordered coffee and a wrap of barbecued oysters and spiced butter. Wes had the same and we found a spare form near the fountain to sit on. We ate in silence for a few minutes until I decided to tell him about the Al'Mayran who spied on my home and the men seen searching Salvation's Climb.

After we ate, we went to see Imala.

'How good of you to come to work,' she said, looking up from her desk at Wes and me. 'You missed a messenger from the embassy. Interviews with Brigadier I'Kalmeen, Major I'Handdru and two of I'Dreng's guards have been arranged for you and Special Agent Kohee to conduct.'

'When?' I said, taking a seat.

'This afternoon, if that's convenient for you?'

'At the embassy?'

'Yes. But they won't be obligated to provide you with written testimony,' Imala said, looking down and turning the pages of a report she'd been reading.

'Figures. Why the embassy? Why not here?'

'Never satisfied, are you, Inspector?' Imala said, keeping her head down.

'Did you know about Nita and Nakni's arrest?'

'If you'd been here first thing, I would have told you.'

'Where will they be held?'

'At CIB Tower. The bureau made the arrest, after all.' Imala looked up. 'Did they find any evidence?'

I shrugged. 'Some love letters to Nakni.'

'It's more than you have.'

I rested my elbows on the desk and leaned forward. 'How about this? Two Kahokeyans and an Al'Mayran were snooping around the base of Salvation's Climb earlier this morning.'

'Do you know who they were?'

'I'm working on it. There was also an Al'Mayran watching my home last night. When I went to challenge him, he attacked me before fleeing, damn him.'

'Are you okay?' Imala said, her tone changing, her concern evident.

'I'll live. But there's more.'

'Oh?'

'The Al'Mayran let loose a red flash that started a fire.'

Imala regarded me for a moment, her eyes unblinking behind her spectacles. 'Did anyone else see this flash?'

'Josee and my cousin saw the fire.'

'But not what started it?'

'No.'

Imala went back to her report. 'The Al'Mayran could have lit a match for all you know.'

'This is pointless. I'll see if I can get any more sense out of Nita,' I said, getting to my feet.

'Don't cause any trouble at CIB Tower, my girl.'

Wes smirked, and I shot Imala an angry look before I turned my back on her.

Wes and I travelled north on Agale Thoroughfare in a cab, past the Al'Mayran embassy, towards the far end of the claw. Not too far from the Wooden House, on a hill, stood the CIB headquarters, a fifty-storey tower rising from a much more extensive, rectangular, ten-storey base. It had been constructed using concrete mixed with white sand, which accounted for its incongruous glow and made it the most notable land-mark to anyone approaching from the continent.

As we neared it, Wes, who had sat in silence with his arms folded, said, 'I admit, the CIB has its problems. But do you think the police exist in a state of benevolent grace, Ani, above corruption or malpractice?'

The cab came to a halt.

'We're not in High Chief Naka's pocket,' I said.

'Neither am I,' Wes protested.

'You are. You just don't know it.'

He shook his head, opened the front-facing doors to the cab, and reached up to pay the driver.

I climbed out and followed him through the main gate in the high curtain wall. Above us dozens of musket-armed guards walked the ramparts. Perhaps I was imagining it, but I felt their gaze as Wes and I passed three separate checkpoints, and I had to fight to control my breath as my chest tightened. My stomach turned; a wave of panic, like nausea, rose in my throat and left a bitter taste in my mouth. Was I now as trapped as the prisoners inside? Irrational? Maybe. But people entered this place and were never heard from again. *Blow the candle out, Ani, lass.*

Wes displayed his badge at each checkpoint, and I had a series of passes pinned to my jacket which allowed me to wander unchallenged within specified boundaries.

CIB HQ had one of the most spacious and well-lit interiors in all of New Capital, with a window or a skylight in every room, corridor, and hall, permitting the sun to shine in from every angle of her daily arc. The tower was the physical manifestation of how the CIB saw themselves: the bringers of light and truth in a world of shadow and lies. Even by the standards of New Capital, the bureau was full of shit.

The holding cells ran along the top floor of the base. Before I could be admitted, I had to clear yet another checkpoint; I was issued with what I hoped would be my final pass. A young jailer in a faded uniform led us down a long, plain white corridor with an A-frame skylight and cells on either side behind solid walls.

'Have both prisoners been brought here?' I said to the jailer.

He shook his head. 'Only the woman.'

'And the young lad?'

'Infirmary. He was unconscious when he was brought in. When he wakes, he'll be interrogated,' the jailer said.

'Then he'll need the infirmary again.'

The jailer looked away.

'Has Nita been interrogated?' I said.

'Not that I'm aware of. They want to speak to the lad first. This is her cell.'

The jailer slid the shutter of the small door window aside and said, 'An inspector is here to see you. Stand and turn around.'

I peeked through the window. Nita was lying on a blanketless cot, still in her nightgown, with her bare feet tucked under the hem. Her bottom lip was swollen where Unaduti had hit her, and her chin was stained with dried blood. She got to her feet, put her arms out, and spun like a dancer. She performed a deep bow.

The jailer shook his head and opened the door.

'Stay here, Wes. Nita won't talk in front of that damn uniform,' I said.

When I entered the cell, Nita said, 'Ani, what do you think of my new digs?' with a wave of her hand.

The room contained no table or chairs, nothing that might make a prisoner feel human – only the narrow cot to rest on and a bucket for her waste. But like the rest of CIB Tower, her room was bright and well-aired, thanks to a large window in the eastern wall. Only this one had a series of vertical razor-sharp steel bars on the outside of the glass.

'Lovely view, isn't it?' Nita said, standing beside me.

The cell overlooked Yawe Bay and Treasure's Rock with its gold-dusted skytowers, still managing to find their lustre in the gloom.

'Gives you a view of what you're losing,' I said.

Nita sat down on the cot, curled her legs up, and pulled her gown over her feet, a wistful smile resting on her face. I sat next to her, took out my handkerchief, and wiped the blood from her chin.

'All better?' she said, when I had finished.

'Hardly,' I said.

'You were always a good girl, Ani.'

'I was a police constable, Nita, and the Stars was on my beat.'

'And you were always fair. We did appreciate that, in case you were wondering. And we never laughed at you. We respected you.'

'Sure.'

'It's true. We respected you because you respected us. And no matter how tough you tried to look, you could never fool me.'

'Nita. Don't be fatalistic. This isn't over. I'm close to building a case against an Al'Mayran. While circumstantial, it's no less convincing than the evidence they have against you and Nakni.'

'A case against who?'

'You tell me,' I said. 'Who dumped I'Advay's body? And did you try to blackmail them with your advocate's help? Two simple questions. Help yourself and answer them.'

'Oh, Ani, you're so smart, but you think you can save everyone in the Known World.'

'I'm just trying to save you.'

'It's too late.'

'How is it too late?'

'Ani, for your own sake, leave things be. I dug my own grave. Don't dig yours alongside mine. If it makes you feel any better, you were right.'

'I don't care about that.'

Nita laughed and kissed my cheek as if a child had said something adorable. 'Save yourself, Ani. This isn't a war you can win. It's not even a fair fight. Please listen to me the way I should have listened to you.' She lowered her voice and leant in. 'Did Memi and her little flock escape?'

I nodded.

'And the rest of my people, who were arrested this morning?'

'I'll see what I can do.'

'Thank you, Ani.'

'It's fine.'

'No, Ani, thank you,' she said, squeezing my hand.

It was approaching midday when Wes and I took a cab to the Al'Mayran embassy. The sun was hidden behind a thick blanket of low-hanging dark grey clouds, the kind that brought continuous drizzle and stirred in the breeze. My mood was no brighter than the day. I had sensed Wes's desire to talk, and so had folded my arms and stared through the cab window. He had got the message, and we rode in silence, but my shame was starting to check my irritation, and when my belly rumbled, I said, 'Let's eat first.'

'How can someone so puny eat as much as you do?' he said, smiling, his eyebrow raised.

'You and I will have to duel one day, Wesu Kohee, and you shall see what puny can do.'

'Swords or pistols? Because if it's pistols you'll have me at a distinct disadvantage. Three pistols, Ani, three!'

'How many shots will it take to down an ape your size? If I hit something that isn't vital, say, your head, it'll be good to know I have two more chances.'

'They can't all be police issue.'

'Just the flintlock. The other two are a pair. My cousin, Oura, bought me them.'

'Beautiful weapons. Not too well used, I hope.'

I shrugged.

'You certainly seemed ready to kill Unaduti this morning,' Wes said, a wry smile spreading across his face.

'I've never felt any compunction about killing villains, even ones in uniform,' I said.

'Oh, come now, you don't have to impress me with such talk. I've only killed once in the line of duty and it didn't sit well with me for months. I still occasionally see his face when I dream.'

'It gets easier. At least, it did for me.'

'Easier? In Xol's name, how many have you killed?' Wes said, turning his bulk in the cramped cab to face me.

I thought for a moment. 'Twelve or thirteen?'

Wes shook his head. His disbelief seemed genuine. 'You don't know. How can you not know? It's a number a person should remember.'

I sighed. 'This woman, a vicious mugger, I ran her through with my sword. She didn't die until weeks later from an infected wound. Do I count her or not?'

'Oh, I'd count her,' Wes said, with more than a hint of facetiousness.

'Then it's thirteen. Happy now?' I said, matching his tone.

Wes shook his head. 'That's not the word I would use. When was the last?'

'A couple of days ago, in the Depths. Two gang members.'

Wes stared at me, agog. 'Xol help me,' he said.

I remembered the scarred face of the young man, the disbelief in his eyes, his unnecessary death from a treatable wound. 'Actually, I regret one of those. Maybe both. This lad attacked me. I'm not sure he intended to kill me. But I couldn't take a chance and struck out with my dagger. I caught him with a wicked slice across the thigh. Then I had to kill a friend of his.'

'And you feel no remorse for the others?'

'Why should I? They dealt the hand.'

Wes paused. He seemed to be searching for words. When he spoke, I heard pity. 'It's not a choice, whether to feel or not.'

'Yes it is,' I said defensively. 'Blow the candle out. That's what my fencing instructor taught me. How can you fight with a clear head otherwise?'

'I don't wish to cause offence, but I'm not sure I could be at ease with that much blood on my hands, Ani.'

I shrugged and said, 'We chose this life of death, Wes. What did you expect to happen?'

A few minutes later, we took a seat in a private booth of dark wood and padded leather in the embassy's circular eatery. The golden-framed glass dome above the centrally placed kitchen let in natural light, but the surrounding booths were in the shade, so Wes and I ate under an oil lamp's warm glow.

I allowed him to order for me, and he chose spiced Al'Mayran lamb stew, the dish that had proved to be I'Advay's last meal, and a pitcher of sugared orange juice. Wes took my bowl and filled it with three ladles of stew. When I fixed him with an unimpressed stare, he added a fourth, shaking his head.

After we sated the worst of our hunger pangs, and my spirits had improved, Wes said, 'I don't like the way you talk about the CIB. I am CIB. When you criticise the agency, you criticise me.'

'I criticise what I see. What did you see this morning?'

'Evidently, more than you. The woman who was hurt struck an agent. Nakni was resisting arrest, attacking all who touched him, quite unnecessarily.'

'He and Nita are innocent, Wes.'

'If that's true, we'll prove it.'

'Is that what Sodia wants you to do?' I said.

'I'm not Sodia.'

'He's a pompous fool with dangerous ambitions and no head for police work.'

'As I said, I'm not him. Although he isn't bereft of virtue. He's loyal.'

'Yes, to High Chief Naka. That's the problem.'

'You're prejudiced, Ani.'

'When it comes to CIB directors, very.'

Wes laughed and said, 'You do like to make an impression, don't you? I was thinking about something you said yesterday.'

'Oh?'

Wes gathered the last of his stew on his fork before he spoke again. 'You said rich people died while plying their trade whereas poor people are killed by theirs. That's not always true, Ani. I know plenty of elderly poor folk and have attended the funerals of young CIB agents, killed in action, who were from wealthy families.'

'Sure, they can die in so-called honourable service,' I said, conceding Wes's point with a nod before going on. 'But when was the last time you heard of a rich man or woman lost at sea on a fishing boat, killed on a building site, crushed in a mine collapse, torn apart by the gears of the Great Lifts or sliced in two by rods of hot steel?

'And, at risk of upsetting you, Wes, what happened to your mother when your father died? Did the company he worked for compensate her? Was your father able to insure his life? Did he leave her the deeds to ancestral homes, or at the very least a handsome widow's pension with a value linked to the ever-increasing cost of living?'

Wes stared ahead, fork poised, lost in thought. 'No. My mother had to sell our home in the Mids on Pastnoon and rent a place on the border with the Depths.'

'And how's your mother now?'

'Well enough. She worked hard. I joined the CIB cadets as soon as I could. Eventually, we could afford a better home.'

'And if your father had lived?'

'Who but Xol can say?'

'You could. You just don't want to.'

Wes ate a mouthful of stew and thought for a moment before speaking again.

'Do you remember your father, Ani?' he said.

'Moments, probably merged: him singing as he sowed an image of Zalema onto my deerskin shirt. The two of us falling asleep together in his chair by the fire. Do you remember yours?'

Wes smiled. 'Quite a bit. He was good with his hands and liked to make my sister and me little toys. I still have some of them. Silly really.'

'No. It's not.'

'Tell me, did you inherit your ability to shimmer from your father?'

'Not going to have me arrested, are you, Wes?' I said with a wink.

'Of course not.'

I nodded and said, 'My father was a shimmerer.'

'How many in your tribe have the gift?'

'Once, we could field an army. Now we number around two dozen, and most are over sixty.'

'I wonder why,' Wes said, more to himself than to me.

I folded my arms and leant back into the padded leather of the booth's seat. 'My uncle says technology is killing magic, and in a way, I think he's right. The more we understand, the less we believe in what we can't. Magic now scares people where it once comforted them.'

'In our line of work, it must be frustrating to have that ability and not be able to use it. Still, it's with good reason, I suppose.'

'Really?'

Wes took a gulp of orange juice and swallowed. 'You would disagree, Ani, but you're hardly unbiased, are you?'

'A hundred years ago, one officer who could shimmer overextended his reach and led his target into crimes she wouldn't otherwise have committed. An abuse of power, I admit. But why should that stop me from using my abilities for, say, basic surveillance? How is that entrapment?' I said, my voice rising.

Wes shrugged and tilted his head. 'It's complicated.'

'It's prejudiced.'

'Perhaps you're right.'

'More than perhaps.'

Wes chortled and shook his head. 'Show me,' he said.

'What?'

'Would you shimmer for me, please?'

'I'm not a circus act.' I was trying to sound more offended than I was.

'You're right. I apologise.'

I shimmered his appearance and said, 'Apology accepted.'

The big man was sipping from his beaker and when confronted with his own face, he gasped and choked on his orange juice.

'In Xol's name, Ani. You wouldn't cast my appearance to fool the Al'Mayrans, would you?'

I didn't answer. I didn't want to lie.

'Ani?' Wes said.

After lunch, Wes took me to I'Dreng's office, an opulent room the captain of the ambassador's guards had decorated with high-quality antique furniture – all dovetail joints, reinforced corners, and drawers separated by fine sheets of wood. On the walls, he'd hung banners and shields with his family crest, and portraits, too, presumably of his ancestors. Judging by their uniforms, they had all been guards or soldiers – the family business of a self-respecting Al'Mayran aristocrat. Of course, the man himself was up there, hands on hips, looking off into the distance, one foot on a felled tree, with the family manor house in the background and his steed by his side.

Today, he was sitting at his desk eating a sandwich. He raised his finger, indicating that we should wait, and took a swig of ice water to wash his last bite down.

Once he had swallowed, he stood and said, 'Each interview will last no more than twenty minutes.'

'I haven't agreed to that,' I said.

'And yet it has been agreed.'

'By who?'

'You should discuss it with Imala.'

'I will. Tell me, what did you do last night, I'Dreng?'

'Excuse me?'

'I thought I saw you last night, on the southern face of Pastnoon Claw, below Magila Bridge.'

'I don't remember ever setting foot on Pastnoon.'

The corners of his mouth were turned up in a smirk. His eyes might never smile, but they did shine with triumph. He was the kind of man who enjoyed being privy to secret knowledge.

He showed us to a small conference room, decorated with plush furnishings, which overlooked the gardens to the south. We were served spicy wrapped sandwiches along with jugs of sugared lemon juice.

'This is nice and cosy,' I said to Wes, when I'Dreng left to fetch the two guards who claimed to have seen I'Advay on the night he was killed. 'We even have a private water closet, and a bell pull should our interviewees grow distressed enough to confess.'

I'Dreng returned, accompanied by a man and a woman, both tall and blond and with the same proud glint in their blue eyes as their captain. They were in uniform, blue-and-golden cowls and brown leggings, and both were armed with swords and fighting daggers.

'These are lieutenants A'Deeyna and I'Edmoond,' I'Dreng said, gesturing first to the woman and then to her colleague.

Neither sat down. They just nodded their heads in unison.

'Lieutenant A'Deeyna, you saw I'Advay at six o'clock in the evening at the entrance to the annex?' I said.

'That's correct,' A'Deeyna said.

'How can you be so sure of the time?'

'I glanced at the clock on one of the skytowers,' she said, keeping her face impassive.

'And I'Advay definitely came from the barracks?'

'Yes, along the eastern path, near the cliff edge.'

'Was he in a hurry?'

'Not that I remember.'

'Did he appear flustered?' I said, rushing my questions to try and make her feel pressured.

'No.'

'In any kind of disarray?'

'He was always a smart man. I don't remember that evening being any different.'

'And he went straight to his offices?'

'As far as I know, Inspector.'

'And you didn't see him again?'

'No.'

'Can anyone corroborate your account?'

'No. I was alone.'

'Is that usual?' I said, turning to Wes.

'At that entrance, yes,' Wes said.

'I see.' I addressed A'Deeyna again. 'Which cane did he have with him?'

'I couldn't say.'

'The golden one, perhaps?'

'I couldn't say,' she repeated. Same tone. Same rhythm.

'You can't remember if he had a golden cane?' I said, exaggerating my disbelief for effect and rolling my eyes at Wes to project my incredulity onto him.

'No,' A'Deeyna said, unmoved by my playacting.

'And how about you, I'Edmoond, can you remember what cane he had?'

'We're so used to seeing I'Advay with different ones, Inspector, you can't remember which day he had what cane,' the young man said in an almost apologetic tone, a polite but insipid smile on his face.

'And you were at the main entrance when he left the embassy?'

I'Edmoond nodded. 'I was in command that evening. We'd just locked the main gate, which we do at nine o'clock. I'Advay left through the wicker gate.'

'Did you see the direction he went in?'

Another apologetic smile. 'No.'

'Or if he caught a cab?'

'No.'

'Did you think he looked afraid or concerned in any way?' I said, the frustration in my voice genuine.

'No, but I always found Mr I'Advay inscrutable.'

'Were there others at the gate with you?'

'Yes, Inspector.'

'Could they have seen anything?'

'Stop fishing, Sulaqua,' I'Dreng said. 'Lieutenant I'Edmoond and I spoke to everyone who guarded the gate that night. All will say the same thing.'

'Yes, I expect they will.'

I'Dreng held my gaze, his top lip hinting at a sneer, but he bowed his head and dismissed A'Deeyna and I'Edmoond.

'I'Dreng, I need access to I'Advay's office and home,' I said.

'In good time, Inspector.'

'Now's good for me.'

'I'll let you know,' he said, before leaving.

'A'Deeyna and I'Edmoond had their lines, played their roles well,' I said.

'Perhaps you're just imagining things,' Wes said.

'Apparently these days I'm imagining everything. In Xol's name – you, my wife, and Imala will drive me to the madhouse before this case is over.'

'I don't see the point in getting angry.'

'I'Dreng has had time to build a history of I'Advay's movements, fabricate them, and conspire with his underlings. He's obviously coached them to corroborate his findings.'

'You have no proof of that.'

There was a knock on the door and a tall middle-aged Coor'Seyan soldier, dressed in regimental scarlet and black, came into the conference room. He had a round belly his robes did little to hide, and his balding pate shone between the remaining strands of dark hair, drawn back into a ponytail. But his most striking feature was the immense horseshoe moustache hanging like a drying winter sock over his thick-lipped, egg-shaped mouth.

'Inspector Sulaqua of the Square,' I said, standing and offering him my hand, which he shook without hesitation.

'Pleased to meet you, Sulaqua. I'm Major I'Handdru. How goes it with you, Wes?'

'Well, Major. And you?' Wes said, warmly shaking the major's hand.

'You know me, as long as I can fill my belly, I'm happy,' I'Handdru said, slapping Wes on the upper arm.

I'Handdru sat down and inspected the sandwiches. 'Do you mind?' he said.

I shook my head, and he took a large bite out of a lamb wrap and poured a glass of sugared lemonade.

'You met with I'Advay on the day he was murdered?' I said.

'I did.'

'What time?'

'Our meeting was scheduled at thirty minutes past three in the afternoon. He was a little late.'

'What time did it end?'

'Around five or ten minutes to six. That's when I left for the feast.'

'The feast?'

'The night of the storm was the Coor'Seyan festival of the Great Wave. The battalion gathered in the mess hall to celebrate.'

'I see. It would have been quiet around the barracks?'

'More so than usual.'

'Your meeting with Areel ran long. You must have had much to discuss.'

'That was the nature of our conversations. We might begin with an agenda point or two but soon meander.'

'Where to?'

'Magic, as always,' I'Handdru said, laughing and wiping lamb fat from his moustache.

'Why do you think he was so interested?'

I'Handdru grew serious and lowered his voice. 'Well, I think he marvelled at real magic and wondered why it's an increasingly rare gift in the Known World.'

'As part of his mission?' I said.

'More than that. It was personal with Areel. He theorised that if magic continues to fade, such abilities will one day pass into myth. And if that were true, what if this drift has been in motion far longer than anyone realises, implying Al'Mayra's fabled magic was, once, long ago, almost certainly real.' He leant forward and whispered, 'And perhaps it still is.'

'Storming? Body swapping?'

'Body stealing, Inspector. Stealing.'

'So Areel believed the Ghost Clan existed?'

'That's not so unusual. I do, too.'

'And you discussed the subject with him?'

'Of course. Quite often. After all, the ability is infamous in Al'Mayran folklore, if unproven.'

'What do you think?'

'Why shouldn't it be real? We accept other so-called magical gifts as fact, why not that one?'

'Very true, Major,' I said, raising my eyebrow and staring hard at Wes, who refused to meet my gaze. 'And Areel believed?' I said, addressing I'Handdru.

'More than that. He talked as if he knew someone with the ability.'

'Do you think he could storm?'

'Alas, we will never know, but I don't think so.'

'And what about other Al'Mayran magic – Ameeleyor, the warrior, and her fire-shooting lifeblood stone? Do you believe the myth?'

'Very much so. You see, Inspector, I've been lucky enough to visit Harnland, and spend time in their great libraries. Now, most of their historians say we defeated their ancient forces with greater numbers. But one scholar, who lived in that time period, writes that the Harn army was burnt alive in a cascade of light, the colour of blood.'

'Did this theory concern I'Advay?' I said.

'I sensed it was important to him, aside from his mission, and certainly more than a disinterested curiosity. The man had his own agenda. I'd put money on it.'

'Did he have a cane with him that day?'

'Yes, a golden one.'

'Are you sure, sir?'

'Quite.'

'And he left your office—'

'The last time I saw him, sadly, it was a quarter to six.'

'And what about the soldier who was killed in the storm?'

'Poor lad. I didn't see what happened to him, if that's what you're asking.'

'You wouldn't lie to me, would you, Major I'Handdru?'

'We all must serve.' Major I'Handdru shrugged and smiled without contempt or triumph. He seemed almost apologetic.

'The major seems to like you,' I said to Wes, once I'Handdru left.

'I make a point of being likeable. Try it sometime.'

The door to the conference room burst open and bounced off the doorstop with such force that the Coor'Seyan who entered raised his hand to protect his face from the recoil.

Perhaps he wasn't quite as tall and broad as his countryman, Mycale I'Krayag, but his eyes, pools of ink, burned with the unrelenting ferocity of a predator searching for weakness. Save for some strands of grey, his swept-back, shoulder-length hair and thick beard were as dark as night. He wore the black-and-scarlet regimental robes of a Coor'Seyan officer, tied with a sash. He had tucked three golden daggers of decreasing size into it.

He undid his belt and threw his longsword and scabbard on the table. He poured a glass of ice water and leant against the window jamb, with his back to Wes and me, staring at the barracks across the gardens.

'What do you want to know?' he said, without turning.

'This is Brigadier Peetor I'Kalmeen,' Wes said.

'Thanks for clearing that up. How's your secretary, Je'mymor A'Soyne, Brigadier?' I said.

'Please don't pretend you care,' I'Kalmeen said.

'I never said I cared. I'm just curious about her condition.'

'She's recovering at home, guarded by my soldiers.'

'Is she still confused about the day she was taken?'

'I haven't asked her.'

'Can you think of a reason why she was kidnapped?'

'No.'

'Or why someone would break into your office?'

He didn't answer.

'Excuse me, Brigadier, but did someone break into your office the night Areel was murdered?'

'No,' he said quietly.

'Pardon?'

'No.'

'And the soldier who died, you're sure it was an accident?'

'A tragic one.'

'I saw the fires of his cremation.'

'What of it?'

'Do you have a personal collection of lifeblood stones?'

'Of course not.'

'Amazing things, the stones.'

'Very insightful.' The brigadier's tone dripped with sarcasm.

'Do you think their power could be used as a destructive force?'

Finally, I'Kalmeen met my gaze. I almost wished he hadn't – I flinched.

'Surely a military man such as yourself would be interested in that?' I said, recovering my composure.

He put his glass down on the windowsill and walked towards the door.

'Your sword, Brigadier,' I said. I picked up the weapon and handed it to him. He seemed suddenly embarrassed by his forgetfulness, so I met his eye until it was he who averted his gaze.

'And your secretary's address, please?' I said, my confidence growing, the advantage mine.

He took out a fountain pen and scribbled on a napkin.

'You were old friends with Areel, weren't you?' I said.

I'Kalmeen nodded.

'Did you still consider him a friend?'

'For my part,' I'Kalmeen said.

'Interesting choice of words. Did you suspect he felt differently, that he didn't return your friendship?'

I'Kalmeen suddenly seemed distant. 'I couldn't say.'

'When did you last see him?'

'Before his meeting with Major I'Handdru.'

'What time was that?'

'I'Dreng has already asked me this.'

'What time?' I said, raising my voice, showing my impatience to a man used to giving orders.

'Between three and half past in the afternoon.'

'Did he have his red cane with him?'

'Possibly.'

'Not the golden one?'

I'Kalmeen's chest swelled. 'By the spirits, I can't recall what damn cane Areel used every day of his life.'

'Not even his last day?'

'No.'

'Where were you after eleven o'clock that night?'

'At the barracks in the mess hall.'

'At the festival?' I said.

'Yes.'

'The whole evening, you never had to leave, just slip away for a moment?'

I'Kalmeen let out an impatient sigh. 'I am the highest-ranked Al'Mayran officer in New Capital. I'm always being called away.'

'Tell me, Peetor, do you miss your friend? Maybe wish you could have saved him?' I said.

I'Kalmeen fixed me again with his black eyes. The veins in his temples swelled, and the muscles in his jaw flexed underneath his beard, but this time, I didn't shrink away. I winked.

'I don't like you, Sulaqua,' he said.

'At least you've been honest about one thing today,' I said.

He left, slamming the door shut harder than he had opened it.

'Xol have mercy. I thought he was going to draw that sword and take your head off,' Wes said.

'The thought occurred to me too. What do you make of him?'

'Well, one thing's for certain, the brigadier, I grant you, is lying.'

'It doesn't come naturally to him.'

I took I'Kalmeen's glass from the sill, emptied its contents out of the window and dropped it into my pocket.

'What are you doing?' Wes said.

'Getting a fingerprint,' I said.

'What does that prove? They were friends. And even if I'Kalmeen wanted Areel killed, do you really think he murdered his friend with his own hands?'

'I think the brigadier prefers to do his own killing.'

Wes and I returned to the landing above the entrance hall. He started down the stairs, but I paused.

'What's the matter?' he said.

'I'm going to speak to the ambassador,' I said.

'Is that wise?'

But I already had my back to Wes and was marching north along the wide corridor, below the A-frame skylight and past the murals of former ambassadors, to speak to their latest successor.

One of I'Rasnee's guards made Wes and me wait in the outer office until he'd spoken with the older secretary whose appearance I'd shimmered the previous day. The guard stood by us while the secretary went to speak to I'Rasnee.

I nodded to the younger secretary, the redhead, who sat at the desk opposite her senior colleague. She flashed a broad smile and said hello. She had opened her mouth, about to speak again, when the older secretary returned.

'You can go in,' he said.

I slapped the guard on the upper arm, and practically ran into I'Rasnee's office.

'What can I do for you, Inspector?' I'Rasnee said from behind his desk.

'Give me access to I'Advay's office. I'Dreng is stalling.'

'He's just exercising an abundance of caution.'

I started to speak but I'Rasnee put his hand up.

'But you're right, it's time you had the access you require,' he said. He called out for the younger secretary, who came running into the room from the outer office.

'Please fetch Captain I'Dreng,' I'Rasnee said to her. Then, to Wes and me: 'The captain likes to be thorough. That's what makes him good at his job. But I'll ensure you get the access you require.'

When I'Dreng entered, his arrogant manner deserted him, and his gaze darted back and forth between I'Rasnee and me.

'Sir?' he said to the ambassador, his hesitancy betraying him.

'Captain, I want you to make Areel's home and office available to the inspector by tomorrow,' I'Rasnee said.

'There are documents that may still need removing or redacting, sir. May I discuss this with you in private?'

'No, I'Dreng, I think not. You've had ample time. We must be more transparent with the city authorities.'

'Yes, sir.'
'Is that sufficient?' I'Rasnee said, addressing Wes and me.
'More than sufficient,' Wes said.
'It'll do,' I said.

CHAPTER ELEVEN

I TOOK THE GLASS Brigadier I'Kalmeen had drunk from to Sudeme at the Square. The forensic pathologist was in his office, scraping the flesh out of a lobster claw, an oversized handkerchief lying across his round belly, its corner tucked into his collar. This was Sudeme's indulgence: he would boil the beasts alive in his laboratory as a treat after he'd completed his day's paperwork or some other onerous task.

'I swear to Xol you enjoy persecuting me, Sulaqua,' he said, gesturing at me with the claw, causing a large piece of loose meat to fall onto his plate.

'Not my intention, Sudeme. Just a happy consequence,' I said.

'What do you want now?' he said, using the handkerchief to wipe grease from his lips.

I put the glass on his desk.

'Don't tell me, you wish me to dust that for fingerprints and compare any I find to the ones taken from I'Advay's corpse and the mausoleum, which, by the way, are a match,' he said.

I laughed.

'Yes, Sulaqua, you were right,' Sudeme said.

'What about the prints on the charm?' I said.

'I'Advay's own.'

I nodded, took the dropped piece of meat from Sudeme's plate and tossed it into my mouth.

'Tell your wife to pick smaller lobsters, Sudeme. Their meat is tenderer. Tell her to buy two if one isn't enough to fill your ever-expanding gut,' I said.

'I think I hate you, Sulaqua,' he said.

Wes and I were unable to find a free cab, so we walked the Magila Bay View nature trail along the cliff edge, enjoying the aromas of spices, baked bread and fried fish drifting from the eateries at the back of Palace Way. The trail was full of tourists and their children, playing and having picnics and queuing at mobile food waggons. If I'd been alone, I would have cut through the crowds at pace, but, as I was learning, it wasn't in Wes's nature do anything quickly. We took our time to reach the end of the claw. We descended the iron-made Corkscrew Steps to the Negotiated Burroughs, and the diplomatic residencies.

Je'mymor A'Soyne was sitting in the paved yard outside her ground-floor flat, under an elm tree at a small white-painted garden table, drinking a cup of spiced tea. There were two Coor'Seyan soldiers on guard at the gate. They knew Wes, and, having consulted with A'Soyne, they let us through to speak with her.

I smiled and said, 'May we sit down, kind lady?'

She attempted to return my smile, failed, and gestured towards the two spare chairs. She was wearing a thin house gown of autumnal colours and her straight and pale blond hair hung loose around her face. Even her freckles were drained of life and the lips of her small mouth were dry and peeling.

'How are you, Je'mymor?' I said.

The sound of her laughter was hollow. 'I've been better,' she said.

'Do you feel up to giving us your testimony?' I said, taking out my scroll.

She nodded. 'Can I say it first? I'd like to gather my thoughts.'

'Of course. Whatever makes you feel comfortable.'

'It happened here. I stopped outside the gate to find my key. That's the last clear memory I have. The rest is a jumble.'

'Okay. Were you kept lying down most of the time?'

'Yes.'

'On a bed?'

'No, I was near to the floor.'
'On a hard surface?'
'A mattress, I think.'
'Were your hands restrained?'
'Yes.'
'By handcuffs or rope?'
'Rope.'
'And the man that spoke to you, are you any more certain he was Al'Mayran?'
'Not really. But he knew my name. He fed me by hand and took me to the water closet.' She began to cry. 'He opened my robe to allow me to pass water and… I was very embarrassed.'
'Did he hurt you in any way?'
'Not really. He kept me drugged by putting a cloth over my nose and mouth.'
'Probably chloroform.'
'That was unpleasant, physically. Other than those occasions, he never harmed me.'
'Did he ask you any questions?'
'No. Not one, Inspector. And when I asked him what he wanted with me, he never answered. I lost track of time. My wits didn't return until I woke up.'
'In the mausoleum?'
'Yes.'
'Do you still maintain you were taken three nights ago, not two?'
She blinked and the tears rolled down her cheeks. She covered her face and turned away.
'Take your time,' I said.
'I don't know anymore, Inspector,' she said, after she regained her composure. 'Everyone tells me I was at the embassy two days ago.'
'But you have no memory of it?'
She shook her head. 'I must be going mad.'
'No, but you might think I am when you hear my theory.'
'What, Inspector, what?'
'I think you were stormed.'

She gasped. 'You think someone stole my body. Are you making fun of me?' she said.

'I'm entirely serious,' I said. 'Did you know I can shimmer, Je'mymor? Do you believe that?'

'If you say so.'

'I can prove it.'

'I'd rather you didn't.'

'So if you accept someone can shimmer, why not believe in storming? And you did say you felt like your body and your voice weren't your own.'

A'Soyne put her hand over her mouth and said, almost to herself, 'No, it couldn't be. Could it?'

'You tell me. As fanciful as it sounds, wouldn't it explain why you can't remember being at the embassy and why you felt so strange? What if this sense you had, of not being in your own body, was the literal truth, and whoever stormed it, stole it, pretended to be you that day?'

'Oh, by the spirits. I almost wish that were true.'

'Now, do you feel up to writing your account?' I said, pushing my scroll across the table and handing A'Soyne my fountain pen.

'Yes, Inspector, I do. And I thank you,' she said, taking the pen and unrolling a foot of paper from my scroll, a new light shining in her eyes.

The sun was in her final descent, and a chill breeze was sweeping in from the south, growing strong across Chief Pawe Skybridge, when Wes and I strode west towards Red Tern Tower, to see if Deta Hinatse, Nita's advocate, was still in his office.

'Even if Hinatse tried to blackmail the murderer with Nita, he won't admit to breaking the law unless we have something on him,' Wes said.

'Nita's life is at stake. Your people will get Hinatse's name out of her. Then *his* life will be at stake. Let's see what he thinks about that,' I said.

'They're not my people.'

We entered the Red Tern Tower rooftop market; residents were eating and drinking outside new brick-built taverns. The smoke from their pipes, along with the aromas from their suppers – lemongrass and chives in particular – was blowing over the bay. We entered reception, ignored the receptionist, and took a hydraulic lift down to the eighteenth floor where I led Wes to Hinatse's offices.

When I knocked, I caused the door to swing open an inch.

'Hello?' I said.

No answer.

Wes and I stepped back, either side of the frame, shared a glance, and drew our pistols.

Blow the candle out.

Put the fear aside.

Focus.

I pushed the door wide open. The waiting room was empty and the blinds were up, revealing the view over the balcony towards the ends of Pastnoon and Sundown Claws. The sun's rays were painting geometric shapes upon the rugs and hardwood floor and the air was fresh with the sea breeze.

Wes nodded, and I stepped forward and pointed my pistol at the secretary's desk. Oza Nequa wasn't there. I checked behind the door, and Wes and I crept forward. He took the southern side, by the window, while I passed behind Nequa's desk.

I crouched by the side of the water closet door, turned the knob, and swung it open, while Wes rested his arms on the back of a chair in the waiting area and took aim.

Empty.

We continued west and met beyond the waiting area at the door to Hinatse's personal office.

I pushed the door open with my pistol and we crept inside, turned back to back, and checked north and south. We split up around Hinatse's desk, and came together by the back wall, where we found the advocate lying dead. His head had been cracked open, and his brains were spilling out onto his private letters, thrown to the floor from the emptied safe above his leather chair.

'Another coincidence, eh, Wes?' I said, testing the carotid pulse on Hinatse's neck.

'I hope you show more grace in defeat than you do victory,' Wes said, holstering his pistol. He struck a match, and lit an oil lamp.

'Not much sign of a struggle,' I said, putting my pistol on the desk.

'They made him open the safe and killed him when they had what they wanted, which was what, I wonder?' Wes said.

'Something that could identify I'Advay's killer. Let's get a forensics team here. The nearest substation is on Noon Claw, not too far north of Chief Pawe Skybridge.'

'I'll go.'

'Don't saunter.'

'Yes, ma'am.'

Wes went back into the waiting area as I searched Hinatse's pockets for the key to his desk drawers.

Seconds later, Wes shouted, 'Halt!'

I picked up my pistol and ran into the waiting area to find Wes struggling with two men at the balcony door. Both assailants had clubs and daggers and were dressed like Kahokeyans in plain animal skins with leather gloves and spook masks – sackcloths painted with skulls with holes for eyes – covering their faces. Wes had one by the neck under his right arm, and was fighting the other off with one fist.

My fear for Wes's safety surprised me. My stomach turned over and bile rose in my throat. I had to blow the candle out, and by the time I had, the man in the hold had tripped Wes. As the CIB agent staggered, the other man clubbed him, a glancing blow, across the crown.

Focus, Ani, focus.

Wes went down. The man in the hold broke free, and he and his accomplice ran west on the balcony. I trained my pistol on the second man and fired through the window. The glass shattered, and the man grabbed his neck as blood soaked his spook mask and seeped between his fingers.

'You okay, Wes?' I said, the relief sharp in my tone.

'Fine. Go, go,' Wes said.

I jumped over Wes and ran out onto the balcony, holstering the spent percussion pistol and drawing the other. The injured man was trying to step over the balustrade onto the wide ledge running around the tower at the base of the next bird-shaped section. He was swaying on his feet, bleeding down his shirt and trouser leg.

'I can't make it,' he said.

'May Xol welcome your spirit,' the other man said, before pushing his wounded friend off the tower.

The poor soul's body broke on the corner of the next ledge, falling onto a diagonal hunk of bedrock before sliding into the waters of the bay. The killer and I took aim at one another and fired.

The pistol ball burnt my hair as it passed close by my head, triggering a surge of adrenaline that coursed through my body. My shot nicked the killer's shoulder. He flinched but stayed on his feet, then turned and ran. I holstered my second spent pistol and jumped the balustrade, through the smoke hanging in the air from his shot. It stung my eyes and made me cough, but I landed on my feet, barely breaking stride.

Be calm.

Focus.

By the time I reached the next balcony, the man was already past it. Beyond lay the painted steel talons of the 250-foot-high hawk above.

The talons were smooth and curved over the ledge, so the man took his time to clear each. I decided to take a chance, hoping to make ground on him, and tried to use my momentum to run over, but I slipped on a fresh pile of bird shit and couldn't stop myself from sliding down the steel slope.

Be mindful.

It was counterintuitive, but I rolled to one side and pushed myself off. My body twisted in the air as I fell, but I stretched my arm out over the ledge and braced myself. I cried out as my shoulder took the strain, and I held on.

My arms burned from pulling my weight up, and my face scraped against the concrete as I raised myself. I was almost there when the soft-soled shoes of the killer dropped onto the ledge before me. He stared down at me, a club raised in his hand. The sun reflected off a pair of dark, almond-shaped Kahokeyan eyes, visible through the holes in his spook mask.

Not a bad life, I thought.

He didn't move.

'What are you waiting for?' I asked.

He cocked his head.

'You do know you're under arrest, don't you?' I said.

The man laughed, slid his club into his belt and reached down. He grabbed my forearm and lifted me up until I was able to get my backside on the ledge. Once I was seated, he put me in a chokehold and squeezed. I tried to stand, but he pushed me down. I grabbed his arm but couldn't pull it away. And although I managed to dig my elbows into his ribs, and heard him grunt, he responded by tightening his grip and whispering in my ear, 'Don't fight. If I'd wanted to kill you, I'd have pushed you off.'

That voice sounds familiar, I thought, before the blackness ate my vision from the edges inward.

'Ani! Ani!' Wes said, shaking me awake.

Wes crouched over me, his concern evident despite the blood running into his eyes from the gash on his scalp, against which he held a fast-reddening handkerchief.

'What happened?' he said.

'I slipped over the ledge. He helped me up,' I said.

'Who?'

'An old man, just passing by, getting some air. The fucking killer, that's who.'

'But why?'

'Beats me. Let's get back inside.'

We returned to Hinatse's office – I insisted Wes stay there while I went to the substation. He made a show of resisting, then lay down on the leather settee in the waiting room with his long legs hanging over the end. I let him rest and took the hydraulic lift to the top of Red Tern Tower, crossed to the other side of Chief Pawe Skybridge and looked out across Magila Bay. Amongst the ferries, fishing boats, merchant ships, and pleasure craft, I spotted a familiar little cutter, whose captain handled her well and navigated the bedrock below the towers and the pillars of the bridges with practised skill.

CHAPTER TWELVE

A MEMBER OF THE forensics team took Wes to Noon Claw Hospital to have his scalp stitched. He didn't want to go, but the practical necessity of stemming the flow of blood into his eyes soon became evident, even to him. I stayed at the crime scene for about an hour to see if there was anything in Hinatse's desk or upon his person to indicate why two Kahokeyans invaded his place of work and cracked his head open. There wasn't, so I took a cab to Titan's Notch on the eastern face of Pastnoon Claw to see Oza Nequa, Hinatse's secretary of letters.

I bumped into the besuited young man on the stoop of his bungalow, one of several hundred long and narrow dwellings built around the stepped cliffside where it curved to meet the mainland above the Depths. He said he was about to leave, to meet friends for drinks and a late supper in a nearby tavern, but made no fuss when I asked to come inside and he immediately offered me a cup of salt tea.

'That would be welcome, I thank you,' I said.

His small home was as tidy and well-presented as its owner, with exposed wooden floors, no rugs, and plain surfaces upon which Nequa had placed ornaments of simple Harn design: stone lanterns, carved pagoda-style sculptures, and figures of dancers, whose smooth and flowing bodies were rendered close to abstraction. There were several family photographic plates on the mantel above the fireplace, and opposite, on the windowsills, were jasmine, citrus, and other fragrant plants which diffused the air inside with sweet and fresh scents that soothed and relaxed.

Nequa handed me a cup of tea, lit the stone oil lamps and joined me around a small oval breakfast table of reclaimed wood. I took a sip of the tea and sighed.

'I have bad news, Oza. Your boss is dead. Murdered.'

He nodded.

'You don't seem surprised,' I said.

'I'm not, Inspector. I was fond of Mr Hinatse, and he was good to me, but I don't believe he was an entirely scrupulous man. There are several clients whose correspondence I knew never to read, and to whom I was never allowed to write,' Nequa said.

'And does that include Madam Nita?'

'Not always. But a tell-tale sign was if I were not required to take minutes.'

'Was that the case three days ago?'

Nequa nodded.

'Anything odd about his behaviour since then – suspicious, nervous?'

'Secretive, but that was normal.'

'Any new clients or visitors who concerned you or who you thought unusual?'

Nequa stroked his thin moustache. 'The morning after your visit, he had me send runners to three clients to rearrange meetings and clear his diary, then he went out.'

'Any idea who he met?' I said.

'None.'

'Anything else?'

'He received a letter two days later marked for his attention. I can't be sure, but I believe it was from an Al'Mayran. He never had Al'Mayran clients.'

'What makes you think it was from an Al'Mayran?'

'The hand that wrote the address. You know, little flourishes here and there.' Nequa sighed and shook his head.

'I'm sorry to bring you bad news,' I said.

'It's not that, Inspector. I'm ashamed to say I was thinking I have to find another job. Am I a horrible person?' he said.

'No. Hinatse was reckless with your life as well as his own. Had you been working this evening, you'd be dead, too.'

Nequa shivered.

'Now, please write your statement,' I said, handing him my fountain pen and scroll.

Night had fallen by the time I arrived at Horizon's Outlook. I found the bridge still up, the oil lamps unlit and no Josee. A cool breeze, an uncommon north-wester, lifted my jacket and chilled my back as I called out for Snuggs. There was no familiar answering call and I soon gave up. I walked onto the western terrace to gaze at the fires on Sundown Claw. They always reminded me of childhood evenings spent playing marbles with Oura or wrestling with Etu, of listening to the tales Ezno and his pals told.

I watched the fires burn for a while, smelling the mussels and fish frying and listening to folk sing, laugh and grow rowdy. I sighed and strolled along the southern balcony to the eastern. I entered the den and went into my study to fetch the pistol-cleaning kit Oura bought me when I became an Inspector.

The flat never felt like home when Josee wasn't there. I lit the oil lamps on the northern balcony and sat on the form opposite the bridge. I laid a waxed linen towel over my legs, took out the percussion pistols I had fired and set to work with solvent to soften the fouling, and a bronze brush to loosen it. Finally, I took the barrels off to pass an oiled patch through the bores with a cleaning rod.

As I was finishing up, leather boots approached. I reckoned they were Al'Mayran by the tapping sound of their soles on the cobbles. It was most likely Josee, but I unholstered the police-issue flintlock pistol I had not fired just in case.

The light from a kitchen window in Shadow Rise fell upon a loose mop of fiery red hair and my wife shouted, 'Sorry, sorry! Sorry I'm late.'

I put the flintlock away and began to reassemble the percussion pistols as Josee ran onto the northern balcony and stood above me, catching her breath.

'Where's Mani?' I said, without looking up.

'At Ezno's. I haven't had time to fetch him yet. I thought I'd come back home first.'

'Where have you been?'

'The Al'Mayran quarter.'

'With?'

'Friends.'

'Does that include Dabreeyor?'

Josee sighed and said, 'Yes,' in an irked tone.

'All day?'

'I introduced her to some of the others and we went drinking.'

'So you're telling me you're drunk. That the plan, is it? Offload Mani to Ezno and get soused all day?'

'First of all, I've spent more time with that poor boy than you have. Second, he trusts me a damn sight more than he does you, because he knows I don't want anything from him. Third, I wasn't drinking all day, because I spent the morning delivering Memi and her friends to Ezno and discussing what we were going to do with them. Lastly, if I do want to drink all day, I will, and with whomever I like.'

Josee stormed off around the dining room corner to the western terrace. I holstered my percussion pistols and, telling myself not to make the situation worse, set off after her. I found her in the drawing room, lighting a lamp.

'I didn't mean to attack you. It's been a rough day,' I said. 'And about Dabreeyor, I don't want to resent her. Really, I don't. It's just… This isn't easy for me—'

'Ani, you don't have to explain your problems to me. I've been living with them for ten years,' Josee said, holding her hand up for me to be quiet.

'That's harsh.'

'Maybe it has to be.' She put her hands on her hips. 'Ani, I love you, and I don't want anyone else. If that's what you need to hear, I'm happy to say it. I like saying it. I like hearing it, too.'

I stared at my shoes and felt my face turn red. I wanted to run. I made myself into a statue.

'But Ani, hear this as well: the only problem in this marriage is what you choose to bring into it. If you want us to last, don't drive me away.'

My eyes stung, but I refused to blink until Josee turned away and I could wipe the tears without her seeing.

She pulled a dust cover off a stack of paintings piled on a sideboard and started to sift through them.

'What are you doing?' I said, clearing my throat.

'I've promised Dabreeyor a picture,' Josee said.

'She's buying one?'

Josee sighed and stared at the ceiling. 'By the spirits, no, Ani. I'm not selling a painting to a friend, I'm giving it to her as a gift.'

'Shall I work for free, too?'

'I've sold plenty this year.'

'Eight.'

'I didn't know you were keeping track,' Josee said, almost under her breath, without breaking from her task.

'Just making sure you understand what plenty means.'

'It's how much they go for that counts.' She turned to look directly at me. 'And I've already made more than you'll earn in a year.'

I felt my face flush and I took a couple of steps forwards. 'And it's all gone into someone else's pocket. You can't save worth a damn,' I said, struggling not to raise my voice.

Josee drummed her fingers on the frame of a painting and pursed her lips before taking a long breath. 'Ani, you need to ask yourself what this is about. Because I know you don't care about money.'

'Four days you've known her, and you're giving paintings away.'

'So it's who I'm giving the painting to that bothers you?'

I felt what little advantage I had slipping away. 'It's beyond me how you make friends so quickly. I don't… I just… I can't relate. Explain it to me. How can she not mean more to you than you say?'

'Because I'm telling you she doesn't,' Josee said, pity creeping into her tone.

'So how do you feel about her? Why has she grown so special to you?'

Josee kept one hand on the frames of the paintings and turned to face me. 'Ani, you and I are different. You keep people at arm's length until

you think you've figured them out. It raises the stakes of every relationship you have. That's not the way I am. So stop projecting an intensity of
emotion onto me I'm not feeling. I just like Dabreeyor, that's all.'

'Yes, in every way.'

'I don't compartmentalise my feelings like you.'

'That's what scares me. You've been romantic with friends in the past.'

Josee smiled and shook her head. 'Romantic is pushing it. I've fucked
some of them for fun.'

'How do you think that makes me feel?'

'Ani, all that's in the past.'

'But fidelity isn't as important to you as it is to—'

'Yes it bloody is, damn you. Do you think I'm disloyal?'

'No.'

'So I must be faithful, constant, right?'

I shrugged.

'I'll take that as a yes. Ani, we took vows. I meant mine, too. You
don't have a monopoly on honour. Are they the same vows and promises
I've made to others in the past? No. They change with each person I'm
with, and I'm with you now.'

I ran out of words. How did you argue a point beyond reason?

'Would it really make you feel better if I stopped seeing her?' Josee
said.

'I don't want that,' I said, trying to sound convincing.

'Good, because she's a lovely, rather gentle woman, who, unless
you've forgotten, you introduced me to.'

'How about going a day?'

'Oh, Ani,' Josee said, returning her attention to the stack of paintings. 'One day?' she said, without looking at me.

'Would it hurt?'

Josee didn't answer. Her face lost its pink glow and she put her hand
to her heart.

'What is it?' I said.

'My paintings. Look,' she said, turning one to show me.

It was one of a series she had painted last winter of ice hanging from

Magila Bay bridge. Now it was covered in crudely scrawled Al'Mayran symbols.

'What do they mean?' I said.

'It's a curse, wishing that when I die, my spirit will be lost forever in the empty blackness of space, away from all my kin.' Josee dropped the picture and inspected the others, throwing each spoiled one to the floor.

'The break-in,' I said. 'They're getting at me through you. I'm sorry.' I put my hand on her shoulder.

'How worried should I be, Ani?'

'Hard to say. These are intimidation tactics. Whether there's any real intent behind them – who knows?'

'Perhaps you should let it go.'

'It's my job.'

Josee sighed. 'I'm tired. Let's fetch Mani.'

CHAPTER THIRTEEN

J OSEE AND I took a ferry to Sundown Claw. While I stood speaking to the captain on the deck, she sat next to me on a bench. When she yawned and stretched, she rested her head on my hip, and I trembled. Then, when we disembarked and stepped onto the dock, she took my hand.

'How is the investigation coming along?' she asked.

'The CIB arrested Madam Nita and I'Advay's young lover, a lad called Nitushi Nakni,' I said.

'What will happen to them?'

'Nothing good.'

We walked in silence for a while, occasionally smiling and greeting members of my tribe who were drinking on their porch or on their way to a tavern. A couple of youngsters saw me through the window of their bedroom, tapped on the glass, and shouted, 'Shimmer, Ani, shimmer!'

I cast the appearance of their father, a rather chubby fellow with a habit of forgetting what he was saying mid-sentence. I put my finger to my lips and made an exaggerated thoughtful face until they fell about laughing.

As we continued south, the hedgeless lanes gave way to narrow fisher-men's trails, which snaked around wooden dwellings and rock formations and cut across patches of grass and wildflowers. Insects flew through the smoke and steam rising from the fires and cooking pots, in search of an unearned meal, while circling gulls called out from above. The majority of folk were still outside, sat together on banks and boulders, in gardens and commons. Their polite conversation, having eased into merriment, grew raucous to rise above the music of fiddles and pipes echoing off the side of the Claw.

Etu was playing handball with Mani outside our childhood home at the far end of Sundown Claw. They were bouncing the cork-and-hide ball off a flat and near vertical stretch of stone marking the western boundary of Ezno's property. My uncle was watching the game and sharing a pipe with Oura on the decking near his rock pool.

'How goes it with you, Ezno?' I said.

'I'm well, my daughter, how goes it with you?' he said.

'Better when you tell me where Memi and her flock are.'

'They've gone west with Etu's girl, Salime, on her boat to pick up a shipment of sweet flowers from the Wa'ki. I thought it was safer. They'll be back in a few days.'

Oura offered me a drag on his pipe once Josee and I sat down. I drew on it, enjoyed the narcotic hum and tried to relax, but I couldn't put the case out of my mind.

'Do either of you know of twin brothers who climb for a living?' I said, passing the pipe to my uncle.

'Kahokeyan?' Ezno said.

I nodded.

'I may do,' Oura said. 'I can't be sure they're the same lads you want. But they live north, on the other side of the bay, in Ulawe's Perch. You remember, Pa, their grandfather was Lo'tse? He and their father were lost while whaling south of the Known World.'

'My, I haven't seen those boys since they were Mani's age,' Ezno said. 'Their mother was a climber, too, a good one, made a living collecting puffin eggs or hiring herself out to the city. I reckon they'll be doing the same.'

'They're called Kana and Taliko,' Oura said.

'Family name?' I said.

'Hiduse,' Ezno said in triumph, punctuating the word with a stab of the pipe stem. 'Taliko and Kana Hiduse.'

Mani wandered over to listen to the conversation. Josee put her arm around him and whispered something in his ear. He laughed, looked at Etu, and nodded.

'I made stew with herring, sprat, and mackerel,' Oura said. 'We've all eaten, but there's enough for a late supper, if you and Josee would like some.'

'I'll fetch the bowls,' Josee said, rejuvenated and on her feet in a flash.

I laughed and nodded to Oura, who followed Josee into the house. While we waited, I smoked with Ezno and watched Mani resume his game with Etu, winning as many points as he lost despite his near comical disadvantage in height. I expected the boy to continue to play rather than watch Josee and me eat, but when Oura and my wife returned with two bowls of steaming hot stew, he came and sat down next to me. I winked at him as I chewed my first mouthful and he laughed.

'Oura's a good cook, isn't he?' Mani said.

'He learnt from the best,' I said, nodding towards Ezno.

'I was thinking about your mother.'

'Oh, what about her?'

'You said she went out at night?'

'I said she was a whore.'

Etu and Josee, who had been engaged in a lively debate about the best taverns in New Capital, grew quiet.

'My ma was a whore, too. Do you think that's bad?' Mani asked.

Everyone was now staring at me, waiting for me to dry up. I ignored them and kept eye contact with Mani.

'No. Absolutely not. Never think that, son,' I said.

'My ma never came back one night. Hani and I reckoned she might have slept somewhere else. But when she didn't come back in the morning, we knew she was dead. But yours might still be alive.'

'Maybe.'

'Can you remember her?'

'No.'

'What about your pa?'

'He died when I was six. I remember him. He was a shimmerer, too.'

'Mine left when I was little. Hani remembers him a bit. I don't. Would you like to meet your ma?'

I nodded.

'I don't think you scared your ma when you shimmered. I think she was scared for you. You wouldn't have been safe in the Depths,' Mani said.

'I like that story better,' I said.

The lad stared off and bit his lip. 'I didn't see who left the dead Al'Mayran by the Stars, but Hani did,' he said, faltering, and continuing with greater conviction, as if a decision, even a decision to talk, were preferable to doubt. 'After we saw you and Josee on the Bridge of Spirits, we ran to Noon Claw to eat the puddings you gave us. We played in the drainpipes, watching the stormwater spill out of the cliff. Hani was spying through a grate onto Sumaka Way when he saw the man. But by the time I looked, he'd gone and the dead Al'Mayran was there. I asked Hani who he'd seen, but he told me to shut up and not speak about it. He says things like that a lot.'

'He's trying to look after you.'

'But I'm getting older.'

'Yes, you are.' I had another spoonful of stew, trying not to appear eager and hoping my family had the good sense to keep quiet.

'When Nita went to see her advocate the following morning, why did she take you and Hani with her?' I asked, as casually as I could.

'I'm not sure. We walked to the cab rank. I was with Nitushi, who was very upset. Hani was up ahead with Nita. They were talking.'

'About what?'

'I don't know, but when we got in the cab, she gave us some money and told us to pretend we'd spent the night at the Stars.'

'And Hani never told you what they talked about?'

'He wouldn't.'

'Do you think it was about the dead Al'Mayran?' I said.

'It had to be.'

'Do you think Nita saw the killer too?'

The boy nodded. 'Are you going to arrest Hani?'

'No.'

'Promise?'

'I promise. I'm not going to turn you or Hani over to the police. I'd let you both go back to the Depths before I did that. I just need to know what he knows. I think I can help Nita and Nitushi.'

'Are you friends with Nita?'

'I didn't think so. But, as it turns out, I am.'

The lad nodded as if he'd never agreed with a statement more in his young life. 'When we're not at the Stars, me and Hani spend most nights in Busted Jaw with our band of the Vermin. Sometimes we sleep with the others in an empty cistern but we have our own spot under the pier.' He jutted his little cleft chin out, looked to the stars and said, 'Want another game, Etu?'

'If you want another arse-kicking, I'm happy to oblige,' Etu said.

Mani trotted over to him and they began to push one another back and forth.

'I think my brother was desperate for a new playmate,' Oura said.

'Now he has an intellectual equal,' I said.

'You do the boy a disservice,' Oura said.

'Poor Etu,' Josee said.

'Oura, would you and Etu take my wife and Mani home?' I said.

'Where are you going?' Josee said.

'Busted Jaw.'

'I don't need an escort.'

'There's safety in numbers. Oura, could you spend the night? The settee in the drawing room is very comfortable.'

'You should know,' Oura said.

'Do I get a say in this?' Josee said.

'No,' I said.

Many of the folk who had travelled to Pastnoon Claw for the evening were returning home to Sundown by the time I took another ferry across Lo'tse Bay. I stood at the bow, listening to their conversations, watching the reflected fires and lamplight dance upon the waves and on the crisscross of trailing wakes left by passing vessels. A gust brought sulphur up from the water swirling around the boat. The odour, so repellent to most rich folk, always comforted me; at the very least it was preferable to the stench of the Depths. Whatever her motivations, I had my mother to thank for that.

When I disembarked, I strolled north along the tidy tree-lined lanes of Pastnoon Claw's eastern face, where the middle-classes of New Capital lived. Good families on the whole, neither rich nor poor, but they had money enough to look down on those from the Depths and tell themselves criminality was never an option they would choose, even if they were desperate. They lived in charming homes on pleasant lanes surrounded by small parks and communal areas. There was no industry and few businesses save for the odd corner shop, respectable tavern and artisanal eatery, all refined establishments free of advertising banners. The grass in the beer gardens was kept short, the shrubbery trimmed, and the furniture was painted or varnished and made with interlocking joints that did not creak. But if you kept walking north and descending the levels, you eventually wandered into the Depths.

The area became less well populated, until the number of uninhabited properties grew higher than those occupied. These neighbourhoods were buffers, abandoned by the city. No one came here to refill and light the oil lamps or clean the lanes and ways, and gangs of orphaned and abandoned children made homes for themselves amongst the urban ruin.

I quickened my pace as I left the warm glow of lamplight and entered the blackness. As I hurried on, the chatter from the packed taverns faded and was replaced by the whistles and birdcalls of lookouts. When I reached Busted Jaw, I closed my eyes, pictured Mani and shimmered his appearance.

At the centre of the neighbourhood was an open-air theatre surrounded by dwellings once home to a thriving community of performers. But that was two millennia ago. Now, as my eyes adjusted to the dark, I saw caved-in roofs, rotting and peeling shutters, broken windows, and unchecked weeds sprouting from the overgrown grass of the commons.

There were no campfires, at least not out in the open, and only a handful of children, whose scurrying shadows I spotted dancing on the walls, cast by the moonlight. Those who couldn't find a home in an abandoned flat or in some part of the decaying arena had built shacks from repurposed wood, fashioned tents out of lost sails, or filled barrels and crates with straw to curl up inside. The stench of rotten food, body odour, and human waste permeated the air, a reminder that feral living should never be romanticised.

Shona lived in a place like this, although she never brought me. I often wondered why. Had she feared for my safety? Or, more likely, I now realised, had she felt the shame and degradation of her poverty? I had once envied her freedom. Now, as an adult, I couldn't bear to think of her fragile body shivering in the night or her ragged clothes soaked with rain, clinging to her skin in the icy sea breeze.

I asked her once to come and live with me on Sundown, but she refused and grew angry. Perhaps I should have seen her humiliation and known how to comfort her and overcome her objections. But I was a child, and I never found the courage to ask again. Not before it was too late.

What would have become of her, had she lived? Like the children that grew up here, by the time I knew her, she had already learnt she was of no value to the city. Was it any wonder her kind flocked to the gangs, who at least had use for them? *Never preach morality to those who aren't taught it.* Or, worse still, those who were shown proof, time and again, that principles didn't earn material benefit. Like everything else in New Capital, nurturing the soul was a privilege afforded to the wealthy, who seemed to value the practice least of all.

I put such thoughts out of my mind and kept my eyes focused straight ahead as I made for the empty cistern, built on stilts near the dilapidated northern wharf. I tried not to look at the older Vermin members who were supposed to be keeping guard. They were more interested in drinking, smoking and gambling than in the return of a small boy, even if it had been days since they had seen his face.

A young girl, no more than nine, approached me. She was short and undernourished. Her deerskin dress was worn but clean, and she had long dark hair. She wore necklaces and bands made of horsetail, and around her waist, she had fastened a shiny leather belt, which was new and most likely stolen.

'Mani,' she said, running towards me and flinging her arms around my chest, thinking my ribcage was her friend's shoulders.

I thought the contradicting reality of my hidden form would create the schism in her mind, and my illusion would be broken, but the imagination of youngsters should never be underestimated.

'Where have you been?' she said, looking straight ahead where she saw her friend's eyes.

'With Memi from the Stars,' I said in Mani's voice.

'Are you back?'

'Only for a little while. Where's Hani?'

'Where do you think? In your spot at the end of the pier.'

She nodded her head beyond the cistern, so I thanked her and headed with a sure foot in the direction she indicated as if I knew where I was going. But once I was out of her sight, I slowed and scanned my surroundings, taking care where I trod on the worn planks. They creaked and splintered underfoot, so I made for relative safety above the supporting beams. I didn't have to search for long. I found the boy lying on a makeshift platform below the deck, eating a bowl of less-than-fresh prawns.

'What in Xol's name are you doing here?' Hani said when he spotted me climbing down.

'I'm here to see you,' I said.

'Well, go back to Nita's.'

'The Stars has been closed. The CIB took Nita and Nitushi.'

'What about Memi?'

'That copper helped her escape.'

'Why are you not with her?'

I moved a little closer so I could whisper. 'I'm staying with the copper and her wife at the top of Horizon's Outlook. I think we can trust them.'

'Probably not, but you're still better off there.'

'Come with me.'

'Fuck that.'

'Why?'

'Because.'

'Then I'm staying too.'

Hani sighed and threw his supper into the harbour waters. He stood, wrapped his arms and legs around a pillar, and clambered up.

'Where are you going?' I said.

'I'm taking you back to that copper.'

I followed Hani along the edge of the crumbling pier, sticking to the beams again, and along the jagged bedrock below the dock. It was hard to see where he was stepping, and I slipped more than once, scraping the skin from my hands and grimacing at the sting. After one tumble, I looked up, and the lad was gone.

'What are you playing at?' he said.

He was no longer out in the open. I stared into the night without blinking until my eyes adjusted and I realised a black oval on the side of the cliff was a huge drainage tunnel. Hani was waiting for me in the opening with his arms folded and his back curved along the pipe's wall.

'About fucking time,' he said.

Hani disappeared into the tunnel, and I set off at a trot to catch up with him. Once we were walking side by side, I said, 'If you're taking me back, why not stay with us tonight, see what the copper has to say?'

'Look, Mani, I know you want us to be together. But I'm older than you, and I don't belong up there. I'll be a war chief soon, and I can make real money. But you can go live with the copper, I won't be angry. You're smarter than me, and you could go to school and get a job and become something.'

'We could both go to school.'

'It's too late, and besides, I can't live with a fucking copper. I've seen their ways too often.'

'But Nita and Nakni are in trouble. The copper is trying to save them. If you told her what you saw that night, you might be able to help.'

Hani stopped dead and turned on me, his finger pointed at what he thought was his brother's face. 'No, Mani. I'm not talking to a copper.'

'Then tell me who you saw, and I'll tell her. That way, you aren't the snitch.'

'Will you fucking listen? I'm not talking about it – not with her, not with you, not with anyone.'

I thought about dropping my shimmer to see if I could reason with Hani as myself, but a splash of water echoed in the tunnel and distracted me. Hani and I stared down the shaft, peering into the gloom, looking for moving shadows.

We heard them again before we saw them, and we saw them too late. Five lads, all around thirteen or fourteen, appeared out of the darkness to circle Hani and me. They attacked from all sides, and they weren't playing.

'Death to the Vermin!' a tall, wiry boy shouted.

As two of his pals pinned Hani to the wet and muddy floor, the boy lifted his axe, where he thought Mani's head was. I grabbed the handle and he froze, caught in the schism as the reality of my true physical appearance and the illusion of the child I was casting fought for dominance in his mind. Reality won, and I lost my shimmer. But before the lad could recover – while he was still blinking and shaking his head – I stole his axe and swung the blunt end into his belly.

In their disorientated shock at my transformation, the two holding Hani let him go, and the lad ran towards the harbour. I tried to give chase, but one of the bigger gang members grabbed me by the neck. I twisted and brought the base of the axe down on his foot.

'Come on, she's a fucking shimmerer!' the tall, wiry boy said, and they all fled and vanished deep into the tunnel.

I followed Hani out of the drain, but when I emerged, there was no sign of him. I doubted he would have returned to Busted Jaw, and even if he had, and I could shimmer another soul's form to return to the Vermin's domain, I would not be able to extract him by force without his gang falling upon me.

I was standing there on the rocky shore for a moment, staring at the waves, considering what route to take home, when, as it had the night of the storm, the bay flickered carmine-red. The lights had returned to the academy.

'Fuck it,' I said, and spat on the ground.

I made my way along the bedrock until I found a path to the busy harbour at the foot of Pastnoon Claw. I hired a young sailor and his boat to take me across Magila Bay towards Riverlyn Park.

As we crossed, I watched the lights.

'What do you think they are?' the young sailor said.

'Good question,' I said.

By the time I was back on dry land, the lights had stopped flashing, but I wasn't deterred. I strode through the park, which was filled with lovers and drinkers, and no doubt the odd mugger, to Pawe's Lament. I passed behind the Magila Bay waterfall and headed for the steep path to the science academy. The cliffside was unlit, but the darkness helped focus my attention, and I made it to the little overhang where I'd found the charred splinter of stone in less time than it had taken me in daylight.

I stood catching my breath, listening to the roar of the waterfall and gazing across the bay at the skybridges and towers. They were discernible by the lights from the flats within and from the rooftop taverns, still doing good business despite the hour. With my eye, I followed the line of Magila Bay bridge to the final pillar, around which my home, Horizon's Outlook, my sanctuary in the Known World, was built. But the jagged slope of Pastnoon Claw obstructed my view, and I could not tell if Josee were home.

I kicked through the overgrown grass, looking for more burnt fragments, but someone had cleared them away. It was the same on the last third of the path, all the way up to the academy.

The lamps in the Octagon Hall had now been extinguished. Whoever had been working late had gone for the day. The gardens to the west were empty, and if there were guards outside the nearby entrance, they were hidden under the portico's roof. With a final look around, I ran across the lawn, keeping low, to the scaffolded section of wall.

Repairs were underway, and several new stones had been laid at the base of the keyhole wound, but there was still a hole at the apex, covered from the inside by planks of wood from a pallet. I climbed the scaffolding, thankful the crash of the waterfall drowned out the creaking joints of the frame. Once on the top platform, I lay on my back and kicked one of the planks loose. When no one came running, I twisted the plank away, pulled it through the gap, and laid it on the platform.

The smell of smoke and roast pork escaped. Through the gap was a collapsed wall, part of an octagonal corridor running around the central lab. On the walls to my left, revealed by the moonlight pouring through the glass dome, were lines of scorch marks and deep fissures, as if someone lost control of a hosepipe spitting fire. I leaned forward to poke my head through the gap and get a better look. There, on the floor of the lab, in a stretched oval of moonlight, was a tripod. It was not unlike the kind used with a camera obscurer, but whatever had been mounted upon it was missing.

I twisted to squeeze my shoulders and my upper body through the narrow gap, hanging onto the burnt and jagged edge of the wall. Unfortunately, the section I was clinging to gave way. While I managed to grab another hold, stone pieces smashed on the marbled floor below, echoing around the corridor, the hall beyond, and against the glass dome above.

I heard voices from the west. Probably the guards from under the portico. I pulled my upper body back through the gap, banged my head, and jumped off the scaffolding. I hit the ground hard, bending my knees until I came to rest in a squat with my backside on the lawn. When I caught a glimpse of the guards, I sprinted across the lawn and leapt off the cliff edge.

I missed the path and fell for what seemed like an eternity, the lights of the towers and bridges flashing before my eyes. I put my hands out, searching for a hold as the adrenaline surged through my body and my heart tried to rip through my chest. Stalks from thick grass clumps whipped at my palms and fingertips until I managed to grab a wad and slow my momentum. I flipped onto my belly, but the stalks snapped, and I slid, cutting my chin and taking the skin off the heels of my hands.

My baldric and the grips of my pistols dug into the earth and caught on pointed rocks, slowing my descent down the steep incline and allowing me to draw my dagger. I thrust the blade into the cliff and brought myself to a halt. I clasped the handle and pommel with both hands and searched for secure footing.

My head pounded, and although I wasn't cold, I shook uncontrollably. My teeth rattled, and the blood flowing past my ears had grown so loud I could no longer hear the waterfall. Gradually, like regaining consciousness after a blow to the head, I became aware of my surroundings again and heard voices shouting from the clifftop.

'I can't see a fucking thing,' one said.

'Me neither. Come back up. They're either dead or gone. Looked like a youngster anyway.'

'Dressed in a suit?'

'Perhaps you're mistaken, eh?'

'Could be.'

When the voices faded, I clambered east until I found the path, sitting on a step, holding my head in my hands, begging Xol to cure me of the need to always be proven right.

CHAPTER FOURTEEN

DIDN'T WANT TO disturb Josee at such an early hour, nor did I want to talk with her and see the disapproval in her eyes, so when I returned home, I spent the night on the swing seat on the western terrace. But I slept poorly and woke at sunrise before the first high water of the day.

Wisps of brilliant white clouds, indicative of fine weather, could already be seen high in the sky, and the calm sea glistened as if a mesh of flickering silver light had been laid upon it. I felt like the day was betraying me. I wanted it to be murky and cold and wet and stinging my face with rain, spat out by implosions of the blackest clouds. But the Known World had no interest in reflecting my turmoil.

I entered the drawing room and, avoiding the spoiled paintings still lying on the floor, I crept past Oura, who was asleep on the settee. In the bathroom, I washed my hands and face. I fetched a clean suit from the bedroom and changed on the southern balcony so I didn't wake Josee.

It was hours before I was due to meet Wes at the embassy and search I'Advay's office, and I had no desire to spend the best part of the morning in the Square. Instead, I went to the fish market below the Al'Mayran arcade and bought a pair of lightly battered mackerel wrapped in crispy seaweed. I ate them as I rambled north through Magila Market, turning east when the incline of Noon Claw became gentle enough to climb. I returned to Riverlyn Park, and I climbed a nature trail up to the top of the Claw.

I showed the Coor'Seyan soldier at the embassy gate my police emblem and made my way along the curving drive towards the blood-red, gold, and cerulean painted embassy. Wes was waiting for me inside the grand entrance hall, sitting under a painted statue of the warrior Ameeleyor, whose lifeblood stone, atop her staff, was ablaze with a searing light. When Wes saw me, he stood and smiled, bounding over like a giant horse from the Kahokeyan plains.

'How's that head?' I asked.

'It's nothing,' he said, running the tip of his finger over half a dozen looped stitches.

We walked around the embassy to the annex and through the rear entrance, where the guard, A'Deeyna, said she had seen I'Advay return from the barracks at six o'clock on the evening of the storm. When we reached I'Advay's office, I paused outside the dark mahogany door and pressed my hand upon the carvings in the panels, tracing the spirits with my fingers.

'There'll be nothing in here. I'Dreng will have seen to that,' I said.

'I know, Ani. But perhaps he missed something or didn't recognise its significance. There's only one way to find out,' Wes said.

He handed me the key, and I unlocked the door and swung it open, but stayed on the threshold. A single glance confirmed what I had feared. Areel I'Advay's work had been spirited away, and not with care. Filing cabinets had been broken open and the drawers left empty on the floor, some in pieces. Everything was disturbed.

Wes placed his hand on my shoulder and slid past me.

'Come, Ani,' he said.

I kept my hands in my pockets and didn't peek inside the ransacked cabinets that once contained I'Advay's writings and illustrations. Instead, I examined the paintings he had chosen to hang on his walls. They depicted a world where the spirits of the Al'Mayran dead swirled around the living, protecting them, guiding them and becoming one with them. Many showed the lights of the Red Mountains, but they weren't the usual representations of awesome wonder. They depicted the faces of revellers at festivals, their faces joyous in the red glow. I suspected they were I'Advay's own work and mediated on a theme clearly dear to his sacred heart: Once bathed in the light, the Al'Mayrans of flesh and blood were no different to their non-corporeal counterparts.

One painting in particular caught my eye. It was of the warrior Ameeleyor. Unlike the statue in the entrance hall, here her fight was over, her enemy slain, and she was on her knees, weeping, a pile of dust in her hands. The title on the border read: *Death of a stone*. The next painting also depicted Ameeleyor, now dead herself and being carried from the battlefield.

'Ani, look at this,' Wes said.

'Where are you?' I said.

'The bathroom.'

'Oh, for Xol's sake.'

'What was that?'

'Nothing.'

I followed Wes's voice down a narrow hallway and into a small room, which had a bed, a chest of drawers and a wardrobe in it. Along the northern wall, there were two doorways. One led to a water closet, no bigger than a cupboard, and the other to a tiled bathroom, where I found Wes. He was standing with his fists on his hips, staring down at a white, enamelled, roll-top bath. He looked up when I entered, his eyes ablaze with curiosity, and said, 'Indoor plumbing.'

As if I didn't understand the concept, he picked up the shower head and turned the tap on and off, sprinkling the tub with water.

'There must be a boiler somewhere,' he said. 'What a fascinating modern world we live in.'

'Do you think Areel I'Advay's bathing habits pertinent to his murder?'

'What? Oh, I'm sorry, Ani. You see, I have a bath in my flat, only I have to fill it using the pan, having heated the water on the stove. It's so time-consuming.'

I shook my head and was about to leave when I noticed a small side table with a vase of dead and withered flowers sat upon a runner. The runner had been dragged off centre. I pulled the cloth back to the middle of the tabletop and revealed a series of fresh dents and cracks in the wood.

'How odd,' Wes said. 'Something was smashed here.'

I got onto my knees and lowered my face until my chin was on the tabletop. The splintered and exposed wood was covered in red stains as if the fibres had soaked up droplets of wine. I crawled under the table into the shadows and ran my hand over the tiled floor until my fingers brushed a thin layer of dust gathered along the wall. When I crawled out, I held my hand up to the frosted-glass window and my fingertips sparkled red.

'Lifeblood stones,' Wes said.

I dragged the table to one side, took out some wax paper from my pocket and pressed it flat against the patch of dust until the sticky side was coated.

'I'Advay had traces of the stones under the nail of his little finger. I believe they got there when he smashed a stone here and brushed the smaller fragments away, like so,' I said, sweeping my hand, thumb up, away from me and over the table.

'Why did he do it?' Wes said.

I tried to imagine the same hand that had painted pictures of raptured Al'Mayrans covered in the lifeblood glow destroying the very source of that sacred light.

'Sheer desperation,' I said.

The embassy temple lay to the north on a hill, which had been sculptured into a flat-topped mound. I knew from Josee's art history books that the circular design was millennia old: half a dozen stepped and painted platforms, like the layers of a cake, represented the Red Mountains, the twisting blue and gold columns above were the rising spirits, and the stained-glass dome they supported was a window to a transcendental world.

I waited for Wes at the top of the steps, taking in the view from east to west: Yawe Bay and the financial towers, the cliff edge, the annex where I'Advay's office was located, the main embassy building and the stables, set apart and lying just north of the grand entrance.

We entered the temple and weaved an improvised path across the marble floor through the forest of columns, which were laid out in concentric circles to give the illusion of unbroken walls. At the centre lay the altar, a bespoke golden frame holding a lifeblood stone the size of a sloop's anchor.

'I had no idea,' Wes said.

I laughed at him.

'Couldn't someone steal it?' he said.

'Good luck with that. It's a fucking boulder,' I said.

'Language, Ani. This is a sacred place.'

'Someone might be able to chip a piece off though,' I said, ignoring his reprimand and crouching down to take a closer look.

'How could you tell?'

'See how smooth the surface is?' I said, running my hand around an ovoid section jutting out like a stepping stone in a river. 'That's because when the Al'Mayrans come here to talk to their ancestors, they touch the altar. If a piece has been broken off, it should be obvious.'

I lay down on my back and checked the underside.

'A little rougher, but no sharp wounds,' I said.

'Ani,' Wes said.

'Wherever the stone in I'Advay's office came from, it wasn't from this altar.'

'Ani.'

'Someone within the embassy grounds must have their own supply.'

'Ani, for Xol's sake.'

'What?'

'No two are alike,' the gentle voice of a rather elderly sounding man said.

By my head, near Wes's soft-soled shoes, was a pair of sandalled feet. I slid out from underneath the altar to find the cleric staring down at me. He was slight for an Al'Mayran, barely taller than me, although his back was bent with age and his narrow shoulders sloped, stealing inches from his height. He had brushed his white hair behind his ears, and it hung loose to his ankles. His papery, almost translucent skin revealed the veins and arteries that carried the blood to and from his sacred heart, and he appeared so frail it was a wonder his body could support even the lightweight robe of sapphire spirals he wore.

His face was a melted candle of flesh. His eyes were bright blue, and when he held you in his gaze, it was like finding solace.

'Forgive me, sir, I meant no offence,' I said.

He chuckled, adjusted his arms, folded in his sleeves, and said, 'What offence could you possibly give, my dear?'

'You'd be surprised,' Wes said with a cough. Finding his manners, he said, 'Brother Jaymee, this is Inspector Sulaqua.'

The cleric bowed. 'Investigating the murder of poor Areel I'Advay, no doubt?' he said.

I nodded.

'But what brings you here? You weren't just admiring the stone, were you?' he said.

'I wondered if it had been vandalised,' I said.

'By the spirits, what makes you suspect such blasphemy?'

'We found traces of a stone on I'Advay's body,' I said, opting not to mention the remains we'd just found in his office.

'I don't believe it. He was such a devout man.'

'Brother Jaymee, how can it be a sin to break a stone if you have rocks like this in your temples?' Wes said.

'The ones used in the altars roll down the mountains without the assistance of a human hand, then they're taken, whole and unaltered.'

'What about the dust burnt in cremations and used in rituals?' I said.

'Likewise discovered, often following great labour, like panning in a river or searching miles of labyrinthine caverns. But they are never mined.'

'Why?'

'Because we believe them to be alive.'

I took a moment to process the notion. 'Literally alive?' I asked, as if I had not heard right.

'Not in the way we understand, perhaps, but alive nonetheless.'

'Sentient?'

Brother Jaymee smiled and chuckled. 'Entirely.'

'Self-aware?'

The old man thought for a moment. 'Aware of far more than you and me, my child.'

I stared at the altar and tried to imagine a mind within, a thought process, capable of ideas and opinions. 'And you believe our spirits, if such things even exist, join with them, are absorbed into them, upon the death of our physical selves?'

'I believe the stones perceive the universe in a very different way to us, and they see an aspect of ourselves beyond the physical, beyond even consciousness.'

I told myself not to be deferential to Brother Jaymee. To treat him like any other interviewee I needed answers from. 'Our souls?'

He made the effort to shrug. 'Soul, spirit: these are convenient but inadequate labels for what we don't understand.'

'But this aspect lives in our hearts?' I said, pointing to my chest.

'I doubt that.'

'Are you being blasphemous now, Jaymee?' I said with a deliberate hint of accusation.

Beside me, Wes shuffled his feet and stared at the columns surrounding us.

'Not at all,' the cleric said, laughing. 'Symbolism and ritual provide conduits from the everyday to the abstract. If I live as if my spirit is in my heart, every moment of my existence is an acknowledgement of the divine. Besides, why take a chance?'

'And what about the warrior Ameeleyor – just a myth? Her staff?'

Wes coughed and I rolled my eyes at him. But Brother Jaymee grew serious.

'I've been around the stones since I was a boy,' the old man said. 'I don't question their power.'

'Or their danger?'

'A matter of perspective.'

'What about today? Could someone create a weapon using one? Or is that a ridiculous question?'

'No, not ridiculous at all, Inspector.'

Wes had been focusing on his feet. Now Brother Jaymee had his attention.

'Oh, come now, a weapon?' he said.

Brother Jaymee nodded. 'I'm entirely serious, Wesu. The stones could be exploited for such means. But it would be a great sin.'

I took a step forward. 'But Ameeleyor, the warrior, she didn't sin?'

'No, the stone chose to come to her aid.'

I nodded and paused, wondering what to ask next. 'Have you seen the lights in the science academy?'

'I have.'

'And?'

'Something about magnetism and the amber effect, I am told,' Brother Jaymee said gently, with his blue eyes fixed on me.

'Are you convinced?'

'Not particularly.'

'I thank you, Brother Jaymee.'

We left the cleric in peace and strolled through the columns, trying not to get turned around.

'If I'Advay didn't get the stone from here, where did he get it from?' Wes said.

'Brigadier I'Kalmeen's study,' I said.

'You think I'Advay killed the Coor'Seyan soldier to steal it?'

'I do now.'

We passed the last circle of columns and came out on the edge of the temple's platform just as I'Dreng reached the top of the steps.

Seeing him ignited my anger, so I tried to blow the candle out, but it burnt all the brighter. *Ignore him*, I told myself. *You don't have any proof he spoilt Josee's paintings and threatened her spirit.*

'How dare you come here,' I'Dreng said, spittle forming on the corners of his mouth.

'Easy, Normain, my friend. Brother Jaymee didn't mind,' Wes said.

'I mind, Kohee. You and Sulaqua had permission to search I'Advay's office, not an Al'Mayran sacred house. What are you doing here?'

When I'Dreng blocked my path, the wheels of the Great Lift roared in my ears and one of their immense chains tightened around my neck. I focused on the embassy and passed I'Dreng by walking down the grass-covered hill. When the captain was behind me, I exhaled and returned to the steps, the grind of the wheels fading.

I'Dreng barked, 'Don't ignore me when I ask you a question,' and ran down the steps to grab my shoulder and twist me around.

The wheels came off.

I punched him in the stomach, and as he doubled over, I swept his foot away and pulled him to the ground by his cowl. I knelt on his chest.

'Do you like to paint?' I said.

'What are you talking about?' he snarled, trying to rise, grasping for my jacket.

I forced him back down. 'I asked you if you like to paint. You know, Al'Mayran symbols and such – threats, curses, that kind of thing?'

'I have no idea what you're talking about.'

Wes stood over us. He started to put his hands on me, thought better of it, and crouched down.

'Ani, think about what you're doing,' he pleaded.

I leant down to whisper in I'Dreng's ear.

'Next time you enter my home, just remember, I'm not Al'Mayran, and I don't give a fuck about your sacred heart or what happens to the spirit inside it,' I said.

I freed him and he staggered to his feet.

'I'll see you thrown off this case and out of the police force,' he said.

'Let's all calm down,' Wes said.

'You're through too, Kohee.'

Wes bowed as I'Dreng stalked off towards the cliff edge, holding his stomach.

'What was that about, Ani?' Wes said.

I explained to Wes about Josee's ruined paintings as he and I strolled in the general direction I'Dreng had taken, south-east, towards a wooden viewing platform that overlooked Yawe Bay.

Neither of us spoke for a while as we leant on the oak railings and took in the gleaming spectacle of Treasure's Rock. My eye didn't linger on the jewel-encrusted, gold-infused skytowers of banking and commerce, nor on the brightly coloured flags and banners depicting company logos blowing from their rooftops, but was instead drawn to I'Dreng. He was now standing thirty feet below us on a cliff overhang with Lieutenant Ryeen I'Delboot and half a dozen of his guards. They each carried a rope, hook and pin, and, as I'Dreng shouted orders and directions at them, they practised abseiling down the cliff.

'Will you look at that?' I said.

'I'm looking, I'm looking,' Wes said.

'Is this a regular training exercise for the ambassador's guard?'

'Not that I've ever witnessed. Besides, look at them. They're terrible.'

As Wes spoke, he looked over my shoulder. I followed his gaze towards Major I'Handdru, who was waving to us from a naturally stepped path well below the clifftop, out of sight from where I'Dreng and his people were training. The sun's rays were reflecting white off his polished head and despite the distance, I could see his giant caterpillar moustache curling. He was smiling at us.

'I think he wants to talk,' I said.

We accessed the path north of the embassy, almost parallel with the temple, and headed south. The route took us below where I'Dreng's guards were practicing.

By the time we reached the spot I'Handdru had waved from, the major had already moved on. I wondered if I had misinterpreted his intentions or if he had changed his mind. We saw him waiting again, some distance ahead at an outward curve in the cliff face. Once he'd confirmed we were following, he disappeared behind the curve.

We found him sitting on a flat boulder halfway between the path and the clifftop. The incline, whilst not exactly gentle, was no longer sheer, and there was a well-worn fishermen's trail leading up to the officers' quarters, the eastern boundary of the barracks.

I'Handdru nodded and said, 'Would you like some salt tea and seaweed cakes?'

'That's very kind of you,' I said.

Major I'Handdru's home was one of a score of stone dwellings built twenty feet from the cliff edge into the eastern curtain wall of the barracks. His was covered with red wine ivy, which made the splintering blue paint on the window frames stand out.

Most of his garden was taken up by a long conservatory doubling as a greenhouse, in which he was growing tomatoes, red chillies, other varieties of peppers, and even a couple of sweet corn plants. There was no fence on either side, but extending from the back of the house was a wooden arbour, with a bench, chairs and table, acting as a northern border.

Wes and I followed him through the conservatory, filled with the sweet grassy scent of tomato plants, into the rear of the house, which he had turned into an office. Judging by the overflowing bookcases and crooked shelves that concealed the walls, he was more of a scholar than a soldier. He had piled more books, along with manuscripts, maps, charts, notebooks and sketches in every available space, including the desktop, the sideboards, and on a decrepit bureau whose drawers sat crooked on their runners.

I'Handdru cleared two chairs for Wes and me by the window and left to make the tea.

'Where's I'Kalmeen's residence?' I asked Wes.

'Next door,' Wes said.

'Just the other side of the arbour?'

He nodded.

The major returned carrying a tray with a teapot and three cups on it. He remained silent while he poured. After he perched his substantial behind on the sideboard below the window, causing the top to bow and the columns of books either side to lean, he said, 'I believe Areel waited in the conservatory until most of the regiment was gathered in the mess hall and only one soldier remained to guard the brigadier's study. Then he slipped by the arbour, killed the poor young chap, and broke in.'

I nearly spat my first sip of tea out, not so much in reaction to the information but due to the abruptness of its delivery.

'Excuse me?' I said, the cup hovering below my lips.

'I misled you yesterday. It's true I last saw Areel on the evening of the storm. But it was I who left, not he, at about a quarter to six. Areel asked to stay to consult a few of my books.'

'Are you certain he murdered the soldier?'

The major sighed and shook his head. 'I have no proof. I pieced it together. The lad was cremated quickly, even by Al'Mayran standards of practice, which many Coor'Seyans don't share. When I found out about Areel's death, I told Brigadier I'Kalmeen his friend spent the evening in my home.'

I lowered my cup, rested my forearm on my thigh, and leaned forward. 'What did I'Kalmeen say?'

I'Handdru cast his eyes down and lowered his voice. He seemed embarrassed. 'To keep it to myself until he got back to me. Captain I'Dreng instructed me to lie to you when he conducted his investigation. He said I should say Areel left before six.'

'What did you make of that?'

I'Handdru's eyes searched, possibly for lies, but I thought answers more likely. 'I couldn't understand it. I spoke to the brigadier again. He said, "Jonee, I will not force you to lie – you must follow your own conscience," the implication being he would lie, which astonished me.'

'Did you ask him why?'

'That's all he would say.'

'And so you lied to us, too.'

The major tapped the pile of books next to him with a clenched fist. 'No, that's the problem: I chose my words carefully so I neither provided a false statement nor contradicted the story I'Dreng wanted telling. But you see, that was even worse. I thought I was being clever, keeping my honour. But I wasn't. Last night my conscience kept me awake. Not only was I a liar, but I was a coward too, one who had neither the courage to be truthful nor the bold commitment to falsehood.'

I leant back in the chair and regarded the major. 'But you can't provide testimony that the soldier was murdered or I'Kalmeen's study broken into?'

'No, and I admit, that's a relief. It lets me off the hook.'

'Well, that's not your fault,' I said, finally taking a sip of tea.

'I have something else to tell you, about Mycale I'Krayag.'

I swallowed. 'Oh?'

'I sing with a choir. We were rehearsing in the temple in the Al'Mayran park. I stayed late, talking with friends, then went for a stroll. That's when I saw them.'

'Who?'

'I'Krayag and Je'mymor A'Soyne. They were arm in arm but furtive. I assumed they were having an affair, and so I stayed out of sight.'

Wes and I shared an astonished glance.

'When was this?' I asked.

'The evening before she arrived at the embassy claiming to have been kidnapped,' the major said.

'Are you sure, Jonee?' Wes asked.

I'Handdru nodded. 'And I'm prepared to enter my testimony in your scroll.'

'I'm not sure that's wise. You may be in danger,' I said.

'As long as I can live with myself, I don't care if I die.'

'All the same. I'd rather you didn't. Not just yet, anyway.'

I'Handdru attempted to smile, bowed instead and rose. He caught one of the piles of books before it fell, stroking the top book like it was a beloved pet. Then he clasped his hands behind his back and shuffled around his conservatory.

Wes and I took the cliff path back towards the embassy. As we passed I'Dreng and his people, it sounded like they were packing their gear away, their training session complete, so we took care that no one saw us emerge above the clifftop.

As we passed the annex building on our way out, Brigadier I'Kalmeen approached on his mount, a typically tall Al'Mayran grey with thick, black feathering on the lower legs. Even as I was telling myself to let the man by, I found myself standing in his path and grabbing the cheekpiece of his horse's bridle.

I'Kalmeen's animal reared, and the brigadier stared at me, more astonished than angry, not quite comprehending that anyone could be so ill-mannered or act with such entitlement. Riding beside him, the colonel of the battalion looked at Wes in disbelief, almost pleading with the CIB agent to intervene.

'Would you agree, Brigadier, that to rise through the ranks of any institution, one must become a politician?' I said.

'What are you talking about, Sulaqua?' I'Kalmeen said.

'I was just wondering if you're still a soldier, or if the lies are getting easier.'

He was about to respond, but he looked towards the bay. I'Dreng was returning with his guards.

'I assume your soldiers don't need to be taught how to ascend or descend a cliff face, Brigadier?' I said. 'They say Coor'Seyans are born clinging to rock, and if they fall, well, they're not Coor'Seyan at all.'

'I'm beginning to think you're quite mad, Inspector,' I'Kalmeen said.

I released his horse's bridle and he rode away, staring back at me, the same look of incredulity in his eyes.

'I'm beginning to think you're mad too,' Wes said.

CHAPTER FIFTEEN

WHEN WES AND I arrived at the Square, I ran up to forensics alone to see Sudeme. He glanced at me over a mound of paperwork before returning to his work with barely a flicker of emotion or recognition on his face.

'The fingerprints didn't match,' he said.

'Eh?' I said.

'The glass you stole from the Al'Mayran embassy. I recovered several fingerprints. None matched the ones left on I'Advay's body, nor the ones from the mausoleum.'

'That's not why I'm here.'

I handed Sudeme the wax paper.

'Whatever this is, I don't have the time,' he said.

'Make time,' I said.

'Tell me, Inspector Sulaqua, do you understand that your rank does not entitle you to speak to me in this way? Many in this institution, far more superior than you in every way, find it in themselves to treat me with respect.'

'You think I don't respect you?'

'I see no sign of it.'

'I've hurried this evidence to you because I have faith in your abilities and your incorruptibility. What else do you want me to do? Fawn?'

Sudeme sighed and removed his spectacles to rub his eyes, then he replaced them, opened the wax paper and stared at the red dust. After a moment's contemplation, he turned his head and fixed me with his gaze.

'Where did you get this?' he said.

'Just confirm what it is, Sudeme,' I said.

'There are several reddish minerals, both metallic and non-metallic, in the Known World,' he said, standing and drawing the blinds until his office fell into darkness. 'But there's only one that does that.'

In the gloom where Sudeme had placed the wax paper on his desk, the red dust burned like dying embers in a fireplace. Without any indication of mounting energy, a burst of red light, a pillar of illumination, fired upwards and dispersed across the ceiling.

'We found the dust in a dark room. It wasn't glowing,' I said.

'Sudden darkness, sudden light,' Sudeme said.

'So it's a lifeblood stone, or what's left of one?'

Sudeme snorted. 'Stone, you say? It's about time the scientific world defined a new category for this matter.'

'Explain,' I said, standing by him to take a closer look at the red light.

He peered down at me, the scientist about to lecture. 'The stones are found in metamorphic rock, formed by temperature and pressure changes, not in sedimentary rocks, which are formed by weathering and cementation.'

'So?'

'Metallic minerals are found in the former, not the latter.'

I processed what Sudeme had said. 'The stones are metal?'

'No, you can't melt them to form a new product, and, unlike metallic minerals, they break down into pieces when hammered, which is what I assume has happened here. And yet they conduct heat, and have their own lustre, their own shine.'

'That's an understatement,' I said, blinking.

'It's also inaccurate. Like the sun, they produce their own light. It is not, however, powerful enough to burn your flesh.'

'Could it be made so?'

'A weapon?'

I nodded.

'Well, the light from the Red Mountains is powerful enough to change Al'Mayra's climate. And making use of our natural resources is what humans do. So who's to say we can't turn the light of the stones into a destructive force?'

'What would such a force be capable of?'

'It would have the potential to be the most powerful weapon in the Known World. It could cut through a company of men and women as they knelt to reload their muskets, or burn through the hull of a ship and sink it.'

I pulled out the chair opposite Sudeme's desk and sat down. My heart was racing, my breathing rapid. I tried to slow both.

'Are you okay?' Sudeme said.

'No.'

'I can never understand you, Sulaqua. I thought you'd be pleased I didn't mock your theory.'

'Have you ever noticed confidence can be undermined by the proof of a theory as much as its rejection?'

'I can't say I have.'

'The cleric at the embassy temple said the stones were alive, conscious, and self-aware.'

'A biologist friend of mine would agree.'

'I think I'm going to leave now, Sudeme,' I said.

'Quite,' he said.

I stood up and turned to leave. 'Oh, the markings on I'Advay's robe – could they have come from sliding down a grassy part of a claw?' I asked.

'Of course.'

'I think it's best for both of us if you keep the remains of the stone safe and unlogged.'

'You ask too much too often, Sulaqua.'

'I'm being cautious, not reckless.'

'As you wish.'

'But that reminds me, I need I'Advay's charm back.'

Sunlight flickered off the silver birch trees growing in the Al'Mayran section of the Negotiated Burroughs. The day was so warm, they appeared to wilt, and their interlocking branches held on to one another for support, while behind them, the large brick-built houses radiated heat like giant ovens.

A couple of cats lay stretched on the walkways, ignoring the birds who had exchanged vigilance for shade, as if a truce had been declared between two warring armies. Even the honeybees seemed tired and lethargic, as if they'd lost their collective instinct to prepare for the long winter months.

'This is it,' I said.

'Pretty,' Wes said, taking in the fenceless grounds of Areel I'Advay's home with its border of green- and purple-leaved beech trees.

There was only a single gap between their trunks, revealing a winding path through a wildflower garden. Above, the blood-red and gold-painted stonework of the house could be seen.

It was only a short distance to the front door, but the trail twisted. All around us, high-growing, red Al'Mayran paintbrushes and wine cups were planted. We rounded one corner and found a statue of an Al'Mayran wrapped in flowers and vines, her face carved into joyful reverie. In her eyes, I saw the work of the same hand that had painted the pictures in I'Advay's office.

'If I were a burglar, I'd grow bored before I finished walking this path and return home empty-handed,' Wes said.

'That's a poor observation for a detective,' I said.

Wes sighed. 'How so?' he said.

I came to a halt and raised my hand, to gesture around us. 'Doesn't this garden tell you something about the man who lived here?'

Wes shrugged. 'Well, of course, I'Advay clearly had a keen artistic eye—'

'But in service of what? A hobby? I don't think so.'

'What then?'

'My wife follows her people's ways with her thousands of little everyday customs, but she spends her days painting the southern sea of a foreign land. Her adherence to tradition is habitual, not spiritual. This, however, this is devotion.'

As I spoke, we came upon another statue, this time of a man, his arms aloft and his mouth wide open. From it poured a growth of bright red wine cups that flowed around his neck and down his chest.

'The poor man looks like he's choking on his vomit,' Wes said.

'The flowers are his spirit. The spirits are the red lights. The red lights are the Al'Mayran people. It's all one. What must it have taken, and taken out of him, for I'Advay to destroy a lifeblood stone?'

I reached out, touched the cheek of the sculpture's face and closed my eyes. For a moment, I thought I could feel a vibration, a hum, a grinding mill of being, transferring from the stone to my hand.

'Come, Ani. We're wasting time,' Wes said.

I took my hand away and followed Wes around the next bend to a circular clearing beside the path. We came upon another figure, this time sat in repose on a marble form. The Al'Mayran was cloaked and hooded and sat so still I believed it to be another statue. But the figure unfolded their arms, took their hands from their sleeves and pulled their hood down.

She was around seventy years of age. Her long curly hair was entirely white but still somehow radiant, and her blue eyes shone so brightly against her pale skin the rest of her face appeared like an unfinished sketch. 'Welcome,' she said.

'Klareesa?' I asked.

She nodded.

'I'm truly sorry for your loss,' I said.

'Oh, we haven't lost Areel. Thanks to Dabreeyor, his spirit is safe in his heart until it can be released. Are you from the police?'

'My colleague is,' Wes said. 'This is Inspector Ani Sulaqua from the Square. I'm Special Agent Wesu Kohee from the CIB.'

'You seem troubled, child,' Klareesa said to me. 'Would you like some spiced tea and ginger biscuits?'

'That would be very kind,' I said.

The house's painted walls were covered in flowering vines. The doors and windows were wide open, and dragonflies, bees and butterflies flew in and out unchecked as if the building were part of the natural land-scape. The air inside smelt the same as outside: wildflowers and honey, with a hint of ginger.

Klareesa showed Wes and me into the parlour at the back of the house before leaving to prepare the tea. In the centre of the hardwood floor was a small Al'Mayran tea table made of twisted wicker. Beside it, there was a neat pile of thin crimson and gold embroidered cushions. I picked one up and handed it to Wes. 'Here, kneel on this,' I said. He copied me as I placed a cushion next to the table and knelt down on it with my backside on my heels.

Despite the dark reds of the curtains and the faded brown leather of the furniture, the sitting room was bright and airy, having been extended by a conservatory. In the rear garden was a fountain in the form of the warrior Ameeleyor. She held her sceptre aloft, and from it, red-tinted water flowed over her body.

The conservatory contained a single wicker chair and footstool. On a table beside the chair sat a drinking glass, stained with dry and congealed wine, which was providing a host of insect life with the drunken feast of their short lives. The scene was incomplete. The owner of the house was missing, never to return.

'I'll admit, I'Advay's presence fills this place,' Wes said.

Klareesa entered carrying a tray with a traditional Al'Mayran tea set and a large ginger biscuit, the size of a plate, made for sharing. She put the tray on the floor and placed the wooden bowl on the tea table along with three cups and three hemp cloths. Once she'd wrapped the long-spouted teapot in another cloth, she held it in both hands and began to pour, directing the flow of tea where the sides of the bowl grew vertical. Only then did she stand and raise the teapot high above her head. It was a remarkable and dexterous display meant to impress the sitters, but also to fill the room with the fragrance of cinnamon, nutmeg and cloves.

I filled my cup from the bowl and used my linen cloth to wipe the rivulets of liquid away before they fell. I took a sip and allowed the flavours to come; the warmth and the tang, the zest and the sweetness.

'Delicious,' I said.

We drank and ate in silence until we finished the first bowl of tea. Klareesa placed her cup down and asked, 'What would you like to see?'

'Areel's office,' Wes said.

'You'll find nothing in there. Normain I'Dreng stripped it bare.'

'Figures,' I said.

'The day I learnt of poor Areel's death, I'Dreng's people barged in and tore through our home. His guards have come every day since, until today. He was here the night of the storm, too, with Lieutenant I'Delboot, asking for Areel.'

'Really? I'Dreng never mentioned that,' Wes said.

'Does that surprise you?' I said, shaking my head. I addressed Klareesa again. 'Tell me, kind lady, truthfully now, did Areel have any enemies?'

'May the lights and the spirits save my sacred heart, but I have come to believe that damn embassy was riddled with enemies, except for Dabreeyor and Ameeleyor,' Klareesa said.

'Even Ambassador I'Rasnee? Why do you suspect him?' Wes said.

'One night, about a week ago, I was woken by raised voices near the fountain underneath my bedroom. I looked out of the window and saw Areel and two other figures.'

'Did you recognise them?' I said.

'I'd lit a lamp, and when I opened my curtains, its light shone into the garden. The other two stopped talking and sank back into the shadows, covering their faces with their hoods.'

'You didn't get a glimpse before they hid?'

'No, but one of their cloaks looked a lot like Ameeleyor's.'

'What were they saying?'

'I only heard Areel's voice clearly. He sounded furious. I heard him say, "I'Rasnee and his ilk will destroy the spirits and Al'Mayra with them."'

'Destroy the spirits? How?' I said.

'I don't know, but nothing would have hurt or angered Areel more,' Klareesa said, piercing me with a stare.

She gathered the cloth around the teapot and stood to pour another bowl.

'Who would I'Rasnee's ilk be?' Wes said.

'I took that to mean the ambassador's political faction,' Klareesa said, mid-pour.

'I thought he was a moderate man?' Wes said, confusion, even sadness, in his eyes.

'From what Areel was saying, I'Rasnee sounded more like a radical.'

'A radical?' I said.

Klareesa knelt down. 'Yes, Inspector. A revolutionary. Those who want to overthrow the king.'

'What about I'Dreng?'

Klareesa sniffed in disgust. 'The ambassador's dog? Him too, the same as that huge brute, I'Remo.'

'And I'Kalmeen?'

Klareesa tilted her head, thinking before answering. 'Him I can't say for certain. But I find it difficult to believe he would have harmed Areel. They were good friends once, long ago.'

I took a sip of tea. 'Did Areel's behaviour change recently?'

'He was greatly troubled in the days before his death.'

'Did he say anything to you?'

'No. He never wanted to worry me. But he was preoccupied, out at all hours, never sleeping when he was home.'

'The CIB have arrested Nitushi Nakni, Areel's lover, for his murder,' I said.

'So Dabreeyor tells me,' Klareesa said, her blue eyes glistening wet.

'What do you think?'

'Nitushi is a good boy. The only source of happiness Areel found in this city.'

'What about Mycale I'Krayag?'

'There was tension between Areel and Mycale. Areel stole much of Ameeleyor's time, which Mycale resented. But he wouldn't do anything to upset or hurt his wife. Besides, he always struck me as hot-blooded, not cold-blooded.' Klareesa paused, started to speak, and scrunched her lips.

'Is there something else you want to tell us, kind lady?' I said.

'Ameeleyor and Mycale came here the morning Areel went missing. They were clearly concerned for his safety. I think they knew he was in danger.'

'Have you told I'Dreng this?'

'No.'

'Good. Don't tell anyone else.'

'But I don't believe Ameeleyor or Mycale killed Areel. I haven't chosen to share this with you to see them arrested.'

'I understand, but I'm not in charge of this case.'

'I see.'

'You told Dabreeyor Areel took his golden cane with him that last day?' I said.

'Yes.'

I took the charm out of my pocket and showed her.

Klareesa smiled. 'That, my dear, unlocks the cane. As I think you already knew,' she said.

After we finished our tea, Wes and I searched I'Advay's rooms, but, as Klareesa had said, I'Dreng and his people had torn through them, and we found nothing of note except the artwork I'Advay had chosen to hang on his walls. Klareesa did provide specific names of eateries in the Al'Mayran arcade which her surrogate son frequented.

As we were leaving, I said to Klareesa, 'Areel was more than an envoy, wasn't he?'

She smiled. 'He was many things.'

I pressed her. 'A spy?'

'A patriot.'

'A good man?'

Klareesa looked at the garden full of wildflowers, now bending in the breeze, and sighed. 'He had much goodness in him.'

'That's not quite the same thing.'

'No, it isn't,' she said quietly, still looking at the flowers tilting and swaying.

I touched her shoulder. 'Forgive me, but do you think Areel was capable of murder?'

She took my hand but did not push it away. 'He fought in a war. He killed the enemy.'

'Was he fighting a war when he died?'

Without a pause, she squeezed my hand and answered, 'I suspect he believed so.'

CHAPTER SIXTEEN

WES AND I returned to the top of Noon Claw via the Corkscrew Steps. We didn't speak about what Klareesa told us. We didn't have to. Besides, one look at Wes told me he was still processing the notion that the people with whom he worked were killers and conspirators. The warm, open manner that usually radiated from his face had clouded over. His jaw was set, his lips turned down, and his brow furrowed. If he were confused, it was up to him to clear his mind; if he were distressed, I didn't want to sadden him further; and if he were angry, I didn't want to get in his way.

'Wes, I believe I'Advay will have taken a cab across the claw from the embassy. Dee's been searching for the driver, and while his diligence and intelligence aren't in question, he's only a cadet and the cabbies won't respect his authority.'

'What of it?'

'It's mid-afternoon. A lot of cabbies who work evenings roll into the cab house about now. We're not too far away. It's time I tried a little intimidation,' I said.

'We'll never find the cabbie if he's an independent,' Wes said.

'Maybe Xol is with us.'

'It's come to that, has it?'

The cab house was little more than a large dining hall with rows of long beer tables with benches either side. There were hundreds of drivers sitting inside, all full of complaints. They debated the costs of self-employment versus the tyranny of bosses: insurance, horse feed and cab maintenance against low pay and the prospect of dismissal without recourse. All hated the long hours, the unannounced city repairs and the customers – always the damn customers, may Xol curse them.

'Block the main exit,' I said to Wes.

'I'm not sure we have the justification,' he said.

I rolled my eyes. 'How did I get saddled with the only incorruptible CIB agent in all the Five Claws? Block the fucking exit,' I said, my voice rising in exasperation.

I left Wes grumbling and ran towards the canteen area. To the shock of all those serving, I leapt over the counter.

'Police,' I said, before the startled staff regrouped.

I found the handbell and rang it with all my strength until the hum of conversation in the hall died down. I climbed onto the counter and shouted, 'I want anyone who was working the top of Noon Claw on the evening of the storm and who took a fare from an Al'Mayran gathered at the far wall.'

There was hesitation, exchanged glances, rumblings about rights and the liberties taken by coppers, all of which I was expecting. But although cabbies could whinge with the best of them, when push came to shove, they didn't risk their livelihoods. So I gave them a shove.

'Move your fucking arses,' I said.

Heads started to pop up, slowly at first, then the dam broke. As if I were herding sheep, I ushered around fifty souls to the back of the hall. Wes was waiting with a smile creeping back onto his open face.

'Anyone take a fare from an Al'Mayran with a golden cane?' I said.

A stocky, short-haired fellow with a barrel chest raised one of his almost comically thick arms.

'Anyone else?' I said. 'No? Okay, give us your names, tell us about the Al'Mayran who hired you, and fuck off.'

The man with the thick arms settled down on a bench with his back against the stone wall and his legs stretched out. He studied me while he waited, and even from a distance, I could see the intelligence in his eyes.

Once the other cabbies returned to their meals and their complaints,

Wes took a seat on the other side of the table from the driver while I sat on the bench by his feet.

'What's your name?' I said.

'Huwaso,' he said.

'Tell me about your fare, Huwaso.'

'I picked the fellow up outside the Al'Mayran embassy sometime before ten o'clock,' he said. 'I assumed he was in a rush to get home and so was surprised when he had me pull over at Windy Park.'

'Windy Park?' I said.

'He told me he'd pay for my time if I waited for him, then he took a seat on a form outside the park. He was clearly hoping someone would show, but the wrong people came.'

'What do you mean?' Wes said.

'He kept looking south for whoever he was expecting, while constantly checking north. And he was wise to. He spotted four Al'Mayrans coming.'

'From the north?' I said.

'That's correct. They were running.'

'As in giving chase?'

'He didn't say as such, but he was on his feet and moving with surprising agility for a man with such a bad leg. He hopped over the thoroughfare and back into my cab. "Drive," he said to me. "By the spirits, drive."'

'He was afraid?' Wes said.

'He certainly had me spooked.'

'Where did you take him next?'

'To the South-Western Great Lift.'

'Did you see him enter the station?' I said.

'I did.'

'What about the Al'Mayrans who were following him?'

'Didn't look for them. I went home and decided to take a day or two off.'

'How can you be sure they were Al'Mayrans?' Wes said.

'All I saw was four long and hooded cloaks. But coming from the direction of the embassy, where I picked the man up, who else could they be?'

Once I'd asked for Huwaso's address, Wes and I paid him to take us across Chief Pawe Bridge to Pastnoon Claw. We walked over the peak and down a serpentine country lane.

'I always liked this side of Pastnoon – a pleasant contrast to the eastern side's assumed urbanism, don't you think?' Wes said.

'Fancy living amongst stinking pigsties and roaming hens, do you?' I said.

'Part of the charm. So you were right about Al'Mayran involvement,' Wes said with a sigh.

'It doesn't mean anything if I can't get Nita and Nakni freed.'

'Who do you think was following I'Advay? I can't see Ambassador I'Rasnee chasing I'Advay along Noon Claw.'

'I'Dreng, one or two of his guards. And did you ever wonder how Liam I'Remo hurt himself in the storm?'

'What about Brigadier I'Kalmeen? Mycale I'Krayag?'

I shrugged and kept my opinion to myself.

Ulawe's Perch was a small mid-level neighbourhood on the north-western face of Pastnoon Claw. Despite its location on a jutting roost, its narrow paths and wooden houses were shielded from the strong southern winds by the undulating topography of the cliff. Like most areas around Lo'tse Bay, Ulawe's Perch was underdeveloped, and there was little in the way of stone or concrete. Trees lined muddy lanes and fragrant wildflowers grew between allotments. Lower down the cliff, seaweed, whelks and clams were farmed.

The storm had left its mark. The resultant floodwaters had scored two muddy trenches, each thirty feet wide, down the claw and swept away every dwelling, outhouse and animal pen in their path. Nothing remained to indicate that only days ago, dozens of houses, some centuries old, clung to the unchanging cliffside. Now they were gone. Had the souls who once lived in those homes escaped? What belongings, if any, were they able to collect, and what did they forsake? Where were their beds, their clothes, their children's toys, the cups they drunk from and the plates they ate off? Were they swept into the sea with the dead and taken into Xol's cabins?

We found an elder sitting on the front porch of his home, a surreal unscathed remnant of a lane torn in two. I asked him where the Hiduse brothers lived, and he directed us north up a steep lane and told us to look for a shack set apart from the rest. Wes and I found the little cabin without any difficulty. It was hard to miss: the Hiduses were practicing their climbing skills on a sheer stretch of rock above their roof.

'Taliko and Kana Hiduse?' I shouted, once Wes and I were standing underneath them.

Neither man replied, although one glanced at us. Instead, they continued their ascent until they reached a natural recess, where they secured ropes and abseiled down.

They were around thirty years of age, stood no more than five and a half feet tall, and had wiry frames and long, raven hair with strands of graphite that aged them beyond their years. As did their leathery faces and weathered almond-shaped eyes, the marks of their chosen occupation.

One of them scowled at Wes and me while his brother tidied their climbing gear away, placing their packs under the back porch of their shack alongside a set of unblemished equipment: axes, pins, hooks, and a coil of unworn rope, that I suspected were new. *Were they about to embark on a new climb, a dangerous or unusual one?*

'Who are you?' the one who had scowled said, putting his hands on his hips.

'Police. CIB,' I said, nodding at Wes. 'Are you Kana or Taliko?'

'Kana. What do you want?'

'To know why you were searching the base of Salvation's Climb with an Al'Mayran.'

'I don't know any Al'Mayrans.'

'What if I bring you in, see if the witness can identify you?'

'Bring us in on what charge? Nosing around?'

'Pretty much. Trespassing. The base of Salvation's Climb is out of bounds.'

'Then go get your warrant.'

I smiled and opened my jacket to reveal my pistols. 'You're leaping into waters more dangerous than you know, Kana, and you'll likely drown,' I said.

'Is that a threat?' Kana said.

'No, but this is: if I find out you've lied to me, I'll arrest you, see you get sentenced, and make sure you're never hired by the city again.'

He sneered. I stepped forward, and Wes placed his hand on my shoulder.

'Take care, Kana,' I said.

As Wes and I were leaving, Taliko said, 'Who was murdered?'

'An Al'Mayran diplomat and a Kahokeyan advocate who thought he could profit from the former's death,' I said.

Taliko shot his brother a glance, and while he tried to keep his expression blank, there was a hint of accusation in his dark eyes.

'Nice bit of rope,' I said to him. 'For your sake, I hope the climb goes well.'

Wes and I walked down the eastern side of Pastnoon and across the Bridge of Spirits, between the twisting spirit sculptures to the Al'Mayran arcade. We checked the list of eateries Klareesa had given us and started with a small establishment on the northern side, which had a gallery overlooking Magila Bay.

I insisted on staying to fill my aching belly with wild rice and roasted duck, followed by a cinnamon slice, all washed down by a pint of coffee. I looked across the bay, between the towers and bridge pillars, towards the Depths. I thought about Shona, and, naturally, Mani and Hani, who, without realising it, I had come to associate with my long-dead love – all three were feral youngsters.

I remembered Josee's disapproving eyes. She was right. How had I come to be exploiting rather than protecting the vulnerable? But if Hani had just told me what he'd seen, perhaps it would have led me in a new direction on the case.

After Wes and I ate, we talked to the eatery's manager. He knew I'Advay but hadn't seen the envoy on the night in question, so we settled our bill, thanked him and moved west to a nearby delicatessen.

The owner recognised me from my outings with Josee. She was also familiar with I'Advay, but she'd closed early the night of the storm to board up before returning home to be with her husband and children.

I took the opportunity to buy Josee some chips of sweet potato and spiced onion. As the owner was serving me, she said, 'I saw your wife today. She was in here earlier buying nutmeg creams.'

'Oh?' I said.

'Yes, with a friend. A tall blond woman. Dabreeyor I think she was called.'

I fell silent as my face burned and the blood roared in my ears. When I tried to speak, my throat constricted, and I swallowed sand. The delicatessen's owner saw my expression and her smile waned like a feather floating to the ground. Beside me, Wes coughed and looked away, his hands behind his back.

'A new acquaintance of ours,' I managed to say, then I left.

I leant against the shop wall and stared through the arcade's bustling midday crowd. *It means nothing*, I told myself, but when I looked at the palms of my hands, I'd broken the skin with my fingernails.

'Where next?' Wes said, standing by me.

'Sophee's Sacred Heart.'

Sophee's was a restaurant Josee and I frequented on occasion, but it was not one of my wife's favourites. Its cuisine was generally subtler in flavour compared to the hot spices and sweetness she preferred.

Although the owner was not at work, the head waiter, a freckled and sandy blond Al'Mayran man called Jeremee, was, and he was in a cooperative mood. He took us away from the lively hum of the restaurant and sat us down at a reserved table in a small room with a window providing views of the arcade.

'Yes, I know I'Advay. He's a regular. Has something happened to him?' Jeremee said.

'I'm sorry to tell you he was murdered on the night of the storm,' I said.

Jeremee pulled a chair from under the table and sat down. 'By the spirits. He was here that night.'

'Are you sure?' I said, sharing a glance with Wes.

Jeremee nodded emphatically. 'Quite sure, Inspector. We only had a few other customers. The rain was really coming down while he was here, and I was concerned about him having to travel home.'

'Can you remember what time he arrived and left?'

Jeremee pinched his chin. 'I think he arrived sometime around eleven o'clock. It may have been earlier. But he left at five and twenty minutes past.'

'How can you be so precise?'

'Two reasons. We were getting ready to close, and he left without paying.'

'Really? Did you give chase?'

Jeremee laughed. 'Oh, by the spirits no. I assumed it was a mistake. He'd been so preoccupied all night. I simply opened a line of credit for him.'

'Where did he sit?'

Jeremee gestured to the table we were at. 'Why, here. He always did.'

'Can you remember what he ate?'

'Oh my, now you're asking.' The waiter put his hand to his forehead and closed his eyes. 'Let me think.' He clicked his fingers and opened his eyes. 'Stew,' he said. 'He had spiced Al'Mayran stew. He said it was the weather for it.'

'Was he alone?'

'Yes, but I got the impression he was expecting someone.'

'Why do you say that?'

'He always liked to watch people as they passed the window, but on that night, I sensed he was looking for someone in particular, and when the staff spoke to him, he was polite but taciturn, unwilling to have his attention drawn away.'

'And he left without paying?'

'Halfway through his main course.'

'Did he have a cane with him?'

'Yes, a golden one. It gleamed wet from the rain.'

Once Wes and I were outside Sophee's Sacred Heart, I said, 'Who was I'Advay so desperate to speak to that he bolted?'

'Someone who lives nearby, who could have passed?' Wes said.

'Someone we need to speak to again.'

It was Ameeleyor who opened the door to her home on Dayna's Lane. She stood blocking our view inside, clutching at the lapels of her robe, tracing the spirits with her fingers. There were heavy bags under her light blue eyes and her pale skin had developed a sickly grey tint.

'What now?' she said, raising her head and peering down her nose at me.

I forced the door open and almost fell into the hallway. When Ameeleyor protested, Wes entered and shut the door behind him.

The weapons were gone from the walls, as was the rug from the hardwood floor. An open chest, packed with clothes and ornaments, sat in the centre of the living room, with another near the kitchen, filled with ceramics and glassware wrapped in paper.

'You can't come into our home like this. You don't have the right,' Ameeleyor said.

'Who is it?' I'Krayag shouted from the floor above.

'The police again, Mycale. That inspector,' Ameeleyor said in a strained voice.

I raced up the stairs, taking them two at a time, and opened the doors of the bedrooms. I happened upon the children's rooms first. In each was the same scene – empty closets, stripped beds, and rectangles of unfaded wallpaper where pictures once hung.

I'Krayag found me in what I assumed was Caysee's room, judging by the mural of the Red Mountains on the wall. He wasn't wearing the long scarlet-and-black robes of his regiment, but a shorter loose-fitting cowl of muted browns over animal-skin leggings and boots. His scarred face was a mask of rage, and his loose hair billowed as he strode towards me and pinned me to the wall, driving the air from my lungs.

I wheezed, managed to smile at him and spat out, 'Going somewhere?'

'That's none of your concern,' he said.

Wes arrived with Ameeleyor following close behind.

'Mycale, no!' she shouted when she saw her husband. She cradled his giant head in her hands, trying to turn his face to hers and catch his manic eyes.

Wes stood at my side and placed his hand on I'Krayag's shoulder. 'Easy, my friend,' he said.

With a glance at his wife, I'Krayag released me and went to stand at the window, looking out at his garden and the small wooded area beyond where he played hide-and-seek with his youngest daughter, little Emellee.

'What do you want?' Ameeleyor said.

'Why did you go to I'Advay's home on the morning his body was found?' I said.

Ameeleyor paused, then shook her head almost imperceptibly. 'I wanted to see him before I went to the embassy.'

'What was so important?'

'As you know, I'd missed work the previous day. I merely wanted a briefing.'

'Why was Mycale with you?'

'He was on his way to the barracks to train, so we travelled together.'

'I'Advay's housekeeper is under the impression you were concerned for his safety.'

'She's mistaken.'

'Really? She doesn't strike me as someone given to dramatic flights. I think you went because you missed your rendezvous with him at Windy Park the night before.'

Ameeleyor looked startled. 'Excuse me?'

'On the night Areel was killed, he waited at Windy Park for someone who never showed. Was it you?'

'As I told you the other day, my husband and I were either here at home or with Ronayld at his shop,' she said. For the first time, a hint of panic entered her voice.

'It's probably for the best you failed to keep your appointment. If you met him at Windy Park, you might both be dead. Who from the embassy would have been chasing him?' I said.

No answer.

'Was the plan for him to hand the stolen lifeblood stone over to you?' I said, pressing Ameeleyor, trying to force her into a mistake.

'That's enough,' I'Krayag said. The Coor'Seyan strode towards me, but Wes moved between us.

'And what about you, Mycale? Did you see Areel that night in the arcade?' I said.

'No,' the Coor'Seyan growled.

'Are you sure? Because I think he came to the arcade to find Ameeleyor. Perhaps he tried your home first. And at the apothecary's, was it Areel who knocked on the door? Only you answered, and you didn't let him in. Rejected, he went to Sophee's Sacred Heart, where he sat at his favourite table and searched the crowd for Ameeleyor. But she didn't pass. She was on her way to Windy Park. So he confronted you again, Mycale.'

I'Krayag tried to push Wes out of the way, but the big Kahokeyan was at least equal in strength.

'But you were in no mood to speak with Areel, were you?' I continued. 'You resented him. Did you get angry? After all, what was your state of mind that night? Payval, your boy, was very sick. Your wife was walking into danger. The man responsible appears out of the falling rain and asks you where she is. That must have pissed you off. Did you lose your temper with him like you just lost it with me? Did you take him by the collar of his robes and hit him, bruising your hands and leaving a mark on his face with that regimental ring? Did you slit his throat?'

'No,' Mycale whispered.

'Of course not,' Ameeleyor said.

'Well, someone did. If it wasn't you, Mycale, who was it? Talk to us. What is this about? Lifeblood stones as weapons? Divisions in your homeland? Radicals?'

'We're just an ordinary couple,' Ameeleyor said.

'Caught in extraordinary events. Do you believe the spirits live in the stones, Ameeleyor?' I said.

'My beliefs are my own. They don't concern you.'

'And when a stone is destroyed, what do you believe happens to the spirits within?'

'No one knows,' Ameeleyor protested.

'How about if one were used as a weapon? What would happen to it? Would it lose its light like the one in your namesake's staff? Would the spirits inside be lost forever?'

Ameeleyor scowled. 'This is nonsense, Inspector,' she said.

'Did Brigadier I'Kalmeen want the weapon, Mycale?'

But I'Krayag didn't answer. He returned to the window and leant against the jamb. Almost resigned now that his anger had passed.

Ameeleyor stood beside him, placed her hand on his back and stared into his face before resting her head on his shoulder. He put his arm around her and gently kissed her forehead.

'Did you kidnap Je'mymor A'Soyne? I said.

No answer.

'Which one of you stormed and stole her body? My money's on you, Ameeleyor. You inherited more than your fair colouring from the Ghost Clan, didn't you?'

Ameeleyor stared down her birdlike nose at me, unblinking, impassive, inscrutable.

'Please leave my home,' she said.

That wasn't a denial.

After Wes and I left Jayson's Haven, Wes went to update Sodia, while I returned to the Square to see Imala. I found her in a pensive mood, smoking on the small terrace outside her office, several twisted cigarette ends already at her feet.

'Any progress?' she said.

'A suspect. The Coor'Seyan soldier I told you about, Mycale I'Krayag,' I said.

She turned away from me and grabbed the rail that ran around the terrace with both hands. 'An Al'Mayran?' she said. She sounded exasperated.

'One close to Brigadier I'Kalmeen.'

She took a drag on her cigarette. 'Any solid proof?'

'Not yet.'

She threw the cigarette aside and faced me. 'Well, Ani, hear this. The CIB have proof of Nakni and Nita's involvement. They found I'Advay's missing cane at the Stars and the Sea, hidden in the basement.'

'The golden one?' I snapped, immediately suspicious.

'No, a red-painted wooden one.'

I tried to keep my voice down. I failed. 'I have several witnesses, all of whom state I'Advay had the golden cane with him the day he was killed.' I took the charm out of my pocket. 'His housekeeper says this charm, which Dee and I found on I'Advay's body, opens that cane.'

Imala was not one to be intimidated, especially by an underling. She took a step closer until her face was inches from mine. 'Well, the CIB also found a letter Nakni received from I'Advay ending their relationship.'

'What?'

'That letter, combined with the red cane and the location I'Advay was found, was enough for the CIB to charge Nakni with murder and Nita as an accomplice after the fact.'

I felt my grasp on the case slipping away. I grabbed Imala's upper arm and shook her. 'Please listen to me. Wes and I found the remains of a smashed lifeblood stone in I'Advay's office. The pieces could have been hidden in the cane. I think I'Advay stole the stone from Brigadier I'Kalmeen's study. We even have a witness who will state four Al'Mayrans chased I'Advay along this very claw the night he was killed.'

Imala remained unmoved, her expression blank, her eyes unblinking behind her spectacles. 'Will any of this build a case against I'Krayag?'

'No, but it casts enough doubt on Nakni's guilt, doesn't it?'

'Time to let a jury decide that.'

Imala walked away and rested on the rail. I took a quick step forward and yanked her back around. 'I'm not leaving Nita and Nakni to rot in a CIB cell, waiting for Sodia and High Chief Naka to rig a jury to convict them.'

'Forget the high chief,' Imala growled, pulling away.

'His scientists are testing a weapon.'

The dam broke. Imala grew angry. 'Oh, for Xol's sake.'

'He's testing a weapon for Brigadier I'Kalmeen or Ambassador I'Rasnee, or both.'

Imala shook her head and laughed with disdain. 'They're conspirators, too, are they?'

'Yes, damn it. They're probably radicals. The weapon brings them what they want.'

'Which is?'

'Revolution.'

Imala took a breath and contemplated me. 'Amazing. The most senior Al'Mayran politician and their highest-ranked soldier in New Capital? You never learn, do you?'

'What's that supposed to mean?' I snarled, squaring up to her.

'Never mind, Ani.'

'Shona? Her killer?'

But Imala wouldn't answer. I dismissed her with a wave and headed for the door.

'Where are you going?' she called after me.

'The CIB,' I said.

'Ani, don't go there, not in this mood. That's an order, Inspector.'

'Ask Sudeme if he thinks the weapon is a ridiculous idea. Maybe you'll listen to a scientist.'

I could still hear Imala shouting my name as I slammed the door to her office shut and strode past Medele.

I showed my police emblem to a security guard sitting in his hut at the CIB Tower main gate. He was an older man with calm manners, who spoke softly and exuded neither agenda nor institutionalised resentment.

'Who are you here to see, Inspector?' he said.

'Special Agent Wesu Kohee. If he's here.'

'He is. At least, he hasn't left by this exit. Do you have an appointment?'

'No. We're working a case together.'

'The Al'Mayran envoy?'

I nodded.

He rapped his fingers on the frame of his window as he thought. 'You were here a few days ago,' he said.

'That's right,' I said.

He prepared a pass for me to pin to my jacket and let me into the yard. I looked up at the guards on the ramparts of the curtain wall as I passed and gave them a nod before I cleared the next two checkpoints. It was like a greenhouse inside the base of the tower, with the sun glaring through the skylights and windows, cooking the agents trapped within.

Reception sent me to Wes's department first – security services, located within the wide base of the building, but he wasn't there. One of his colleagues told me he'd gone to see Assistant Director Sodia in the murder department located in the tower above.

I avoided the hydraulic lifts and walked up the fire escape steps, but I had to stop to take my jacket off and throw it over my shoulder.

I was breathing hard and the antiseptic smell of the white-walled tower brought back memories of hospitals and sick and dying friends. At least in a hospital there were murals of Xol and Zalema and other animal gods to gaze at. There were no such distractions in the tower, just plain surfaces. My collar felt tight around my neck, my head heavy, and everywhere I went, I had the nagging sense of being observed, and once again, I had to fight off the sense of being trapped in my enemy's lair.

I found Wes in Sodia's glass-walled office at the far end of the murder department. The blinds were open and he was talking to the director, nodding often, and constantly trying to rise from his chair.

Sodia's secretary, a young and bespectacled man, waved me into the outer office when I knocked. He linked his fingers on his desk and titled his head, waiting for me to speak. But before I uttered a word, there was a tap on the dividing glass wall. Wes opened the door to Sodia's inner sanctum and beckoned me inside.

I nodded to the secretary before I entered. As I passed Wes, he fixed me with a glare. It was an expression I knew well. *Don't cause trouble.* I winked in response.

'Inspector Sulaqua, how goes it with you?' Sodia said. He squinted at me through a pair of clip-nose spectacles. The sunlight flooded through the window behind him and shone off his bald head.

'Well, sir, and you?' I said.

'Good, good. Excellent in fact, now this business with I'Advay has been cleared up.'

'Yes, sir. That's what I wanted to talk to you about. I was wondering if I could ask Nita and Nakni some questions?'

'Really?'

'Yes, sir.'

'To what end? We've found the envoy's cane, you know.'

'I understand that, sir.'

'And a letter from I'Advay ending his affair with the young man.'

'Yes, all very damning.'

There was a knock on the door and Unaduti entered, nodded to Sodia, shot me a hateful look, and left.

'Fine, I will permit your visit,' Sodia said. 'Good day to you both.'

Outside Sodia's office, as we were walking through the murder department, Wes leant over and whispered, 'So you're capable of respect after all. Perhaps you should attempt diplomacy next. Although I have no wish to exhaust you.'

'Fuck you. How's that for respect?' I said.

We took a hydraulic lift down to the holding cells. We were alone, so I asked Wes, 'Is that it, then, are you off the case?'

'I'm to compare reports with you first, but yes.' He nodded.

'Did you argue with Sodia at all?'

'I was going to point out to him that we have witnesses stating I'Advay had a golden cane with him the night he died. But suddenly, I didn't want to provide any names.'

Before I could ask Wes what he meant by that, the lift came to a halt and the doors opened, revealing the locked entranceway to the cells. The young jailor, whom I had seen earlier in the week, rose from behind his desk.

'We're here to see Nakni,' Wes said.

The jailor nodded to us but didn't speak. He unlocked the doors of the secured entranceway, led us to Nakni's cell, and let us in.

The room was a perfect copy of Nita's: no table or chairs, just a narrow cot without a blanket. The lad had recently used his bucket, and the stench of his waste was trapped in there with him. He was standing with his back to the door, staring out of the window. He glanced in our direction as the jailor let us in, but didn't turn. A glimpse of his face was all I needed to see it was inflamed with black and purple bruises and one of his eyes was swollen shut.

'Did you receive all that resisting arrest?' I said.

'Resisting everything,' he said.

'They've found one of Areel's canes at the Stars, Nitushi.'

'They found it somewhere, that's for sure,' he said in sardonic tone.

'And a letter from Areel saying he no longer wished to see you.'

'A letter I don't remember receiving.'

'Be clear with me, for Xol's sake.'

'I can't speak in front of the CIB.'

'Then you won't be allowed to speak to me either.'

'Are you my saviour, Sulaqua?' Nakni said, turning to face me with his arms folded.

'I'm your only chance to make it out of here in one piece.'

'It's a little late for that,' he said, gesturing to his face.

'Tell me about the letter.'

He took a deep breath. 'I've never seen it before and don't believe Areel wrote it.'

'Did you see Areel that night?'

Nakni shook his head.

'Do you think he was coming to see you?' I said.

'We had no plans to meet, and while Areel had many virtues, spontaneity was not amongst them,' Nakni said with a wry smile.

'The boy, Hani, do you know what he saw?'

Nakni said nothing.

'What about Nita?' I said.

I took a step closer, and he flinched. I held my hands up. 'Do you know who killed Areel?' I said in a gentler tone.

'No. That's the truth,' Nakni said.

'But Nita does?'

He looked away.

'Answer me, Nitushi, for Xol's sake,' I said.

'Ask her,' he said.

'I will, but you need to help yourself.'

'I owe Nita. All of us at the Stars do.'

'Her advocate, Hinatse, is dead. Murdered.'

'Xol help us. I begged her, I did.'

'Begged her to do what?'

'I can't, Inspector,' he said, his eyes pleading with me not to press him further. 'Tell Nita he's dead. It's up to her. Are those boys okay?'

'As far as I know.'

He breathed a sigh of relief. 'That's something at least.'

I touched his shoulder and said, 'Hold fast, shipmate.'

Once the young jailer locked Nakni's cell door, Wes ordered him to take us to Nita. The jailer nodded, and as he strolled down the corridor, he worked through the ring of keys on his belt. Before unlocking Nita's cell, he slid the shutter in the door open and said to her, 'On your feet. Turn around.'

Silence.

'I said on your feet and turn around. Can you hear me?' he repeated. 'Damn it. Answer me.'

I pushed him out of the way and looked through the door's window. Nita lay on her back, still in her gown, her face turned to the wall, her body at an angle, one foot hanging from the cot.

My stomach dropped and acid rose in my throat. I felt the press of Xol's tentacles wrapping around my head, crushing my temples, and a sound like the forging of steel roared in my ears.

'Open the fucking door,' I barked, grabbing the jailer's lapels.

'What is it, Ani?' Wes said.

The jailer had the key poised in his hand. I ripped it away from him, unlocked the door, and ran to check on Nita.

I turned her head.

Her eyes were open. Her skin was cold.

I put my ear to her chest.

Silence.

I closed her eyes, kissed her forehead, and threw the passes I had been given onto the cell floor. I barged the jailer out of the way and stormed towards the secure door at the far end of the corridor. The candle was ablaze, the anger fuelling the furnace my heart had become.

Wes picked the passes up and followed me. 'Ani, wait,' he shouted.

'Your people killed her,' I growled, without breaking a step or slowing.

'We don't know that for sure. And they're not my people. Ani, please.'

The young jailor pushed past me to open the door and fetch help. I ran after him, then took the fire escape steps down to the tower's base. I ignored the outstretched hand of the guard at the first checkpoint. He shot me an angry look as I jumped the barrier and I heard him remonstrating with Wes, who was shuffling through the passes to find the right one.

I repeated the scene at each checkpoint, daring the guards to chal-lenge me, the need for violent expression almost overwhelming. But Wes was there each time, preventing trouble before I could cause it. Once we were in the courtyard, I quickened my pace and ran through the gate, away from the bureaucratic violence that had, with obscene calm, extinguished the life of a most unusual woman. Whatever Nita's faults, she had refused to spend her days subjugated by the tyrannical administrators of state interest, and she deserved better than to die at their hands.

CHAPTER SEVENTEEN

R ONAYLD I'KRYSE DIDN'T own the only apothecary shop in New Capital. There were several. One could be found in Little Palace Gardens, a collection of stores off Agale Thoroughfare, not far from CIB Tower. I had bought a small bottle of chloroform from there, now hidden in my pocket as I strode down Agale Thoroughfare, shimmering Wes's appearance, heading for the embassy.

This time, I didn't have to fight the visions foretelling the end of my freedom. I saw well enough the disgust in Imala's unblinking gaze, the sorrow in Josee's expression as I was taken away from her, and the hate in the angry stares of my fellow prisoners. I saw this possible future as if it were already true, only this time, I didn't give a fuck. Not even about poor Wes, whose kind face I had stolen.

Blow the candle out?

Fuck the candle.

Set it all on fire.

The Coor'Seyans didn't blink as I passed them at the gate, nor did the workers and visitors coming and going through the grand entrance hall. I took great care not to bump into anyone and risk creating the schism and losing my illusion.

Typical of I'Dreng, there were no guards outside his office. Before I entered, I checked I was alone, shimmered Ambassador I'Rasnee's form, and walked in without knocking.

I'Dreng looked up from behind his desk, ready to berate the underling who dared interrupt him without an invite. But when he saw his master, the expression on his face morphed from irritation to confusion.

'Sir, is a guard with you?' he said, standing.

'Sit down, Normain,' I said in I'Rasnee's voice.

'What is it, sir?'

'Sulaqua. We need to deal with her. She's close to learning the truth about the weapon.'

'She can suspect all she wants. She and Kohee have no proof. Even her own high chief has denied it to her face. Now I'Advay's whore has been charged, this will soon be over.'

'No. She's going to keep pushing until she uncovers something.'

'What would you have me do?'

'Kill her like you did I'Advay.'

I knew it was a mistake as soon as I said it. I'Rasnee would never order a killing without leaving room for reasonable denial.

I'Dreng cocked his head and squinted. Was the schism forming in his mind?

'Sir?' he said, rubbing his eyes.

My shimmer was failing. Reality was taking over.

I had to act.

I leapt at I'Dreng, snatching my chloroform-soaked handkerchief out of my pocket and slamming it over his mouth. In the same, swift motion, I stepped behind him and pulled his head to my chest. I lost the shimmer as I fell to the floor, but it didn't matter. I'Dreng couldn't see me, and when I wrapped my legs around his arms, and kept them pinned to his sides, he couldn't move either, not with the drug taking effect. In seconds, his struggling subsided and he slipped into unconsciousness.

I shoved him aside, half wishing he were dead. I found his keys, unlocked the drawers of his desk, and rifled through them.

Nothing.

I unlocked each filing cabinet in turn, yanking the drawers out, letting them fall to the floor. All I found were staff files, thick with reviews, rotas, training plans and I'Rasnee's schedule. No I'Advay. No lifeblood stone. No weapon. Nothing.

For some reason, his damn portrait caught my attention. I stared at his proud face and his affected pose and knew. I took the painting down to reveal the safe.

'Shit,' I said.

I wasn't getting in without the combination.

In a fit of anger, I picked up I'Dreng's fountain pen from his desk, flipped the lever, and threw the ink over his portrait. It was either that or his actual face.

'Fuck you,' I said, standing over his unconscious body.

I gave him another dose of chloroform, shimmered his appearance and left, locking him inside.

I made my way to I'Rasnee's office, swaggering like I'Dreng, full of self-importance. The guards outside stood up straight and saluted as I passed. I didn't even nod in response, nor did I acknowledge the secretaries who seemed used to such entitled behaviour.

I rapped on the door to I'Rasnee's office.

'Enter,' I'Rasnee said.

I swung the door open, let it shut behind me, and marched to I'Rasnee's desk.

'Whatever is the matter, Normain?' he said.

'Sulaqua, sir. She's a menace.'

'We knew she would be. What's changed?'

'She needs to be taken care of.'

'By the spirits, Normain. Whatever is the matter, my friend?'

I'Rasnee surprised me by leaping to his feet and running around the desk, his face full of genuine concern. I had underestimated the friendship between the two men. I shouldn't have. They were from the same class, and that, at least in private, transcended nominal station.

I'Rasnee put his hand out, palm towards me, and continued to approach with the intention of placing his hand where he thought I'Dreng's heart would be – a greeting or sign of great affection. Unfortunately, what I'Rasnee thought was I'Dreng's chest was my head, and the moment he touched it, he would break my illusion and I would be revealed.

I backed away, almost tripping.

'Normain?' I'Rasnee said, squinting as if trying to look at the sun.

'Sorry, sir, I've forgotten something,' I said.

I returned to the secretaries' office and quickened my step to a trot.

'Normain, wait!' I'Rasnee had followed me, blinking, the schism taking effect.

In the corridor, Liam I'Remo was walking without crutches towards me, so I turned left.

Behind me, I'Rasnee shouted, 'Liam, whoever that is, it's not I'Dreng!'

I quickened my step around the next corner and came face to face with a middle-aged Al'Mayran woman. Startled, she moved aside and, as I passed, I shimmered her appearance, no longer worrying if anyone saw me. I joined a group of Al'Mayrans heading towards the entrance hall.

As we reached the top of the stairs, a woman shouted, 'Look, that's not me,' in an angry tone.

I glanced in her direction and the woman, whose appearance I was casting, pointed me out to I'Remo and the two guards from outside I'Rasnee's office.

The group I was with stalled halfway down the stairs to see what the commotion was. A number of Kahokeyan visitors were trying to push past them, so I squeezed between the two parties and, hoping all were looking the other way, shimmered the appearance of the last man I passed: a slight Kahokeyan with cropped grey hair who wore a conventional black suit.

I made it as far as the portico and was about to descend the steps when one of I'Rasnee's office guards shouted, 'There!'

I didn't wait to find out who he meant. I jumped off the steps and ran north to the stables; a young Al'Mayran lad, not too far from manhood, was leading a grey mare into a stall. I shimmered his form and waited.

When one of the guards appeared, I pointed towards the northern wing of the embassy, and shouted, 'That way, that way! He went that way!'

As soon as the guard passed, I took one of my pistols out and struck his head with the grip. He went down, and I returned to the front of the portico, now casting his image. I'Remo was standing at the entrance to the southern garden. When he saw me, I shrugged and shook my head. He gestured that I should turn back and circle the embassy. I nodded and set off as instructed, but when I'Remo disappeared from my view beyond the portico, I changed direction towards the embassy gate and freedom.

It was a fair walk, made longer by tension. To distract my mind, I blew the candle out and focused on my shimmer. Still, little concerns burst forward like tiny fireworks popping: What if the guard had woken? What if I'Remo had found him? At least the Coor'Seyans were at the gate.

When I was thirty feet from the exit, running footsteps sounded on the drive behind me.

'Stop that man!' someone ordered.

Two of the soldiers started to close the gate while their comrades scanned those who were exiting and entering. But they didn't know who they were searching for, so I pointed to a random soul, a young blond Al'Mayran chatting happily with his female colleague, and shouted to the Coor'Seyans, 'Him! Quick, grab him!'

As the blond man was wrestled to the ground, I ran past, and, turning my body sideways, leapt through the closing gate to Agale Thoroughfare.

There was a party of older Kahokeyan children crossing the road with their tutor on the way to the department of education – a stone building with a columned entrance in the shape of Xol. I ran behind them and shimmered the appearance of a tall and gangly boy, dressed in fashionable animal skins, who had long, loose hair and a spotty face.

A cab driver, who had stopped to let the group cross, and his fare, a young woman in a white summer dress sown with little stars, saw my appearance change. I winked at them and put my finger to my mouth, but they couldn't help pointing and drawing attention to me as they blinked and tried to clear their vision.

There were raised voices coming from the embassy. It was stupid, but when I reached the opposite walkway, I glanced back. I'Remo noticed and came running.

I cut down the side of the department of education, using a row of beech trees to shield the direction of my flight. All the while, heavy foot-steps closed in. I chanced another glimpse behind me and saw I'Remo and the guards emerging from the treeline. I was seconds away from being caught, but the cliff-edge path I was heading towards was too far away. Out of desperation, I clambered over the wall into the grounds of the department of education, swinging my legs out of I'Remo's grasp before dropping onto the other side.

I took off around the back of the gardens, behind patches of high-growing bushes, past a groundsman who was on his knees, busy weeding the soil below a willow tree. I took on his appearance as I emerged back onto the lawn, just as I'Remo and the guards cleared the wall opposite. Ignoring them, and those who were challenging their entrance, I found a side gate, left the gardens, and turned south on Agale Thoroughfare. I blended in with the flow of pedestrians, a drop of rain in a river.

I held my jacket and tie in my hand as I strolled through Malaye's Heart and up the steep lane leading to Horizon's Outlook. As I neared the top of the hill, a figure appeared, silhouetted against the lemon sky. It was Dabreeyor A'Mendayse, and she waved and smiled when she saw me. But I only nodded in return, unable to duplicate the enthusiasm of her greeting.

'Are you well, Inspector?' she asked.

'Not really,' I said.

'I'm sorry to hear that.'

'You've been out with Josee?'

'Most of the day. We went to see an Al'Mayran play in the park. I hope that's okay?'

'Why wouldn't it be?'

'Because you seem angry.'

'I am, but not at you.' I puffed my cheeks out and exhaled hard, breathing in the iodine and sulphur from the Coiled Sea, which was floating through the sweltering atmosphere.

'What do you know about radicals in Al'Mayra?' I said.

'Just rumours. Modernisers who have lost patience with the king,' Dabreeyor said.

'Do you think they believe in the stones?'

'Everyone is different. Some may believe; others will just see superstition.'

'And Areel?'

Dabreeyor smiled. 'He was definitely not much of a moderniser, let alone a radical.'

'And Ambassador I'Rasnee?' I said.

'I'm not sure. He strikes me as a practical man, so by definition, that makes him a moderate, but a radical? I can't see it. Well, I must go. Josee is cooking dinner for you both. I must say, it smells divine.'

'I'm surprised you aren't dining with us.'

'I have no wish to outstay my welcome, Inspector. Not after Josee has been kind enough to keep me company all day.'

'She's always been generous with her time.'

I said goodbye to Dabreeyor and crossed the drawbridge. It was late, and the sun was already low, so I sat at the table on the western terrace and watched as the horizon caught fire. I said a prayer to Xol for Nita, and took solace that I had shown her some kindness in her last days. I set about loading my pistols with powder and ball.

'Ani, how long have you been home?' Josee said, stepping onto the terrace from the dining room with the day's post in her hands.

'About half an hour,' I said.

'Why are you out here all alone? What's wrong?'

'Nita is dead.'

Josee sat next to me, put the envelopes and a small box on the gateleg table and lowered her head.

'That poor woman. I'm so sorry, Ani,' she said.

'I brought you these,' I said, placing the bag of sweet potato chips and spiced onion on the table.

'Thank you, they'll make a nice appetiser. I've slow-cooked a pot of crab for dinner.'

'I have to leave now.'

'What? You've just arrived. You can't disappear again. I haven't seen you since yesterday.'

'Well, now you won't see me until tomorrow.'

'Why are you lashing out at me?' Josee said, snatching at the box. 'Where's Mani?'

'Etu will be here with him any moment.'

'Fine. What did you do today?'

'I saw a play.'

'On your own?'

Josee sighed and undid the string around the box. 'As I think you already know, I was with Dabreeyor,' she said.

'After promising me you wouldn't see her.'

'I didn't promise anything.'

'Xol knows you implied it. You certainly let me believe it. And you weren't going to admit it. You were going to lie.'

'And this is why. I bumped into her and she invited me to the play. What was I supposed to do, refuse?'

'Why not?'

'Oh, fuck off, Ani. I'm done with this conversation. We've had it too many times. I'm not having it again,' Josee said, throwing the string from the box aside.

I holstered the last pistol I loaded, the flintlock, and stood up.

'You're really leaving?' Josee said.

'I thought you wanted me to fuck off?'

'You're such a bloody child.'

As I stalked away with the vice once again tightening around my temples, Josee let out a sharp cry, pitched somewhere between shock and disgust. I turned as she clamped her hand over her mouth and squeezed her eyes shut tight, causing her freckles to twist into lines and tears to run down her face. She had dropped the box. It was lying on its side, Snuggs's head beside it, his heart torn in two and stuffed in his mouth.

I sighed and cast my eyes down. Snuggs had been missing for days. I'd been expecting something like this. Still, I wish I'd been the one to open the box and spare Josee the shock.

She walked to the corner of the terrace where she stood, silhouetted by the burning sky as her robes swelled in the breeze. She put her hands on the balustrade and turned her face to the sun, as if the warm rays would renew the energy lost by such a cruel blow.

I searched for words. I found none.

'What evil have you brought into our home, Ani?' she said, gazing out at the Coiled Sea.

I didn't answer, just picked up Snuggs's head and put it back in the box.

'Say something,' Josee said.

'What?'

'Something. Anything. Tell me you're sorry for Snuggs, poor little thing, who never harmed anyone, not even a bird.'

'Of course I'm sorry. And I'm angry. But this is calculated intimidation.'

'Is that all you feel when you look at such butchery? Anger?'

'I've just seen a lot of trauma.'

'Too much. It's not good for you. What if that were Mani? What would you feel? Or are you impassive to dead children, too?'

I saw Shona floating in the sea, and the boy I had stumbled over while chasing Hani in the Depths, but I couldn't find the words.

Mani ran onto the terrace with Etu chasing him. He smiled at me and went to stand with Josee. After taking one look at her face, he said, 'What's wrong?' When Josee didn't answer, he stared at me.

I turned away, picked the box up and handed it to Etu. 'Stay the night, will you?' I said.

I followed a different route down the eastern face of Pastnoon Claw than I had the previous night, but the winding lanes I strolled along were all the same. Oil lamps were battling the dusk, families were still gathered on common greens and in tavern gardens, and children were squeezing the last drop of joy they could from the fading evening. I entered the Depths and quickened my pace as the twilight succumbed to darkness.

I didn't want to appear as Mani again in case his brother had told the rest of the Vermin to look out for me. Instead, I chose to shimmer an old drunk I knew. While I hoped his presence wouldn't cause any alarm, I skirted around Busted Jaw anyway, walking past the storm drain where the rival gang ambushed Hani and me, and climbing up the pier.

I found the lad in his improvised home: the platform he had built between two pillars below the wooden deck. He jumped when he saw me and reached for his knife.

'It's Inspector Sulaqua,' I said, revealing myself to him.

He barely blinked as the mirage disappeared. The lad was hard, no doubt about it.

'You almost died last night. Why come down here again?' he said, pointing his blade at me.

'No, Hani, *you* almost died. I saved you.'

'I wouldn't have needed saving if you'd stayed in the Heights where you belong.'

'I live in the Mids, Hani, not the Heights, and I grew up on the lower levels of Sundown Claw.'

'A fucking paradise. You're not like me and Mani.'

'I was born here. My mother was from the Depths.'

'You spit on her every time you come back.'

'I came to tell you Nita is dead.'

The boy held my stare in silence for a few seconds. He said, 'People die all the time in the Claws.'

'I thought you'd want to know. After all, she took you and Mani in.'

'We worked for her.'

'The point is she was killed because of what she knew.'

'She was killed because she was an idiot.'

'Agreed. But if you have the same information as her, do you think your fate will be any different? Sooner or later, they'll come for you, too.'

'I took an oath.'

'To who?' I said.

'It doesn't matter.'

'Wrong. That's all that matters. You don't prove your worth to someone who has none.'

'You don't understand anything.'

'I know you're making the same mistake Nita did, thinking you can survive this storm without shelter.'

He pointed the blade at me again and raised his voice. 'It's different. I'm not trying to make a bargain,' Hani said.

'Bargain? You mean blackmail? Who, Hani? Who did she try to blackmail?' I said.

'Like I said, Nita was an idiot,' he said with a snort.

'And what about Nitushi? Does he deserve to die, too?'

'If it's Xol's will.'

I grabbed the boy by the arm and twisted his hand until he dropped the knife. It ricocheted off a pillar before splashing into the water below.

'Xol helps two kinds of people,' I said. 'Those who exercise their agency and those who have it taken from them. You fall into neither category. It's your will, not Xol's, because you have a choice: save an innocent man or let him die.'

'No, you have a choice. Let Hani go or die.'

I spun at the sound of the new voice and drew a pistol from my baldric, but the skinny, long-haired lad, who was crouching on a beam, fired before I could get my shot off. The ball grazed my shoulder, and it splintered the post above Hani's head. As the fresh wound burned, I considered shooting the boy, but he was so young, no more than fourteen, and his skinny form, revealed by the light cotton shirt he wore, was yet to fully develop. He was serious though, taller than I, and no doubt knew how to fight.

'No, Itzel, wait,' Hani said.

I turned to see another boy, dressed only in deerskin leggings, who was about the same age as the skinny lad but shorter, stockier, and with cropped hair. He'd approached along the beams from the opposite direction and was trying to keep his balance while handling an old musket that was far too big for him.

'I don't want to hurt anyone,' I said.

'I think you're confused, copper,' the skinny lad said.

As he spoke, two more of the gang, a boy and a girl dressed in animal-skin rags, swung from the deck above. Their matted, unkempt manes trailed behind them, falling to their shoulders, emphasising their wild appearance. Both had pistols. As soon as their feet touched the makeshift platform, they pointed them at me.

'Don't kill her, Dasan. She's an inspector,' Hani said to the skinny lad.

'Why are you talking to her?' the girl said.

'She's been after me for ages. She's the one I ran from. What was I supposed to do, take her on myself?'

'I guess we'll have to deal with her for you.'

'No, take her to Kononwa.'

'Hani's right,' Dasan, the skinny lad, said. 'Now, copper, drop your baldric and your sword and dagger and climb, very slowly, onto the deck.'

Beside me, Hani whispered, 'Now we're even.'

Kononwa lived near the dock in an incongruously well-kept, two-storey terraced house with a garden full of flowers and vegetables enclosed by a neat wooden fence. Dasan knocked on the door while the rest of the gang held back and Itzel pointed his musket at my head.

'Put that down, will you? Where am I going to run to?' I said.

'Nowhere, copper,' Itzel said.

'Not if you accidentally blow my fucking head off.'

'If I blow your fucking head off, it won't be by accident.'

'Very reassuring.'

'Just lower it,' Hani said.

With a snarl and a shake of his head, Itzel obeyed. 'I think you like this copper too much, Hani,' he said.

'Both of you be quiet,' Dasan said.

There was the creak of a bedroom window opening and the flash of a musket barrel in the moonlight.

'Who is it?' Kononwa said from the darkness.

'Dasan and his band. We've captured a copper.'

'Stay there.'

A moment later, a lamp flickered to life in the bedroom, and footsteps sounded on a wooden staircase, followed by the rattle of a key turning in a lock. The front door swung open, and there stood Kononwa, bare-chested, with a long-barrelled musket pointing at the ceiling and its butt resting in the crease of his arm. The gleam of the oil lamp he had set on the kitchen table highlighted the warm tone of his skin around the edges of his bandaged arm.

He smiled and shook his head. 'Come in, Sulaqua, and sit down. I'll make us some coffee. Then we'll go and wake Yoyu. Give the inspector her weapons back, she isn't our prisoner.'

The young girl who had wrapped my sword, my fighting dagger, and my pistols in a worn and flea-ridden blanket dropped my weapons at my feet.

'Thanks,' I said.

She curled her lip and spat on the ground.

'Charming,' I said.

'Here, take this and buy some fresh fish for your band's breakfast,' Kononwa said, throwing Dasan a sixpence.

'Many thanks, Kononwa. I knew it was best to come to you and not kill her,' Dasan said. He spun on his heel and faced me. 'Don't enter Busted Jaw again. We might not be so kind next time. A copper's body sinks as well as any other.'

The gang strolled away. Hani stole a furtive glance over his shoulder at me as Dasan put his arm around the girl.

'Not the sharpest fishing spear in the ocean that Dasan, is he?' I said.

'He caught you,' Kononwa said.

'He did. Now what?'

'You're under my protection, so come in and wait. Yoyu will rise in a couple of hours. It's best if I take you to him, unless you want to take your chances out there.'

Kononwa put a pot of coffee on the stove and carefully dressed my wound under the light of the oil lamp, having first disinfected it with alcohol. We talked about summer vegetables and how lucky he'd been that his garden hadn't been damaged or washed away in the storm.

The regimental sword of a Five Claws Eastern Cavalry officer was on the wall over a worn but pretty double larder, and I wondered what brought him into the service of a man like Yoyu. But the sword could have been a parent's or a fallen lover's, so despite my curiosity, I decided not to pry. What right did I have to trespass uninvited into his past? It wasn't relevant, and I didn't want to repay his kindness with an implied slight, even though I suspected him to be a killer for hire.

The black sky was turning purple by the time Kononwa escorted me to Yoyu's Manor. Mackerel clouds were sweeping in from the south and the first light of the rising sun was reflecting off their bellies and on the rooftops of Noon Claw.

The harbour in Magila Bay was already teeming with life. Trade ships, some local, some foreign, had either docked or were in the process of anchoring to unload their cargoes. The captain of a Harn ship, transporting high-quality ceramics, was engaged in a heated debate with a group of stevedores around an open crate with a cracked corner spilling straw onto the deck of the vessel. The captain's voice became shrill and frantic but was falling on deaf ears, and his attempts to move the indifferent loaders by waving broken pieces of porcelain at them seemed destined for failure.

Scores of children were running from ship to ship in search of fallen merchandise or an opportunity to thieve. Some of the sailors laughed at their efforts and cheered them on, even threw them pieces of salted meat and biscuits; others shooed them away, as they did the predatory gulls.

Kononwa nodded at the guards outside Yoyu's Manor before taking me up to the second floor. He asked me to wait in the hallway, so I sat on a spindle-back chair and considered how Yoyu might fit into the case and how much I dared to provoke him to find out. I figured too many people had seen me enter his manor for him to have me killed, so what did I have to lose?

Kononwa came out accompanied by a young woman who tore down the hall, her open gown flowing behind her, before she disappeared into another room.

'In you go,' Kononwa said to me.

Yoyu was on his balcony, looking at the harbour. His hands were folded behind his back which emphasised the bulk of his massive shoulders. He was barefoot and wore a pair of deerskin leggings and a loose-fitting white hemp shirt decorated with a pattern of meticulously sown yellow butterflyfish.

'Good morning, Inspector,' he said without turning. 'I can't say I am pleased to see you.'

'Same here,' I said.

'Why are you down here again?'

'Police work.'

'Does that normally include harassing children? What did you want with the lad?'

'What's it to you?'

'Nothing, I'm sure.' He rotated his bulk to look at me and smiled.

'Once again, I would inquire about a possible change in police policy, but I fear I would be repeating myself.'

'Then I'll be on my way.'

'I may raise this matter with a city official.'

'Why not with your master, the high chief himself?' I said.

'You think High Chief Naka and I have cause to talk often?'

'I think you're his obedient dog. I think he comes to you to get his killing done when he can't use the CIB. Ever heard of an advocate called Hinatse?'

'I believe the gentleman was well known in certain circles. Notorious, one might say. Nevertheless, I do hope no harm has befallen him.'

'What scraps has Naka promised you in return? You're a fool if you think it's the weapon.'

I didn't expect the truth from Yoyu, nor did I anticipate the slow, thunderous laughter that drummed in his chest and rocked his shoulders.

CHAPTER EIGHTEEN

When I emerged from Yoyu's Manor, sunlight was breaking through the gaps between the theatres and galleries along Noon Claw's skyline, and the clouds were still glittering in the dawn's glare, making them appear to bobble as they glided by. The sea, too, was sparkling, the gentle waves flashing as they split upon the bow of Kononwa's little cutter.

'Beautiful morning,' Kononwa said.

I nodded.

'Sometimes I come out just to sail, feel the breeze, the glide, you know?' he said.

'When I was a little girl, I'd often go out with my uncle during the school holidays. He'd put me to use. I helped to clean and salt our catch, but what I really loved was to lie on the bowsprit and pretend I was flying close to the waves.'

'You're Lo'tse?'

'That's right.'

'And you're a copper. How does that happen?'

'Want to tell me why you're a crook? And a murderer?'

'Who says I'm either?'

I raised my eyebrow and he laughed.

'You do have a way about you, Sulaqua,' he said.

I shrugged and lay back to feel the sun on my face. I must have fallen asleep because the next thing I knew Kononwa was tapping my shoulder with his fingers.

'Come on, Sulaqua,' he said, in a low voice.

He'd already tied bowlines from the cutter to a piling on a jetty near the South-Western Great Lift. I nodded and rubbed my eyes, then stepped onto the platform and helped him unmoor.

'Tell me, Kononwa, were you sailing by Red Tern Tower a couple of nights ago?'

'Why do you ask?'

'I'd been to see an advocate called Hinatse. He was dead. When I was leaving to report to a substation, I thought I saw this vessel.'

'Perhaps you were mistaken.'

'Perhaps. How'd you get that wound on your arm? Pistol ball?'

He laughed and went about setting his rig. 'Stay safe, Sulaqua,' he said.

'You too, Kononwa,' I said, once I had walked out of earshot.

I took the lift to the top of the claw but was too tired to walk, so I hailed a cab and had the driver drop me off near a street vendor. I bought a bowl of prawns and fried bread. Once I had eaten, I entered the Square, walked through the courtyard and climbed onto Imala's small terrace. I lay down on her form and fell asleep.

I dreamt of dead children and headless cats and of my home on Horizon's Outlook on fire with Josee trapped inside, staring through the flames at me. Shona emerged from the sea and asked me whether I was Ani, her childhood friend. Her flesh was fetid and hanging from her bones. Tiny bobtail squid and sea spiders emerged from the holes in her frail body.

'Don't you recognise me?' I said.

'You've changed so much,' she said.

I wanted to ask her what she meant, but Imala woke me and handed me a mug of black coffee.

'You look terrible, child,' she said.

I made room for her on the form, and the two of us sat in silence for a few minutes as we drank. Imala rolled a cigarette and smoked it with long and deep draws. Once she'd finished, she stubbed the end out and dropped it into her empty mug.

'You've been in the Depths, using magic to investigate. And you saw Yoyu,' she said.

'How'd you find out so quickly?' I asked.

'Yoyu must have sent word to Naka. One of the high chief's errand boys subsequently informed the police chief at her home. She waited for me outside my office, less than thirty feet from where you were sleeping.'

'What did she say?'

'She asked why I was unable to restrain you. I reiterated to her you had good reason to suspect the boy Nakni was innocent of Areel I'Advay's murder and that I'd given you permission to prove your theories.'

'Thank you.'

'I also told her you were the best inspector I had.'

'What did she say?'

'She told me a shimmerer assaulted I'Dreng at the Al'Mayran embassy, ransacked his office, and beat one of his people.'

I took a sip of coffee and stared straight ahead.

'There was also an attempt to gain access to the academy the other night,' Imala said.

'Good coffee,' I said.

'Damn it, Ani, I know it was you.'

'Prove it.'

'Now you sound like a criminal, which you are. And for what? Nothing you find out while shimmering can be used as evidence.'

'I'm well aware of that,' I said, before finishing my coffee.

'Then why do it?'

There was more emotion in Imala's voice than usual. Had I heard concern? Was it genuine? I stared at her, unsure how to react. 'Is this a trap?' I said, putting my mug down. 'Are you trying to trick me into a confession?'

She shook her head. 'I'm worried about you, child. This path you've taken, where does it lead?'

'To the truth, I hope.'

Imala took a deep breath. 'But at what cost?' she whispered. 'To you, to me, our careers, maybe your life.'

I felt my anger rising and I noticed I was squeezing the edge of the form and my knuckles had turned white. 'And what about Nita's life?' I hissed.

'I know, Ani. I'm sorry.'

'The CIB killed her.'

'You'll never prove it. Let her go. You can't bring her back.'

'I'll settle for bringing her justice.'

'From what I understand, she brought her fate on herself.'

'Are you saying she deserved to die?' I sneered at the suggestion and spat on the ground.

'No, Ani, she didn't deserve it. Perhaps she could have avoided it.'

'And Nakni?'

'You may have to let him go, too.'

'Is that an order?' I said, the disdain potent in my voice.

'No. Advice. You can't spend your life swimming against the tide. You'll tire and drown.'

'You give up too easily. And it's the innocent who drown,' I said, standing and tidying my shirt and jacket.

Imala rolled her eyes. 'Oh, such nobility. Keep pretending you fight for the poor. You'll fool most, but not me, Ani, not me. I've known you since you were a child. When you destroy yourself, just remember it was to spit in the eye of the rich and powerful and prove to them that Inspector Sulaqua is always right.'

'Are you done?' I said, staring at my feet.

'I knew I'd be wasting my breath.'

'Am I off the case?'

'I couldn't very well protest your innocence one minute and punish you the next. But if you're caught shimmering to investigate, you won't be reassigned, you'll be off the force and lucky to stay out of jail. And I'll end up in procurement or transport coordination. No more shimmering, child, do you hear me?' She wagged her finger at me.

'Don't talk to me like that. You're not my mother,' I snapped.

'But you're ungrateful enough to be my daughter.'

'Perhaps it's time I reported to another chief inspector.'

Imala laughed, a squeaky and underused cackle. 'Who would have you?'

Wes had been chatting with Medele in the secretary's little adjacent office while I had been with Imala. He smiled when he saw me, but for once, his avuncular nature seemed forced. I greeted him with a nod and walked past him and into the department. The few conversations flowing between my colleagues dried up when I appeared. I suspected tales of my adventures were spreading like Red Bee Balm in the shade.

'Let's get out of here, Wes,' I said.

My legs felt too heavy for stairs so Wes and I strolled over to the paternoster lifts. As we passed the cadets' desks, Dee made sure he caught my eye. I smiled and beckoned him with a flick of my head.

'Yes, ma'am,' he said, standing to attention before me.

'If I'Advay was murdered at the arcade, there are only so many places where you can slit a man's throat and carry his body unseen to Salvation's Climb,' I said.

'Very true, ma'am,' Dee said.

'Would you like to join Special Agent Kohee and me on a hunt?'

Wes, Dee and I took the South-Western Great Lift down the side of Noon Claw. We leaned on the balustrade and stared out at Magila Bay and the bridges and skytowers. It was not yet mid-morning, but the sun was high and scorching our dark hair, so I took my jacket off, unbuttoned the top of my shirt and rolled my sleeves up to my elbows. Dee copied me, taking his long tunic off, but Wes shifted uneasily and fiddled with his collar.

'Take your jacket off, man. That uniform doesn't seem to fit anymore,' I said.

'By that, I assume you mean I no longer fit the CIB?'

I shrugged.

Wes smiled. 'I'll take that as a compliment.'

'Oh?'

'A friend of mine is a medical examiner. He was on duty yesterday.

He told me an outside doctor was brought in to perform Nita's autopsy, someone neutral apparently.'

'You don't sound convinced.'

'It stinks, Ani, even to me. All I could do was tell Nakni about Nita.'

'That was good of you.'

'I have other news,' Wes said, sighing and looking away.

'Clearly.'

'The infiltration at the embassy is big news.' When I didn't speak, he went on: 'Sodia sent for me. He told me to report back to him if I witnessed you shimmering during this investigation.'

'What did you say?'

'That I would.'

'Will you?'

'No. I'm done, Ani. I'm out.'

'Why did you ever join?'

'As I told you, I grew up on Pastnoon, eastern side, and after my father died, my mother, my sister and I had to move into a small flat near the border with the Depths. I was a big lad, and I joined a watch to tackle the youngsters who came up to the Mids to go mugging. It felt good, you know, helping, so I joined the cadets. Back then, before Naka, it was different. The CIB focused on gangs and organised crime. Like you, I found a mentor. My Imala. But her generation is almost gone, and I'm an atavistic presence in a conquered land.'

'I know the force isn't perfect, Wes. But of late, we've been lucky with personnel, from the top down.'

'Why did you join?'

A Kahokeyan family sat near us. Wes and I watched as their youngest daughter practised her tribal dancing in a tasselled white dress adorned with a picture of a leaping dolphin on the chest.

'I had a friend: Shona,' I said. 'A first love, if you like. We were still youngsters, not much older than that lass. It was all very innocent. But feelings are feelings. She was murdered, and I saw her killer throw her body into a sack and toss it into the Coiled Sea. I followed him to a hotel atop Noon Claw, then I went to the Square and found Imala. She was just a junior inspector, not long out of uniform, but she believed my story and went with me to the hotel.

'The woman on reception showed us to the owner's office. That's when I saw the portrait of the killer. He was the owner's son, and he had an alibi. Of course, it was fish shit. Imala wanted to arrest him, arguing they had a witness: me. But her chief inspector said I was just some poor child from Sundown who was either mistaken or lying. The following day, Imala, Ezno and I looked for Shona's body. We didn't hold out much hope, but Xol, and the tide, were with us, and we found the sack. Imala made sure Shona was turned over to Ezno, who asked me if I wanted her buried at sea like a Lo'tse. But I said Shona was from the Depths, and they burned their dead, so we cremated her atop Sundown.'

'And you've been looking for justice ever since,' Wes said, a gentle smile on his kind face.

'I let people think that. But the truth is, I like looking into the eyes of the rich and powerful as I put the fear of Xol into them.'

Wes laughed.

'I like knowing they have to listen to me, no matter my tribe or class. And when I arrest one of them, it's like a narcotic hit,' I said.

'That's still justice, Ani,' Wes said.

'Perhaps. And while I'm being so honest, you should also know my family are harbouring Memi and some others from the Stars, and my wife and I have one of the brothers Nita took to see Hinatse.'

'In Xol's name, Ani,' Wes said, raising his hand to his forehead.

CHAPTER NINETEEN

Eᴀsᴛ ᴏғ ᴛʜᴇ arcade was one of many corridors, hewn out of the southern face of Noon Claw, leading to Salvation's Climb. Decades ago, a brick wall was built to block access to the cliff passage from Carmeyn's Way, a seafront walkway below the Bridge of Spirits, but the wall had been partly destroyed by youngsters or criminals, and it was easy to navigate its remains.

As usual on a warm, still morning, the seating areas along Carmeyn's Way at the back of the cafes and restaurants were crowded with Al'Mayrans, either taking a break from shopping or meeting friends to share coffee and gossip. All along the way, folk were standing, trays and cups in their hands, searching for an open table or queuing at rear serving counters and bars. Others were gazing at the Coiled Sea or watching ships pass under the bridge as their children ran wild, weaving through tables and chairs and jumping over stone forms. All the while, the music of unabashed laughter and buoyant voices accompanied the chaos.

'The murderer would have accessed the steps here,' I said.

'Hard to imagine someone dragging a body this way,' Dee said.

'With a storm approaching, this place would have been deserted,' I said.

'Say that's true – what evidence could survive days of this onslaught?' Wes said.

'The man had his throat cut. Where did all that blood go? All we need is a drop,' I said.

Wes, Dee and I searched the length of Carmeyn's Way. Dee stayed close to the balustrade above the Coiled Sea, Wes scoured the middle of the path, while I made a nuisance of myself in the seating areas. I checked under tables and canopies, in entranceways and nooks, along windowsills and down drainpipes – two hours of work for naught.

'The odds weren't in our favour, Ani,' Wes said.

'I never claimed they were,' I said.

'That wasn't a criticism.'

'I need food and strong coffee.'

'I swear you have a parasitic worm in your guts.'

'If I do, she's hungry.'

My lack of sleep was catching up with me, and I couldn't organise my thoughts well. I suggested an eatery at the far eastern end of the arcade with plenty of shaded seating outside. I had a bowl of fried Al'Mayran chicken with chilli and ginger, while Wes tore through a brace of spiced rabbit and Dee made short work of a cod loin that hung over the edges of his plate. But it was the coffee I wanted, and I ordered a large pint mug of it with a sweet pastry made from the leaves of the morning star plant – a rather potent stimulant.

We spoke little during lunch, except to comment on the heat of the day and the cloudless sky. Before long, I was washing the final piece of pastry down with the last of the coffee. I rubbed my eyes and stretched. When my gaze returned to the crowd, I spied Josee approaching the eatery arm in arm with Dabreeyor.

They hadn't spotted us yet, so I threw a shilling on the table and grabbed Wes by the arm.

'Let's get back to it,' I said.

'I think you should avoid coffee, Ani Sulaqua,' he said, winking at Dee as he rose from his chair.

Despite his jest, he didn't resist, and we were soon clear of the eatery's colourful, spirit-decorated awning. But I glanced back, and when I did, Josee saw me. She waved, but I turned away, pretending I hadn't seen her, and strode on.

We returned to the spot where we started, our backs to Noon Claw and the cliffside path, looking down Carmeyn's Way towards Pastnoon.

'Let's check the open arches. We should have done that first,' I said. 'Think about it. It's the night of the storm. It's raining, a few people are running home, but nobody's using Carmeyn's Way. So those arches, the passages onto the way, will have been dark and deserted.'

Beside me, Wes nodded.

'As I said yesterday, if I'Advay was eating in Sophee's Sacred Heart, staring out of the window, looking for Ameeleyor, he could have seen Mycale coming from the apothecary's shop. He leaves the restaurant without paying, crosses the arcade, and the two argue in one of the open arches,' I said.

We checked the easternmost arch first, the one least likely to be the murder location. Unfortunately, the sun was overhead, and the curved walls appeared black in the shadows. Wes persuaded the owner of the shop next door, a cobbler, to lend us a lantern. But even under lamplight, we could see no suspicious marks or stains except for those left behind by centuries of piss and shit.

The next arch was no different, so we passed the back of the apothecary until we reached the third open arch. We entered the gloom; it was so dark I could barely see the weathered stone walls at all.

As Wes fiddled with the lantern, a young Al'Mayran woman with two small children, a girl and a boy, passed us. She attempted to hide her puzzlement at our behaviour behind a thin and artificial smile. The little boy, whose hand she held, was equally mystified. He stopped and stared at Wes and me with his thumb in his mouth. Wes winked at him but his mother dragged him away. Wes raised the lantern to reveal a curved, six-foot-long projection blood splatter. It was as if it were being sprayed before our eyes.

'In Xol's name, will you look at that?' Dee said.

'I'm looking, I'm looking,' Wes said.

The splash had darkened and congealed but was unmistakable to any police officer who had examined a murder scene before – a head-height, carotid arterial spray. The three of us stepped back in unison and studied the ground. A streak of dried blood was running along the bottom edge of the wall.

'Someone mopped this up,' I said.

'There are transfer stains higher up,' Dee said.

'But no further stains to indicate which way he was carried. Damn it, how many people have passed through here since I'Advay was killed? Hundreds? Thousands?'

'It was too dark for them to see the wall, and the curve of the arch prevented anyone from walking through the blood,' Wes said.

'Or they just didn't give a fuck,' I said.

I sent Dee back to the Square to fetch a forensic company and enlisted a young Al'Mayran couple, who had been enjoying the freedom of the day, to help me block access to the arch using several stone forms. Wes cordoned off the other access points to Carmeyn's Way, much to the disgust of the Al'Mayran public and the owners of the nearby establishments who considered it their backyard. When he was finished, he finally took his uniform jacket off, sat on one of the forms the young couple and I had moved, and wiped his brow with a handkerchief. I sat with him and waited for Dee, who soon returned with Sudeme and several members of his company.

'Come on, big man, we need to talk to the shop owners,' I said to Wes.

On one side of the arch, there was a florist's owned by an elderly Al'Mayran woman. She shared the flat above the shop with her husband, an old soldier, who provided Al'Mayran martial arts lessons to the local children in a studio near the park. They had lived in New Capital for thirty years and understood a thing or two about the nature of southern storms. On the night of the hurricane, they closed early and boarded up their shop. The florist had a gentle and guileless manner, and I heard nothing in her account that rang false. We left her promising to lay some flowers in the arch in memory of the unfortunate Areel I'Advay.

Next, we crossed to the other side and to the dressmaker's shop, which, like the florist's, I remembered from when I was a child. The Al'Mayran man who ran it was in his early forties, was of slim build and had thinning sandy-brown hair combed over his shining pink pate. He wore a pair of wire-rimmed spectacles and sported a neat beard trimmed to a point below his chin. Unusually for an Al'Mayran, he wasn't wearing the traditional robes of his people, but instead had chosen to dress in a suit, combining it with a waistcoat, a lemon shirt and a purple tie. I presumed he was born in the city and felt a greater connection to the modern trading world than he did to his ancestral homeland. In contrast to his chosen attire, his shop was stocked with some of the most beautiful and intricately patterned Al'Mayran robes I had ever seen. As I recalled, it was his mother who founded the shop, and I wondered if it were her hand still at work producing their wares.

'Can I help you?' the owner said once we were inside his shop. His piercing stare darted from Wes to Dee and to me, like a cat following a dangling ball of wool.

'I hope so, sir. I'm Special Agent Kohee of the CIB. This is Inspector Sulaqua of the Square, and this is Police Cadet Deewhalee Huno. What's your name?' Wes said.

'Patreek I'Donowld. What is this about?'

'A rather unpleasant matter, I'm afraid to say, Patreek. We have reason to believe a man was murdered next to your shop on the night of the storm.'

'By the spirits, how terrible.' I'Donowld's body grew rigid, and he slid his hands into his trouser pockets.

'Did you see anything unusual that night?' Wes said.

'No, no. Not at all. I bordered up early,' I'Donowld said.

'Very wise. I don't suppose you heard anything?'

'Above the thunder and rain?'

'Before the storm hit, perhaps?'

'No, nothing at all, I'm afraid to say. Is that all?' he said, taking his hands out of his pockets and picking up a pair of tailor's scissors.

'Are you closing?' I said.

'No.'

'Do you have an appointment with a customer?'

'Not for an hour, why?'

'You seem eager that we leave.'

'I'm not used to talking to the police.'

'Take us to your mother.'

'My mother?' he said, fidgeting with the scissors and cutting a price tag away from a robe folded on the countertop.

'She's still with us, I hope?' I said.

'Oh, yes, yes. She rarely serves customers but the designs you see are hers,' I'Donowld said.

'Very beautiful. A talented lady. Take us to her.'

'Of course. I should close up first.'

'Lock the door and flip the sign, Cadet,' I said to Dee, without taking my eyes from I'Donowld.

I lifted the flap in the counter and pushed the gate aside without an invite. We all followed I'Donowld up a flight of steep and narrow wooden stairs to a room overlooking the arcade. Surrounded by rolls and heaps of material, a half-finished robe over her lap and a needle and thread in her hand, sat his mother, the woman I remembered from when I was a child.

Her flaxen hair had grown white, and she had become frail in her advanced years, but she remained a bold seamstress, and she worked with assured speed.

'How goes it with you, kind lady?' I said.

She looked up from her task and narrowed her blue eyes, scrunching her nose and pursing her lips as she studied me. 'I am well, I thank you. And you, young lady?'

'Good. I thank you,' I said.

'Mother, these are the police. They have questions for you. Inspector, this is my mother, Ms A'Leezbeth,' I'Donowld said.

I introduced us and took a seat opposite the old lady on an uncomfortable, creaking wooden chair. Wes and Dee stood behind me while Patreek I'Donowld hovered, twitching and fondling his beard, at his mother's side.

'What's the matter?' Ms A'Leezbeth said.

'It appears a man was murdered in the archway beside your shop on the night of the storm,' I said.

Her reaction surprised me. She looked neither afraid nor shocked and didn't raise her hand to her mouth, but instead turned to her son and said, 'By the spirits. I told you, Patreek, but you wouldn't listen, you young fool.'

'Mother,' he protested.

Ms A'Leezbeth leant forward before continuing. 'I told him, Inspector. May the spirits be my witness, I told him.'

'Told him what, kind lady?' I said, trying to control my breathing.

'I heard two men quarrelling something terrible that night. And even though we'd boarded the shop up, I pulled one of the shutters aside to take a look.'

'What did you see?'

'A customer of ours. A usually soft-spoken gentleman who walked with a cane, arguing with a vicious-looking brute, a Coor'Seyan I would say, judging by his dark hair.'

'Can you describe the Coor'Seyan?'

'He was about this young man's size,' she said, gesturing to Wes. 'He had black hair, of course, which he wore loose and wild. You wouldn't forget him in a hurry.'

'How so?'

'He had a scar sliced right across his face.'

'Had you seen this man before?'

'No. But the other fellow I knew.'

'The man with the cane?'

'A magnificent golden one.'

'Did he have it with him that night?'

'He did.'

'And you say he and the man with the scar argued?'

'Yes.'

'What about?'

'Sounded like a fight over a woman to me, although I didn't think the gentleman with the golden cane was so inclined.'

'Did they come to blows?'

'Not that I saw,' she said, turning, once again with disgust, to glare at her son. 'But only because he dragged me away from the window and closed the shutter.' She raised her arm, gestured at I'Donowld with a long and bony thumb.

'And you saw no one else?' I said.

'Oh, thanks to him, I saw nothing else that entire night.'

'Did you hear the quarrel continue?'

'For a few minutes, but I couldn't tell you what was said.'

I used Dee's scroll and stayed with the old lady until she had written, read, re-read and signed her account. I handed the roll back to Dee and sent him to the Square. Once he left, I sat with Wes on a marble form on Carmeyn's Way and stared out at the blue and sparkling sea, and at the ships sailing in and out of Magila Bay under the Bridge of Spirits.

'Mycale is finished then,' Wes said.

'So it would seem,' I said.

'And Nakni should be released.'

I nodded.

'But you don't look happy,' Wes said.

'I can't reconcile Mycale I'Krayag's hot temper with the cold manner of I'Advay's murder,' I said. 'And if Mycale was coming from the apothecary's shop when he met I'Advay, he can't have been amongst the four Al'Mayrans pursuing him atop Noon Claw.'

'But Mycale would have been strong enough to carry I'Advay's body up those steps.'

'True. Let's have a look along the passageway.'

Wes and I stepped over the remains of the destroyed wall onto the cliff path leading to Salvation's Climb. Like its counterpart in Rose Town, where I'd stood with Dee on the first morning of the case, the arcade corridor was exposed to the south, with only a waist-high stone balustrade for protection. There were more ruins farther on, vestiges of ancient eateries, echoes of a bustling past sounding in the forsaken present, where, long ago, a hungry pilgrim might have found respite from a weary climb.

Even though the path was reasonably secure, having been carved out of the cliff, Wes and I fell into single file and only stepped near the balustrade to negotiate the remnants of an old stall. We took our time on the route but saw no footprints nor any blood.

'Wind and rain would have lashed every corridor from the beach to the summit,' Wes said.

When we reached the centre of the cliff, where Salvation's Climb emerged through the floor, I risked stepping forward to peer over the balustrade. The concrete flight directly below was torn away in the storm, and the falling debris had collapsed others below, leaving a hundred-foot drop to the next.

Wes stood beside me and said, 'Even if Mycale is our killer, he's still a braver man than I.'

'Fear drove this climb, Wes, not bravery,' I said.

'Fear of what?'

'A forsaken spirit.'

The flight leading to the next level was still mostly intact. We stood on the granite landing, and I had Wes hang on to my belt as I leant forward and tried to inspect the steps, the rail, and the octopus-shaped balusters.

'Can you see anything?' Wes said.

'I can't,' I said. 'Fuck it. May Xol welcome my soul.'

I placed my foot on the staircase and began to transfer my weight.

'Ani, no,' Wes said.

'Just let me check this flight,' I said.

'If you don't find anything, you'll want to continue, and sooner or later, your luck will run out.'

But I had stopped listening. A third of the way up, the risers and treads had started to crack and fall away, and there was a faint transfer stain on a baluster, shielded from the general direction of wind and rain.

'I see blood, Wes.'

'You're joking,' he said.

'The killer had to walk closer to the barrier here to avoid the southern edge, which is falling away. When he did, I believe he caught this baluster – smeared it with the bloody robe maybe.'

I lay down to get a better look and spread my weight, but the step I put my elbow on gave way, taking two others with it and leaving my head, shoulders and arms dangling in the gap. My momentum was taking me over, but Wes grabbed my legs.

'Enough, Ani, please. For the love of Xol,' he said.

'Has anyone ever told you, Kohee, that you have a nervous disposition?' I said.

'Ease my agitation and come back down.'

'Not yet. The baluster has come loose. I'm going to pull it away.'

'We'll be disturbing evidence.'

'Sudeme won't be climbing these steps to take a sample of that blood, so let's take a sample to him.'

Wes crawled back onto the landing while I tied one end of my belt around the baluster. I stood and pulled, but I couldn't shift the post.

'Here, let me try,' Wes said.

We swapped places, and it was my turn to grow nervous as I watched the big man risk his life for my pig-headed nature, hauling on the belt with his entire weight on the fragile concrete.

'Come on, Wes, put some effort into it,' I said.

He grumbled before he tried again. This time the baluster gave way and came rolling down the steps into my waiting hands.

'There, are you happy now?' Wes said.

'Give me my belt back,' I said.

After we handed the baluster to the disbelieving Sudeme, I invited Wes over for dinner. I didn't tell him Josee and I were arguing. Like most visitors, he was charmed by the location of our flat. The drawbridge in particular delighted him, as it usually did me. But crossing that evening, I felt like a child being dragged to the doctor's.

Josee was in the kitchen, dressed in her shorts and tunic, as was her habit when cooking in the summertime. She looked up from the vegetables she was chopping and was about to speak when she spotted Wes behind me. He smiled, blushed and maintained determined eye contact with Josee as he shook her hand.

'I hope there's enough food for a guest?' he said.

'Of course. Two guests, in fact,' Josee said.

'Who else is here?' I said.

'I invited Dabreeyor.'

Wes shot me a look.

'Josee has developed quite a rapport with her,' I said, the sarcastic tone of my voice, which I regretted immediately, a nail across a blackboard.

'She needed a friend,' Josee said with a graceful smile.

'Is Mani at Ezno's?' I whispered.

Josee wheeled, taken aback, her eyes flitting between Wes and me. 'No. He's here.'

'With Dabreeyor? What did you tell her about the boy?'

Josee smiled at Wes but I could tell her expression was forced. She adopted a nonchalant tone, but her eyes betrayed her anger. 'That he's the son of a tribal friend, and we're taking care of him while his mother is at sea.'

'So Mani's going to keep that front up, is he?' I snapped.

Wes spun on his heel, his hands behind his back, and looked around the kitchen.

'He liked the idea,' Josee protested.

'I like the idea of being an artist; it doesn't mean I have the talent.'

'Isn't this a little hypocritical, darling?' Josee said, a rare false note sounding in her voice when she said 'darling'.

'How so?'

Josee looked over my shoulder at Wes. The big man was inspecting a shelf above the kitchen table packed with jars full of pickled vegetables and sweet preserves.

'I have no desire to offend Wes, but you promised not to drag Mani into your investigation. And now a CIB agent stands in our kitchen – forgive me, Wes – one who clearly knows who Mani is,' Josee said, her eyes widening to emphasise her point.

Wes waved her apology away and found some smoked fish dangling from a hook on the wall to occupy his interest.

'I trust Wes,' I said with a shrug.

Behind me, he coughed.

'I trust Dabreeyor, but I haven't told her who Mani is,' Josee said, folding her arms.

'No, you just expect a boy to maintain a subterfuge.'

'We decided it was for the best.'

'We?'

'Ezno, Etu, Oura. We all agreed.'

I raised my voice. 'Oh, a family meeting, was it? With my family.'

Josee made her apologies to Wes, took my hand and led me through the dining room onto the western terrace, where Dabreeyor was playing marbles with Mani.

'Could you give us a minute, please, Dabreeyor?' Josee said.

'Of course,' Dabreeyor said, quickly picking up on the situation. She caught Mani's eye and flicked her head towards the dining room. Mani scooped up his marbles and hurried away with her.

Josee blew out a puff of air before she spoke. 'Ani, you're never here. But decisions still need to be made. Our family – one I thought I was part of – decided we need to explain Mani's presence.'

I raised my hands. 'To whom? My tribe know he's not Lo'tse. Your lie isn't going to convince them. Besides, I'd vouch for every one of them before…'

'An Al'Mayran?' Josee said, putting her hands on her hips.

'I was going to say any outsider. That includes other Kahokeyans.'

'And me? Am I an outsider?'

'Of course not, but let's be honest, discretion, like fidelity, is not a value Al'Mayrans hold dear, is it?'

Josee snorted. 'Don't make this about Dabreeyor.'

'Why not? For someone you've known less than a week you're trusting her with a lot.'

'I could say the same thing about Wes,' Josee said, gesturing with her hand towards the dining room and the kitchen beyond.

'He's a law officer. We've been in danger together. That's when you find out who a person is.'

'He's a fucking CIB agent, Ani. How often have you told me they're brutal and corrupt?'

'Wes is different,' I offered as justification. But my words sounded hollow.

'And you've determined that in less than a week?' Josee said, turning my phrase against me.

I dug in. 'Yes.'

'But I can't do the same with Dabreeyor?'

I looked over Josee's shoulder at the tip of Sundown as I chose my words. 'You lack judgement. You go through life as if everyone's your friend until they prove otherwise.'

'I keep forgetting Inspector Sulaqua is infallible.'

My eye followed the sea's horizon. 'I don't confuse feelings for evidence.'

'Meaning?'

'You like Dabreeyor, in every way, whether you can admit it or not. That clouds your judgement. Wes is a colleague, nothing more, and, let's be honest, I'm never going to fuck him, am I?'

'I wouldn't care if you did.'

I fixed Josee with a hard stare. 'That's the problem,' I snapped.

As Josee opened her mouth to speak again, a carmine-red beam illuminated the twilight sky and set fire to the dining room window frame. Josee and I stared, agog, as the ray of light changed course, looping down and shattering the window, then up, scorching an inch-deep trail across the brickwork. I dragged Josee onto the northern balcony, and we ran, our heads down, to the eastern side of the flat. We were soon joined by Wes, Dabreeyor and Mani, who fled through the kitchen door.

Wes shouted something.

I paid him no mind and concentrated on Josee. Her eyes were wide open and manic, her face contorted by fear. I twisted her head until she focused on me.

'Don't move,' I ordered.

I sprinted back to the western terrace, leapt onto the coping of the balustrade and scoured the rocky slope of Pastnoon Claw where I had fought the cloaked Al'Mayran. Plumes of dark smoke rose and billowed above a newly burned pathway, tiny fires alight amongst the bushes and foliage.

My flesh prickled. The wheels and chains of the Great Lifts roared in my ears. I jumped from the balustrade and ran past Wes, who was heading in the opposite direction. He was still shouting, but his voice was drowned out by the blood rushing in my ears, as loud to me as an industrial explosion. I raced across the bridge, running through Shadow Rise with my percussion pistols in my hands. The thought of blowing out the candle and extinguishing my anger was an insult as great as the attack on my home.

The folk of Shadow Rise saw me. They hid from me. They pulled their children out of my way and held them close. The playground was clear, the flames beyond almost out, but the smoke was thick. I choked as I cleared the wall onto the steep cliffside and ran, without thought or concern, towards the newly made and blackened path.

I waited for an attack, for another searing beam of light to slice me in two. But it didn't come. I searched, pistols pointed forward, without stealth or circumspection, through smouldering trees and bushes for an Al'Mayran armed with a weapon that would transform the Known World. But he had fled, taking death by conflagration with him, leaving my nerves shredded, my mind full of visions of an inferno, sparked into creation as effortlessly as water flowed from a tap.

I floated as though in a dream back through Shadow Rise, like I was being carried through a mirror realm – a half-seen phantom on the edges of perception. No one dared speak to me as I passed. Even Wes fell silent as I crossed the bridge to find Dabreeyor cradling my wife. I ran onto the western terrace, towards the Coiled Sea, my eyes stinging, my tears taken by the wind, and shot my pistols into the darkness.

CHAPTER TWENTY

MANI TOOK HIS supper into the den while Josee went to bed without eating. But I had found my appetite, if not my voice, so I had dinner in the kitchen with Wes and Dabreeyor, a surreal repast during which we only spoke for the sake of custom and manners. After we had eaten, they remained, it seemed to me out of obligation, and passed the time by cleaning the pots.

I noticed their eyes meeting on several occasions, and when they thought I wasn't looking, they exchanged flirtatious smiles, resulting in Dabreeyor's pale face turning a fetching pink. Ordinarily, I would have found this amusing, but it only served as proof my jealousy was unfounded. I was thankful when Oura arrived to spend the night, and they could be freed from the weight of societal duty.

After they left, I showed Oura the damage on the western wall.

'In Xol's name. So this is what your mysterious weapon can do?' he said, putting his finger into one of the grooves.

I nodded.

'So you were right all along. As usual,' Oura said.

'That matters little, not without the weapon or the man who fired it.'

'What are you going to do?'

'Search the Octagon Hall.'

'You mean break in? Shimmer?'

I shrugged.

'You'll break the law to find evidence against our own government that would be inadmissible in court?' Oura said, cocking his head.

'That's about the size of it.'

'Ani, you're not going to want to hear this, but perhaps it's time to heed these warnings and leave well enough alone. If these people are as powerful as you think, you won't be able to stop them.'

'I don't accept that.'

'It's not just up to you anymore. You've dragged us all into this now.'

'You can sleep in the den tonight if you prefer. Mani doesn't use the settee. Wind the bridge up after I leave.'

'Ani. Ani, wait.'

I left Oura cursing my name and took Runner's Trail down Pastnoon Claw to the dock. I found a sailor willing to take me to Riverlyn Park on the other side of the bay. From there, I took the now familiar route behind the waterfall and up the steep cliffside path to the academy.

The repairs to the keyhole wound were almost complete, but the scaffolding was still up and there was a roll of tarpaulin on the ground underneath.

Unfortunately, the high chief's guard had increased security, and there were extra men and women at the rear entrance and others patrolling the circumference of the hall. Amongst them was the older, well-built guard with the shaved head, whose partner I'd fought with.

I watched him and his colleagues for half an hour until I determined their routine. During the next interval between patrols, I ran across the lawn and hid in the shadows below the scaffolding.

It was another thirty minutes before the older guard reappeared, during which I crouched behind the tarpaulin as others passed by. When I stood to follow him, my thighs cramped, and I had to shuffle, but I kicked a stone and it ricocheted off the wall with a loud crack.

I was shimmering the older guard's form before he turned, and in his shock at seeing himself, he was slow to react, giving me the opportunity to get the chloroform-covered handkerchief over his face before he could draw his axe from his belt. But I hadn't gathered enough momentum to knock him over, and when he grabbed my arms, he nearly prised them away before the sweet-smelling liquid could take effect. He was still struggling as we fell. Thankfully, the roar of the Magila Bay waterfall drowned out his muffled cries, and he soon lost his strength and passed out.

By now, I was breathless and sweating, but I couldn't rest. I had to drag the guard to the scaffolding and dump him behind the roll of tarpaulin. My back strained from the effort and my thighs burned with acid until they grew numb and unresponsive. In the end, I had to lay him on the ground, take hold of his wrists, and pull him by his arms for the final few feet. I collapsed beside him, gulping for air. As I recovered, I searched for his keys, and only when I found them did I manage to stagger to my feet and resume his patrol.

Just like at the rear of the Octagon Hall, the front entrance was crowded with extra warriors. I doubted they would let even one of their own inside unchallenged, so I continued north, then west to the gardens. At the bottom of a flight of steps dug into the earth behind a hedge, I found a small door to the basement.

I tried five keys before the lock turned. The room beyond was dank and musty, lit only by a faint moonlight glow through a tiny wire-mesh window. In the shadows, I picked my way past scythes, spades, rakes and hoes, and sacks of compost and gravel. Luckily, the far door was unlocked.

I poked my head into the dark corridor and checked both directions. No one was present, so I continued west, running my hand along the stone wall until I found the doors to a stairwell, faintly lit by the moonlight from a small window. I let my eyes adjust, ensured no one was there, and ran up the steps.

On the corridor above, which ran around the domed laboratory, the lamps were lit but dimmed. Their warm light carried only a short distance, leaving pockets of shadow along the marble walls. I listened for voices or footsteps approaching in the gloom but heard nothing. The silence was dreamlike but familiar to anyone who had wandered alone in a communal space.

The corridor was lined with marble busts and statues of great scientists, rendered with unusual realism for Kahokeyan art. When my shadow fell upon their faces, their expressions seemed to change, spooking me, and I felt a wave of relief when finally, I came upon the wider passage to the lab.

Before I entered, I cracked open the high, wooden double doors and listened, but only stillness greeted me. Inside, splashes of moonlight, rendered abstract through glass utensils, fell in fractured patterns upon the surrounding walls, cabinets and shelves. But what drew my eye most of all was the same strange tripod I'd seen before, standing under the glass dome in a shower of light.

The tripod had extendable legs, adjusted for use by a person, at least in Kahokeyan terms, of average height. That left the wide lever mount, set upon a pivoting joint, level with my chin. I still couldn't picture the weapon and there was little else to glean from an examination of the tripod, so I searched elsewhere.

In addition to the keyhole wound visible from outside, the blast had demolished the dividing wall to the surrounding octagonal corridor. Steel bars, rising from baseplates screwed to the floor, stood to reinforce the ceiling, and although repairs were underway, there was much work still to be done.

The scorch marks on the sections of wall still standing ran south and were similar to those that now scarred my home, if a little wider and deeper. Below them lay dust and chunks of brickwork and what I thought was animal fat.

To the north, there was a safe, and by it was a wooden workbench, covered in metal strips and granules, four soldering irons, and a burner lamp. What caught my eye was a small steel chamber, covered in rubber, with copper wires sticking out. I picked the chamber up to examine it, straining my eyes in the moonlight. Was this part of the weapon?

Someone began to sing, and I jumped, then froze, listening as the tune grew louder. I dropped the chamber and ran towards the double doors as the singer entered the opposite side of the lab.

'Hey, you! What are you doing?' she shouted.

I glanced over my shoulder at a middle-aged Kahokeyan woman with cropped grey hair. She carried an oil lamp and was dressed in the long dark brown lab coat of an academy scientist.

I took off down the wide passage and sprinted around the corner into the octagonal corridor. The woman followed, screaming for others to come to her aid.

As we ran, voices echoed off the marble walls, and with every corner I took blind, I expected to collide with a guard charging in the opposite direction. When I reached the stairwell, I threw open the doors and searched in the moonlight for the first step and the rail of the bannister.

As I ran into the basement, my shadow danced in the glow of the scientist's lamp shining from above. I made it back to the storeroom filled with gardening equipment, and I crouched in the gloom, soaking my handkerchief with chloroform as I waited. When the scientist entered, I pounced, throwing her to the floor and smothering her with the kerchief until she fell unconscious. I opened the external door, shimmered her appearance, and stepped out into the warm night, creeping up the steps below the hedge and back into the rear garden.

'Good evening,' a voice said.

I jumped and spun, somehow keeping my shimmer intact, to find the high chief emptying a pipe into the soil at the other side of the hedge.

'Sir, is something the matter?' I said, snatching a breath as if surfacing from the Coiled Sea.

'Quite the opposite, my dear. I love to walk alone at night. I lose track of time and stay out late, much to the disgust of my doctors. They tell me I must get eight hours every night. Maybe that's true of most people, but not me. Do you know why?'

'No, sir,' I said, putting my hand in my pocket, searching for my sodden handkerchief.

'Because this city rejuvenates me. I stand on the cliff edge and gaze upon her, bathing in her radiance until I am quite recovered.'

I nodded and smiled and wondered if he could see me shaking, and if he could, did he find this unusual or was he accustomed to folk trembling in his presence?

He reached out and patted my shoulder.

If the scientist I was shimmering had not been close to my own height, Naka's hand might have missed and struck my face, betraying my illusion to him. As it was, he touched me close to where he intended, and in the dark, did not notice any visual inconsistency. Nevertheless, I froze, horrified, without breath or heartbeat, until he said, 'Well, goodnight to you,' and walked away, humming an old folk tune.

It was still dark when I reached the Square. I nodded at the officer on reception as I entered, taking a paternoster lift to the floor where Sudeme's office was located. I used my jacket as a pillow and fell asleep outside his door.

Shona came to me again in my dreams. This time she was whole and alive and not dead and rotten, and I was a child again, like her, unchanged by time's unrelenting advance. She sat with me on Salvation's Climb and we were joined by Hani and Mani and a thousand other nameless children of the Depths. Together we watched the horizon across the Coiled Sea, but what we were looking for, I couldn't tell you. There was a sense of ease and solidarity. When I looked upon their faces, they smiled at me, but in their eyes, I saw disappointment tinged with resignation.

'It is the way of things, Ani,' Shona said. 'Don't be too hard on yourself.'

I was about to ask her what she meant when Sudeme woke me by patting my shoulder.

'What time is it?' I said.

'A little after six. What are you doing here?' he said.

'The blood from the baluster and from Carmeyn's Way, is it the same type as Areel I'Advay's?'

'It is. The next time I reject one of your theories, Ani, remind me of this.'

I waved my hand in dismissal. 'Does Imala know?' I asked.

'She does. And the dressmaker's description of the Coor'Seyan was enough to convince the police chief and a sympathetic but rather nervous city judge to issue an arrest warrant.'

I nodded, rose, and stretched my aching body, groaning as the knots in my neck and shoulders strained. I tried to walk, but my legs felt like they had been drained of blood.

'This doesn't please you?' Sudeme said.

'I'm pleased for the lad, Nakni. But maybe I've replaced one innocent man with another.'

'Come in, Ani. Have a coffee, share my breakfast. I could afford to lose the weight.'

'I broke into the Octagon Hall last night, Sudeme. I found a small steel chamber, a component from a larger device, covered in rubber, threaded with copper wires.'

Sudeme put his fingers to his temple and stared at me, eyes wide, mouth hanging open.

'Rubber?' he eventually repeated.

I nodded.

'The amber effect,' he said.

'Naka mentioned that to me. What is it?' I said.

'It's already an outdated term, but it describes the energy you can create in a piece of amber by rubbing it with certain materials, like wool. This energy can be conducted by copper. Rubber, on the other hand, prevents its flow.'

'There were scorch marks on the walls of the lab so deep I could have put my fist into one.'

'Xol protect us.'

'And last night, someone directed a beam of light at my home that made the same markings,' I said.

'Oh, Ani, was anyone hurt?'

'No. Someone was just trying to scare us. Had they wanted to kill us, that light would have sliced us in two.'

'You have to tell Imala. Otherwise, she'll be blindsided. She's bet her reputation on you. I hope you appreciate that.'

'I do,' I whispered.

'Then show her.'

'In Xol's name, you're mad, Ani. And I'm a fool,' Imala said, standing from her desk. 'I tell you not to break into the Al'Mayran embassy again, and you break into the academy instead. Are you sure you maintained your shimmer before Naka?'

'As sure as I can be,' I said.

She clasped her hands behind her back and began to pace. 'And Josee saw this... beam?' Imala said.

'She did,' I said.

'And you're convinced the same weapon blasted the hole in the academy's wall?'

'Something like it.'

'What a mess. You can never leave well enough alone.' Imala stopped pacing and pointed at me. 'It's you, not some weapon, that leaves behind a trail of destruction, my girl, everywhere you go.'

I shrugged Imala's criticism off. 'But I was right. I'Dreng as good as confirmed the existence of the weapon when he thought I was I'Rasnee. Josee's now seen its power too. Sudeme believes in the scientific possibilities. It's real. You have to accept it.' I nodded as I spoke, more for my own benefit than Imala's. 'I was right. I was right about I'Advay's murder, about Salvation's Climb, and I was right about the weapon.'

Imala wasn't impressed. If anything, her tone grew angrier. 'And so we add the high chief to our list of suspects, along with Ambassador I'Rasnee. To which judge do you suggest I apply for a warrant? For Xol's sake, Ani, even when you're right, you're wrong.'

'No,' I shouted. 'It's everyone else who's wrong.'

Imala croaked and cackled. 'If you can explain to me how that improves our options, I'll arrest Naka myself.'

I got my emotions under control and tried a different tack: being reasonable. 'Can't you escalate this?' I offered.

'To whom?' Imala asked, lifting the palms of her hands towards the ceiling.

'The chief of police. She seems honourable.'

Imala pursed her lips. She stood beside me, leant on the edge of her desk, and folded her arms. 'That's one person. And if you can for a moment imagine she may not be willing to risk her life for us, what then?'

Imala's manner had calmed. I matched her tone. 'So what will you do?'

'Arrest I'Krayag. It's the right thing to do anyway, based on what you've uncovered in your investigation.'

'I'm not sure he's guilty.'

'That's for a jury to decide.'

'But if you give me a few more days, I may be able to find the young lad who saw I'Advay's body being dumped. If his description doesn't match I'Krayag's—'

Imala shook her head. 'There's no getting that boy out of the Depths, even if we could find him.'

'I've found him twice. I can find him again.'

'How?'

I took a deep breath before answering and looked through the window. 'Josee and I have been protecting his brother.'

'You've what?' Imala said, her eyes widening behind their spectacles. 'In Xol's name, you're unbelievable.'

I tried to stop my anger from rising, but I was on the defensive. 'Don't get any ideas. I'll release him to the Depths before I give him to you,' I growled.

'I wouldn't want him or his brother, anyway, no matter what they saw,' Imala barked. She paused, looked at the door to Medele's adjacent room, and lowered her voice. 'You of all people should know a testimony from a child of the Depths will not be taken seriously. Ani, hear me, please. I beg you. Drop this. Your evidence is enough to charge I'Krayag. I will do all I can to ensure it frees Nakni. But as for the others – I'Dreng, I'Rasnee – there's no touching them. And Naka, well, we have more of a chance of arresting Xol himself.'

'That's not enough.'

'And it never will be. You have to find solace elsewhere.'

I sighed and shook my head. 'I'm not sure I can,' I said. 'Can you?'

'It comforts me to think Shona's passing led you here, to a place where you're of inestimable value to the people of this city. That is her legacy. Don't destroy it. Don't destroy yourself.'

I stepped out onto Imala's terrace, where I could listen to New Capital's song, intoned by the wheels of cabs, the strain of masts, and the grind of the lifts upon their tracks. The edges of my vision closed in and the world began to roll. I grabbed for the iron rail of the barrier and sat on the form, lowering my head until the spinning stopped. Imala came to stand beside me and placed her hand on my shoulder.

In all, there were twenty police officers and CIB agents, including Wes, Imala and me, along with an armoured police waggon, gathered on the south-facing bend of Dayna's Lane in Jayson's Haven. We were waiting for the command to turn north past the self-closing flood barriers and arrest Mycale I'Krayag for the murder of the envoy, Areel I'Advay.

Imala gave the signal, and we marched in something approximating unity to I'Krayag and A'Jozaf's family home to divert their and their children's lives forever. We were armed with swords, fighting daggers, traditional double-bladed axes, pistols and muskets. We could have been going to war instead of taking one man into custody. But Mycale I'Krayag was no ordinary man. He was a fierce warrior with a hot temper, and even I thought the show of force justified.

As it turned out, I'Krayag was waiting for us, kneeling on the walkway outside his front door in his tunic and shorts with his robes at his side to show he was unarmed. Behind him stood a man I hadn't seen before. He was a tall and slim Al'Mayran in a golden and cerulean embroidered robe of high quality. He was clean-shaven with a cleft chin and had tied his long, straight strawberry-blond hair into two ponytails twisted together.

While Imala read I'Krayag his rights, I asked the man his name.

'Garen I'Fanadhar. I'm Mycale's advocate,' the man said.

'Is that true, Mycale?' I said.

I'Krayag looked at I'Fanadhar and spat on the ground.

'Your client doesn't look too happy about it,' I said.

Wes allowed the Coor'Seyan to dress before handcuffing him and helping him into the armoured police waggon.

'Where are Ameeleyor and your children, Mycale?' I said.

No answer.

'Why didn't you leave with them?' I said.

But he looked away as I'Fanadhar sat beside him.

'My client will not answer any questions regarding his wife's where-abouts,' the advocate said.

After Wes shut and locked the waggon's door, he said to me, 'I never thought Mycale would give himself up.'

'Perhaps if he were guilty, he would have resisted,' I said.

Back at the Square, Ms A'Leezbeth was waiting with her son in the viewing room to identify I'Krayag. We had drafted in two Coor'Seyans and two other Al'Mayrans, a blond and a redhead, to take part in a sequential identity parade. I questioned the fairness of the process, especially considering I'Krayag was the only one with scars on his face, but it went ahead anyway. A'Leezbeth surprised no one, least of all I'Krayag, when she picked him out.

I returned to my desk and sat staring at a blank evidential form in my typewriter with my hands behind my head.

'You hate paperwork too, I gather?' said Wes, as he sat at the desk beside me.

'Ordinarily, no,' I said.

Sudeme stepped out of a paternoster lift and made his way towards us, a faint smile on his face. 'Your suspect's fingerprints match the ones I recovered from I'Advay's body and the mausoleum. You have your man, Ani, for the murder and the kidnapping.'

'Thank you, Sudeme. For everything,' I said.

Sudeme's eyes widened. He looked at me in wonder and said to Wes, 'Is she feeling quite well?'

'Just magnanimous in victory,' Wes said.

I sent Dee to the canteen to fetch a wrap for I'Krayag, then I had a couple of uniformed officers escort I'Krayag to an interview room with I'Fanadhar. Wes and I were about to join them when Imala took my arm and led me aside.

'I'll be there in a minute,' I said to Wes.

Once Wes was out of earshot, Imala turned to me. 'Keep it simple, Ani. Nothing about lifeblood stones and weapons.'

I didn't answer. Beyond her, Sodia had just emerged from a paternoster lift.

'Do you hear me, Inspector?' Imala said. 'I'Fanadhar says I'Krayag is ready to confess. Let him. Keep the official record clean. Then we can all move on.'

'All?' I said.

I pulled away from Imala and caught up with Wes. We entered the interview room and sat opposite I'Krayag. There was a knock at the door and Dee entered. He placed a glass of iced water and a wrap containing fried squid in front of I'Krayag, but the Coor'Seyan touched neither.

On the wall of the interview room, under the ceiling coving, covered by a wire-mesh grill, was what appeared to be an air vent but was really a duct leading to the next room, where Imala and Sodia were listening.

I collected my thoughts and studied I'Krayag as he fingered the scar on his face and brushed his long dark hair behind his ears. For once, he seemed calm and impassive, resigned to his fate; a proud, scarlet- and black-clad soldier on a mission from which he did not expect to return.

'Before we begin, my client would like to make a statement,' I'Fanadhar said.

I gestured for I'Krayag to begin.

'On the night of the storm, my wife and I went to see the apothecary, Ronayld I'Kryse, to fetch medicine for my son who was very ill,' I'Krayag said. 'I left thirty minutes after eleven o'clock with the draught for my son while my wife stayed a little longer to help I'Kryse tidy. As I was walking through the Al'Mayran arcade, Areel I'Advay approached me. We quarrelled, and he struck me with his cane. I have a temper, and in my rage, I beat Areel to the ground and slit his throat.'

'What did you do then?' I said.

'I delivered the remedy to my son.'

'You went home?'

'That's correct.'

'What did you do with the body?'

'I left it in the arch. After my wife returned, I went back and carried Areel up Salvation's Climb to Rose Town.'

'Why not throw the body in the sea?'

'Guilt. I'd killed Areel's body. I didn't wish to kill his spirit.'

'Why not leave the body in the arcade to be found?'

'I knew Areel visited Nitushi Nakni at the Stars and the Sea. I thought by leaving his body there, I was less likely to become a suspect.'

'So much for Coor'Seyan honour, eh?'

I'Krayag bristled.

'Thousands of Al'Mayrans use the arcade. Why would we come looking for you?' I said.

'Because of my connection to Areel. I thought it safer to throw you off the scent,' I'Krayag growled.

'Safer? Climbing those steps with a body in the middle of a storm?'

'I didn't consider those risks.'

'And you were alone?'

'Yes?'

'And your wife?'

'She stayed with our son. She knew nothing of the incident.'

'Yet when I interviewed her, she supported your previous account of the evening and said she left the apothecary's shop with you, not separately.'

I'Krayag turned to I'Fanadhar as if to say, *Are you going to intervene?* But his advocate just nodded for him to continue.

'Maybe you confessed to her, and being a loyal and loving wife, she helped you carry Areel's body up the steps and provided you with an alibi,' I said.

'That's not what happened,' I'Krayag said, his voice rising. The muscles in his neck flexed and the vein along his temple swelled.

'I don't believe she stayed behind to help I'Kryse tidy up,' I said.

'I swear on the sacred spirits, she wasn't with me when I met Areel,' I'Krayag said.

'Perhaps so, but she didn't remain at the apothecary's shop. Swear that to the sacred spirits.'

He didn't reply, but he made fists with his hands on the table.

'We'll put Ameeleyor's whereabouts aside for now. I have another question for you: why did you kill Areel?' I said.

'Why did I kill him?' I'Krayag said.

'Yes. What provoked such murderous rage?'

He wiped his lips and said, 'I believed he was having an affair with my wife.'

'Excuse me?' I coughed, rolling my eyes at Wes.

'He was having an affair with my wife.'

I held I'Krayag's gaze and was impressed when he didn't look away.

'Was he inclined towards women at all?' I said.

'Some people are not concerned with gender.'

'But were you aware of him having romantic relationships with women in the past?'

'I was only concerned with the one he had with my wife.'

'When did you realise their association had developed?'

'I'd suspected it for some time.'

'Has she had affairs before? Is this a habit?'

I'Krayag's pale face turned red. 'No,' he growled.

'How can you be sure?' I said. 'Al'Mayrans spread themselves thin – believe me, I know. Was she promiscuous before you met? How many men do you think she took to her bed before you? How many came after?'

I'Krayag slammed his fist on the table, prompting I'Fanadhar to place his hand on his client's arm.

'What is the purpose of these questions?' I'Fanadhar said. 'You have your confession. What more do you require?'

'The truth would be nice. Talk to me, Mycale. Who's making you confess? Have you struck a deal? And what do you get in exchange? Is it Ameeleyor's safety?'

No answer.

'I'm right, aren't I? Ameeleyor was Areel's ally, but in what fight? A holy war? Who was their enemy?' I said.

'My wife is not involved,' I'Krayag snarled.

'So she can't storm?'

'I beg your pardon?' I'Fanadhar said.

'Storm. To steal a person's body, swap their mind and spirit with yours.'

Beside me, Wes winced.

'This is ridiculous,' I'Fanadhar said, searching Wes's face, almost beseeching him to control me.

But I wouldn't stop.

'Your client's fingerprints were on I'Advay's body but they were also found in Jayson's Mausoleum, where Je'mymor A'Soyne woke up, disorientated, missing time, claiming she'd been kidnapped.'

'I don't know what you're talking about,' I'Krayag said.

'Someone saw you in the park with A'Soyne, only I think it was Ameeleyor wearing A'Soyne's face that they saw. And where was A'Soyne?

A prisoner, twice over, trapped in the attic of I'Kryse's shop and in Ameeleyor's body.'

'This is nonsense. Agent Kohee, I implore you, protect your associate. Stop her from making a fool of herself,' I'Fanadhar said.

'And where did this parasite come from?' I said, addressing I'Krayag but flicking my head towards I'Fanadhar. 'Who hired him? Why was he already at your home today?'

'Just leave my wife out of this,' I'Krayag said.

'But she's already in it. For example, where did she go when she left I'Kryse's on the night of the storm?' I said.

'Home,' I'Krayag said.

'Not to rendezvous with Areel in Windy Park?'

'No.'

'Because we know Areel waited for someone there. What was so urgent they had to meet on the night of the storm?'

'There was no meeting.'

'Only because Areel was spooked by four Al'Mayrans and took flight, first in a cab to the South-Western Great Lift and then down to the arcade, where you cast him away when he called at the apothecary's. He found you again. Did he tell you he had the proof for your wife?'

'What proof?' I'Krayag said.

'The lifeblood stone for the weapon,' I said.

'I have no idea what you're talking about,' I'Krayag said, crossing his fingers and turning his palms away from me.

'Of course you do. Ameeleyor was working with I'Advay to stop the testing and building of a weapon that functions through the destruction of lifeblood stones. Areel knew about the involvement of Ambassador I'Rasnee and your friend, Brigadier I'Kalmeen, both disloyal revolutionaries who wish to dethrone your king.'

'I would call this speculation except it's so preposterous as to be pure fantasy. I think you're overworked, Inspector,' I'Fanadhar said.

But I'Krayag was glaring at me now, his face the colour of beetroot, his body shaking from tension. His clasped hands were pushing down on the table so hard the legs and joints were creaking.

'It's no fantasy,' I said. 'We found the powder from a crushed lifeblood stone in I'Advay's office. He stole it from the traitor Brigadier Peetor I'Kalmeen.'

'Brigadier I'Kalmeen is the most loyal man I have ever met,' I'Krayag said, his voice low, guttural.

'If that seditious dog is a bastion of loyalty, it says a lot about the qualities of the Coor'Seyan soldier.'

The table broke, and I'Krayag dropped to his hands and knees. He sprung forward and pounced on me, knocking over my chair and slamming my head into the hardwood floor. The shock came before the pain, and the interview room pitched like a ship struck by one powerful and violent wave after another.

My throat constricted, my aching head about to burst. I'Krayag was strangling me. I held his forearms but couldn't pull him off, and all I could think about was how his muscles felt like iron in my hands. But Wes was on him, seizing him around the shoulders and dragging him away.

I closed my eyes to stop the world from spinning and listened to the door opening and the angry voices of others entering the room. I'Krayag screamed, and in his cry, I heard the desperation of a being, who, like me, could not accept the Known World the way it was, and I felt so very sorry for him.

CHAPTER TWENTY-ONE

I SAT IN THE listening room next to where I'Krayag had attacked me, touching the growing lump on the back of my head, now throbbing like the beat of a whale's heart, as Wes wrapped some ice in a linen cloth.

'Well, there's never a dull moment with you, Ani,' he said, handing me the bundle.

'Do you think I got to him?' I said, taking the ice and holding it to the back of my head.

Imala entered the room, followed by Sodia, who pushed past her and stormed over to where I sat.

'You're a disgrace,' he said, pointing his finger at me. His voice was raised and shrill, his round face trembling with rage.

'She has her confession,' Imala said.

'But it's not enough for her. She wants Ambassador I'Rasnee, too, Brigadier I'Kalmeen, and Xol knows who else. She won't be happy until our relations with the Al'Mayrans are in ruins.'

'I doubt that will happen, Assistant Director Sodia. We have the confession of a man, only indirectly connected to the embassy, who acted out of personal malice. Furthermore, I'm happy to let the Al'Mayrans have him. Incarcerating him here for the murder of his countryman serves no purpose. I'm sure the chief of police will agree with me, as will the high chief. But you are, of course, welcome to discuss it with him at your next meeting.'

'And what about the shimmerer's attack at the embassy and the break-in at the academy?'

'Can you prove the shimmerer's identity?'

'We all know she's one such freak,' Sodia said, gesturing at me with his thumb.

'Does Ambassador I'Rasnee wish to pursue the matter?'

'That's beside the point.'

'Really? It seems key to me. Now, may we discuss the release of Nitushi Nakni?'

As Wes and I passed through the gate at CIB Tower, I waved to the guards atop the curtain wall. There were four close by, above or near to the gate, more walking the eastern wall, and they all kept checking north.

'Try not to make it obvious, Wes, but look at the sentries on the wall. Something's wrong,' I said.

Wes glanced east. 'Those aren't the regular guards, they're Unaduti's people.'

'Why would they be on guard?'

'Xol only knows.'

'What is it they keep looking at?'

'Could be the general population yard. But there are also small exercise areas for those in solitary confinement.'

'Like Nakni?'

'Indeed.'

'Come on, let's take a look.'

As the spiked iron-fence enclosures to the east came into view, we heard shouting. I took off, sprinting around the corner of the tower's base, with Wes and the guards from the gate calling after me. At first, the yards appeared empty. Then I spotted Nakni, bare-chested, clambering up the corner of one pen, his legs bent, his hands gripping a single iron bar, one foot on the fence and the other on the curtain wall. As I neared him, several CIB agents appeared. From where exactly, I couldn't tell, but Unaduti was leading them, his pistol drawn and aimed at Nakni.

The shot rang out. Nakni's shoulder exploded with red. His arm swung uselessly to his side as he tried to keep hold of the fence with one hand. He didn't have far to climb, but now he had to risk letting go of the fence each time he tried to advance. And all the while, blood ran in rivers down his body and dripped from his fingers to the concrete below.

'Don't fire. That boy is innocent!' Wes shouted. 'Open this damn gate.' He snatched the keys from one of the guards.

I watched, helpless, on the other side of the fence as Unaduti's people ignored Wes and continued to fire. One shot passed through the lengths of Nakni's trailing locks. Another grazed his back, cutting a groove along his skin.

Two of the agents posing as guards on the curtain wall knelt to take aim at Nakni with their muskets, just as the lad slung his good arm over the top of the wall, above the rampart's walkway and onto the glass shards embedded in the cement. He screamed as he hung there, unable to climb up or down, trapped.

'Don't shoot. We're here to release him,' I said, drawing my pistols.

Wes opened the gate to the pen and ran in, waving his arms and shouting, 'Hold your fire, hold your fire!'

I followed him, a percussion pistol in each hand, past Unaduti and his people towards where Nakni was hanging. The nearest agent on the wall fired his musket. The ball splinted a shard of embedded glass close to Nakni's face, and he fell. Wes dived, arms outstretched to prevent Nakni's skull from smashing on the concrete, but the poor boy's legs crumpled beneath him and the sickening sound of his bones snapping echoed around the yard.

Shut it out, Ani. Your empathy won't stop his murder.

Wes covered Nakni's broken body with his own as I spun and aimed one pistol at the advancing Unaduti and another at the musket-wielding guards atop the wall.

'Out of the way,' Unaduti said.

'Fuck you,' I said.

'He was trying to escape.'

'He's innocent. A Coor'Seyan has confessed.'

'I don't care. He was still trying to escape.'

'Well, he isn't now. I'm getting him to a hospital.'

'He can be treated here.'

'Forget it.'

Unaduti took a step forward.

'I'll blow your fucking brains out,' I said, taking aim at the centre of Unaduti's forehead.

'You wouldn't dare.'

'Actually, I'm having difficulty resisting,' I said, the truth of my words alarming me.

Blow the candle out, Ani.

Unaduti sneered. He started to take another step. My finger squeezed around the trigger of my pistol. Xol knows I wanted to kill him.

'Enough, for Xol's sake, enough, Unaduti!' Sodia came running towards the pen, his face reddening as he gasped for air.

I relaxed my finger and lowered my pistols.

'What is the meaning of this?' Sodia said, placing his hand on Unaduti's chest and pushing the agent back.

'Your dog just tried to murder an innocent man,' I said.

'He was escaping,' Unaduti growled, trying to push past his boss.

'Never mind that now,' Sodia said, holding his agent back with his outstretched arm. 'Get the lad to our infirmary, Kohee.'

Wes picked Nakni up, but instead of taking him back into the tower and to the CIB's infirmary as ordered, he carried the injured man out of the pen and across the yard towards the main entrance.

'Kohee, where are you going with that prisoner?' Sodia shouted.

'Consider him released,' I said.

By the time I arrived at Noon Claw Hospital with Dee and a dozen other cadets he trusted, Nakni had come out of surgery and was recovering in a private room. Wes was at his bedside, sitting on the only chair present, his arm resting on a small cabinet with an empty vase on it.

As I entered, he stood and said, 'I'm going back to the tower to see what I can find out.'

'Is that sensible?' I said.

'Let them try anything with me.'

A few minutes after Wes left, Nakni's surgeon, a tall woman who was younger than me, entered the room with a portly male nurse.

'What's the damage?' I asked.

'Besides the cuts and pistol wounds, he's broken the tibia and fibula of both legs, and the femur of the right, which required realigning,' she said.

The nurse was attempting to wake Nakni from his chloroform-induced stupor with ammonia smelling salts.

'He's not waking,' I said.

'He will. He has a strong heart. And we heard no arrhythmia,' the surgeon said.

'Will he fully recover?'

'As far as I can tell, there's no injury to the spinal cord, so he'll be able to walk. But whether he'll regain full mobility is a different matter.'

'Did he say anything before you operated on him?'

'Nothing comprehensible. He was in far too much discomfort.'

The nurse continued to hold the ammonia salts under Nakni's nose until he woke and swiped the offensive hand away. He coughed and tried to sit up, staring wildly at his surroundings. Then he cried out and fell back on the bed.

'I'm going to administer a tiny dose of the elixir of the poppy,' the surgeon said.

I adjusted the curtain so the light through the window wasn't falling onto Nakni's face. I sat down beside him and beckoned Dee, who was hovering in the doorway, to come in.

'Dee, I want you and your fellow cadets to guard this man in teams around the clock,' I said.

'You think he's still in danger?' Dee said.

'I'm not taking any chances. And nor should you. Remember, teams, Dee, no fewer than three of you at any one time. There's safety in numbers.'

When I was alone with Nakni, I waited for the poppy to take effect. I watched as his groaning quietened down, and his breathing eased. I wondered if he was drifting back to sleep, but he surprised me.

'I suppose I should thank you for saving my life,' he said, keeping his eyes closed.

'Why were you trying to escape?' I said.

'Let's just say I was persuaded to.'

'A set-up?'

'Forget it. It doesn't matter.'

'Give me a name. We might be able to prosecute.'

'My word against half a dozen CIB agents?'

'Just tell me as a friend.'

'I was taken to the exercise pen, later than normal, by one of the jailers on duty,' he said. 'Unaduti was waiting for me there. He said, "I can kill you here, and move your corpse to the bottom of the wall, or give you a head start." So I ran. Then you arrived and saw the rest.' He sighed. 'Why did you come?'

'To see you released. We've arrested Mycale I'Krayag for Areel's murder,' I said.

'Mycale?'

'Yes.'

'Why would he hurt Areel?'

'He says Areel was having an affair with his wife.'

Nakni laughed, and began to cough.

'I thought so,' I said. 'At any rate, you're free now.'

'Free of what?' he said, staring at his splintered legs.

'Would you rather be dead?'

He looked away and rubbed tears from his eyes.

'I'm sorry, Nitushi, truly I am. For your loss, for your pain. But I tried to help you and Nita,' I said.

'I would have told you, but Nita… she saw an angle, and I owed her,' he said.

'She and Hinatse tried to blackmail the killer?'

'Yes.'

'So who killed Areel?'

'That's what's so funny, she never told me. All the beatings the CIB gave me, their attempt to silence me, all pointless.'

He blinked and tears escaped.

I sighed and looked around the room. I believed him, and the disappointment stung. 'Why wouldn't she tell you?' I said, my question aimed more at the now dead Nita than at poor Nakni.

'Afraid of what I would do, I suppose.'

I hadn't expected him to answer. But with Nita gone, I wondered what else he might share. 'Do you know if Ameeleyor was aligned with Areel – politically, religiously?'

'I think so. They were both devout, true believers in the stones.'

The lad grimaced and tried to adjust his body to face me.

'Okay, rest now. You'll see some odd faces about. I'm arranging an unorthodox guard for you.'

But now he wanted to ask questions. 'Have you seen Memi?'

'Not for a few days. But she's safe with the others who escaped from the Stars.'

'And those who were arrested with me?'

'All either released or in the process of being released.'

'Then it's over?'

'So it would seem. Unless you'd like to tell me anything further.'

He shook his head and closed his eyes. A few minutes later, he began to snore.

When Wes returned, I joined him in the hallway outside Nakni's room. The big man's face was still flushed with anger, although now a certain sadness, something close to grief, was rising to the surface. He took my arm and led me away from Dee and the other cadets until we stood out of earshot.

'What did you find out?' I said.

'That I'm without a tribe,' he said, staring past me, at the wall.

'Excuse me?'

'The regular perimeter guards were told this morning to attend a surprise training session. Then Nakni's exercise time was delayed; no reason given to either him or the jailers.'

'By Unaduti?'

'By the usual chain of command – no questions asked. There's more. A new emergency directive has been issued: find Ameeleyor A'Jozaf.'

Mani was laughing as I crossed the drawbridge at Horizon's Outlook. The boy darted past the open kitchen door towards the western terrace, chased by Josee. She stopped when she saw me approaching and whirled to greet me, her smile broad and welcoming. She was about to speak when the light in her eyes dimmed, and the warmth faded from her face. No doubt she had remembered we were supposed to be fighting.

'Ani, how goes it with you?' she said.

'I couldn't tell you,' I said.

Oura emerged from the pantry, blindfolded by his handkerchief.

'Ani, is that you?' he said.

'Who else?' I said.

He took the blindfold off and hugged me.

'Thank Xol you're alive,' he said.

'Barely,' Josee said. 'You don't look well.'

'The heat,' I said.

'You don't normally suffer.'

'I hurt my head.'

'Where?'

'It's of no concern.'

'It may not be to you.'

She started patting my skull less than gently, and I tried to pull away, but she seized me in her powerful arms and held me close as she searched for the tender spot. I rested my head on her shoulder in surrender and squealed when she discovered the swollen lump.

'By the spirits, how did you do this?' she said.

'A suspect didn't care for my line of questioning.'

'Then you have your murderer?'

I didn't answer. I just embraced her.

'Oh, Ani, whatever is the matter?'

'I think I'll leave you two alone,' Oura said.

'Thank you, cousin,' I said.

'Forget it, we're family,' he said.

After Oura had gone, Josee had me lie down on the settee in the den with the door to the eastern balcony open to let the breeze in. She gave me a bundle of ice for my head and wrapped a cold cloth around my neck. She pulled my trousers off and helped me out of my shirt, inspecting the wound where the pistol ball grazed me.

'You have been in the wars, haven't you, love?' she said.

'Superficial wounds,' I said.

'Only by a matter of inches. Who shot you?'

'Just a lad from the Depths a couple of nights ago. One of Mani's tribe, more scared than I was probably.'

Mani was peering into the den, hanging onto the doorframe, reluctant to step inside.

'Who was it?' he said.

'Dasan,' I said.

'You met Dasan?'

'I did.'

'Dasan is our leader.'

I wasn't sure what to say, but I wanted to keep the conversation going. I smiled at the boy and said, 'I know.'

'I like him.'

'He seemed a little dim to me.'

'But he's brave,' Mani said, letting go of the doorframe and standing at the threshold of the den.

'Your brother certainly is.'

'Hani will lead us one day, and we'll take over the Depths.'

'That's a lot of territory to win.'

Mani shrugged as if such a daunting task were nothing. He pursed his lips and stared at me, suspicion in his eyes. 'Did you shoot Dasan?'

'No.'

He smiled and nodded. 'Did you meet anyone else?'

'A thin little girl who wears horsetail necklaces.'

He pointed at me, suddenly excited. 'That's Jacira. Was she wearing the belt I got her?'

'A shiny leather one?'

He nodded again.

'She was,' I said.

Mani ran into the den and jumped onto the end of the settee.

'I wouldn't sit too close to my feet, lad, they stink,' I said.

He pinched his nose and made Josee laugh.

'I'm going to prepare a bath for you. Come and help me, Mani,' she said.

'Not too hot, please,' I said, shutting my eyes.

After I bathed, I put on one of Josee's robes and joined her and Mani on the western terrace. We ate a prawn salad and washed it down with freshly squeezed and iced orange juice, mixed with honey and crushed mint. The sun was dipping over the far western claw, and the sky above the horizon was a blended watercolour of layered yellows, oranges and violets, which grew deeper and dimmer until starlight broke through the gloom above.

After we finished eating, Mani went to play marbles on the southern corner of the terrace, leaving Josee and me alone. I looked at the damage to our home and then at my wife.

'I'm sorry,' I said.

'That doesn't matter, love. You're alive. That's all I care about,' Josee said.

'No, I need you to know I'm sorry about everything: that I couldn't leave this case alone, about your paintings, poor Snuggs, our home, but mostly about Dabreeyor.'

'You don't need to do this, Ani.'

'It feels like people are always leaving.'

'I'm not going anywhere.'

The doorbell rang.

'Except, apparently, to answer the door,' Josee said, getting up.

I watched Mani knock the last of his marbles out of the ring he'd chalked. I stood up, groaning as my aching body complained, and walked over to where the boy was playing. I knelt next to him and chose a marble to use as a medium-sized shooter.

'Come on, lad, I wager I can beat you in three goes or less,' I said.

'You need a bigger marble,' he said.

'Maybe, maybe not. You go first.'

Mani picked the biggest of his collection and used his index finger to flick it. But he couldn't generate the necessary power or control the direction. My method was to place my middle fingernail on the ground and quickly rub my thumb against it in a clicking motion. My first shot almost cleared the ring.

Mani's eyes widened, but he neither smiled nor frowned.

'Show me,' he said in a flat but firm tone.

Before I could, his attention was taken by Josee, who had returned to the western terrace accompanied by Hani. The boy was limping badly and nursing his right arm, which had been cut from elbow to wrist.

'What happened?' Mani said, leaping to his feet and running to his older brother.

'Itzel and some others tried to kill me, and when Dasan sided with me, they killed him instead,' Hani said.

'How'd you escape?'

'I jumped from the pier.'

'You could've landed on the rocks.'

'It was either jump or die.'

'Let's talk about this later,' Josee said. 'Take your shirt off and sit down so I can clean and bandage that cut.'

I crawled over and removed the lad's coal-stained deerskin shoes so I could check his ankle. It was warm and swollen, and he winced when I prodded him, but I couldn't find a break.

'Keep your foot up, lad,' I said.

I poured him a glass of orange juice which he snatched from me and gulped down. As Josee bathed and bandaged his cut, I bound his ankle as tightly as I could. When I was finished, I took the last of our ice from the box and wrapped it in a wax cloth for him.

'Why did your tribe try and kill you, lad?' I said.

He didn't speak.

'Why not tell me? What do you owe them now?' I said.

'I shouldn't have told you anything. That was a mistake. I should leave.'

He tried to stand, but Josee pushed him back into the seat.

'You're not going anywhere tonight,' Josee said. 'You will stay here with your brother and be pampered. Ani, shut up. No more questions.'

I was too tired to argue, so I knelt back down and spent the rest of the evening playing marbles with Mani while his brother fell asleep next to Josee. She remained with the lad all night, just to prevent him from leaving, but I couldn't stay awake and so made room for Mani on the bench and went to bed early, my head still sore and my body fatigued.

The following morning, I woke before everyone else, so I got dressed and visited Ezno. He gave me some seaweed, and I stole four mackerel he had caught in the rocky breakwaters where Sundown Claw curved east into the Coiled Sea. Once I arrived back home, I put a griddle pan on a high heat and made a dressing for the seaweed from sweet vinegar, fennel seeds and mixed herbs.

Josee was still asleep on the western terrace with Hani, but Mani was awake and playing with his marbles. The lad was a quick learner and had already perfected the technique I had shown him, having discarded the larger shooter for the one I'd used.

I rubbed Josee's shoulder until she woke. Her reaction disturbed Hani, and he opened his eyes.

'I always wondered who lived in these flats,' he said.

'Artists and weirdos,' Mani said.

I served the griddled mackerel, and we ate in silence, not really sure what to say. It was Hani who overcame his reticence first.

'Mani says you arrested a Coor'Seyan,' he said.

'We have,' I said.

'Does he have dark hair?'

'As black as a Kahokeyan's.'

'He's not the man I saw.'

'Oh? I didn't think you saw his face,' I said, trying to appear disinterested as I finished off my mackerel.

'I didn't, but his hair stuck out from under his hood. It was blond.'

'I see. Was this person big?'

'Quite big.'

'What colour were his robes?'

'It was hard to tell in the rain. Blue and gold I think.'

'I see.'

'Will you make me testify?'

'No, Hani, I won't. But thank you for telling me.'

'Will it help?'

'Well, it's convinced me to help the Coor'Seyan. After all, he's an innocent man.'

CHAPTER TWENTY-TWO

It was another hot and cloudless day, and folk were strolling and dawdling to their appointments in the neat brick offices of Advocate's Row, just off of Agale Thoroughfare, roughly halfway between the Square and the Al'Mayran embassy.

The advocates, who usually took pride in their appearance, and whose dress code consisted of expensive suits, buttoned-up shirts, and throat-strangling ties, were climbing out of their cabs and private carriages with their suit jackets and ties in their hands, and their shirts open at the collar. They stood on the walkway, fixing their appearance before entering their place of work.

I hadn't been waiting long before I spotted the armoured police waggon heading north along Agale Thoroughfare. It was being pulled by a pair of eight-feet-tall draught horses and guarded by three armed officers, two on the rear platform and another up front with the driver. Sunlight glinted off the barrels of their muskets and off the metal chaffrons protecting the horses' heads.

As the waggon neared, I raised my police emblem and flagged the driver to pull into the edge of the thoroughfare.

'What's your name?' I said to her.

'Jula, ma'am.'

'Give me a lift to the embassy.'

'That's a little irregular.'

'I'm going there anyway. Are you going to make me pay for a cab?'

I walked around the horses and climbed onto the driver's box, squeezing in next to an older sergeant of slim build.

'How goes it with you, Taka?' I said.

'I am well, Sulaqua,' he said. 'How's life in the murder inspectors' department?'

'Of late, a little stressful.'

'I can only imagine. Come back and walk a beat, we always need good officers.'

'Sounds too much like hard work.'

For a while, as we drove north, I chatted with Taka and his colleagues, but as we neared the embassy, I grew quiet and looked out for the scarlet-and-black robes of the Coor'Seyan soldiers whose turn it was to guard the main gate. When we arrived, Jula steered the waggon through the opening and brought us to a halt on the drive.

'Wait here,' I said to her.

I hopped off the waggon and ran over to the captain's cabin.

'Thank Xol it's you, I'Seth,' I said when I saw the young lieutenant inside.

'Inspector, what can I do for you?' he said.

'It's what you can do for I'Krayag.'

'We were expecting the police to bring him, but not you specifically.'

'I'm not supposed to be here. These officers are expected to hand their prisoner over to the ambassador, which means I'Dreng.'

'He's been watching from the embassy steps all morning, along with several CIB agents.'

I looked over my shoulder, down the drive to the portico. I could make out blue- and gold-clad guards and several uniformed Kahokeyans, including the giant form of Wesu Kohee, who appeared to be engaged in an increasingly animated discussion with a man I suspected was Unaduti.

'If we hand I'Krayag over to I'Dreng, I've reason to believe he'll come to harm. His life, and even his wife's, may be in danger,' I said.

I'Seth set his jaw and narrowed his eyes. 'What do you need me to do?' he said.

I explained my plan to I'Seth, who nodded, a solemn expression on his brooding face. When we left his cabin, we saw I'Dreng, his guards and the CIB agents clear the embassy's steps and run in our direction.

I'Seth ordered a young lad to race to the barracks and alert I'Kalmeen; he had the rest of his company block the path by standing in a line shoulder to shoulder. His people moved with quick grace and no small amount of flair, and once in formation, they looked a formidable opponent, their black-and-scarlet robes billowing in the breeze and the tips of their silver-and-gold spears catching the sunlight.

'Xol help us,' I said, hurrying back to the waggon.

'What's happening, Sulaqua?' Taka said, as I passed where he and Jula sat on the driver's box.

The skin above the sergeant's nose and around his eyes wrinkled with anxiety and confusion as he watched the unfolding situation. He suddenly looked very old to me.

'Nothing to worry about, Taka, just further debate between the Al'Mayrans as to who will receive the prisoner,' I said. 'Best bring him out.'

'We're supposed to drive up the embassy steps and hand over—'

'The prisoner is a Coor'Seyan soldier, the former regimental sergeant major, and it appears his people would like him back,' I said, gesturing to the line of guards.

'I see. This is most irregular.'

'They're Al'Mayran, Taka, so what difference does it make to us who we deliver him to? Besides, do you want to get in the middle of a foreign civil conflict?'

He studied me for a moment, his head shaking and his mouth open.

'Whatever happens, it's my responsibility, okay?' I said.

'Yes, ma'am,' he said.

I'Krayag's hands were chained together, as were his feet. This limited his gait to a shuffle. He didn't look at me as he was brought out of the waggon, and there was nothing in his behaviour to indicate he had tried to crack my head open on a hardwood floor yesterday. Outwardly, at least, he was composed and appeared once more to have resigned himself to the role of scapegoat and martyr.

In the time it took to release I'Krayag from his bonds, I'Dreng, his people and the CIB agents – who, along with Wes, included Unaduti and the barrel-chested Sewati – had reached the Coor'Seyans' line.

'What is the meaning of this, I'Seth?' I'Dreng said.

'I have my orders,' the young captain replied firmly.

'Whose orders? The only orders you need to obey are Ambassador I'Rasnee's.'

'He doesn't command my battalion. Brigadier I'Kalmeen does.'

'I'Kalmeen has no authority in this matter.'

'He does when it relates to one of his men.'

As I'Seth and I'Dreng argued, I stood by I'Krayag.

'How goes it with you today, Mycale?' I said.

He ignored me and kept his eyes fixed straight ahead on his comrades.

'I'm fine, I thank you,' I said. 'A bit of a sore head and a nice lump, but I'll live. Of course, only time will tell if my intellect, such as it is, has been impaired.'

His eyes briefly flickered in my direction, then regained their focus.

'You know, a witness says the Al'Mayran who dumped Areel's body had blond hair and wore robes of blue and gold,' I said.

'What witness?' I'Krayag said, without looking my way.

'A different one than the witness who saw you with Je'mymor A'Soyne in the park.'

'I have nothing further to say.'

'Will you keep your silence when I'Dreng is questioning you? Do you really think he'll keep his word and not harm your wife?'

No reaction.

'I suppose you might hold out for a little while, to protect Ameeleyor and your children,' I said.

'Leave my family alone,' I'Krayag said, finally facing me.

'I'd like to, but what about Ambassador I'Rasnee? I'm sure it's his influence that has the CIB scouring the city for them.'

That got his attention.

'That's right, Mycale. Whatever deal you struck isn't worth fish shit. Your wife is being hunted as we speak.'

Unaduti, whose eyes had kept darting towards me as I spoke to I'Krayag, stepped forward to join I'Dreng. As he did, Wes walked away from the stand-off onto the embassy's lawn. I met him out of earshot of my fellow police officers.

'What's happening, Ani?' Wes said.

'You have eyes, don't you?' I said.

'Why is Mycale unchained and out of the waggon?'

'I take it Unaduti is in command?'

'For all intents and purposes.'

'And he's coming to speak to me.'

Unaduti held his palms up to the Coor'Seyan line and took his time walking around them.

'Are you behind this, Sulaqua?' he said.

'Looks like an Al'Mayran affair to me,' I said.

'Hand the prisoner over.'

'To who?' I said.

'Captain I'Dreng.'

'The Coor'Seyans are in the way.'

'They won't attack the New Capital police.'

'I'm not taking that risk.'

As Unaduti and I debated the point, the rest of his agents circled Wes and me.

'Get the prisoner,' Unaduti said to them.

'Yes, sir,' Sewati said.

I reacted before the stocky CIB agent could and placed my hand on his chest with my body at a right angle to his. He smiled and held his arms out at his sides, but his eyes were alight with anger.

'What are you about, Sulaqua?' Unaduti said.

'We're here to deliver the prisoner to an Al'Mayran,' I said.

'What do you think I'm trying to do? This is ridiculous. Captain I'Dreng, come and get I'Krayag.'

I'Dreng didn't move at first. He was still squaring off against I'Seth. But he took a step to his left, and when I'Seth didn't react, he walked without hurrying around the Coor'Seyans. I'Seth scanned the south for reinforcements, and when he saw none, he followed I'Dreng, telling his men and women to hold their line.

'This is getting dangerous, Ani,' Wes said.

'Then stay out of it, Wes,' I said, backing away from Sewati with my hand on the grip of my sword and my focus as sharp as the blade's point.

The candle was out.

Doubt was my only enemy.

I'Dreng and I'Seth approached me together, walking in unison, facing forwards as if they were taking part in a parade.

'Hand the Coor'Seyan over, Sulaqua,' I'Dreng said.

'Okay, okay. Mycale, please come here,' I said.

I'Krayag pulled away from the two officers guarding him, both of whom started to follow.

'Just the prisoner,' I said, fixing Taka with a stare.

He nodded at his fellow officers.

'Now take the waggon and leave, Taka,' I said.

'But Sulaqua…' Taka said.

'You've done all you can.'

I'Krayag walked in a half-circle that led him away from I'Dreng and behind me.

'I think we should stay, ma'am,' Taka said, eyeing I'Dreng.

'Please leave, Taka. You'll only get your people hurt if you stay,' I said. I could have added *and cloud my judgement.*

With a shake of his head, Taka ushered his officers into the back of the waggon and climbed onto the driver's box with Jula, who turned the vehicle on a sixpence and drove out of the embassy, taking my concern for their safety with her.

'You're all alone now,' I'Dreng said.

'Not quite,' Wes said, joining me.

'No need, Wes. I don't want to cause you any trouble,' I said.

'You're nothing but trouble.'

I was about to speak again when a horn sounded to the south. Across the lawn, Brigadier I'Kalmeen approached on his mount from the barracks, with his colonel at his side and what appeared to be his entire battalion, marching in formation, behind them.

'Yield,' I'Seth said to I'Dreng.

I'Dreng appeared to accept the changing circumstances and took a step back. But it was a feint. He drew his sword and directed its hilt at

I'Seth's face. The young captain's nose twisted and split from the impact, which knocked him off his feet. As the blood covered his face, he fell to the ground and lay unconscious, his eyes wide open.

There was a brief pause, during which everyone grasped the significance of what just happened. And then it began. The Coor'Seyans reacted first. They came running towards their fallen commander with their spears pointed and I'Dreng in their sights. The captain of the ambassador's guard paid them no heed. With I'Seth down, he made for I'Krayag. I drew my sword and my fighting dagger and stood in his way, calm as you like.

On paper, I'Dreng had the advantage over me in both height and reach. But his height made him lazy, giving him a crutch he relied on too much, turning his strength to weakness. He never learnt subtlety, never developed, couldn't see his reach made him vulnerable to the smaller more agile fencer with the shorter and lighter blade. The result: he tended to remain too stationary, save for powerful lunges that were slower than he thought. I parried them with increasing ease while his growing frustration made his moves all the more readable.

Panic kills.

Discipline is a weapon.

Act.

I countered the next lunge and created a line to jab the point of my blade into the thigh of his leading leg. The shock and pain caused him to hobble back. I suppressed a surge of giddiness that fired, like a jellyfish sting, through my body. I refocused and advanced, feigning a high attack. I'Dreng lost his stance completely and bent his arm, trying to block. I advanced again and kicked him between the legs. He went down.

The shooting started.

It was I'Dreng's men and women who fired first. They had no hope of closing the distance on the charging Coor'Seyans, so they drew their weapons on the soldiers and shot them in the back. Most of the pistol balls hit their mark. One stray ball found a gap and struck me, glancing off a rib.

Numbness gave way to burning heat like an ice-covered lake melting in spring sunshine. I kept hold of my fighting dagger but fell onto one knee, driving the point of my sword into the earth for balance.

Ignore the pain.

Blow the candle out.

Around me, the chaos escalated. Half the Coor'Seyans were on the ground, clasping wounds, with one young soldier doubled up, holding her stomach, blood seeping between her fingers. Another clutched his ear and screamed. Those who remained on their feet turned and rushed I'Dreng's men and women. The ambassador's guards drew their swords, and the clash of steel rang out across the embassy's grounds.

I searched for Brigadier I'Kalmeen, and saw Wes wrestling with Sewati and Unaduti. The older man had his arm around Wes's neck, trying to drag the big man down. As he did, Sewati landed blow after blow into Wes's midriff.

A burst of anger extinguished the pain. I dropped my sword, got to my feet and ran. When I was about four feet away from Sewati, I jumped and curled my legs to strike him like a cannonball. We both hit the ground hard, and the air left my lungs and was replaced by an intense ache that rose to my neck as I gasped for air.

By now, I'Dreng was getting to his feet and searching for I'Krayag. He spotted the Coor'Seyan skirting the melee, walking with a serene calm towards Brigadier I'Kalmeen as if the fight beside him wasn't happening. I'Dreng drew his pistol and took aim. Despite my burning lungs and the acid seizing my muscles, I managed to rise and scramble clear of the other CIB agents just as they tackled Wes to the ground.

'Mycale, take cover!' I shouted in a hoarse voice between gasping breaths.

The Coor'Seyan neither looked my way nor turned to spot his pursuer. He threw himself flat on the grass just before I'Dreng's pistol ball embedded itself in the wall beyond. I drew my percussion pistols and fired one, aiming just past I'Dreng's ear to get his attention. I pointed the other at his face.

Brigadier I'Kalmeen and eight mounted Coor'Seyans rode into the heart of the confusion. They circled I'Dreng's men and women, who, despite their opponents' injuries, were close to defeat. They seemed relieved to have an opportunity for honourable surrender and threw their weapons to the ground.

The CIB, however, did not capitulate. Perhaps they saw little reason to fear the Coor'Seyans, or maybe they were just determined to finish their mission. Unaduti, whose right eye was now swollen shut, had drawn his pistol and had the barrel pointed at Wes's head. Behind him, his agents were nursing various strains and aches, all of which Wes was responsible for.

'Hand the prisoner over to I'Dreng,' Unaduti said.

'What do you say, Wes? Shall we let Mycale choose?' I said.

Wes's expression was dark, his nostrils were flared, and spittle had gathered in the corners of his mouth. His chest rose and fell, and his hands were clenched at his sides. His good humour and gentleness were gone, replaced by rage and enmity.

'Why not?' he growled.

'Who will it be, I'Dreng or I'Kalmeen?' I said to I'Krayag.

'I am a soldier,' he said.

'Then go to your regiment.'

I'Dreng pushed me aside, aggravating my wound, and lunged for the Coor'Seyan. The pain triggered my anger, and for the first time since the fighting began, the sounds of the world fell away, and the din of turning lift wheels rang in my ears and the fires of industry burned in my heart. Xol's tentacles wrapped around my head and squeezed my temples until I thought they would crack. All I wanted to see was I'Dreng dead at my feet, a hole in his brow and his brains soiling the lush green grass.

I became a passenger, a witness to actions I couldn't control, unable or unwilling to blow the candle out.

The next thing I knew, I had I'Dreng's blond ponytail wrapped around my hand, and I was snapping his head back with as much fury as I could muster. He spun and fell, and I drove my knee into his face. The sound of his nose breaking was as stirring to me as the driving beat of festival drums, and the way his nose crumpled against my hard bone turned my anger to intoxication. Hurting him felt too good, and when I had him on the ground, I rammed the muzzle of my pistol down his throat until he gagged.

'That's enough, Inspector,' a deep voice said. 'Sulaqua, that is enough.'

And then Brigadier I'Kalmeen was dismounting beside me and putting one hand on my shoulder and sliding a thumb between the hammer and percussion cap of my pistol.

'Come, Ani, it's over. Mycale is with his regiment. You saved him. You brought him to me,' he said. 'Don't sully such an honourable act with murder.'

CHAPTER TWENTY-THREE

Wes and I sat at a dark wooden table in the den of Brigadier I'Kalmeen's cliffside home. There was a blue stained-glass window in the eastern wall looking out on Yawe Bay and the financial towers of Treasure's Anchor. The hardwood floor was free of carpets or rugs, and the black settee was plain leather. The walls, however, were covered in red-painted plaster, shaped into the swirling forms of spirits, upon which I'Kalmeen had hung Coor'Seyan weapons, a whaling spear, and a ceremonial silver fishing net. Pride of place was given to a painting of his homeland on the Al'Mayran coast. It depicted heavy rain, teeming from grey clouds and lashing against the Palace of Ash, once home to the Coor'Seyan monarchs of old, kings and queens who had been Harns more than Al'Mayrans, descendants of invaders, who, it was said, launched their attack riding on the backs of giant blue whales.

Opposite me, Wes was quiet, seething, the mists of his rage slow to lift. In contrast, my anger had subsided, replaced by relief that I'd delivered I'Krayag to his regiment. The decision may have cost me my livelihood, but I told myself it was worth it. Although a nagging doubt had already set in, and my heart felt hollow when I thought of my dismissal – the nature of sacrifice, I supposed.

I'Kalmeen fetched a decanter of dark Al'Mayran wine made from the fire grape and placed three glasses on the table along with a bowl of ointment and a roll of bandages.

'Is that purifying oil?' I said.

'I'm afraid so, Inspector. Now, show me your wound, please.'

'I need a drink first.'

'I'll pour,' Wes said, rubbing his eyes and shaking his head as if to clear the fog.

I drank my wine in a single swig and shook the glass for a refill.

'Go easy, Ani,' Wes said.

'It's a little late for that,' I said.

I took my jacket off, unbuttoned the lower half of my shirt and pulled it aside to reveal an insubstantial gash.

'Ah, it's nothing,' I said, drawing my shirt back together. But I'Kalmeen pushed my hand away and dipped a soft cloth into the ointment.

'I'm in your debt for what you did for Mycale,' he said.

'You can repay me by answering some questions,' I said.

'You never stop, do you, Inspector?' he said with a sigh. He patted the cut with the ointment.

I jumped and squealed and gritted my teeth as he cleaned the wound. When he was satisfied, I helped him wrap my torso with the bandage.

'Are you a radical, Brigadier?' I said.

He laughed and said, 'Far from it.'

'What about I'Rasnee?'

'I try not to concern myself with the politics of others.'

'Did you hire Garen I'Fanadhar as I'Krayag's advocate?'

'No.'

'Heard of him?'

'He's embassy council.'

'Not connected to your regiment?'

'No.'

'How did he come to be with I'Krayag this morning?'

'I have no idea.'

'I'Krayag is innocent, isn't he?'

'I suspect so.'

'You know so. And furthermore, you know who killed Areel.'

The brigadier sat back in his chair, sipping wine and staring out of the window. 'What does this Al'Mayran affair matter to you? The Kahokeyan lad, Areel's lover, has been released,' he said.

'He can hardly walk.'

'That's not an Al'Mayran's doing. Your own people did that.'

'The CIB aren't my people, and if you'd been honest with me a few days ago, maybe you could have prevented Nakni's injuries and the death of an innocent woman.'

'Is your life so simple, Inspector?' he said with a wistful smile.

'I try to keep it so.'

'Well, I don't have that luxury.'

'Let's discuss lifeblood stones,' I said.

'Must we?'

'We found the broken pieces of one in I'Advay's office.'

'What does that have to do with me?'

'He stole it from you, knowing full well you and Ambassador I'Rasnee were planning to supply them to High Chief Naka to build a weapon. Did you order your men and women to hunt down I'Advay, or did you notify the ambassador who sent I'Dreng and I'Remo?'

'I'Dreng is an animal and I'Remo a mindless idiot.'

'Did they kill I'Advay?'

I'Kalmeen ignored my question. 'What drives you, Sulaqua? Do you always need to be proven right? I may have misjudged your character, but I won't answer these questions. I will, however, be grateful to you for the rest of my life for delivering Mycale. What will happen to you now?'

I leant back in my chair and folded my arms, studying I'Kalmeen. I figured he wasn't ready to confess his part in all this, and I saw little use in pressing him further, at least for now.

'Suspended. Brought before a tribunal. I could be finished,' I said.

'I sincerely hope not. You are very gifted. And what about you, Special Agent Kohee?' I'Kalmeen said.

'I'm through with the CIB. Never mind them,' Wes said. 'Despite what Inspector Sulaqua thinks, there are good men and women who work there, but our leaders set a tone of fear, malice and corruption I can no longer ignore.'

'What will you do?'

'See if I can join the police.'

I laughed.

'I'm serious, Ani,' Wes said. 'If they'll have me.'

But I couldn't stop chuckling.

When Wes and I said farewell to I'Kalmeen, I tried to read his face, but all I saw was anxiety. Whatever tormented him, returning I'Krayag had not eased his burden.

Perhaps I was drunk on the wine or intoxicated from the fight, but while Wes went to his office in the embassy to fetch some personal belongings, I paid I'Rasnee another visit.

The guards outside his offices hadn't taken part in the melee, but, judging by their scowls and abrupt manner, they had learnt of it.

'Wait here,' one of them said.

I smiled at his comrade while I waited, never breaking my gaze, almost daring him to respond as the stench of sweat rose from my clothes and all the bruises and tiny cuts and grazes I had suffered began to ache and sting.

The first guard returned, nodded, and let the door slam in my face.

'Thanks,' I said, pushing it open.

The older secretary stood as I entered, but I ignored him as I passed his desk and heard him say, 'Of all the gall.'

I'Rasnee was sitting at a small breakfast table with I'Remo stood behind him. The ambassador was drinking tea and eating a fruit scone while signing some papers. I sat opposite him at the table and winked at I'Remo, whose face was turning purple.

'How's the ankle? Able to run on it? How about jump over a garden wall?' I said, taunting him.

When I'Rasnee finished his scone and washed it down with the dregs of his tea, I'Remo took the cup and saucer and placed them on a silver tray, which he took into the secretaries' office before returning to his master's side.

'What do you want, Sulaqua?' I'Rasnee said.

The man had lost weight, and his face bore the mutilations of strain. His skin had grown ashen, almost cadaverous, and hung from his bones like wet paper.

'Are you a radical, sir?' I said.

'I beg your pardon?' he said, either no longer willing or unable to maintain the politician's civil facade.

'Are you a radical, a revolutionary, looking to overthrow your king?' I said.

'I refuse to validate such a ridiculous question by answering it,' he said.

'You could just say no.'

'No, Inspector, I am not a radical. I am loyal to my king. Is this why you're here, to insult me, after starting a fight and attacking Captain I'Dreng?'

'He started it.'

'Because you refused to hand I'Krayag over.'

'I handed him over, just not to you. Tell me, how did Garen I'Fanadhar come to be I'Krayag's advocate?'

'How should I know?'

'He's embassy council,' I said, laughing and gesturing towards I'Rasnee.

'Anyone is free to hire him. I have no idea how or why I'Krayag came to do so. Are we done, Inspector?'

'Almost. One more thing: the lifeblood stone weapon, the one that doesn't exist, somebody fired it at my home last night, practically sliced through the wall.'

'Your point?'

'I want you to remember I can appear as anyone I wish and go anywhere I please.'

'Is that a threat, Inspector?'

'Sleep well, Darnell,' I said, rising.

As I was leaving, the double doors of the secretaries' office swung open and I'Dreng entered. His eyes were circled with black ink. Upon seeing me, he reached for his sword.

'Normain, no!' I'Rasnee shouted.

'Any time you want a rematch, pistol or sword, you let me know,' I whispered to I'Dreng as I passed.

I waited for Wes at the main entrance. Lieutenant I'Seth, his company now bolstered by what appeared to be half the battalion, had resumed his duties.

'I thought you might have rested this afternoon, Lieutenant,' I said.

'I'm fine, I thank you,' he said.

'And what about your people? That young woman received an ugly stomach wound.'

'Seleenor is being operated on. I'm told, spirits willing, she will live. The rest of my company, those who were hurt, are either being treated or are recovering in the regimental hospital. Their injuries, like mine, are not life-threatening.'

I breathed a sigh of relief. 'I can't tell you how much it pleases me to hear that, Lieutenant.'

Wes emerged from the embassy and stood on the portico, shaking his head. He made his way down the steps and onto the driveway. He had a desk drawer under his arm filled with his possessions, including a set of Coor'Seyan daggers, a pile of papers wrapped and tied with string, and a miniature statue of Xol.

'Shall we go to the Square?' he said when he reached the gate.

'What for? I can be just as easily dismissed tomorrow. Let's get drunk instead.'

I could see Dabreeyor A'Mendayse sitting at my kitchen table as Wes and I crossed the drawbridge. Mani was showing her his new marble technique, and she was doing an excellent job of feigning interest. I didn't spot Hani at first and wondered if he had made his escape. But I saw the top of his head through the window. He was standing beside Josee, helping her prepare dinner.

I waved and winked at Mani as I entered the kitchen and patted Hani on the shoulder.

'How's the ankle, lad?' I said.

'It's nothing,' he said.

He limped onto the western terrace, carrying a serving bowl of seaweed salad.

I stood on my toes, kissed my wife on the cheek and put my arm around her waist.

'What's got into you?' she said.

'Booze mostly,' I said.

'That I can cope with. At least you haven't been beaten or shot today,' Josee said, taking a tray of prawn flatbread out of the stove.

'Oh, I've been shot,' I said, lifting my shirt to show her the bandage. 'See?'

Josee dropped the tray onto the worktop and covered her face with her hands.

'Are you trying to kill me or yourself?' she said.

'Sorry. I didn't think,' I said.

She flung her arms around me and squeezed so tightly I began to reconsider if my rib was broken. But I said nothing. There was nowhere else I wanted to be.

I didn't leave her side for the entire evening, although we said little to each other or to our guests. Wes talked for us. He rediscovered his avuncular nature and made the boys laugh until they cried. As the sun set, Dabreeyor took his hand and showed him a traditional Al'Mayran folk dance in honour of the spirits who resided in the red rocks. And for the first time in days, Areel I'Advay and his golden cane full of broken lifeblood stones seemed distant and abstract and unimportant.

CHAPTER TWENTY-FOUR

I ROSE WITH THE sun and slid out of bed, taking care not to wake Josee. I threw on one of her robes and wandered onto the southern balcony to greet the sea and almost trod on Hani. The boys were used to hard floors and the night sky above their heads and did not sleep well in the den. They had turned Josee's work area into their own private space, demarcated by a line of small and coal-stained deerskin shoes from the doorjamb to the balustrade. I stepped over the improvised border onto neutral territory, leant on the railing, and read the sky.

Off in the distance, low-floating cauliflower clouds were riding a strong westerly breeze, which drove plunging waves into a crisscross of breaks, forcing deep water to the surface. The flat-bottomed clouds might, if inclined, shower the cliffs of New Capital today, treating one claw with a refreshing downpour while leaving its neighbour dry and thirsty.

Josee had bought some smoked haddock the day before and thrown them into the box with replenished ice, which the boys helped her carry and chop. I decided to bake them for breakfast and went into the kitchen to light the oven. But through the window, I saw Etu arrive at the cantilevered platform on Pastnoon Claw.

'What do you want?' I shouted from the northern balcony.

'Kana Hiduse is lying dead at the bottom of Salvation's Climb,' he said.

Hiduse had fallen on his belly with his arms and legs stretched out. He could have been sleeping, except his bed was made of his own guts, and his eyes were open, seeming to express a lack of comprehension, a refusal to accept this was the end, that he couldn't possibly be falling.

'Someone should tell his brother,' Etu said.

'His brother already knows,' I said. I squatted to lift Hiduse's shirt with my fountain pen. 'There's an exit wound in his back. He's been shot.'

'Is that the weapon?' Etu said.

My cousin pointed at the barrel of a percussion pistol lying between the broken pieces of a concrete step.

'Don't touch that,' I said.

I combed the area where Etu had found the barrel until I discovered the snapped grip. The exposed wood was unstained, the splinters sharp, and the carvings of the red spirits still clear. It had belonged to an Al'Mayran.

I reported the death at the nearest police substation in the Al'Mayran fish market and returned home. I explained to Josee that the case wasn't over, that we still might be in danger. Much to her disgust, she agreed to let Etu and Oura stay with her and the boys all day. But only if I would meet her for lunch in the arcade.

The lanes and thoroughfares atop Noon Claw were stippled with damp, after a recent shower, but the stones and cobbles were drying fast. As were the folk I passed on my way to the Square, none of whom opted to carry umbrellas. Their suits and robes and deerskin dresses were blotched with damp stains, but their wearers didn't seem to care.

I found Wes sitting on the steps of the Square. He was out of uniform, dressed in animal-hide trousers and a purple linen shirt. His elbows were resting on his long legs, stretched out in front of him, one foot over the other.

'Have you quit?' I said.

'Yes, I told Sodia,' he said.

'How'd he react?'

'I think I rather took the wind from his sails. He would have preferred to dismiss me, but I robbed him of that pleasure, and I'm delighted to have done so.'

'Listen, Wes. I have news.'

'I warn you, Ani, she's in a foul mood,' Medele said as I placed a bag of boiled sweets on his desk.

'Did she almost form an expression?' I said.

'That's not the attitude to take in there.'

'It'll make little difference.'

I knocked on the door to Imala's office and entered without waiting for an invite. The chief inspector was outside on her terrace, pacing and smoking, with half a dozen twisted cigarette ends forming a trail at her feet.

'So you've surfaced,' she said, glancing in my direction before continuing to pace.

'Yes, ma'am,' I said.

'You're suspended, pending a hearing with a tribunal which will decide your fate.'

'I understand.'

'I hope it was worth it.'

'I think it was.'

'I don't see how. Why couldn't you just allow I'Krayag to be delivered to the ambassador's people?'

'I feared for him and his wife and children.'

'Why do you care?'

'He's innocent.'

'He confessed,' Imala said, her voice rising.

'The confession is fish shit.'

'What does that matter to you? The Al'Mayrans were satisfied and Nakni was freed, all without any lasting damage to the relations between Al'Mayra and New Capital. We could have put this behind us.'

'Tell that to Kana Hiduse.'

'Who?'

'A local climber. He was found dead this morning at the bottom of Salvation's Climb.'

'When did a Kahokeyan falling from the steps become news?'

'When he's been shot by an Al'Mayran pistol.'

Imala turned and stared at me, her arms at her sides, ash from her cigarette falling to the ground.

'Maybe someone was looking for the cane. Maybe they found it,' I said.

'Hand your weapons and emblem in to Medele,' Imala ordered, disappointment evident in her tone.

'This is the only police-issue weapon I have,' I said, unholstering the old flintlock pistol from my baldric and tossing it to Imala along with my emblem. 'Everything else is mine. You can't have them.'

'I assume you have a permit for those percussion pistols?' Imala said.

I shrugged.

'I could have them taken from you,' Imala said.

'Try it,' I said.

'You're a stubborn and unnecessarily provocative fool, Ani. And you will live to regret your actions. If you aren't a police inspector, who are you?'

I snorted a hollow laugh and turned on my heel, already feeling something akin to grief rising in my heart. On the way out, I took one of Medele's boiled sweets. I looked for Dee in the cramped cadets' space.

'Any issues at the hospital?' I said to him.

'No, ma'am. Nakni is never alone. He has many visitors from the Stars.'

'Good. Keep him under protection until someone orders you to stop.'

'Anything else?'

'No, lad. I've been suspended.'

'Oh, Ani.'

'Tell Nakni's people to stay close to him.'

I gave Dee a gentle slap on the cheek and left, my eyes already stinging with tears, before he could finish expressing whatever heartfelt sentiment he felt compelled to make.

Outside, Wes was still waiting on the Square's steps. I ran down and kicked him in the back.

'Come on, big man,' I said.

'Is it done?' he said.

'It is.'

'And how are you?'

'I have no idea,' I said, looking through Wes rather than at him.

'What now?' he said.

'I'm meeting Josee in the arcade in a couple of hours. That gives us time to visit Taliko Hiduse.'

'Why not?' Wes said, slapping his thigh.

Smoke was billowing above the rooftop of the cabin the Hiduse brothers had shared. Wes and I found Taliko in the garden around the back, burning clothes in a steel barrel. He jumped when he heard us coming and spun around, reaching for a pistol tucked in his belt.

'Can I help you?' he said, trying to disguise the fear in his voice.

'We'd like to speak to your brother Kana again,' I said.

He winced at the mention of his brother's name.

'My brother isn't here,' he said after a pause.

'When will he return?' I said.

'I can't say.'

'Where has he gone?'

'Away.'

'Away where?'

'Down the coast, surveying.'

'So he's not lying dead at the bottom of Noon Claw?'

Taliko Hiduse bent over as if someone had punched him in the stomach.

'An Al'Mayran hired you to climb Salvation's Steps, yes?' I said.

He nodded.

'Ready to tell me his name?' I said.

No reply.

'Mycale I'Krayag?' I said.

Taliko cast his eyes down and shook his head.

'Ronayld I'Kryse?' I said.

Taliko looked up, surprised.

'He hired you to find something on the steps. What?'

'We were to help him climb. He did most of the searching.'

'But you weren't alone. Other Al'Mayrans were there too?'

He blinked. 'I saw none.'

'One of them killed your brother,' I said.

'Kana slipped.'

'Before or after he was shot?'

'He slipped. It happens.'

'Of course. Good luck to you, Taliko. Because if the high chief or the Al'Mayrans learn your name, you'll need it.'

Neither Wes nor I were surprised to find the closed sign on display at the apothecary's. I knocked anyway and didn't stop until the narrow staircase creaked. The door opened ajar, not enough to ring the bell, but wide enough to allow dank air and sulphur to escape and for Wes to force himself inside.

Ronayld I'Kryse stood in the centre of his shop floor. His right arm was tucked into the opening of his gown, resting upon the sash around his waist. He raised the other hand and backed away. He looked even sicker than usual, his face ashen and his sunken eyes with their yellow film encircled by blackened skin.

'Taliko Hiduse says he and his brother were on Salvation's Climb with you last night. Why were you there and what happened?' I said.

'I don't know what you mean,' he said.

'Don't fuck with me today, I'Kryse,' I said, resting my hand on the grip of a pistol.

'Okay, okay,' I'Kryse said, lowering his hand, palm facing forward, like a defence against an attack. 'We were there. I'd hired Kana and Taliko to help me climb. But we weren't alone. Two of I'Rasnee's guards, I'Dreng and I'Delboot, were waiting for us. They jumped us on the steps and killed Kana. They almost killed Taliko and me.'

'How did you survive the ambush?'

'Kana, Taliko and I had been climbing for a while and were coming up to the corridor at the base of Mowate's Towers. The shaft has been filled in there, and you have to use a rope and pin to climb past. Kana was in the lead when I'Dreng and I'Delboot attacked. He didn't stand a chance. They shot him and he fell. Taliko and I were on the same rope; we fell too. But the pin and hook held, and he and I were able to swing into the shaft. Kana wasn't so lucky. He dangled below us, too badly wounded to climb. As Taliko and I were trying to hoist him up, I'Delboot cut the rope and Kana fell. I'Delboot and I'Dreng then abseiled down to continue their attack.

'Taliko and I hid in the shadows and when they came, I slit I'Delboot's throat, but I'Dreng shot me.' I'Kryse nodded towards his shoulder. 'Taliko buried his climbing axe into I'Dreng's chest, and I stabbed him in the thigh. Somehow, he staggered to where his rope still hung, and he slid down it. I don't believe he could have survived with those wounds.'

'Did you find the cane?'

'No. I swear.'

'Fine. Now, where is she?' I said.

'Who?' I'Kryse said.

I aimed a percussion pistol at his face.

'Don't shoot, Inspector,' Ameeleyor said, appearing at the bottom of the narrow stairs behind the counter.

'Can we speak?' I said, holstering my pistol.

'Fine, but not down here.'

Wes and I strode past I'Kryse, through the open gap in the counter to the foot of the staircase. Ameeleyor led us to the top floor and up the ladder through the ceiling hatchway into the attic.

Since the last time Wes and I had been here, it had been cleaned out. Now, instead of pallets, tools and spare stock, there was a battered table, a few second-hand chairs with torn seats, a faded rug and a pile of folded blankets with cushions on the wooden floor by the mattress. Much of the gloom had lifted. Oil lamps burned behind translucent throws and robes, causing soft but multi-coloured light to fall upon the grey curved walls.

Caysee, the eldest daughter, sat with her sister, Emellee, at the table, drawing pictures of their father. Payval, their brother, lay on the mattress, reading a book called *The Coor'Seyan Line*, which had a picture of a mounted battle on the cover.

'Mycale is with the brigadier,' I said.

'Oh, thank the spirits,' Ameeleyor said, covering her heart with her hand. 'Your doing?'

I nodded.

'I'm in your debt, Inspector,' Ameeleyor said, with a warm smile.

'Will you tell me what this is all about?' I said.

'Everything, Inspector, everything. It's all at stake.'

'What does that mean?'

'The weapon is real. It drains lifeblood stones for power and murders the spirits within. Those manufacturing it want to overthrow our king. War will follow. And it will spread throughout the Known World.'

I sighed and nodded.

'You seem disappointed, Inspector. I thought you'd be pleased to hear the truth.'

I shrugged. 'Depends on the truth. Besides, I'm not sure what to do about it.'

'We need to continue what Areel started.'

'We? It's we now, is it? Why don't you try filling in some gaps for me first?'

Ameeleyor rolled her eyes.

'Fine,' she said.

'How did I'Advay learn of the weapon?'

'I'Kalmeen showed him a non-functioning prototype. He wanted to persuade Areel to establish a supply line of stones through the High Temple.'

'So I'Kalmeen is a revolutionary?'

Ameeleyor furrowed her brow. 'I don't think so. Mycale says the brigadier is torn up inside – he sees the weapon as essential, but hates himself for plotting with revolutionaries.'

'Such as Ambassador I'Rasnee and I'Dreng?'

Ameeleyor nodded.

'You're certain?' Wes said.

'I have no doubts,' Ameeleyor said.

'What about Naka, the high chief, is he supplying the scientists?' I said.

'And the knowhow.' She put her hand on my shoulder and stooped to look into my eyes. 'They have to be stopped, Inspector.'

I held my hands up and backed away. 'I'm not sure that's possible.'

'Inspector—'

I cut Ameeleyor off before she could complete her protest. 'Your part in this is over. If you leave this shop without protection, you're dead.'

'Ma?' little Emellee said, looking up from the picture of her father she was drawing.

'No one's dying, sweetheart,' Ameeleyor said, leading Wes and me to the far wall.

I lowered my voice. 'The CIB is looking for you. The only option I can see is to smuggle you out of the city or maybe into the barracks.'

Ameeleyor shook her head. 'I can't return to Al'Mayra without the proof Areel had,' she said. There was neither protest nor request in her tone. She was merely stating a fact.

I was going to argue but Wes stepped in. 'Is that what you were to collect from him at Windy Park, the night he was killed?'

'The prototype, the plans, and the stone I'Kalmeen had. But Areel never arrived. Mycale and I found out why the following morning when we visited his home.'

'Then what did you do?' I said.

'I didn't know if it was safe for me to go back to the embassy – at least, not in my own body.'

'So I was right about that, too. You can storm.'

'Yes, Inspector. You've been right all along.'

Wes slapped me on the back. 'And you took Je'mymor A'Soyne's body?' he said.

Ameeleyor nodded. 'The following evening with Ronayld's help.'

'How does that even work?'

'If someone else is descended from the Ghost Clan, I can sense their mind, so to speak. All I have to do is make physical contact with them. Once I've taken over their body, mine becomes an anchor, and I can swap back any time I want.'

'Amazing,' Wes said.

'Enviable,' I said.

'I'd rather be able to shimmer. I could be anyone, then,' Ameeleyor said, looking at me.

'It has its limits, believe me,' I said. 'After all, it's just an illusion. One easily broken.'

'Still, the possibilities.'

'Why did you choose A'Soyne?'

'I'd sensed years ago I could storm her. Given her relationship with I'Kalmeen, she was the natural choice.'

'And so you stole her form and went to the embassy?'

'Yes. To spy on I'Kalmeen and, if possible, I'Rasnee.'

'A'Soyne is traumatised, you know,' Wes scolded, a stern look of disapproval on his face. 'I hope it was worth it.'

'It was,' Ameeleyor said emphatically. 'I learnt that while they suspected me, they weren't sure. And although the prototype was recovered, I'Remo was hurt on Salvation's Climb and he lost the cane with the plans and the stone pieces inside.'

'Anything else?' I said.

'Yes. I'Kalmeen didn't give the order to kill Areel, and he hates I'Rasnee for doing so. It seems they've split.'

'That's good. Do you trust I'Kalmeen?'

Ameeleyor puffed her cheeks out. 'My husband does.'

'And what was Mycale's involvement in all this?'

'He didn't kill Areel, if that's what you're asking. I'd never forgive him if he did. He knows that.'

'But they quarrelled that night? Over you? Your involvement?'

Ameeleyor nodded. 'His guilt is eating at his heart. He turned Areel away from here on the night of the storm, fought with him.'

'Over your involvement with this plot?'

'Yes.'

'Well, your husband is with I'Kalmeen now. You should go to him, or get out of New Capital.'

'If I do either, Areel will have died for nothing. I can't leave without that cane, Inspector.'

'We have to climb those steps, Wes,' I said, when he and I were standing in the arcade outside the apothecary's.

'I'm sorry, Ani, but I'm no climber,' Wes said.

'That's fine. I'll speak to Hiduse.'

'But why climb them at all? What will it serve?'

'It may persuade Ameeleyor to leave.'

'She's made her choice. If you're going to risk your life on the side of that cliff, at least know why you're doing it.'

We made for the Red Plateau restaurant. I was sure Josee would already be there waiting for me, even though it was a quarter of an hour before we were due to meet. But when we arrived, she wasn't there, so I ordered coffee for us and we sat outside, where I could watch the colourful Al'Mayran crowds and spot her emerging from it, smiling and waving.

It was Mani who appeared, already running, like he had materialised from another realm. His long hair trailed behind him, his eyes wide and afraid. I knocked the chair over as I stood and extended my arms to grab him. We fell to our knees, and I seized his shoulders and asked what was wrong.

'They attacked us,' he said.

'Who? Where?' I said, shaking him.

But he could barely speak. All he could do was point at the slope of Pastnoon Claw.

'Malaye's Heart?' I said.

He nodded, seized my hand, squeezing my fingers, and dragged me into the throng.

'I'll get an ambulance waggon to the Heart!' Wes shouted after us.

Mani and I flew up the steps to the Bridge of Spirits and across to Pastnoon Claw, then up the cliff to the Heart's main thoroughfare where it curved south and west.

A whirlpool opened in my guts, draining all the blood from my face and my extremities. I'd never felt cold like it. I was freezing from the inside out. The world shook and spun. My vision rocked as if I were drunk, only terror was my intoxicant. I was ocean-battered, broaching one way then another, about to capsize stem over stern.

It was Oura I saw first over the horizon of the hill. His head was low as he crawled on shaking hands and knees towards Etu, who was lying curled up, clutching his stomach. As I approached, Oura rolled his brother over and cradled him. Etu's shirt and trousers were soaked in blood, and his fingers were stained bright red over his belly.

Oura stared at me as I passed, his face contorting as he wrestled with the unimaginable. The whites of his disbelieving eyes were clear against the crimson stream pouring from the gash on his crown. For a moment, we seemed to share a single thought: this simply could not be happening.

Hani lay a little farther on. His chest was open, his flesh indistinguishable from his shirt, bloody material hanging in tatters from the sharp points of his broken ribcage. His attackers had made a stew of his heart and lungs, and to be sure of their work, they had taken his head off, save for the muscles and tendons connecting the back of his neck to his shoulders. A stray blow had even sliced his mouth open and left him wearing a corrupted reproduction of a once pleasant smile.

Mani collapsed to his knees by the chunks of meat that had been his brother. I didn't stop to comfort him or insult him with my guilt. A glance at Hani's mangled body told me he was dead. But had Hani been clinging to life, I would have hurried by, for Josee lay beyond him in a pool of glistening blood, lit by a sunbeam breaking through the grey blanket above. I looked up at the dark clouds floating by and wondered if they were unable or simply unwilling to let loose their rain and wash the whole damn scene away.

CHAPTER TWENTY-FIVE

PLACED MY FINGER on Josee's neck. Her skin was warm, therefore I told myself she must be alive. Or maybe my hand was as cold as she, and I couldn't tell the difference. But then I felt it: a faint but steady pulse. My wife's sacred heart still beat within her chest.

'Josee, wake up. Please don't leave me. Please get up,' I said, some part of me despising the weakness in my voice.

But Josee didn't move. She lay quite still, save for her red hair, which, like her robes, was billowing in the breeze. And although her bright green eyes were open, they were unresponsive to the world around them and to my desperate pleading.

When the ambulance waggon arrived, I helped to wrap Etu's torso in a bandage, all the while trying to shut out his screams. *Blow the candle out*, I thought. *Xol, please help me blow the damn candle out.* We got Oura to his feet and into the waggon and laid Etu beside him.

Josee was next. But before we lifted her, we crossed and tied her arms to her chest and made a support for her head using her robes. I climbed into the waggon and pulled Mani close to me. I turned his head away from his brother's hacked and divided body, even though it was far, far too late to spare him the ghastly sight.

I estimated less than an hour had passed from the moment I had seen Oura crawling towards his brother across the main thoroughfare of Malaye's Heart to when I sat with my uncle by his bedside at the nearest hospital on Pastnoon Claw. During that period, time hadn't behaved as it should. Although the seconds and minutes dragged, once they elapsed, I could not remember all that transpired. And when I closed my eyes, I saw only frozen moments, like those captured on silver photographic plates: I saw Josee, Oura and Etu bleeding in the ambulance waggon while I held Mani close, Wes at the hospital, introducing me to the surgeon who would operate on Josee, the surgeon smiling as he took her away from me, and the agony carved onto Etu's face as he resisted a nurse trying to dose him with the poppy. Then I saw my uncle arriving with my tribe at the hospital, his eyes as he took in the severity of Etu's wound, and his brave fortitude as he sat with me by Oura's bedside.

'I'm sorry, Ani,' Oura said.

I blinked and tried to push the photographic plates out of my mind and come back to the present.

'What?' I said, straining my eyes to focus on his.

'I'm sorry,' he repeated.

'What do you have to be sorry about?' I said.

'We couldn't protect the boy, couldn't protect Josee.'

'I shouldn't have put you in that position, in such danger,' I said. 'I should have trusted my instincts and insisted Josee go directly to Sundown Claw.'

'Neither of you must blame yourself,' Ezno said. 'The men and women who did this are the only ones accountable.'

'They were waiting for us, Ani,' Oura said.

'In Malaye's Heart?' I said.

'Hiding in the empty houses, waiting for us to pass. They clubbed Josee and me before we knew they were there, then went for the boys. Etu got in their way and gave Mani time to dive into a storm drain. Hani wasn't so lucky. I stood, tried to walk, but the world spun around me, and all I could do was watch as they circled the lad and brought their axes down upon him.'

'How many?'

'Six. All Kahokeyan, I think. They wore spook masks. One of them, a woman judging by her voice, wanted to finish us all off. But the leader, a tall man, said the older brother was the quarry. And they slipped away.'

I kissed Oura on the cheek and squeezed my uncle's hand before I left to check on Mani. He was sitting with Memi, who had arrived with my tribe, and Wes. The youngster rested his head on her breast, his eyes wide open and afraid. I squatted in front of him, put my hands on the sides of his knees and waited for him to acknowledge me.

'Will someone fetch Hani?' he finally said in a quiet but matter-of-fact tone.

'It's being done.'

'He doesn't want to go into the sea or the ground. He wants to be burnt, the way of the Depths. There's a pool where we play, and he wants to go there.'

'I'm sorry, Mani – that I couldn't save him.'

He shrugged and looked away.

'How's Josee?' Memi said.

'They're cutting a hole in her head,' I said.

'Xol preserve us.'

I took a seat next to her and Mani.

'I'm told it's a simple enough operation. Then we wait and see if she wakes up,' I said.

'And how are you?' Memi asked.

'I want to be like the bedrock beneath this city.'

'Oh, Ani. I'm sorry. You don't deserve this.'

'Don't I?'

'Come now, Ani, none of that,' Wes said.

Memi placed the palm of her hand on my face, but I looked away. A few moments passed before she found any words to speak.

'I never thanked you for giving us a place to hide. I believe you saved us,' she said.

'You'll be able to return to the Stars now,' I said.

'It's been taken from us.'

'What?'

'We aren't allowed back in, by order of the CIB.'

'Does it ever end?'

Another hour passed before Josee was out of surgery. An orderly and a nurse wheeled her cot past me, unaware of who I was and what she meant to me. It sickened me to see her pink skin turned grey and her wild hair limp and flattened by the peculiar cap placed on her head.

'Josee,' I said as I stood.

The orderly looked bored and averted his gaze so he didn't have to engage. The surgeon strode into the corridor and spotted me.

I didn't want to crumble before him. Ego, I supposed. But pride helped me batten down my feelings. Besides, if I didn't stow them away, I knew I'd be in tatters.

'How is she?' I asked the surgeon.

'The operation was a success. Textbook,' he said. 'We relieved the pressure, and the swelling has already reduced. I opted to replace a tiny part of her skull with a metal disc, about the size of a guinea. The bone where she was struck had fragmented into too many pieces. But I have relaid the flap of skin over the plate and stitched it.'

'When will she awaken?'

'That's out of my hands and in Xol's command. We must simply wait.'

'Her chances? Are they one in three, two in five?'

'I can't speculate. Is she strong?'

'Very.'

'And healthy?'

'She was,' I said, my voice breaking.

'And her taste for life?'

I nodded and tried not to blink, but the tears spilt from my eyes anyway.

'Then she has a good chance,' he said.

Mani watched over Josee with Wes and me as the interminable afternoon passed. All those from the Stars and the Sea who I had sheltered came to the hospital to pay their respects. They stood outside Josee's room and by her bed and would not leave Mani alone. More of my tribe arrived. They stood guard and talked of war upon those who would hurt us without provocation and declared Josee had too firm a grip on life to depart our world without a fight. They had all heard about Mani's brother, and the same fate would not befall him, they said. But Josee slept through it all, oblivious to the care and affection with which my people held her foreigner's heart.

Uncle Ezno came to tell me Etu had woken and was talking, although he was not making much sense due to his mind being scrambled by the poppy seed. I left Josee's side to visit with him and kiss him and hold him as gently as I could, taking care not to touch the horrendous wound I knew still snaked across his belly beneath his bandages. He smiled and sang and fell asleep again. I patted Ezno on the shoulder and left him with his sons, now lying in beds beside each other, both likely safe from Xol's grasp.

I returned to Josee's room and said goodbye to my wife, placing a kiss on her dry and blistered lips. I strode past my tribe outside in the corridor and headed to the nearest exit. Wes noticed me leaving and followed me outside.

'Stay here, Wes. Keep a sharp lookout,' I said.

He opened his mouth to speak but no words came. He sighed, nodded, and went back inside.

The clouds had blown by, their tears having dried away. It was the height of summer, and by my reckoning, there were five hours of daylight left before the sun set. And this time of year, she fell from the sky very slowly indeed, with the last of her dying light shining upon Salvation's Climb.

CHAPTER TWENTY-SIX

T HE SMOKE ABOVE the wooden shack Taliko Hiduse had shared with his murdered brother had largely died away by the time I returned to the grieving man's home. I sat on a stool on his porch and filled my two percussion pistols with black powder and ball, using the attached ramrods to drive the wads home. As I worked, I could hear Taliko moving inside his cabin. It sounded like he was preparing dinner, maybe his first meal in the lonely world he now lived in. I wondered if the flavours of the dish would taste the same. I realised I might never savour Josee's cooking again.

When I was finished loading the pistols, I stood and kicked the shack's door open. Taliko had just placed a pan on the stove and was pouring a tablespoon of rapeseed oil into it.

'For Xol's sake,' he said, turning, startled, and falling back.

I took aim and fired at a glass jar full of seashells and coloured rocks on the shelf near where Taliko had staggered. The jar exploded, sending shards of glass and parts of shells and whole shells flying and ricocheting off the walls. The pieces showered over Taliko, who raised his hands to cover his face.

As he reeled, I took two quick steps forward and kicked his chest. He hit the wall and slid into a sitting position. When he tried to stand, I pressed the barrel of the loaded pistol to his forehead.

'Taliko, I'm sorry for your loss, but you're completing your climb – with me.'

'You're crazy. I'm done with this affair. I've paid too high a price already.'

'You'll take me up that cliff and we'll find a golden cane or your mother will lose two sons today.'

'My mother is long dead.'

'Then decide whether you want to join her or not.'

'For Xol's sake, what's so important about a cane?'

I holstered my pistols and drew over a small wooden stool to sit on. 'This is personal for me now, Taliko,' I said. 'People I love have been hurt. A young Kahokeyan boy who was under my protection has been murdered, and he's not the only victim. I'm just trying to find a way out of this mess, but I need that cane. I can climb, but I'd rather not try alone. Help me and avenge your brother. What do you say?'

'Those who killed the boy, who hurt your family, are they the ones who killed Kana?'

'They're in this together.'

Taliko glanced to his left, at a photographic plate of his brother and him, arms around each other's shoulders, smiles on their faces.

'I'll help,' he said.

I wondered what the residents of Mowate's Towers made of Taliko Hiduse and me as we walked the narrow path below their flats, dressed in thick leather waistcoats and with loincloths over our trousers, carrying ropes, pins, hooks and axes, and, in my case, armed with percussion pistols and a fighting dagger. Did they think we worked for the city? Or were they afraid we were connected to the comings and goings of pale Al'Mayran foreigners whose purpose on Salvation's Climb was best left a mystery?

I asked Taliko to take me to the cliff aisle where he and I'Kryse left the steps the night before. He had not mentioned we would have to walk along a thin ledge to negotiate the bricked-off entrance.

'How did you get a wounded man out this way?' I said, spreading my body against the wall and staring at the drop below.

'We had other things on our minds. Why, are you scared?' Taliko said.

'No. I learnt to climb when I was a child. I'd just rather not die at the first step.'

'It's only for a few feet. Just don't lean back.'

'Thanks for the tip.'

I followed Taliko along the ledge, over the balustrade and onto the cliff corridor. We made for the remains of the stairwell entrance and stood on the top layer of rubble that had been used to fill in a long section of the vertical shaft below.

'Is this where the Al'Mayrans waited for you?' I said.

'Yes, only their ropes have gone now,' Taliko said.

Taliko hammered three eye pins into the back of the shaft and attached eye hooks to them. He looped his rope around the base of a pillar, fed it through the hooks and tied each off independently. Once he was happy the anchors were secure, he crossed the two strands of rope around his back, drew them underneath his arms and fed them between his legs, ensuring they pressed against the flap of his leather loincloth.

'You know this technique?' he said.

I nodded as he positioned himself on the jutting remains of a granite landing. He pulled on the rope to test it, leant over the edge and walked down the cliff. Once past the blockage, he swung into the stairwell.

'The dead Al'Mayran is still here,' he said.

I copied Taliko's method – stood on the same spot he had, kept the rope taut, and, after taking a breath, leant towards oblivion. Once I adjusted to the pull of gravity on my upper body and found the right tension on the line to keep my feet on the cliff, I began to descend. As soon as I could, I moved inside the shaft and dropped down to where Taliko stood, waiting for me by the body of Ryeen I'Delboot.

'He's a lieutenant in Ambassador I'Rasnee's personal guard,' I said.

I pulled I'Delboot's arms apart and then the lapels of his shirt. His chest had been opened by an unsteady hand, leaving a messy wound behind.

'We didn't do that to him,' Taliko said.

I peered out of the stairwell. The next attached section of concrete steps was fifty feet below, and it was covered in debris.

I still had the rope tied around me, so before Taliko could protest, I went over the edge. It had been a few years since I had climbed, but I used to scale the western cliffs with my cousins and their friends, and the old routines were quickly coming back to me. It took less than a minute for me to reach the next outer flight, which was strewn with rubble and fractured with cracks. I swung straight into the shaft and onto the inner flight. This time, however, no dead Al'Mayran was waiting for me. But I did find dried blood, both large passive stains and several small transfer stains, along with a few thin strips of material torn from an Al'Mayran robe.

'Is he there?' Taliko shouted.

'No, but he was. I believe he made a tourniquet for his leg,' I yelled, tying the rope around me and swinging back out onto the cliff face.

'It'll be dark soon. Perhaps we should stay here, or come back tomorrow?' Taliko said, hauling on the rope I climbed.

I stepped into the stairwell and sat down with my legs dangling over the edge to catch my breath.

I thought for a moment. 'No. Let's climb until the sun sets,' I said.

The storm had destroyed all the external flights up to the top of Mowate's Towers. Taliko and I adopted the same approach he and his brother applied the night before. He used pins and eye hooks to fix three independent anchors, then he ascended the stairwell corner, securing three more points at the next internal flight. I waited for his signal before removing those at my level and climbing up to him to search for the cane. So far, all I had found was blood – lots of it.

'I don't know how that blond Al'Mayran climbed with his wounds,' Taliko said, when we took a rest halfway up the towers.

'Dedication, fanaticism, take your pick,' I said.

'Perhaps he was paying penance like our ancestors, even if he didn't know it.'

'No one has paid penance since the steps were built. They turned the act into an empty gesture. Now we don't even bother to pretend. Climbing the sheer face of this cliff without rope or axe. That was penitence.'

I sighed and looked off to the west. I could see the home I shared with Josee, and beyond it, Sundown Claw. I closed my eyes to shield them from the setting sun and saw head wounds, sliced bellies, and open chests.

'Come on, let's get a few more flights in before nightfall,' I said.

It was foolish, I knew it, but I needed the comfort of the rhythms of the climb, the focus on each moment: place the hand, place the foot, repeat – over and over. But I couldn't find the concentration, nor could I shake the images of my wife's pale and bloodless face and Hani's accusing eyes. I was about to ask Taliko to stop when he shouted from the flight above: 'He's here!'

'Dead?'

'He is.'

'Don't touch him. I'm coming.'

'Let me fix the anchor points.'

'No, hold the rope.'

Taliko cursed me as he took my weight, and I lost all technique and good sense in my haste to scramble up the stairwell. I even let go of the rope as I dragged myself onto the landing.

I'Dreng was sitting with his back against the far wall of the shaft, his injured leg stretched out before him. His head was bowed, but his grey eyes were open, and below them, dark half-circles had formed from the swelling where I had broken his nose. Clasped in his hands, held to his sacred heart, was Areel I'Advay's golden cane.

'Is that the one?' Taliko said.

'If it isn't, this is a coincidence for the ages,' I said, laughing.

'I deserved that. Stupid question.'

'Not at all,' I said, standing and patting Taliko on the shoulder.

I took a seat on the steps above I'Dreng and gazed at him with my arms folded.

'Well, Normain, you met your end well,' I said. 'It took courage to continue looking for that damn cane with a hole in your chest and another in your leg.'

'Who is he?' Taliko said.

'The captain of Ambassador I'Rasnee's personal guard, a mean-spirited brute. But he gave his life in service of something greater than himself, and I don't know how to reconcile that.'

I slid the cane from I'Dreng's stiffened fingers and examined the bottom. Sure enough, the base was hollow for about the length of a thumb, with grooves running down the inside. I took the golden charm from around my neck and tried to match its raised markings to the channels until it slotted into place. I felt a brief resistance as I turned the charm; there was a click, and the crown of the cane came away. I pulled it free of the shank and drew out a thin bloodstained cutting sabre. When I did, a beam of red light struck the wall of the shaft and illuminated the stairwell.

'In Xol's name,' Taliko said.

My throat tightened, and I couldn't speak, so I nodded, coughed and wiped the tears from my eyes with one hand as I put the blade down. I took my leather waistcoat off, laid it beside I'Dreng's outstretched leg, and poured the broken but lustrous pieces of stone upon it. I slid my finger inside the cane and pulled a roll of paper out.

'A weapon,' Taliko said, looking over my shoulder at the diagram. 'But I don't see a firing mechanism.'

'Not one we're familiar with. Look here,' I said, pointing at a chamber where the flintlock or hammer and nipple cap should be. 'The lifeblood stone sits in here, and when you pull the trigger, light comes out of the barrel. Don't ask me how. Sounds harmless, doesn't it, like a lamp, but trust me when I say the light is concentrated somehow, made powerful and hot, capable of burning your enemy where he or she stands.'

I rolled the paper up and reinserted it into the cane. Taliko held my waistcoat and we poured the pieces of the lifeblood stone inside the hollow shank. I slotted the blade back in place and twisted the crown until it clicked.

'We're done for the day,' I said.

'I'm relieved to hear you say it,' Taliko said. He reached inside his shoulder bag and removed a parcel that he unwrapped to reveal two dry-cured puffin breasts.

'You brought supper?' I said.

'I never climb without food, and it seems we're about to receive our drinking water.'

Another gathering of clouds had blown in from the south, partially covering the setting sun and turning the orange sky below them grey with rain. Taliko ran to the top landing and held his canteen out beyond the cliff face. I copied him, just as the shower swept in. I even risked leaning forward to lift my face to the falling drops.

When I sat to eat my puffin breast, I held the cane to me, much as I'Dreng had. For some reason, I reached my hand out and patted the dead man's shoulder.

'What are you thinking about?' Taliko said.

'You don't want to know, my friend,' I said.

I finished my supper and washed it down with rainwater from my canteen. I stood to refill it for the next day's climb. Taliko had lit a small oil lamp and placed it midway up the flight of steps. I brought the lamp a little nearer to where I'Dreng sat, then pulled on the guard captain's legs and pushed his body flat, opened his robes, and stood over him with my climbing axe poised to strike.

'I hope I get this right, Normain,' I said.

'What are you doing?' Taliko said.

I brought the axe down onto I'Dreng's breast and heard the crack of bone breaking under the impact. Two more blows and I had made a hole big enough to allow me to slide the pick of the axe through. I began snapping his ribs away.

'You can't make him any deader, you know?' Taliko said.

'By what this man believes, I'm saving him,' I said.

I used my fighting dagger to reveal the organ underneath and cut the veins and arteries that connected it to the rest of the body. Next, I opened the cane and poured a small amount of the stone pieces into my hand.

The gravity of the ritual suddenly gave me pause, and my hand shook as I coated I'Dreng's heart. After that, I could not replace the organ nor cover the hole in the man's body fast enough to relieve my unease, and when I was finished, I held my hands under the falling rain until I had washed them clean of his blood. I went dizzy and sat on the edge of the landing to stop myself from falling.

There I rested until the sun set and the moon was bright in the sky, until my thoughts turned to my wife's sacred heart, which I hoped still beat within her chest. And when I lay down to sleep, I heard my people's prayers to Xol, imploring him to gift her more seasons with the living.

I saw Shona first, followed by Hani. They looked upon me with sadness and I tried to apologise to them and rid myself of the guilt, but I couldn't speak. I felt Josee beside me, comforting me, whispering in my ear that, in the end, the life and death of the body was nothing compared to the eternal spirit or to the great mystery of the unknowable universe to which we all belonged.

CHAPTER TWENTY-SEVEN

ALIKO WOKE ME at dawn, after he had climbed to the level above and secured anchor points. I followed him up the rope, and we carried on with the same pattern of climbing and searching we established the previous day. By mid-morning, we had reached the corridor at the top of Mowate's Towers where Hani and I had emerged from the storm drain.

'Do we continue?' Taliko said.

'Only to the Negotiated Burroughs. There may be other evidence,' I said.

'Why not any farther?'

'Whoever dumped the body in Rose Town lives in the Burroughs.'

'Are you always this confident?'

'Where my job's concerned,' I said, feeling a pang of grief in my heart and a sickness in my stomach. *My job*, I thought. *My calling*. As Imala said, without it, who was I?

'There's much less damage above here,' Taliko said, gazing up. 'As long as we secure ourselves as we go, we can use the steps. Just don't stand below me. Inspector, are you listening?'

'Yes, Taliko,' I said, blinking.

'Are you okay?'

'Let's just get going.'

It was strange to walk again, and oddly more tiring without the aid of adrenaline. Perhaps the fatigue was just setting in, but I began to sympathise with the souls who climbed the steps years ago. Although they had not risked their lives, it wouldn't have been easy, so who was I to judge?

Despite Taliko's warnings, our progress became routine – that was, until a collapse left him hanging in a cloud of dust. Thankfully, that was the only incident, and it took us mere minutes to reach the next corridor. Above that, we would need to alternate between walking the remaining steps and climbing the stairwell corner.

'Someone's coming down,' Taliko said.

'What?' I said.

'See for yourself.'

Taliko held on to my loincloth as I looked up. At first, I saw only shadows, cast by the rising sun, but then I spotted a face peering down at me. It was Kononwa. I heard a woman's voice too and glimpsed others moving behind him. Something metal glinted, the crack of a pistol report echoed in the stairwell, and I saw the tell-tale puff of black and grey smoke. The ball chipped the balustrade beside me as it passed.

'Who is it?' Taliko said.

'They want the cane,' I said.

'Come, we can rappel back down to the top of Mowate's Towers.'

I handed the cane to Taliko and said, 'That hulking CIB agent you saw is with my tribe in Pastnoon Claw hospital. Give this to him and tell him to meet me at the Al'Mayran embassy gate.'

'Where are you going?'

'To speak with those men and women.'

'For Xol's sake, come with me. What good will it do to die fighting them? You have the cane.'

'I'm not dead yet. Besides, it'll buy you time.'

'Don't make me the cause of your suicide.'

'You're right. I'm sorry. Thank you for your help, Taliko Hiduse. And if I haven't said it, I'm sorry for Kana. Go now, or else this will all have been in vain.'

Taliko shook his head and with a final look at me, began his descent. I waited until he'd rappelled as far down the cliff as he could using the rope he'd secured, then I dropped it to him, leaving the eye pins in the stone. Above me, Kononwa and his people were having to fasten their own line to negotiate a missing flight.

I sat cross-legged, enjoying the warmth of the rising sun on my face, and refilled my two percussion pistols with powder and ball before slotting them back into my baldric. I wiped my hands on my trousers and realised they were not actually wet with perspiration, and my throat was not dry. I was not afraid.

Why?

Were my emotions numbed? In the wake of the attack on Josee and poor Hani, had I deadened my feelings? I didn't think so. Josee was with me, as she had been during the night when I'd felt and reciprocated her love. Perhaps, if she were already dead, I wanted to join her? But that didn't seem right either. All I knew in that moment was the morning sunlight warming my heart and the tranquil sea, glistening under a cloudless sky, soothing my nerves.

Josee would have enjoyed the vista, although its lack of drama perhaps wouldn't have inspired her to paint. Instead, if she and I were at home, we may have squeezed fresh orange juice and splintered some ice and sat on our southern balcony, drinking, with our bare feet resting together, neither of us speaking very much.

Above, a woman screamed, followed by the crack of bone breaking upon hard rock.

I smiled. Not out of malice. I just knew Xol was with me.

They said his greatest gift was clarity of action, knowing what to do without having to consider it. I had no intention of waiting for Kononwa to find me, nor of climbing the steps and offering him a free shot at my head. Instead, I walked to the nearest landing and looked for handholds on the cliff face. Several waited for me, more visible and inviting than any I'd used thus far. The thought that I had no rope to protect me from falling scarcely fluttered through my mind as I lifted my body away from the platform and hung a thousand feet above the sea and the shore below. And when I raised my head, I saw my path as sure as if it were a trail cut into the thickest forest.

I climbed west of the steps, where Kononwa and his men and women were least likely to notice me. I was out of sight when they were in the stairwell, and they turned their backs on me when they came out. In those moments, all they had to do was glance right, and they might discover their quarry less than three feet away in the most vulnerable position possible. Indeed, at one point, Kononwa himself stepped out as I was passing. He was so close, I could have reached out and tapped him on the shoulder, but it never occurred to him to look my way.

I counted five others in his group, three men and two women, including Kineks, the young woman with the tattooed face I shot the morning I chased Hani into the Depths. Her poor luck had continued. In addition to her still bandaged shoulder, she now limped severely, presumably having fallen on the steps. Helping her was a tall man with mid-length and thinning tresses, who carried a rope coiled diagonally around his torso.

At the next landing, I stepped over the balustrade. Then I went on the hunt.

My soft, deerskin shoes made no sound upon the stone as I entered the shaft above where Kineks and her companion were making their slow progress, unaware I was now pursuing them.

Blow the candle out.

When I emerged from the shadows into the light, with my pistols drawn, I shot them both in the back. The tall and lean man crumpled, the ball having found his heart. But I must have caught Kineks in a lung, because she fell to her knees, wheezing. She glared over her shoulder at me, and the expression in her eyes was like none I had seen before: a combination of impotent rage and utter disbelief that Xol had twisted the course of legitimate events to steal her righteous vengeance and hand it to me. I almost felt sorry for her, despite the harm I knew she intended me. But if I were her antagonist, it was she who had written her story's finale, here on Salvation's Climb.

Still, I felt no particular malice towards Kineks, whose story I did not know, nor did I wish to imbue the strike that ended her life with any unnecessary symbolism. I simply had not brought my own sword, and so I killed the young woman with hers, hoping she might find some peace with Xol she had not found in the Depths.

I lifted the rope from around the dead man's body, checked that his and Kineks's pistols were loaded, took them, and raced back up to the landing. Below me, I could hear shouting and knew Kononwa and his remaining companions were coming. But I didn't panic, my course of action clear, as if Xol had lit the way.

I looped the end of the rope around the balustrade, crossed the strands under my arms and brought them between my legs. I laughed with astonishment that I was now trusting the treacherous steps to keep me alive and caressed the stone rail as I stepped over. Once the line was taut, I leant away and twisted, lowering my body until I was horizontal. I ran down the cliff face.

I knew the rope I was using was visible where it dangled, and that I had exposed my tactics, so I moved as fast as I could and hoped those chasing me were either in the shaft or were too preoccupied to notice. One vacant external flight went by, followed by another, and on the third, I found Kononwa. His mouth fell open when he saw me.

'How goes it with you, Kononwa?' I said.

A stocky man with a shaved and tattooed head stood with him. At that moment, all this stranger represented to me were the odds that needed shortening in the gamble I had taken. I drew a pistol, used the painted black band across his eyes as a target, and put a hole in his skull. I swung to the level below.

As soon as my feet touched the granite landing, I stood free of the line, unholstered the other pistol and aimed towards the gloom of the shaft. The forms of two people were rising in the darkness.

I didn't have a clear shot, but fired anyway. One of the figures disappeared. The other emerged into the light. She was slim, athletic, dressed in deerskin leggings and a shirt and had waist-length hair that trailed in her wake. She charged up the steps, drawing her sword as she ran. I pushed my stolen pistols into the band of my loincloth, drew my fighting dagger and sprung upon her. She tried to thrust with her sword, but as she ran, her arm swung back, and when I tackled her, I managed to push its point aside with my sleeved arm.

We fell hard, both of us winded. But her body cushioned mine, and her head split on a stone edge, stealing her wits. The struggle was brief. I pinned her down and slid my blade between her ribs.

I couldn't explain what happened next. Perhaps it was caution alone directing my hand, or Xol guiding me. I didn't hear Kononwa above me, nor did I see him take aim. Nevertheless, I lifted the dead woman and used her as a shield to block his shot.

Her body slowed the ball as it passed through, and it was stayed by my padded leather waistcoat. Kononwa sighed, shook his head, and took an axe from his belt.

I picked up the dead woman's sword in my right hand and transferred my fighting dagger to my left, just as Kononwa turned onto the landing above. I whipped the sword through the air to gauge its weight and balance. It would do.

'Are you coming?' I said.

There was deliberation in Kononwa's eyes. He had lost his people, and the odds he had once no doubt believed well in his favour had evened. He took one last gamble and hurled his axe at me. It was a beautiful throw. The kind only years of practice could produce. The head spun in the air, glinting in the morning sun, and even as I crossed my sword and dagger to check the axe's flight, I couldn't help but admire the skill of the man who launched it.

At that point, I think we both knew it was over. Even so, Kononwa knelt and began to fill his pistol with powder. I watched him as I climbed the steps, noted the calm manner with which he rammed the first wad in place, the speed with which he took a ball from his pouch and dropped it into the barrel, and the deftness of his hand as he drove the second wad home. It was all for nought. Just as he raised the pistol, I was upon him. I drove the point of my sword through his firing hand, causing him to shoot wide. I followed my thrust with two more jabs of my sword, stabbing his forearm and his thigh. He fell back, raising his uninjured arm in surrender.

I pressed the tip of my sword to his throat.

'Who sent you?' I said.

'Let's not play that game, Sulaqua,' he said, trying to stand by pressing his body against the balustrade, which started to crack.

'Stay down,' I said.

'I'm not a dog,' he said, staggering to his feet.

I backed away from him, keeping my sword and dagger ready to strike.

'I know Yoyu sent you. What if I could guarantee your safety? Would you testify to that?' I said.

'I won't go to prison, Inspector,' he said, lifting his injured leg over the balustrade with his working hand before grasping the rail.

'Wait, Kononwa! What are you doing?'

'I'm off to my reckoning with Xol.'

'Don't be foolish. That's not necessary. Come with me. Make a deal and live.'

'You're the fool if you think Yoyu will see justice. He's not from the Depths. He is the Depths. As Naka is the Heights.'

'So who are you? Decide. Are you the man who killed his friend on Red Tern Tower or the man who saved my life that day?'

'I killed my friend because I knew he'd give me up. But I had no orders to kill you, and it seemed a shame for you to die like that. What a fool I am. Still, I can't regret it.'

'What about the lad? Did you butcher him, too? Do you regret that?'

Kononwa hung his head and sighed and would not meet my eye.

'What about my cousins, my wife?' I said.

'Our target was the boy, and, if we had an opportunity, his younger brother. I don't know why, but we were told not to kill your people. Kineks, it seems, had her own agenda,' he said.

'She attacked my wife?'

'Yes.'

'But you cut open the boy's chest and cleaved his face in half?'

'Whatever he saw the night of the storm, he should have kept to himself. He died by his own hand.'

'No, it was you, Kononwa. You.'

'What choice did I have?'

'You could have come to me. You could have run, but you were too afraid to leave the Depths. That's your cowardice.'

'And Xol hates cowards. Perhaps he'll reject me. He was certainly with you today. But I'm not bitter. I don't resent your victory. I'm glad it was you who beat me. And I'm truly sorry for the boy and for your wife. Believe it or not, I would gladly become one of Xol's outcasts if he were to return her to you. If I see him, I'll tell him that. Goodbye, Ani. You fought well.'

And with a step, he was gone.

I didn't hear him scream, nor did I care to peer down and see his broken body on the rocks below. Instead, I chose to imagine that Xol reached out a tentacle from the water and caught him in his fall, drawing him beneath the waves of the sea to be with the spirits of his kin.

Six lives gone. Six more I had killed. Did Kononwa's death add to my tally or his own? *It's a number a person should remember*, Wes had said. Too true. Perhaps, when my fencing instructor told me to blow the candle out, he should have added: *once the fight is over, be sure to relight it, Ani, girl.*

Before I carried on up the steps, I returned to collect the eye pins and hooks I'd left nailed in the rock where Taliko and I parted. I used them and the dead man's rope to secure myself before I negotiated the missing flights below Rose Town. I searched as I went but discovered nothing, and so found myself back where the case started, where I had stood with young Dee, staring down Salvation's Climb, wondering at the heart and mind of one who would risk their life on them.

When I reached the corridor at the Negotiated Burroughs, I headed west towards the path that once turned north to join the main thorough-fare. The route was now blocked by a stone wall without gate or door, forcing me to drag my weary body over it. A lethargy beyond my control seeped into my muscles and clambering over felt like slapping drenched laundry against hard rock.

On the other side, a hedge of Kahokeyan orange blossoms ran along the walkway. Behind them were the gardens of several single-storey dwellings with domed roofs and spires. I could hear the voices of two women, one of which I recognised all too well.

I peered through the nearest entrance and saw Dabreeyor A'Mendayse leaning against a column on her porch, talking to her neighbour, an older Al'Mayran woman who was kneeling on a padded mat to tend her rose bushes.

A balloon of bubbling acid inflated in my stomach, and my skin prickled like I'd been wrapped in a coarse woollen rug. Beads of sweat formed on my brow, and I fought the need to vomit.

Dabreeyor A'Mendayse.

She seemed taller and even more powerfully built than the day she'd performed the lifeblood ritual for Areel I'Advay. I had assumed her affection for I'Advay drove her to carry out the ceremony. It never occurred to me that it was her spirit, more than his, she was trying to save.

I closed my eyes and saw a strand of her curly blond hair, lit by the flash of a lightning bolt on a stormy night as it hung from the hood of her blue-and-golden robe. And I saw a young boy watching her through the rain as she laid the body of a dead Al'Mayran man down near his lover's home.

All my recent history with her unravelled and was rewoven into a different pattern. Dabreeyor manipulated me into giving her my address. She established a friendship with Josee, to track my progress and disturb my jealous mind. Had she known who Mani was from the first moment she laid eyes on him? Had she waited for his brother to appear before issuing the kill order? And when she walked arm in arm through Malaye's Heart with my wife, had she reflected on how the quiet little neighbourhood would be an ideal spot for an ambush?

The older Al'Mayran woman noticed me first. She looked up from where she knelt and said, 'Can I help you?'

'No, I was just passing and heard Dabreeyor's voice,' I said.

'Ani, where did you come from?' Dabreeyor said.

She stood away from the column, her back straight, with her arms flexed by her sides like a fighter's. She smiled, but it was a flickering reproduction of warmth, and it fell from her face quicker than it appeared.

'From Salvation's Climb. I didn't realise your home was so very close,' I said.

'Is it really? I suppose it is, but with the wall there, I never think of it,' she said, her voice artificial.

'Oh, the wall's easy to scale, for a healthy man. Or woman.'

'You seem tired. Perhaps you'd care to come in for some refreshment?'

'You'll have to excuse me, I have a busy day ahead. A couple of breakthroughs in the case, you know – I'm sure you'll be pleased to hear.'

When I reached the end of the thoroughfare, I turned to see Dabreeyor A'Mendayse standing on the walkway, watching me. The sun was lighting her pale yellow hair and her bright blue-and-golden robe, making her appear as the ethereal creature I remembered. Although she didn't wave, I knew she could see me, so I raised my sword to salute her, then pointed the tip of the blade at her heart.

CHAPTER TWENTY-EIGHT

'Kalmeen's housekeeper showed Wes and me into her master's den. When we entered, the brigadier was admiring the whaling spear hanging on his red-plastered walls and running his fingers across the silver fishing net that hung alongside it. He had the air of a man whose thoughts and feelings were far away in both distance and time. But he smiled at us when we entered and offered us a seat around the dark wooden table. He joined us a moment later, after one final, wistful gaze at the net and spear.

'What is this about, Inspector?' I'Kalmeen said, looking at the wrapped parcel I placed on the table.

'First, I wish to apologise to you, Brigadier.'

'Oh, indeed?' he said, laughing and shaking his head.

'Yes. I've insulted you on several occasions to provoke you into a misstep or admission, and for that, I'm sorry.'

'You're certainly adept at triggering my temper, but you were doing your job. Besides, haven't we recently struck a conciliatory note?'

'We have, but I'm here to manipulate you in another way.'

'Consider me forewarned, Inspector, and intrigued. What have you brought me?'

I untied the string around the cane and rolled the linen away. Upon seeing his late friend's possession, I'Kalmeen became impassive. Perhaps there was a hint of longing in the wetness of his dark eyes, but they didn't narrow, nor did his brow furrow, nor his jaw clench. Instead, he reached

for the cane, faltered, recovered, and ran his finger across the crest. For
the first time, I began to wonder at the nature of his relationship with
I'Advay.

'You were lovers?' I said.

'Once upon a time, during a bitter war that cost us both dearly,'
I'Kalmeen said with a heavy sigh. 'Areel was different back then. At least
I thought so. Religious, yes, but pragmatic. I still don't know what happened to him. Terrible wounds often affect the mind. They change the
individual. Or perhaps his faith carried him through the ordeal and delivered him to the other side. Either way, after he recovered, the spirit was
all that mattered to him and became the only freedom worth fighting for.
We rekindled our friendship here in New Capital, nothing more, and he
remained somewhat distant. I see now he was spying on me, on all of us
with modernising views.'

'My condolences, Brigadier,' Wes said.

I'Kalmeen nodded. 'Have you opened it?'

I took the charm from around my neck, unlocked the cane's base and
poured the pieces of the lifeblood stone onto the table. I pulled the diagram free and offered the plans to the brigadier, but he didn't take them.

'The prototype was recovered when they killed Areel, yes?' I said.

I'Kalmeen winced and nodded.

'Who killed him?'

'I'Remo and A'Mendayse.'

'You make me sad, Brigadier. I didn't want to believe Dabreeyor was
involved,' Wes said.

'She was radicalised as a child. Her village was slaughtered by the
Harn. Poor Areel, he never suspected. Dabreeyor was the lure, and Liam
delivered the killer blow. But in a way, I suppose, I am responsible.'

'How so?'

'I sent a message to I'Rasnee that the plans, the stone, and the model
were stolen. I should have realised what he might do. It was naive of me.'

'So they found I'Advay in the arcade, after he'd argued with Mycale?'

'That was just an unfortunate coincidence,' I'Kalmeen said. 'Mycale
has nothing to do with this. In fact, I'Remo and A'Mendayse saw the
quarrel and waited until Areel was alone. They carried his body up the

Climb. Only there was a collapse. I'Remo was hurt, the cane lost, and Dabreeyor was left alone to drag Areel's body as far as she could. She'd planned to perform a preservation ritual in her home. But she improvised and left him in Rose Town instead. She knew he would be discovered and the preservation ritual performed. Having the blame falling on Areel's lover was a stroke of opportunistic genius. Or it would have been, if any other inspector were assigned.'

'What did you do when you found out about Areel?' Wes asked.

'What could I do other than fly into an impotent rage? Areel was already dead. I'Rasnee assured me a preservation ritual would be carried out, so...'

'You went along with the plan?' I said, flatly.

'To my shame, yes. You arrived at the embassy the following morning. We weren't expecting that. We knew the police would come eventually, and we would have reported Areel missing a day later, but we thought we would have more time to recover the cane and its contents.'

'Why? Why do you need a weapon like that? You're not a bloodthirsty man. Why are you even involved?' Wes said, imploring the brigadier.

'I had – I have – my reasons,' I'Kalmeen said.

'And you won't share them with us?' I said.

'I'm not sure it's my place.'

'I don't understand.'

'There is much I don't understand in the Known World, Inspector. But I don't find mystery intolerable.'

He took a pinch of the lifeblood stone pieces and rubbed them between his fingers until they glowed. He dropped them into the pile, and a beam of red light rose from the table to the ceiling.

'I don't know if I believe the spirits truly reside in the stones,' he said. 'This is probably just a natural phenomenon. And not everybody believes as Areel did, you know. There are religious academics, allies of I'Rasnee and his ilk, who argue when a stone is spent, the spirit within returns to the mountains, the same as when we perform a cremation. Others believe the spirits are willing to die, otherwise they wouldn't provide their light.'

'I used some from the cane to coat I'Dreng's heart,' I said.

'So Normain is dead,' I'Kalmeen said, without surprise or emotion of any kind. 'And you conducted a lifeblood preservation ritual?'

'My approximation of one. I don't know if it was – what can I say? – valid.'

'I'Dreng wouldn't care. Maybe now he can prove the radicals' point and sacrifice his spirit for his cause as well as his body.'

I shrugged.

'So why are you telling me all this, Inspector? How do you wish to manipulate me?' I'Kalmeen said.

'By my reckoning, over a dozen people have lost their lives because of this affair. People I love have been hurt. My wife may never wake up, and, if she does, I don't know if she'll still be my wife. I'm here to return the plans for the lifeblood pistol, what's left of the stone, and the cane, to you. In addition, I'Dreng and I'Delboot's bodies, along with Areel's, will all be released to you personally.'

'If?' I'Kalmeen said, raising an eyebrow.

'Consider placing I'Rasnee and his guards under arrest. Stop the man from hurting anyone else. Whatever your motives for aligning with I'Rasnee, I don't believe you're a murderer.'

I'Kalmeen rested his arms on the table and leant forward, a wry smile on his face. 'An Al'Mayran coup in New Capital? An odd request for someone who wishes to prevent further bloodshed.'

'Will blood be spilt? Will I'Dreng's guards fight without him?'

I'Kalmeen arched his fingers to support his chin. 'I doubt it. They're hiding away in their guardhouse.' He looked straight at me, and I had to fight not to shrink away. 'But what about the high chief's response?' he said.

'Without I'Rasnee, you're Naka's closest link to Al'Mayra,' I said, pointing at his sacred heart.

'And my superiors back home?'

I shrugged. 'Wouldn't you be defending the king? Turn on I'Rasnee in the king's name, go home, confess, plead for mercy?'

'And if I don't receive it?'

'Then die with honour.'

'In Xol's name, Ani,' Wes said.

I kept my attention on I'Kalmeen.

'I have to say, Inspector, I don't seem to be doing very well in this bargain,' he said.

'I'm betting my family's future you don't believe that.'

Brigadier I'Kalmeen and I strode down the long corridor towards I'Rasnee's office while Wes and half a dozen soldiers waited out of sight. I was shimmering I'Dreng's appearance to ensure the two guards outside the door remained at their posts as we approached.

'I'll take the one on the left. He looks smaller,' I whispered.

I nodded to the guard I had chosen, a rather portly fellow with thinning blond hair, as if I were going to pass him without a word. But instead of moving my hand towards the door handle, I drew a pistol and shoved the muzzle under his chin. I lost my shimmer, but it didn't matter.

'Don't move,' I said. 'There's a good lad.'

I checked if I'Kalmeen needed help. He already had a knife at the other guard's throat.

'If you say a word, it will be your last,' I'Kalmeen hissed.

Wes and the Coor'Seyans sprinted down the corridor to join us. They gagged the guards and tied their hands, and we entered the outer office.

Both secretaries were at their desks. The young woman gasped and covered her mouth. I held a finger to my lips to quieten her. The older secretary stood and said, 'What is the meaning of this?' in a not-too-quiet voice before Wes persuaded him to silence with a wave of his pistol.

'Is the ambassador in?' I said to the woman.

She nodded.

'Who else?' I said.

'A CIB agent,' she said.

'What about I'Remo?'

'He left a few minutes ago, just after the CIB agent arrived.'

'Do you know where he went?'

'No. I swear by the spirits, I don't.'

'Okay, I believe you. Now go and stand by the wall with the guards and don't make any trouble for the soldiers. Understand?'

She nodded.

Wes and I raised our pistols and flanked I'Kalmeen, who pulled the doors to I'Rasnee's office open. The ambassador was sitting at his desk, but when he saw us, he stood and knocked his chair over. Unaduti, who was sitting opposite, turned and reached inside the jacket of his uniform.

'I wouldn't,' Wes said, standing over his erstwhile colleague.

'By the spirits, Peetor, have you lost your wits?' I'Rasnee protested, clearly alarmed.

'Maybe I've come to them,' I'Kalmeen said calmly.

'Are you here to assassinate me?'

'No. We're going home, Darnell.'

'What?'

'It's over, man. Do you understand? No weapon. No revolution. No Al'Mayran empire.'

I'Rasnee tried to sit back down on his chair and fell to the floor. No one laughed. When I'Kalmeen tried to help him to his feet, he refused to move and started to shout: 'Fools! You're all fools. We need the weapon, Peetor, you know that.'

'That's up to the king.'

'That senile old man will never agree. The temple won't let him.'

'Maybe with good reason, Ambassador,' Wes said. 'Think of your ancestors' spirits.'

'I refuse to be lectured by a Kahokeyan oaf. The spirits are willing, Kohee; they give themselves to us, protect us.' He turned to I'Kalmeen. 'You must see that, Peetor. Even Areel's spirit will now understand, thanks to Dabreeyor.'

'Sounds like self-serving fish shit to me,' I said. 'And even if it's true, the weapon is an abomination. Now, where's I'Remo, Ambassador?'

But I'Rasnee didn't answer, he just put his gaunt face in his hands, so I turned to Unaduti.

'I'Remo left after you arrived. Why?' I said.

Unaduti shrugged and smirked, folded his arms, and put his feet on the desk.

'Go fuck yourself,' he said.

I saw Nita dead and Nakni broken, and heard fires roaring in my ears and the sound of a blast, like an explosion of molten metal from a furnace. I whipped my pistol across Unaduti's face and broke his nose.

'Where did I'Remo go?' I said, pressing the muzzle to his temple.

'The woman – he went for the woman,' Unaduti said, dragging a handkerchief from his pocket to stem the flow of blood.

'Ameeleyor,' Wes said.

'By the spirits, go,' I'Kalmeen said. 'I must arrest I'Dreng's guards. I'll follow as soon as I can.'

I expected to find the apothecary's shop ablaze or reduced to rubble with a gathering of local Al'Mayran shoppers huddled around its remains. But the unremarkable building still stood, a model of normality, with the same tinted windows and faded green-and-yellow sign.

I opened the door and triggered the sprung brass bell. The lock had been forced. Wes and I exchanged a glance, drew our percussion pistols, and stepped inside. Although the hum of sulphur and cat piss was exacerbated by the dank air, none of the beakers and bottles had been disturbed, and the only sound was the writhing of lizards, caterpillars and cockroaches in their glass tanks.

A child screamed.

I tossed the flap in the counter aside and ran through, then up the narrow and steep wooden stairs to the next floor. I almost tripped over the body of Ronayld I'Kryse outside his office. There was a smouldering hole burnt into his head from which smoke, along with the stench of cooked human flesh, rose. On the wall above where he lay were the now familiar lesions of inch-deep scorch marks.

'Open this hatch!' Dabreeyor shouted from the floor above.

With my pistol raised, I ran for the next flight of stairs, but I was slow to spot the enormous form of Liam I'Remo squeezed into the stockroom doorway. There was a burning lamp above him, and his shadow fell upon me before he did. I fired into his belly and saw the flap of his cowl where the ball entered his midriff. He barely flinched as he pinned me to the opposite wall with one giant hand around my neck and the other stabbing at me with a dagger. I grabbed his forearm but only succeeded in slowing his thrust.

The tip of I'Remo's blade had almost pierced my leather waistcoat when Wes shot him in the shoulder. I'Remo winced but didn't falter, so Wes tackled him, sending the dagger flying to the floor. The big Al'Mayran elbowed Wes in the face and split his nose. I reached for my second pistol and took aim at I'Remo's head. I almost had him too, but he kicked my feet from under me, causing me to fire wide and low into his bicep. He roared, picked me up and threw me along the hall; my head hit the post of the bannister.

For a moment, I saw Josee on our southern balcony, her face silhouetted against the sun. I reached for her, but she floated away across the Coiled Sea. 'Get up, Ani,' she said.

'Get up, Ani!' Wes said.

I opened my eyes to a spinning and blurred world. In the distortion, the misshapen form of I'Remo sat on top of Wes. He was hammering the Kahokeyan with his fists and spraying blood from his wounds onto the walls around him.

'Go, Ani, go!' Wes shouted as he shielded his face with his forearms.

I tried to stand, but my legs wouldn't hold me, so I crawled up the staircase as it rocked like the deck of a ship in a storm. Ameeleyor was ahead of me, dragging her body like a snake, leaving a red trail behind her from a terrible wound across her abdomen.

I locked eyes with her as I passed and saw in them a flicker of recognition. But she couldn't spare the energy to talk to me. What little she had left, she needed to save her children.

Before I reached the top of the stairs, I concentrated my thoughts on the appearance of I'Remo and shimmered his form. I clung to the bannister and pulled myself onto the landing. Dabreeyor turned and glanced in my direction. She was standing below the attic hatchway, her back to the living room, holding a pistol of blue-tinted metal to little Emellee's head.

'Come out now, Payval, and we can all go to the embassy,' she said, beckoning me over with a flick of her head.

As I neared, I got a better look at the pistol. There was an enclosed chamber where the hammer, nipple and percussion cap should have been. The barrel looked as if it had been trodden rectangular and there was no ramrod attached.

'Where's my mother? What have you done to her?' Payval yelled through the thin gap in the hatch, his voice breaking.

'She's fine. But it's time to grow up and use your own judgement. If you stay in there, you'll force me to take actions I have no wish to. Caysee, are you listening?'

'We're coming down. Just don't hurt Emellee,' Caysee shouted.

When the hatch started to creak open, I leapt forward, and I think I may have shouted. The warning gave Dabreeyor time to push Emellee aside and seize me, and when our bodies collided, I lost my shimmer.

'Ani, you are full of surprises,' Dabreeyor said as she flipped me onto my back and threw me to the floor. 'I'm sorry about Josee. I tried to spare her. I tried to spare you.'

She pointed the pistol at my head, and I stared down the barrel at a warm glow, like the dying embers of a fire. I grabbed her wrist with both hands and pushed. I redirected her aim just as she fired, and the red beam burnt a line into the wooden floor beside me. Dabreeyor straddled me and leveraged her weight advantage to redirect the beam. I managed to cross my forearms with my elbows planted to slow her, but she was too strong, and the light stream kept coming.

I turned my face away as smoke filled the hall, stinging my eyes and making me choke. There was heat on my skin, and I wondered what my own flesh would smell like when it burnt. But when the light fell upon me, the temperature was little more than hot water from a tap. The stone powering the weapon was spent, drained of its energy, its spirits dying perhaps.

Dabreeyor dropped the pistol, wrenched her arm free, and brought her fist down on my right eye. I felt like I was falling. She hit me again, and I thought I was going to be sick. The third blow brought a dark swirl, circling around the edges of my vision.

Through the closing aperture, I saw Ameeleyor rise behind Dabreeyor. They fell beside me, rolling and struggling until Dabreeyor gained the upper hand, drew a dagger from her robe, and slit Ameeleyor's throat.

I tried to grab Dabreeyor's arm again, but my fingers grasped at the empty spaces where my fractured sight perceived her to be. She swatted my hand away, sat on my chest and brought the knife down towards my neck. My resistance faded with the last of my strength. I wondered if my spirit would unite with Josee's in the Red Mountains or join her in Xol's caverns beneath the sea. As long as we were together, I didn't care.

The blade bit into my skin. Warm blood trickled down my neck. The pressure I expected didn't come. Dabreeyor slumped to one side, Ameeleyor's hand clasped around her ankle. When I gazed into Ameeleyor's eyes, I saw confusion and disbelief before their light dimmed forever.

Dabreeyor shook her head, studied the knife in her hand and threw it down the corridor.

'Are you okay, Inspector?' she said.

'What?' I said.

'Are you badly hurt?'

'I hit my head.'

'I know. But you'll be okay. My family owes you another debt we can never repay.'

'Your family?'

'Yes.'

'I don't understand.'

'Yes, you do.'

'Ameeleyor?' I said.

She nodded.

'You stormed Dabreeyor?' I said, disbelief in my voice.

'I did, but where I found the strength, I couldn't say. The spirits must have been with me,' Ameeleyor, in Dabreeyor's form, said, placing her hand over her new heart.

'And so Dabreeyor, she's dead?'

'Her spirit is safe in what was my heart.'

'My head hurts too much to think about this fish shit,' I said, lying back.

'Payval, Caysee, it's your mother. Come and help me,' Ameeleyor said.

'Ma?' Caysee said, opening the hatch.

'Yes, sweet pickle.'

Caysee climbed down the ladder and lifted her little sister away from the bloody corpse that once contained the spirit of their mother. Payval lowered himself from the hatch and dropped to the floor.

The woman who looked like Dabreeyor took the children into her arms. I was going to say something, but Wes, his face beaten, his fists bloody, a nasty knife wound in his thigh, came stumbling up the stairs with Brigadier I'Kalmeen and Mycale I'Krayag behind him. I'Krayag screamed when he saw his wife's former body lying cut open on the floor. But then he saw his children, clinging to the woman with the face of his wife's enemy, and he fell to his knees, a dawning recognition in his tearful eyes.

'It's me, Mycale,' Ameeleyor said, putting her hand to his face.

They embraced, and the last thing I saw before the black circles closed in was Ameeleyor slipping the pistol into her robe.

CHAPTER TWENTY-NINE

I CAME ROUND ON the settee in I'Kryse's living room. Ameeleyor was pressing ice wrapped in a towel to my forehead and I'Krayag was strapping Wes's thigh. Payval was kneeling beside his father to assist. Caysee was sitting in an armchair comforting her little sister, Emellee, who buried her face into her big sister's neck.

'I'Remo?' I said to Wes.

The big Kahokeyan shook his head.

I sat up and the world spun.

'You have to rest,' Ameeleyor said in Dabreeyor's voice.

'This is too fucking weird,' I said.

'It will take some adjusting to,' Ameeleyor said, turning to her husband, who smiled back at his wife's new face.

'I have to see Naka. This isn't over until I do,' I said.

'I'll come with you,' Wes said.

'Where?' I'Kalmeen said as he entered the room.

'The Wooden House,' I said.

'Can you even walk, Agent Kohee?' I'Kalmeen said.

'No, he can't,' I'Krayag said.

'I'll go with you, Inspector.'

'No, Brigadier. Unless your entire regiment comes with us, we risk Naka taking you. You go with your regiment, it's an act of war,' I said.

'Then we'll accompany you as far as the embassy. The regiment's doctor can attend to Agent Kohee.'

'Good,' I said, lowering my head to see if the room would stop revolving. It didn't.

When I'Krayag finished strapping Wes's leg, he slapped the Kahokeyan's shoulder and stood. On his way out of the room, he stopped and stared at me. He opened his mouth, about to speak, but nodded instead, and left.

'Tell him he's welcome,' I said to Ameeleyor.

I took a cab from the embassy and travelled north along Agale Thoroughfare. Once I'd collapsed into the seat, I closed my eyes and fought the nausea off. But a clamp pressed against my temples and a noose tightened around my neck. Every time I swallowed, I ate sand.

Images of Naka flickered through my mind: a hole in his head, my sword through his heart, him lying in pieces like Hani. The man deserved nothing less.

Agale Thoroughfare narrowed and rose as we neared the ivy-covered timbers of the Wooden House, the high chief's residence, sat above the crests of the Yawe and Magila Bay waterfalls across the Kahokey river from the mainland.

The cab came to a halt, and the driver tapped on the roof.

'This is as far as I go,' she said.

I opened the doors, reached up to pay her, then climbed out on wobbly legs.

The driver pulled on the reins, swung her horse and cab around on a sixpence and set off south. I watched her until the vehicle was consumed by the mid-afternoon traffic, and I headed for the Wooden House.

There were scores of guards standing in a line along the threshold before the open doors, all dressed in deerskin trousers and sleeveless shirts. Their captain came forward to meet me on the moss-covered, green-stained portico.

'Your business here?' he said.

'I'm Inspector Sulaqua, here to see the high chief,' I said.

'Do you have an appointment?'

'No, but he wants to see me.'

The captain nodded to one of his people, who ran off to pass on the message. While I waited, I sat on the steps, trying to catch my breath, and holding my head again as the nausea returned. When my mouth watered and my stomach convulsed, I ran to the wooden rail and vomited into the Yawe Bay waterfall.

I was still leaning over the rail, my head down, waiting for the world to stop spinning, when someone called to me. 'Inspector Sulaqua, are you quite well?'

I recognised the polite and cheerful voice of High Chief Naka and a sensation, like a cold wave passing over me, made me shiver. He was watching me from the Wooden House's steps along with his guards, blending in with them, dressed in an animal-skin shirt and trousers.

I spat and said, 'Fine.'

I staggered over to him and leant on the wall as I climbed the steps.

'What did you need to see me about?' he said.

'The murder of Areel I'Advay,' I said.

His small mouth turned up at the corners, and his eyes sparkled.

'Yes, yes,' he said.

I followed him through the timber entrance hall with the hanging tribal banners to the inner courtyard, its walls lined with hundreds of warriors. They stood to attention as we passed the giant wooden sculpture of Xol.

At the other side of the courtyard, we climbed a thin wooden staircase by the side of the northern wing and went into the house through an unadorned door, which opened onto a corridor. As with the entrance hall, the interior walls of the high chief's residence were covered in timber, their vertical lines only broken by large, curtainless glass windows with simple trim.

Two men were on guard in the corridor. They lowered their heads as Naka passed them.

'At ease, friends,' he said.

We headed west, occasionally passing more guards, all of whom bowed. Naka nodded back, smiled, sometimes patted them on the shoulder and asked how they were. We even stopped for him to inquire about the health of one young woman's mother, whose name he knew and who was injured in the storm.

'When she is well enough, she must come for tea,' he said.

'She would be honoured, sir,' the young woman said.

'Oh, the mother of a Wooden House guard is always welcome inside it. The honour would be mine.'

We turned north and ascended another staircase, passing a window at the landing that overlooked the Magila Bay waterfall and the academy beyond. Naka took the stairs two at a time, and I pushed myself to keep up with him, hanging on to the rail all the while, trying not to fall. I was out of breath by the time we reached his office. We stopped outside for him to chat with more of his people before we went inside.

I had been in the workplaces of powerful men and women before and assumed the high chief's office would be similarly grandiose and imposing. Instead, it was a room where my uncle and his understated sensibilities would have felt at home. There were no rugs, let alone a fitted carpet, and no ornaments or sculptures save for one: a giant wooden claw. The furniture was of traditional design, too. There were half a dozen plain chairs with woven seats, a small coffee table made of reclaimed wood and a well-used bureau with a new brass mechanical clock on top, the only nod to the modern world I could see. Even the man's desk was small and unassuming, and the chair behind it was neither raised nor stately; nothing to symbolise the throne of the most powerful person in the Known World.

I watched in amazement as Naka stood at a sideboard, squeezing fresh orange juice into a pitcher. Beyond where he stood, there were glass doors and a terrace commanding a magnificent view of the Great Kahokey River where it split.

'Please sit, Inspector. Would you like a glass?' he said, smiling at me.

I didn't know if I could keep anything down, but my mouth was dry and tasted of bile, so I nodded as I sat. He placed a glass in front of me and I took a sip, allowing the wave of sickness to pass before drinking a little more.

'You look terrible, Sulaqua. Who did that to you?' he said.

'Dabreeyor A'Mendayse, the woman who murdered Areel I'Advay,' I said.

'Of course, the new developments. The last I heard you'd arrested a Coor'Seyan soldier.'

'He was coerced into his confession to protect his wife from Ambassador I'Rasnee.'

'I see. How did you uncover this?'

'Brigadier I'Kalmeen told me. He was also involved, but is now full of regret. He's arrested I'Rasnee, and intends to sail home to Al'Mayra to confess to the king his part in a conspiracy to supply New Capital with lifeblood stones to power a terrible new weapon that would be used in a revolution. Now, with I'Rasnee neutralised, and I'Dreng, Liam I'Remo and A'Mendayse dead, the supply chain of stones is broken. The weapon your scientists are testing will never be.'

Naka laughed and slapped his desk with the palm of his hand. 'My, you are something special, Sulaqua. Yes, yes,' he said, grinning.

My headache became a roar, the heart of a burning furnace. I stood, drew a pistol, and aimed it at Naka.

'Special indeed,' he said, drinking from his glass without a hint of fear in his expression.

'Now all I have to do is kill you, and my family will be safe,' I said.

'You assume a lot, Ani. To begin with, I have no intention of harming your people. However, if you kill me, who knows what my warriors will do on Sundown Claw?'

'If you're dead, you can't give them any orders.'

'I won't have to. My people love me, as I love them, as I love all my children.'

'Yet you had one butchered only yesterday – a boy, no more than eleven.'

'I would never do such a thing.'

'Not in person, but I knew the killer. He worked for Chief Yoyu,' I said.

'The community leader from the Depths?'

'Don't pretend Yoyu isn't your dog.'

'I rather think Yoyu is no one's dog.'

'Either way, you've probably taken my wife from me, too. And you've destroyed other lives, and for what? More power? How much is enough?'

'Ani, I think you're confused about what a high chief does. You see, I make bargains, that's all, day in, day out, and all for the benefit of the Five Claws and her people. In doing so, I may have to facilitate the wishes of those with whom I have entered into agreement, even if those terms are personally egregious to me. Of course, if for any reason my associates cannot reciprocate, our pact is nullified. Do you see?

'For example, take Ambassador I'Rasnee. However much I may have liked Darnell, even considered him a friend, if he is found guilty of these terrible crimes, I will consider our relationship terminated, and my obligations to him annulled. On the other hand, who knows what my successor would do?'

I holstered my pistol and staggered onto the decking outside with the glass of orange juice in my hand. I held onto the rail of the balustrade to steady myself and accidentally dropped the glass into the river below; the current took it over the Magila Bay waterfall.

'Shona, forgive me,' I said, remembering the disappointment I had seen in her eyes.

'Who is Shona?' Naka said, standing beside me.

'An old friend. Another dead child from the Depths. She was murdered, and her killer went free because he was rich and powerful, just like you. The only difference is, now I'm the one letting you go.'

'It pains me to see you so troubled. Let me do something for you.'

'I don't want anything from you except a promise my family won't be harmed in any way.'

'That's easy. I don't bear them any malice. No, pick something else. Anything else. Name it. If I'm as powerful as you say, perhaps I can facilitate your wish, Ani.'

'Give the Stars back to her people,' I said, astonished at my willingness to bargain with a monster.

'Excuse me?'

'The Stars and the Sea. It's a brothel in Rose Town. Its owner, Nita, and her bodyguard were accused of I'Advay's murder. As I'm sure you're aware, she died before she could be freed. Now the CIB are refusing to hand the Stars over to the people who worked for her, even though it's their home as much as it was hers.'

'How unjust. Consider it done.'

'Just like that?'

'Yes, yes.' Naka took a deep breath, stood on his toes, and raised his face to the sun. 'I will miss Darnell, I can't lie. A remarkable man, and a patriot. But perhaps I can reach an agreement with Brigadier I'Kalmeen.'

'I think I'm going to be sick again,' I said.

'I want to show you something, Ani. Follow me, if you're well enough.'

We left the Wooden House by a western entrance and took a set of steps down to the narrow bridge spanning the Magila Bay waterfall. Once we crossed over, we headed for the Octagon Hall.

The guards at its entrance reacted to Naka like the others had, by bowing or nodding, but the scientists inside, all dressed in long, dark brown leather lab coats, barely seemed to notice their master as he hurried by.

The tripod was still erected in the lab under the glass dome, only now there was an iron tube, about three feet long, not unlike a telescope, fixed to its mount. The weapon was unlike either the one in the diagram or the one Dabreeyor used. If they were pistols, this was a musket. Its chamber was the same as the one I'd found, covered in rubber and threaded with copper wires.

'We need space to test the weapon, you see,' Naka said to me. He addressed the two scientists present, a fat middle-aged man and a frail-looking elderly woman: 'A demonstration for the Inspector, please.'

The fat man pushed a wheeled table, which had the carcass of a pig upon it, about fifty feet in front of the musket. He hurried out of the way as the woman took aim. When she fired, a beam of carmine-red light, six inches in diameter, bridged the gap. There was no sound until the hide of the pig crackled and smoked. A flame took, and the woman let go of the trigger to allow the fat man to dampen the fire with a blanket.

'We are months, maybe years away from a functional handheld design,' Naka said. 'And despite the size of this model, all we can presently do is roast pork for dinner.'

'I don't understand. I've seen the pistol, seen what it can do. This contraption couldn't do that,' I said, nodding towards the destroyed corridor wall and the keyhole wound beyond.

'It didn't. Show Inspector Sulaqua the other musket.'

The elderly woman helped the fat man push a stone wall mounted on a dolly behind the table and extend outriggers to keep it stable. She removed the blanket from the singed hog carcass while the fat man unlocked a windowless iron cabinet. I couldn't see what he was taking out, but when he turned, he was holding a musket unlike any I had seen before. It was made from blue-tinged metal, and the barrel was short and thick with a wide muzzle. The butt and stock were wooden, stained oak, I thought, and the breech large and round.

The fat man pointed the weapon at the pig and fired. This time the animal exploded in flames, and the wall behind it blew apart.

'Xol save us,' I said.

'Indeed, Inspector,' Naka said. 'And that's with a lower setting and a dying stone. You saw for yourself our experiment with the higher settings.'

'The explosion?'

'What you thought was an explosion, Inspector. In reality, a single, momentary beam of light; no more than a flash. But it destroyed the inner wall, cut a passing laboratory assistant in half, and blew a hole in the outer wall. Thank Xol one of the skytowers wasn't in the firing line.'

'I don't understand. You said you were months away from a working design.'

'We are. Our best effort is this clumsy device,' Naka said, gesturing with his open hand towards the iron tube on the tripod. 'You see, we didn't build this powerful weapon. We don't know how.'

'Then who did? The Al'Mayrans?'

'In a way.'

'You're showing me all this and speaking in riddles. I'm tired, hurt, and not in the mood.'

'In the Known World, lifeblood stones can only be found in Al'Mayra, yes?'

'Everyone knows that.'

'Come with me.'

I followed him out of the lab, down the wide corridor, and through another set of doors to a narrow hall. He lit a handheld oil lamp, took a key from his pocket, and unlocked a door to a pitch-black, windowless room.

'The working musket and pistol were found about a month ago, west of the city, far beyond your people's home on Sundown Claw, by a fisherman who had the good sense to take them straight to the fort near his village,' Naka said. 'Luckily, the colonel stationed there sent a company of men and women out to scour the beach where it was discovered. This proved to be a wise decision because the weapons weren't all that was found.'

Naka raised the lamp and illuminated the remains of a vessel that was twenty feet in length and unusually narrow. I didn't recognise the design and wondered if it was a canoe, but when I looked again, I realised it was one thin hull from a multi-hull craft.

'Was any other wreckage found?' I asked.

'No. Although my experts believe there were three hulls in all, joined by crossbars with a small cabin in the centre. We have no notion of its rig.'

'I've seen drawings of double-hull vessels used by fishermen and women on the islands of Alsea. It's said they can cross oceans on them.'

'This is not Alsean.'

'How can you be sure?'

'Because we found its sailor.'

Naka spun on his toes and swung the lamp aloft to reveal a steel-framed glass tank with the body of a man inside it, suspended in formaldehyde. He was seven feet tall but broad, with heavy limbs in proportion with his frame. At first glance, I thought his long straight hair and his eyes were white, but on closer inspection, the lamplight revealed the pale gold of his locks and the soft blue of his irises.

'The Ghost Clan,' I said.

'Very astute, Ani. We assume the legend is true. They left their homes in Al'Mayra to find other lifeblood stones. I would say they succeeded. Exactly when they lost their piety and chose to charge such monstrous weapons with their sacred stones is another question.'

'When my uncle was a boy, his grandfather and the crew he sailed with once spotted a strange vessel far to the south, beyond the Known World, but they lost it amongst the icebergs.'

'There have long been rumours of undiscovered peoples. The

continents of the Known World cover what, maybe a quarter of the globe? Why would we be alone?'

'This is why you want the weapon, why an honourable man like I'Kalmeen conspired against his king: a fucking arms race with an unknown enemy. What if these people greet us peacefully?'

'It wasn't peace that drove the creation of those weapons. So while I hope for peace, Ani, it is my responsibility to prepare for war.'

I wanted to be sick again. This time, because I wondered if Naka were not justified in holding his views. Had I inserted myself on the wrong side of a conflict I didn't fully understand? Did we need the weapon after all? *No*, I told myself, *no*. It would destroy the Known World, not save it.

'What keeps you awake at night, Ani?' Naka said. 'Is it dreams of murdered children and dead whores? What luxury.

'My experts, historians, masters and scientists spend their days debating these discoveries and sending me conflicting reports of their conclusions. Some say the musket and pistol must be the most advanced weapons the Ghost Clan possess. Others suggest they might just as plausibly be standard-issue. My people argue about the boat, too. It could be a long-range craft for a small crew to go exploring far across the oceans, knowing they may never return home. Alternatively, it could be a utility craft carried by a much larger vessel, capable of Xol knows what firepower. And this dead man, imposing, isn't he? But is he an exceptional individual, that is to say, an anomaly to his race, an extraordinary physical specimen, their greatest warrior perhaps? Or is he just a common sailor of average build?

'That is what keeps me awake at night, Ani – the fate of this city, of the Known World. When I dream, I see an army of men and women, a million strong, capable of reading each other's minds, all armed with terrible muskets and pistols. They sail from the south and burn our homes from the cliffs, and all the children and whores in New Capital, along with everyone else, perish in the flames.'

The Known World was spinning again, gathering pace, the momentum dragging at my body. This time, as the black whirlpool tightened, I was helpless to prevent it from closing, and I sank to my knees and tried to dig my nails into the stone floor, desperate to remain anchored to all I knew and not be torn away, lost forever in a vast universe.

I sat on the southern balcony of my home, watching Josee paint a self-portrait. The sun was setting, and the sky and the sea were the colour of lifeblood stones. Hani and Mani were playing marbles at my feet, and the younger boy, who was using the thumb-clicking technique I'd shown him, was beating his older brother, who did not seem to mind.

'Sorry I couldn't save you,' I said to the dead boy.

'Xol calls us when he calls us,' Hani said with a shrug.

Xol himself lifted an enormous tentacle from the Coiled Sea and rested its tip over the balustrade to allow Shona to join us. When I thought about or dreamt of my first love, I saw my contemporary, someone my own age and height. Now I saw a child. She hadn't changed; I had. She touched my face and smiled warmly, taking Hani's hand.

'Come and play with me again,' his brother said.

'Maybe I will, but you don't need me,' Hani said.

'But I miss you so much.'

'You'll make other friends. And you'll lead them, you'll see. And when Xol finally calls you, you can join me and Ma.'

'Is my mother there?' I said.

'No, Ani,' Shona said.

'Did Xol reject her?'

'I don't know, but he rarely denies a home for the children of the Depths.'

'Forgive me,' I said.

'You couldn't have saved me.'

'Not for that, for conspiring with Naka. I'm just like everybody else in this damn city now.'

Shona smiled at me and said, 'Try and find some peace, Ani.'

Xol lifted his tentacle and carried her and Hani away into the sea.

'Do you have to go too, Josee?' I said.

'Ani, you're dreaming,' she said.

'Sorry?'

'Ani, wake up, love.'

I opened my eyes to see Josee with that silly cap on her head, sitting beside my bed in Pastnoon Claw hospital. She was holding my hand, and her green eyes were alive and bright, although focused inwards, like a perplexed drunk lost in their own secret consciousness.

'Are you real?' I said.

'I think so,' she said.

Her face blurred as the tears came and ran down my cheeks. 'I'm so sorry, Josee, about Hani. He—'

'I know. Oura told me. Listen, love, you either condemn the men and women who cut him down and no one else, or you apportion me a share of the blame too. If I hadn't been so insistent on visiting the arcade, he'd be alive today.'

'You don't know that.'

'Either way, I'm not going to waste my time imagining a million variations of a day I didn't live, and nor should you.'

Mani ran in, his long black hair trailing behind him.

'Is she awake, is she awake?' he said.

'She is. Be careful, I think she's tender all over,' Josee said.

'Is it true you made Salvation's Climb?' Mani said, climbing onto the bed.

'It is,' I said. 'With a little help.'

'Wes says you cut down the bastards that killed Hani, all six of them?'

'Five of them. One stepped off the cliff.'

'Josee said you'd be climbing the steps. She dreamt it, didn't you, Josee?'

'Did she now?'

'I dreamt I was there with you, lying beside you, whispering in your ear as the sun set,' Josee said.

I was about to speak again when High Chief Naka opened the door to my room and walked in, flanked by two of his guards. Imala followed, trying to catch my eye, the tension in her face evident, the warning clear: *for Xol's sake, please stay calm, Ani.* Wes hobbled in on crutches, also wearing a fearful expression, his gaze restless, switching between me and the back of Naka's head.

Josee squeezed my hand, crushing the bones together and only relenting when she got my attention.

'Look who brought you here, and stayed,' she said with a forced smile.

My heart was pummelling my breastbone. Air was rushing past my ears as the Known World tried to spin free of its axis again. I closed my eyes, drifted in darkness, my mouth watering, the nausea rising.

'Ah, the patient awakes,' Naka said.

'What?' I said, opening my eyes and trying to gather my wits.

'I was worried about you, Ani.'

'You shouldn't be here. Not here,' I said, searching Josee's face, hoping my wife could tell me I was trapped in a nightmare. I didn't know how else to explain Naka's toxic presence. The violation was too much to bear. How could it be real? 'Why are you here? How dare you!'

'Forgive the intrusion, only you gave me quite a scare, collapsing as you did,' Naka said.

When I stared at the high chief, I saw his violent death, over and over, like a flip book: I put my sword through his heart, across his throat, in his eye. I fired a pistol ball into his head and the back of his skull exploded, emptying his malignant brain of all his dark ruminations. The lifeblood stone musket was in my hand and I was slicing him into pieces, each smaller than the last, until there was nothing of him left but a puddle of tissue and blood.

Josee tightened her grip on my hand while Imala's eyes grew wider than I thought possible.

Stay calm, Ani, stay calm.

Blow the candle out.

'Pardon?' I said.

'You gave me a scare, Ani,' Naka said, smiling.

'I feel just terrible about that,' I said, my sarcasm making Imala wince.

'The high chief has requested all disciplinary actions against you be dropped and you be reinstated, ready to return to work the moment you're well enough,' Imala said.

'And I've asked that you be partnered with Wesu here,' Naka said, slapping the giant Kahokeyan on the back.

Wes smiled but his eyes betrayed his disbelief.

'I'll be sad to see him leave the CIB, but what a team you two will make. I just feel it in my bones,' Naka said, clenching his fist like he had scored a point at handball.

He took a step closer to my bed and put his hands behind his back.

'I may call on you one day, Anika Sulaqua of the Square. I'm always on the lookout for people of your calibre,' he said. 'But until then, I shall leave you and your family in peace. On that, you have my word.'

'I guess we'll see about that, won't we?' I said.

'Yes, yes,' he said, a glint in his eye. He bowed, spun on his heel, and set off at pace. His guards held the door open, revealing Dee and Ezno and other members of my tribe waiting in the corridor beyond. He smiled at them and their mouths hung open, shock upon their innocent faces.

Josee and I were discharged from Pastnoon Claw hospital three days later, leaving behind Etu, whose wound still worried the doctors. I made sure I spent my remaining hours there with him, gloating and laughing at his misfortune. He would not have had it any other way.

Uncle Ezno insisted Josee and I stay with him and our tribe in Lo'tse Bay until we fully recovered. He presented his case with reason and conviction, but he need not have bothered. I was in no mood to argue.

As the days passed, Josee put on a spirited performance for my sake, but she was not herself yet, and was often forgetful and confused, with an inward look in her eye, an ever-present reminder of her injury's nature. She was quick to temper, too.

Today, I had fussed over her more than she could bear. She grew so angry she threw me out of the house, demonstrating, if nothing else, that her strength had returned.

I decided to take a ferry across the bay and return to our flat to check all was well and gather some more belongings. Hani only stayed with us two nights, but his ghost haunted the place, particularly on the western terrace where he had played marbles with his brother and on the southern balcony where they created a bedroom under the stars. Despite Josee's advice, I was unable to forget my role in his death and often reflected on my failure.

He had not belonged to any recognised tribe, and any death rites the Vermin invented over the years were not sanctioned by the city. Ordinarily, his kind cremated their fallen brothers and sisters in some sheltered and secret place where the fire would not be noticed. It was the least I could do, therefore, to arrange a funeral pyre for him out in the open on Sundown Claw; his friends could gather with my tribe, sing songs, and praise his courage.

Earlier in the week, once Josee felt up to travelling, she and I had taken Mani to the pool where his brother wanted his ashes scattering: a disused mill dam at the bottom of Riverlyn Park that had long since been reclaimed by nature.

There was plenty of shade to be found under the willow trees and places to play hide-and-seek in the long grass near the banks. Mani emptied the urn with his brother's remains inside, his face blank, seemingly unmoved. I think I understood him. I had barely known Hani, but I couldn't associate the dust in the breeze with the flesh and blood being I remembered. How, I wondered, could he? We sat for a while by the pool and watched hawker and darter dragonflies compete for midges and saw a diving beetle catch a tiny red shiner fish.

The boy didn't cry once. I imagined he found the improvised ceremony too abstract and vague to connect with, so we returned home after an hour with a hollow feeling in our hearts and a nagging sense of unfinished business. But such was the nature of death.

I sighed at the painful memory of that day and tried to push all thoughts of Hani aside. Why dwell?

'Come on, Ani,' I said. 'Snap out of it. You can't bring the boy back.'

I sat down at the corner of the southern and eastern balconies and hung my legs between the balusters. It was another cloudless summer day. The sun was high over the city and its light was glistening on the buoyant sea, turning the froth of the breaking waves silver and highlighting the sails of the passing ships all the way from Magila Bay to the horizon. I watched as vessels from all over the Known World came and went and heard the voices of sailors float by, carried like gliding birds in the gentle but constant breeze. I sighed and breathed in the aroma of salt, brine and mild sulphur from the living sea and its fleshy vegetation.

The doorbell rang and, startled, I stood up with a jolt and set off to answer it at a trot. But I felt the complaint of every ache and wound I had received and slowed to a saunter. When I entered the kitchen, Brigadier I'Kalmeen was visible through the window, standing on the platform on Pastnoon Claw, looking magnificent in his black-and-scarlet robes.

I hadn't wound the drawbridge up, so I beckoned him over.

'How goes it with you, sir?' I said when he crossed.

'Good, I thank you. And you? Are you healing?'

'Yes. All my excuses are fading with my bruises, and I'll have to return to work soon.'

'And what of your wife? How is her recovery coming along?'

'Slow, but I'm hopeful.'

'And Kohee?'

'Distant. He killed I'Remo with his bare hands. It doesn't sit well with him.'

'Nevertheless, a remarkable feat.'

'What can I do for you, sir?'

'You can start by not calling me sir. I'm used to thinking of you as a dangerous and reckless antagonist who provokes me at every opportunity. Your pivot to obsequiousness is making me dizzy. Call me Peetor.'

'You may call me Inspector Sulaqua or just Inspector, whichever makes you more comfortable.'

'Ah, that's the Ani Sulaqua I'm used to. I've brought you a gift. Or rather, I'm returning one. I hope my bringing it won't offend or trouble you.'

He pulled Areel I'Advay's golden cane from his robes and offered it to me. I took it and held it up to the sun, turning it so the light glinted upon its raised symbols.

'Come in, Peetor,' I said.

'No, no. My people grow worried when I'm absent.'

'I don't blame them, but I insist. I have two bottles of spiced Al'Mayran citrus ale left. No ice, though.'

'How can I say no to Al'Mayran ale?'

I took the bottles from the pantry and led the brigadier onto the western terrace. He helped me open the gateleg table and untie a couple of chairs from where I'd battened them down.

'What an odd home you have. Lovely and welcoming but odd. I've never seen a flat wrapped around the pillar of a bridge before,' he said, once we were sitting and drinking our ale.

'Space is a premium in the Five Claws,' I said as I ran my fingers over the figures of the cane, wondering what they meant. 'Why don't you want this, Peetor?'

'Good question. I suppose it's not representative of the Areel I choose to remember. When I think of him, he's a young and cheerful man. One who carries his religion lightly and whose duties don't burden him.'

'Would you be offended if I gave it to someone else?'

'Not at all.'

We fell silent, both of us lost in reflection, sipping at our ale.

'Naka came to see me yesterday,' I'Kalmeen said.

I coughed and almost choked on my ale. 'Oh?'

I'Kalmeen lowered his voice. 'He told me he'd shown you the Ghost Clan sailor and the musket.'

I nodded.

'He speaks very highly of you,' I'Kalmeen said.

I put my bottle of ale down on the table and rubbed my eyes. 'In Xol's name, I don't know what I've done, other than thwarting his plans, to win his favour. But now I have, I'm even more frightened of him than I was before,' I said.

I'Kalmeen chuckled quietly. 'That's probably wise.'

'What did he want?'

'To wish me a safe voyage, and to give me the musket so I can show the king.'

'He still wants the stones?'

'He does,' I'Kalmeen said with a nod.

'And you?'

I'Kalmeen took a sip of ale. 'I'll leave that up to the king and the temple.' He looked my way. 'Which is what I should have done in the first place.'

'What will happen to you?'

He shrugged. 'Dishonourable discharge, prison – only the spirits know.'

'Your people would be foolish to lock you away.'

'Oh, Al'Mayra has no shortage of fools.'

'No, nor New Capital.'

'To the foolish and foolhardy,' he said, raising his bottle.

'Tribes we all belong to,' I said, clinking the brigadier's bottle with
my own.

CHAPTER THIRTY

A WEEK LATER, WES came to Sundown Claw to check on my family and me. It was another hot day with little more than wisps of brilliant white cloud floating in the sky like curls of unstirred cream atop a mug of coffee. Etu had been released from hospital the previous day and Dee joined us for lunch to celebrate. We ate crab and fried seaweed under the awning my uncle erected and spoke of anything but the case of the dead envoy with the golden cane.

Wes had already disposed of his crutches but still walked with a limp. He fussed over Mani and chatted with Dee and my uncle and cousins, taking particular care to ask Etu and Josee if I were caring for them properly.

His humour seemed forced to me, his conversation too precise and considered and without its usual buoyant flow. After lunch, he played marbles with Mani, but when he looked upon the boy, a sadness crept into his eyes, and he hid his face. I went over and joined them for a game.

'Are you sure Josee is quite well?' Wes said.

Mani and I exchanged a glance and looked around for my wife before we spoke.

'She's getting better, sort of,' Mani said.

'And by that, the lad means short-tempered and irritable,' I said.

'She tried to draw the tip of Pastnoon Claw yesterday,' the boy whispered.

'It didn't go well, I gather,' Wes said.

'We thought things were getting back to normal, didn't we, Ani? So we left her to it and went for a walk. Only for her sketchpad to come flying over our heads and into the sea,' Mani said, making a splashing motion with his hands.

'It'll come back to her,' I said.

'But what if it doesn't?'

I had no answers for him, and I wasn't going to lie. But the prospect turned my heart to ice.

I'd been wearing traditional deer and sealskin clothes and had taken to leaving my hair free and loose while I waited for my suits to be mended. In doing so, my identity as Inspector Sulaqua of the Square retreated. And in staying with my uncle and our people out on Sundown Claw, where I was Ani to every man, woman and child, I felt the pull of my tribe and their way of life more than usual. But as I stood in my childhood bedroom and slipped on my suit trousers, buttoned up a crisp cotton shirt and straightened my waistcoat, the inspector returned, a latent but living being, never lost, never dead, just sleeping. Imala was right: if I wasn't an inspector, who was I?

Josee walked in as I was drawing my hair back and tying it into a ponytail. She watched as I slipped my baldric on and holstered two new percussion pistols. She picked out a tie and fastened it for me.

'Very dashing,' she said.

'It seems your brain wasn't entirely scrambled after all,' I said, examining the tidy knot she'd made.

'That's not all I remember.'

'Oh?'

'I've been thinking of our early courtship.'

I laughed. 'A kinder term than I'd use to describe night after night of heavy drinking and aggressive fucking, but go on.'

'Well, do you remember our third night and our first alone?'

'The night you fell in love with me?'

Josee snorted. 'Hardly. No, the moment I decided you might, just might, be worth my time. Until that point, I hadn't found you to be much fun.'

'In Xol's name, you're delusional, Josee. We must see the doctor immediately,' I said, taking her hand, stepping forward, and trying to drag her towards the bedroom door.

She easily resisted and pulled me back. 'No, no. The memory is strong,' she said, turning me to face her. She put her hands on my shoulders. 'You were your usual dour and grumpy self, and I was wondering if there was anything more to you than this sullen persona.'

'I don't know who you're describing now,' I said.

Josee laughed. 'A fight broke out, and three men set upon another, smaller and weaker than they were. Before I knew it, you were on your feet and diving into the brawl to help defend the young lad, your tiny fists flying.'

'I believe he and I lost that fight.'

'Oh, you were both soundly beaten,' Josee said, nodding.

'Now I'm sure you're not yourself. The Josee I know hates violence.'

She rolled her eyes. 'Yes. I thought the whole show rather pathetic, and I was ready to go home and never see you again.'

'So what stopped you?'

She drew me nearer. 'The young lad asked you why you'd come to his aid. Can you remember what you said?'

'I've had a few knocks on the head myself since then.'

'You said no one should have to receive an arse-kicking alone.'

I felt my face burn. 'Just something clever to say.'

'That wasn't what impressed me.'

'Oh?' I said, looking at my baldrick and fixing how it lay, even though it was not out of place.

Josee lifted my chin with her forefinger until I met her gaze. 'No one should have to receive an arse-kicking alone. I thought about that all night. It was that one word. The last word. The qualifier. Alone. No one should receive an arse-kicking alone. It gave the sentence all its power and told me all I needed to know about you.'

'What did it tell you?' I whispered.

'It told me this woman hates bullies, and although she has friends and family and a whole tribe who love her, she had in some way, all her life, felt like she was fighting on her own.'

'Sounds like self-pity.'

'No. You weren't bitter, a little angry maybe, and I hated seeing you fight. But at least it showed me you'd happily have both your eyes blackened so a stranger might, at least for a few minutes, not feel quite so all alone.'

'You give me too much credit. You always have.'

'By heck, Ani, you are daft, lass.'

I grabbed the lapels of her robe, stood on my toes and kissed her.

'Just when you're leaving,' she said.

'I won't be long. We can resume this conversation later,' I said.

'Indeed? I thought you believed me too fragile.'

She handed me my jacket. I kissed her again and brushed a curl of red hair away from her eyes.

'Never,' I said.

Wes, Dee and I took a ferry to Noon Claw and rode the South-Western Great Lift up to Rose Town. I took Areel I'Advay's cane with me and held it to my bosom as I gazed at Magila Bay.

'Why have you brought the cane?' Wes said.

'I'm going to see if Nakni wants it,' I said.

'Because it was his lover's or because he needs it?'

'I never thanked you for saving my life,' I said, changing the subject.

'On which occasion?'

'Specifically? Saving me from Liam I'Remo. And I'm sorry his resultant death has brought your spirits so low.'

'I've killed before, but killing Liam was different. To squeeze the life out of someone, to feel their muscles and sinew straining in your grip, and to watch the light in their eyes fade and vanish – that I can't forget.'

'I thought it'd be Hani – his butchered corpse and split face that would haunt me,' I said, 'but it's his murderer, Kononwa, calmly stepping away from Salvation's Climb that I see when I dream. He said he'd ask Xol to return Josee to me, even if it meant being cast out. Did he keep his promise, I wonder, and does his soul now drift with the tide?'

Wes coughed and shared a furtive glance with Dee.

'I wish I'd climbed the steps with you,' Dee said.

'As do I,' Wes said.

'You weigh too much, big man,' I said.

Memi was standing outside the Stars and the Sea when we arrived. She had her back to us and was running her hand up the side of one of the building's decorative pilasters, looking up at its capital, carved into our octopus god.

'How goes it with you, Memi?' I said.

She turned her head and grinned, then came running to hug me. I was wholly unprepared for such a greeting, and I held my arms out straight like an unaffectionate cat as she embraced me. Dee broke into giggles and Wes's chest thundered as he chortled.

'What have I done to deserve this?' I said.

'I know it was you that gave us back our home,' Memi said.

'No, no. Occasionally the administrative state makes a just decision.'

She held my face and looked into my eyes. 'I know it was you.'

I stared at my feet and pulled away. 'At any rate, we're here to see you and bring this to Nitushi,' I said, holding the cane up.

'I'm waiting for him now. Two of the girls went to fetch him in a four-seater carriage. They do like to fuss over him.'

'How is he?' Wes said.

'Struggling to walk. He'll appreciate having Areel's cane.'

'I hope so. I don't wish to upset him,' I said.

'He'll appreciate it, Ani.'

'Then you give it to him.'

'No, I can't.'

'Please, I insist,' I said, offering it to her.

She accepted it with a shake of her head and said, 'You don't fool anyone, you know, Inspector.'

'Only myself. Tell me, Memi, have you been given access to all of Nita's estate?'

'I signed the paperwork this morning. She was wealthier than I'd imagined.'

'Are you surprised?'

'I can't say I am.'

'And what will you do with it?'

'Share it out. The Stars will become a cooperative.'

'Profit sharing on Noon Claw? Xol help us.'

'We open next week.'

'Memi, have you thought about doing something else for a living?' Wes said.

'Of course I have.'

'And the younger ones, what kind of life is this to set sail on?'

'Perhaps you should save your judgement for another day, Wes,' I said.

'Forgive me, I meant no offence.'

'Most of the young men and women who find their way here are like I was, uneducated and homeless,' Memi said. 'I wasn't blind to Nita's exploitation. But she cared too, in her way. More than many of those who run the orphanages and poorhouses do. Have you been inside such places, Agent Kohee?'

'I have, and I'm no longer with the CIB, Memi.'

'Glad to hear it. They don't deserve a man like you. Maybe I can't accept all the strays this city has, but if someone is made of the right stuff, I can give them a family and a future, or, at least, the chance of one. That's more than most receive.'

Wes bowed.

'Nitushi is home,' Memi said, peering over my shoulder.

The hired carriage was ridiculous. Pulled by four horses, it was ornately carved, covered in gold leaf and with a footman who looked almost as embarrassed as the honoured beneficiary who sat within. Beside me, Wes wept with laughter.

'Don't let them see you being so amused,' Memi said.

Wes turned and wiped his eyes, his muscular frame still shaking as he brought himself under control. His disposition changed when he saw the footman and the driver set the wheelchair upon the cobblestones. Nakni's left leg was splintered below the knee, his right from hip to ankle, and he needed support from both the young women who accompanied him to climb out of the carriage.

As one of the girls raised a leg rest for him on the wheelchair so he could sit, Memi walked over and kissed him on the cheek. I couldn't hear what she said when she handed him my gift, but his lips broke into a slight smile, and his eyes shone. He nodded at me.

Wes pulled the wheelchair up the steps and into the Stars. A heated and poorly coded debate soon began around the embarrassed Kahokeyan giant, who stared off into the middle distance, pretending not to listen. After some argument, Nakni put an end to the discussion and decided to rest before he attended the so-called surprise party, which he had already guessed awaited him. Wes lifted the young man into his arms, and, with infinite care, carried him up the staircase to the small room where Nakni had shared his life and love with Areel I'Advay. Nakni gripped the cane until his knuckles turned white.

I didn't join them. Instead, I strolled south along Sumaka Way until I reached the wall with the iron gate leading to Salvation's Climb. The lock was still broken, so I stepped out onto the corridor and gazed east towards the remnants of the steps. Even though I'd now climbed them, my memories of the ascent were dreamlike and elusive: Kononwa was floating in the air as he offered me his apologies, and I'Dreng's heart was beating in my hands. I recalled how I had sensed Josee's presence, as if she'd been holding me during the night, even though she had been miles away in a hospital bed fighting for her life.

'We thought you'd be here,' Wes said, peering through the gate with Dee. They each took a tentative step forward and shuffled towards me, their backs against the wall.

'What are you thinking about?' Dee said.

'Wondering if it was all worth it,' I said.

'Don't do that,' Wes said.

'What did we achieve? I mean really achieve? Did we find justice or just take a questionable side in a foreign civil war?'

'You solved I'Advay's murder.'

'A murderer himself. What if I'd just left it alone and learnt my lines like I was supposed to?'

'Nitushi would be dead, Memi and her family in prison,' Dee said.

'Hani alive, my wife...'

'You saved Ameeleyor and Mycale and, most likely, their children too,' Wes said. 'That's what I hold on to and why I will continue to fight.'

'What fight?' I asked, derision rising in my voice.

'The only one that matters – the one that never ends.'

'Oh, spare me, Wes. There are no great forces of good and evil doing battle for our souls. Like our gods, we're each born capable of anything.'

'I can't accept that world view. It leaves only chaos.'

'For there to be chaos, we must also have order, and I've never seen that in New Capital.'

When I looked upon Wes, the darkness had returned to his face, and I cursed my cruelty.

'My wife's people believe there will be order one day,' I said, putting my hand on his arm. 'At the end of time, after the universe has crumbled into dust. Until then, I will fight with you, Wesu Kohee.'

'That I can live with,' he said with a gentle smile.

Dee and I sauntered home. The young cadet tried to make conversation, but my mood was still low, and I was unable to reciprocate. Eventually, he gave up.

I'd never seen the sea bluer, so we paused on the bridge to take in the view. I leant on the balustrade and happened to look down. Below me, sat on an upside-down bucket, peeling a mountain of potatoes, was the tall and skinny girl whose gang Josee and I fought on the night of the storm.

She'd put on weight, and her clothes were new, and like their wearer, clean and neat. She must have felt my gaze upon her because she looked up. When she saw me, she gasped and furrowed her brow, fear in her eyes. I smiled and winked, and her face broke into a wide grin. My feet didn't touch the ground all the way to Sundown.

EPILOGUE

The day after Wes, Dee and I had stood together on Salvation's Climb, another storm hit New Capital. It veered east and did not make landfall, but its tails skimmed Noon Claw and swept the remnants of the steps away. Over the remaining weeks of a long and hot summer, Josee and I watched as the stairwell was bricked shut and filled with concrete. Now an advertising banner covers the scar. I am told the price of a single square foot of space is the equivalent of most people's annual income.

A week later, Wes officially joined the Square. He started with a rotation in uniform, but Imala wanted Wes in the inspector's department as soon as possible, and she got her way. She partnered him with me, hoping he might provide a counter to my wilder speculations and tame my provocative behaviour. I believe she considers the results to be mixed at best. For my part, I enjoy Wes's company, value his mind and appreciate his kind heart. He's a regular guest for dinner at the flat and rarely misses lunch with Josee and me on Xol's Day.

Business is booming for the reopened Stars and the Sea. Memi has found meaning in the role of mother and is generous to both her clientele and her staff. The seediness of her chosen profession will never be lost on me, and its long-term impact on some of the fragile souls who drift her way remains to be seen. I comfort myself in the belief that New Capital continues to fail their kind and they're as well falling under Memi's wing as any other.

Although Nakni still lives at the Stars – Memi wouldn't let him leave – he has retired from its trade and, despite his years, has found work as an apprentice sign painter. He needs Areel I'Advay's golden cane to walk, but he walks nonetheless.

As for Josee's health, my wife's recovery that summer was gradual but constant. Mani and I judged her progress by her efforts to paint, although neither of us is an impartial critic. Late in the season, after we returned to Horizon's Outlook, Josee wisely decided to put down her pencil and pick up her brush. On the second attempt to reclaim her artist's eye, she spent only an hour painting, during which Mani and I worked each other into a state of near-hysterical anxiety, both believing the success of the resultant composition would indicate whether the woman we loved would return to us whole. Whether this was fiction or not is irrelevant; Josee was satisfied with her work and, therefore, so were we.

From then on, Josee's obsession with the sky, the Coiled Sea, and the rising and setting sun returned. Form and realism feature less in her work than they did, and, if possible, colour and energy more so than ever.

On one late summer's day, when the winds were violent and the rain lashed against our flat, she stood at the drawing room window before our southern balcony and painted the dark and heavy waves as they broke and crashed. When she was finished, she went outside into the torrent and sat down and wept. I ran to comfort her in her despair and found her laughing. I didn't need to ask why. When I looked at the painting, I saw the sea in motion, almost as if I were a child again, aboard my uncle's fishing boat, riding the waves with Xol winking at me from the depths.

Mani came to believe Josee's recovery was dependent on his presence and feared his departure would trigger a relapse from which she would never return. I have to say, I didn't think his logic at fault. But, as always, I underestimated my wife. While I parade my cynic's heart for all to see, she is the deep and secret stoic of the Known World, and she accepted Mani leaving our home in the same way she welcomed him into it: with love and understanding.

Even before he left, I had sensed the pull of the Depths in Mani for a while. He would disappear for hours, then days. Regardless, with the start of the new academic year approaching, Josee and I had discussed which school we would enrol him in, and he had played along to humour us. But in hindsight, our conversations had been an act, a fantasy of a possible future never meant to be. And truth be told, what fate would it have been for a young and freedom-loving warrior from the Depths to struggle in an environment he had never known? Even if Mani's heart had been in it, and his efforts and energies directed with zeal, what could he have accomplished? Could he have become a scholar or a scientist, maybe reach the heights of industry or even cast a spell with his poetry? Unlikely. At best, he would learn to be like everyone else in my tribe and spend his days on a fishing boat with my cousins. Not a bad life by any means, but not one I had chosen and not one I could condemn him to against his will. Better then, in the end, that he spends his years with those he knows and trusts best.

He still visits Josee and me, often with another hungry youngster, such as his friend Jacira, the little girl who wears horsetail necklaces and bands, and to whom he'd gifted a shiny leather belt to show his affection. My wife cooks for them no matter how many appear. She makes them leave their dirty soft-soled deerskin shoes on the northern balcony before they enter the kitchen and, on more than one occasion, has insisted they take a bath before they eat. I arrived home from work one day full of love and lust only to find my ambitions thwarted by a mob, for there is no other word for it, of perhaps a dozen wild-eyed boys and girls, all with empty bellies that needed filling. Josee shrugged, and I had to shake my head and laugh.

But I notice a change in Mani these days. He has found his brother's grit, and I'm often reminded of the evening I showed him my way of flicking a marble and the speed and determination with which he learnt. I worry about him and wonder what fate will bring his way. Will a harsh and violent life in the company of men like Yoyu drive him to murder like it had Kononwa? Or will memories of the home Josee and I shared with him create a yearning in his sacred heart for a gentler way of being? Xol will reveal all.

Until then, Mani will remain with the rough but spirited orphans he has known all his life. He will grow to manhood with them and learn how to fight for them. One day he may die for them. And why not? After all, they were his tribe.

As for me, I can't say if I've changed. My manners certainly haven't improved, although my jealousy has abated. More importantly, High Chief Naka has, thus far, kept his word. But, as I understand it, Brigadier I'Kalmeen was not imprisoned upon his return to Al'Mayra with the weapon. What this foretells, I cannot say, but whenever I stroll home alone at night across the Bridge of Spirits, or walk with Josee to the arcade for a late supper in one of her favourite eateries, I always check the dome of the Octagon Hall, just in case it starts flashing carmine-red again – the colour of lifeblood stones.

www.ingramcontent.com/pod-product-compliance
Lightning Source LLC
Chambersburg PA
CBHW020859060726
47591CB00004B/998